Three h
abou
d

**Julia James
Kim Lawrence &
Diana Hamilton**

in

Seduced by the Billionaire

Seduced by the Billionaire

featuring

THE GREEK'S ULTIMATE REVENGE
by Julia James

THE ITALIAN PLAYBOY'S PROPOSITION
by Kim Lawrence

THE BILLIONAIRE AFFAIR
by Diana Hamilton

*M&B™ and M&B™ with the Rose Device
are trademarks of the publisher.
Harlequin Mills & Boon Limited, Eton House,
18-24 Paradise Road, Richmond, Surrey TW9 1SR*

SEDUCED BY THE BILLIONAIRE
© by Harlequin Books S.A. 2008

The Greek's Ultimate Revenge, The Italian Playboy's Proposition
and *The Billionaire Affair* were first published in Great Britain in
separate, single volumes.

The Greek's Ultimate Revenge © Julia James 2004
The Italian Playboy's Proposition © Kim Lawrence 2003
The Billionaire Affair © Diana Hamilton 2001

ISBN: 978 0 263 86659 9

10-0208

*Printed and bound in Spain
by Litografía Rosés S.A., Barcelona*

THE GREEK'S ULTIMATE REVENGE

Julia James

Julia James lives in England with her family. Mills & Boon were the first 'grown up' books she read as a teenager, alongside Georgette Heyer and Daphne du Maurier, and she's been reading them ever since. Julia adores the English and Celtic countryside, in all its seasons, and is fascinated by all things historical, from castles to cottages. She also has a special love for the Mediterranean – 'The most perfect landscape after England'! – and she considers both ideal settings for romance stories. In between writing she enjoys walking, gardening, needlework, baking extremely gooey cakes and trying to stay fit!

**Don't miss Julia James's new novel,
The Italian's Rags-to-Riches Wife,
out in February 2008 from
Mills & Boon® Modern™!**

PROLOGUE

'NIKOS! You've got to do something! You've got to! The little trollop has got her claws into Stephanos so deep he can't see straight!'

Nikos Kiriakis looked down at the woman lying in the hospital bed. She looked dreadful, and it stabbed at him painfully. Her face was pale and drawn, and she looked ten years older than her thirty-nine years. Though it had been only a minor operation medically, psychologically it had taken a much greater toll.

And, as if that wasn't enough, now it seemed her husband had chosen this moment of all times to be unfaithful.

Nikos's dark gold-flecked eyes hardened. His older sister had been a devoted wife to Stephanos Ephandrou—she didn't deserve this. Not now.

Not when a doctor had just told her that the results of a laparoscopy were showing that both her Fallopian tubes were irreparably damaged. That her desperate years of trying to give Stephanos the child he longed for had been, as she had so feared, totally in vain.

Nikos had tried to take the most optimistic line with Demetria when she'd relayed the results to him just now. Told her that at least the doctors now had a reason for her continued infertility, and that there were methods of assisted conception available that held out hope for her still, even at her age. She might still be able to give Stephanos a child—she must not give up trying.

Then Demetria had dropped her bombshell.

'He doesn't even *want* a child from me! He's got another woman!'

Her voice had been strained and bitter. Very bitter.

Stunned, Nikos had heard her out. Of all the men he knew, Stephanos Ephandrou had seemed to be the last husband to run a mistress. He had always been devoted to Demetria, had even said when he married her that he was glad her first marriage had borne no children rather than view it as what it was—a warning that perhaps all was not well with his twenty-nine-year-old bride's reproductive system.

Stephanos had married her after he'd finally persuaded her to divorce her chronically philandering first husband— her late father's choice for her, a socially suitable match for a Kiriakis, who had seen no reason to stifle his sexual proclivities on that account. And now it looked as if Stephanos was cut from the same cloth as Demetria's first husband— or worse. For what could be said about a man who was prepared to chase after another woman when his own wife was battling with infertility?

He lowered his tall frame, clad in an impeccably cut business suit, carefully onto the side of Demetria's bed. His handmade jacket eased across his broad shoulders as he took her hands, rubbing them gently.

'Demi, are you sure you're not imagining things? Stephanos would never be so cruel, so dishonourable.'

His sister clutched his hands, flexing her thin shoulders forward from the pillows supporting her.

'I'm *not* imagining things! He's found some blonde twenty-five-year-old and he's set her up where he can go and visit her whenever he can. He's there with her now. He's obsessed with her—he's changed completely. I can tell. I can *tell*!'

Her voice rose dangerously.

'You've got to help me, Nik. You've got to!'

Nikos let go of her hands.

'You say you know where he has installed her? Tell me everything else you know about this,' Nikos instructed calmly. He was subduing his own instinct, which was to seek out Stephanos and beat him to a pulp. But that wouldn't help his sister.

Demetria swallowed heavily and took a difficult breath.

'Her name is Janine Fareham. She picked Stephanos up at Heathrow the last time he was in London. He flew her straight out here and set her up.'

'In Athens?' Nikos asked sharply. His mind was racing. To pick up a rich, middle-aged man at an airport and be installed in luxury by him the following day was fast work—the girl must be skilful indeed! Unconsciously, his sculpted mouth curled in disdain.

Demetria was shaking her head.

'No, he's put her in that latest resort of his on Skarios.' Her voice became strained and bitter again, 'Maybe that way he thinks I won't know what he's up to!'

Nikos frowned slightly.

'How *do* you know?'

'Philip,' Demetria answered simply. 'I made him tell me. Stephanos was behaving so strangely—I knew something was up.'

Nikos nodded, not all that surprised. Philip was Stephanos's right-hand man in the office, and usually the soul of discretion, but he had a soft spot for Demetria and Nikos could just see her badgering him to confirm her suspicions. Silently he cursed the other man—this was definitely one time when ignorance would have been the better option. Demetria just simply didn't need this kind of heartache right now.

Demetria clutched at his hand again.

'You will do something, won't you, Nik? Please—you must—you just must! I can't talk to Stephanos. I just can't. He's trying to be nice to me—but it isn't working. He's so strange, so withdrawn. He can't look me in the eye. It's that woman's fault! She's got him totally in her clutches! She's one of those whores that use rich men and don't care what damage they do!'

Her voice was rising once more, and there was a note of hysteria in it. Again Nikos took her hands and squeezed them lightly.

'She's got him infatuated with her. I know it. And how can I blame him?' Her voice broke almost into a sob. 'Look at me—middle-aged and barren. I'm useless to him—useless! No wonder he doesn't want me any more.' A hectic flush spread out over her cheeks and her eyes were anguished.

Silently Nikos reached out a hand and pressed the call button, then leant forward and kissed his sister on the cheek.

'You are a wife any man would be proud to have. This is nothing but idiocy on Stephanos's part,' he told her firmly. He got to his feet and looked down at the stricken woman. 'Infertility takes its toll on a man, too, Demetria,' he said quietly. 'I think this is nothing more than temporary madness—Stephanos will come back to you; I am sure of it.'

Demetria clutched at him again.

'Get rid of her—Nik. If anyone can get her to leave my Stephanos alone it's you! Please, for my sake, I beg you. Get her claws out of my husband! Do whatever you have to—whatever it takes.'

The hysteria was definitely identifiable now, and Nikos felt his emotions mount. Demetria was the only family he had left now, since their parents' death, and he'd seen her through so much unhappiness—so much. He'd seen her through the ordeal of divorcing her first husband, backing her all the way and telling Stephanos not to lose hope, that the woman he loved would free herself if he just stood by her. He would not turn aside now, when their marriage was in such danger, however much of a besotted fool his brother-in-law was being.

Nikos knew exactly what his sister was asking of him. His face tightened and he looked across at her.

'You can do it, Nik! I know you can.' There was a terrible hope in her voice now. 'Women always fall at your feet. Always! Make this one do the same. Make her besotted with *you* so she leaves my Stephanos alone. Please, Nik, *please*!'

'I could speak to Stephanos,' he said slowly.

His answer was a violent shake of her head, panic in her eyes.

'No! No! I can't bear him knowing that I know. I can't. If you could only just get rid of her, get her claws out of him, he'd come back to me. I know he would. Oh, Nik, please. *Please!* If I could get pregnant—oh, dear heaven, if I could just get pregnant—then he'd be happy with me again! But if that harpy hangs on to him he'll never come back to me. Never!'

This was bad, thought Nikos. Demetria should not be upsetting herself like this, not at such a time. She'd been under such strain for so long, her desperation for a child eating into her.

But she was asking him to interfere in her marriage—come between a husband and his wife.

His expression tightened again suddenly. No, she was only asking him to come between a husband and his mistress...

A long, slow breath was exhaled from him as he soothed her hands.

His long lashes lowered over his eyes.

'What I can do, I will,' he promised her.

Her expression relaxed a fraction, the hectic look fading a little from her eyes.

'I knew I could count on you—I knew it!' There was relief in her voice now—relief and gratitude. 'You'll go right away, won't you, Nik? Won't you? You'll go and find her and get her claws out of Stephanos?'

'Very well.' His voice was sombre. Then he took another breath, quicker this time. 'But you, Demi, must promise me that you will start treatment immediately! No more prevaricating. The doctors have told you what can be done—there is considerable hope; you know there is. But these things take time—the doctors must have told you that—and you must delay no more.' His eyes narrowed suddenly. 'It might be a good idea,' he said slowly, 'to consult a fertility expert abroad—somewhere requiring quite a journey. Say, America. Get your doctor here to recommend someone in America. Tell Stephanos that he is the best and you insist on seeing him—and that he must come too. He will do that for you, I am sure. But I need time, Demi—you understand?'

Her eyes had lit up as she understood what he was suggesting. 'Sophia's daughter's wedding!' she added suddenly. 'I told her we couldn't come—but I think, oh, I really think that we might be able to make it after all. We could go on to Long Island after I've seen a consultant in New York.'

The hectic flush was fading now, and hope was filling her again—he could see it. She was speaking rationally—eagerly.

Her brother gave a tight smile.

'Two weeks. I need at least that long to do what you want,' he told her. 'Make sure Stephanos is away from Greece for two weeks. And Demi?' His eyes were hard. 'Keep him out of contact with the girl! I don't want her distracted.' His eyes hardened even more. 'Except,' he finished, his mouth twisting, 'by me.'

'Two weeks,' she promised him. Already her expression was less gaunt, her eyes less haunted. 'Oh, Nik,' she cried suddenly. 'You are the best, the very best of brothers! I knew you would help me. I knew it!'

As he handed Demetria over to the care of a nurse and left the private room, to stride on long legs down the lushly carpeted corridors of the exclusive clinic, his face grew grim. Stephanos was being a fool, all right. Even if he hadn't been married, and to a wife tormented by infertility, at fifty-two he had no business running after a girl of twenty-five. He was more than twice her age, for heaven's sake!

His expression darkened even more. But of course men in their fifties trying to recapture their youth were prime meat for girls like the one who had snared his brother-in-law. And if they were rich, as Stephanos Ephandrou undoubtedly was, they were even more attractive.

His eyes took on a cynical light. Well, if it was meat such girls wanted to feed on, then he was primest of the prime! On the Richter scale of desirable protectors he had to score even higher than Stephanos. His wealth was as great as Stephanos's, he had no inconvenient wife to circumvent, and, best of all, he was nearly twenty years younger than Stephanos.

He gave a cold, sardonic smile. Demetria had known exactly what she was doing when she'd turned to him for help—she knew very well what his reputation with her sex was. It was something she usually vigorously berated him over, as it came between her and her hopes for him finally marrying and settling down—as she longed, with sisterly affection, for him to do.

Well, he hadn't earned that reputation emptily—and now he could put it at his sister's service.

As he swung out of the clinic and climbed into his low-slung car, occupying one of the guest parking spaces, Nikos's face hardened.

Time to go and visit Miss Janine Fareham—a visit that he intended her to find quite, quite unforgettable. And one that would finish her affair with his brother-in-law once and for all.

CHAPTER ONE

JANINE eased herself over onto her stomach and sighed languorously, giving her body to the sun. In front of her the sunlight danced dazzlingly off the azure swimming pool. Beyond, slender cypresses pierced the cerulean sky.

The sound of children splashing and calling in the pool was the only noise. She felt the warmth of the sun like a blessing on her naked back.

The hotel was a haven of peace and luxury, brand-new, and Stephanos had shown it off to her with pride—the latest addition to his hotel empire.

A smile played around her lips.

Stephanos. It had been amazing, encountering him like that at Heathrow. He'd stopped dead, transfixed by her looks—and that had been it! He'd simply swept her off and taken her with him back to Greece. Her life would never be the same again.

A shadow flickered in her face. She just wished he could spend more time with her! Oh, he'd been completely honest with her, and she understood—of course she understood— that it was impossible for him to formally acknowledge her existence. All she could have of him would be snatched moments, all too brief. That was why he'd installed her here.

'Even if I cannot be with you, my darling girl, I want you to have the very best I can give you!' he had said to her.

She smiled fondly at the memory. Then the smile faded. His phone call last night, brief and hurried, as all his calls had to be, had not been good news. But she'd done her best to reassure him.

'I shall be fine,' she'd told him. 'You mustn't worry about me while you are in America.'

The trouble was, she thought ruefully, that Stephanos obviously *did* worry about her. His protectiveness was touching—he seemed so fearful that she would disappear from his life as unexpectedly as she had entered it. She smiled to herself again. He need have no fears. None at all. Nothing could part her from him now—she wanted to be part of his life for ever, however much of a secret it had to be.

She closed her eyes, letting the heat of the afternoon feed her drowsiness. For once she would enjoy this luxury beneath the golden sun.

So totally different from the life she usually led...

Nikos stood on the terrace, looking down over the pool. His eyes beneath the dark glasses were hard. So that was the girl, splayed out on a lounger. The girl who was wrecking his sister's marriage.

He paused a moment in the dappled shade, where the grapes were already ripening to a rich purple, and gazed down at her.

Emotions warred within him. The first was bitter anger—anger that the creature down there had the power to make Demetria weep in his arms, filled with despair.

The second was quite different.

She was, quite simply, delectable.

He had a vast experience of women, but this one was, he could see, in the very top rank. Her face was turned sideways, eyes closed, lashes lying long against her cheek as she lay relaxed on the lounger, but he could see that it was breath-catchingly lovely. A long, sun-bleached mane of pale hair swept across the pillow of the lounger, gently wisping across her smooth forehead. As for her body—

His eyes swept on, down the exposed length of her. She was naked apart from a tiny bikini bottom that barely covered her softly rounded cheeks. Her bikini top had been unfastened so that its ties would not mar the tanned perfection of her back. She did not look to be particularly tall, but she was very slender, with the kind of natural grace that girls of her age and type had in abundance.

She was sun-kissed, soft-limbed and sexy.

Oh, yes. Very, very sexy.

He could see immediately why Stephanos had not been able to resist her.

But Stephanos was married and should have *made* himself resist her. He, Nikos, was hampered no such impediment. Indeed, quite the opposite. He had given his betrayed sister his word on that.

His mission was very clear. He would quite deliberately, quite calculatingly, seduce Janine Fareham away from Demetria's husband.

Relief—no, more than relief eased through him. Satisfaction. Carrying out his mission would be no ordeal at all. In fact, he felt his body stir, and indulged it for a moment. It would be a positive pleasure.

For a brief while he let himself luxuriate in surveying her in all her enticing blonde beauty. Then, as he let his eyes feast on the nymph-like, softly rounded curves of her near naked body, as if a knife had come slicing down another image imposed itself, vivid and painful. His sister's gaunt, strained face as she begged him to help her sprang in front of his eyes.

His eyes hardened and he began to walk forward.

In her half-dozing state it took a moment for Janine to register that she could hear footsteps. A second later a shadow fell over her. Her eyes flew open and she looked up.

A man was standing there, looking down at her. He was very tall and dark. A generation younger than Stephanos. Was it one of the hotel staff? What did he want?

'*Kyria* Fareham?' The voice was deep and accented.

There was something about the tone that told her instinctively that this man was not a member of the hotel staff. This was a man who gave orders, not took them.

And he certainly didn't look like a guest either. Guests were all casually dressed—but this man was wearing an immaculately cut lightweight business suit and looked as if he had just walked out of a board meeting. Her eyes travelled on up to his face.

She felt her heartbeat lurch.

Eyes veiled by dark glasses bored down on her, surveying her as she lay there displayed for him. Suddenly she was acutely conscious that she was almost naked—and he was dressed in a formal suit. The disparity made her feel vulnerable, exposed.

Instinctively she pushed herself up to a sitting position, taking the sarong she'd been lying on with her, swinging her feet down to the warm paving. Even then she felt at a disadvantage. He still towered over her. For a Greek—and his looks and accent told her he had to be—he was very tall: easily six feet.

She stood up, knotting her sarong hurriedly around her in a fluid movement.

As her eyes focused on him properly she felt her breath catch. Her lips parted soundlessly, eyes widening.

She was looking at the most devastating male she had ever seen in her life.

What nature had bestowed on him his obvious wealth had accentuated. The superbly tailored suit fitted him like a glove, and she could see it had most definitely not been an off-the-peg purchase. But the man wearing it did not look off-the-peg either. He looked, she assessed instantly, *expensive*. His dark hair was expertly cut, feathering very slightly across his wide brow, and the dark glasses he wore did not need to have the discreet designer logo on them for her to know they had not been purchased from a market stall.

His nose was strong, and straight, with deep lines curving from it to the edges of his mouth.

His mouth—

Sculpted. That was the only word for it. With a sensuous lower lip she had to drag her eyes from, forcing herself to gaze into the blankness of his shaded regard.

There was something about this man that was making her heart race—and it was not just because he'd all but woken her out of a sun-beaten slumber. She felt the world shift around her and resettle.

As if something had changed for ever.

Then a different emotion surfaced. She'd been too busy gaping at this fantastic-looking man to take on board that he seemed to know who she was.

'Who wants to know?' She countered his enquiry warily. If he wasn't from the hotel who else knew she was here, except for Stephanos?

She pushed her hair back over her shoulders, feeling it tumbling warm and heavy down her back, and gazed at him, lips parted slightly.

Theos, thought Nikos, absorbing the sensuous gesture, she was perfect. Just perfect. The dream image of a sexy blonde.

But she wasn't cheap or tarty. Nothing so resistible! She was beautiful—head-turningly so. In an instant Nikos's expert eye took in the fact that she had one of those faces where every feature complemented every other, from her chestnut eyes, set in a heart-shaped face, to her generous mouth below a delicate nose. A golden tan gilded her flawless skin and her hair hung like pale spun gold down to her slender waist, faintly visible through the gauze of the turquoise sarong.

Desire flashed through him. Instant and insistent.

For a moment he felt consumed by it, overwhelmed. Then, with deliberate control, he subdued his reaction.

It was good that he desired her, it would make his task

so much easier, but that was the only reason he should feel desire for her. It was a means to an end, that was all, and the end was the removal—permanently—of this girl from his brother-in-law's marriage.

And to that end it was also necessary that this girl should be sexually vulnerable to him, Nikos. His eyes flickered over her again.

She was sexually aware of him all right. He knew the signs. Knew them well.

Beneath his regard Janine felt colour stealing out along her cheekbones. Heat flushing into her blood.

She could feel herself reacting to this man. She couldn't stop herself. There was something about him that was more than his devastating looks, more than that potent aura of wealth, or even the potent frisson of the power that a man like this must surely wield in the world he moved in. There was a raw sexuality beneath that tailored suit, hidden in those veiled eyes. She felt it licking at her.

Making her want him.

The realisation shocked her.

How could she be responding so strongly to a man she'd just set eyes on—whose eyes she couldn't even see yet? But she was, and she couldn't stop it. She felt her breasts tighten, her pupils flare, the colour flood to her cheeks.

Nikos watched her responding to him. That was good, very good. He wanted her responsive, wanted her physically aware of him—wanted her vulnerable to him.

There would be no problem seducing her, he knew.

Women came easily to him. They always had. Despite Demetria's bewailing, in his twenties he had indulged himself to the hilt. Now, in his thirties, he was more selective, preferring to choose women who could move in his world, who were sophisticated and discreet. Who understood what he wanted—and then moved on when he gave them the indication, as he always did.

Such women would neither know nor care that he was

about to make a temporary diversion, in a call of duty, to seduce away this female who threatened his sister's marriage, who was making a fool of a man who, up till now, he had always held in the greatest respect.

Now he let the female he was about to seduce, deliberately and calculatedly, respond to him, heighten her awareness of him, begin to make herself vulnerable to him.

He smiled.

Janine felt a kick go through her, powerful and shocking. The sculpted mouth parted, lines indenting around it, showing strong white teeth. It was an easy smile, yet it sent a frisson through her.

'We have a mutual—acquaintance,' he said, pausing minutely over the word. 'Stephanos Ephandrou.' He could see her stiffen fractionally as he dropped the name into the space between them.

'Oh?' responded Janine. Out of the blue he had mentioned Stephanos—what should she say? She knew Stephanos wanted her to be discreet about their relationship—yet here was a complete stranger who seemed to know there was a connection.

Her concern showed in her eyes. Nikos saw it and felt a stab of anger. Any lingering doubts he might have had that Demetria had somehow imagined her husband was having an affair vanished. The girl *was* carrying on with Stephanos. No doubt about it. His name had registered with her as loudly as if he'd rung a bell in her ear!

He forced his natural anger down. To display it now would ruin his strategy. Janine Fareham must have no idea of his hostility to her—indeed, she must think quite the opposite.

He bestowed another smile on her, and knew without vanity that it had distracted her attention from wondering why he seemed to know that she was connected to Stephanos Ephandrou.

He had been in two minds as to which approach to take

with her. He could, indeed, have simply engineered her acquaintance and set out to seduce her as a complete stranger. That approach had its advantages—it would have been simple and straightforward. But a female who made her living from the protection of rich, besotted older men might well be worldly enough to be wary of quick seductions that would jeopardise her lucrative relationship with her current protector. Instead, Nikos planned to use his acknowledged 'acquaintance' with Stephanos as a lever with which to gain the girl's confidence as swiftly as possible.

'Perhaps you will take a coffee with me and I can explain?' he went on, in that same smooth tone. He glanced towards the little poolside bar set back under the shade of some olive trees.

Still wary, but feeling she was being effortlessly manipulated by an expert, Janine let herself be ushered towards the seating area of the bar. It was a breath cooler under the trees, but she still felt her skin was flushed. The heat that was filling it, however, did not come from the sun.

She sat down on one of the canvas-backed chairs and the man did likewise, pausing only to beckon to the barman, who was already hurrying forward. Whatever it was that this man had, thought Janine, he had a lot of it! He wasn't the type to get ignored by a barman—or anyone else.

And certainly not women. Janine watched as a couple of female guests with small children in tow, seated at a table further off drinking fizzy drinks, immediately turned their heads in their direction. Their eyes were not for Janine. One of them said something to the other in Greek, and they laughed before turning their attention back to their children.

Janine didn't blame them for looking. The man sitting opposite her in his hand-tailored suit, would turn female heads wherever he went! Sexual magnetism radiated from him like a forcefield, pulling at everything in sight with a double X chromosome!

The barman was hovering, ready to take their orders.

'A frappe, please, no sugar,' requested Janine abstractedly. She had already discovered that iced frappes were the ideal way to take coffee in the heat of the day, and were delicious and cooling. Her companion ordered coffee— Greek, she assumed.

The barman nodded acquiescently and hurried off.

Nikos turned his attention back to the girl. She was still wary, he could see—but still radiating sexual awareness. Not that she was flaunting her reaction to him. If anything, judging by the way she was sitting—pulled back in her chair, legs slanted neatly out of the way, her hand resting on the knot of her sarong, shielding her breasts—she was trying to conceal it.

Her lack of immediate sexual forwardness—despite his blatant appreciation of her charms—confirmed that he had been right to acknowledge Stephanos's presence in her life. The girl had landed herself a very soft number indeed— and she clearly realised it would be folly for her to risk her position as Stephanos's mistress, with all the guaranteed cashflow that it promised, for the sake of a brief interlude with a passing stranger. However much sexual pleasure she might gain from the encounter.

Hence her wariness.

Time to dispel it.

He slid his dark glasses off and slipped them into his jacket pocket. He relaxed back in his chair.

'Perhaps I should explain that I am here at Stephanos's suggestion,' he told her smilingly. 'Stephanos is a close friend and business associate, and when he heard I was coming to Skarios he suggested I stay at his hotel and asked me to seek you out,' he went on, the lie coming smoothly and fluently. He felt no guilt about lying to her. He only had to remember Demetria's tears and pleadings to absolve himself of all such guilt.

Janine made no answer. She was simply staring.

She felt her stomach clench. Dark, gold-flecked eyes

flickered over her, long lashes sweeping down over his cheeks. Her lips parted in a silent exhalation.

If she had thought his mouth hard to tear her gaze from, those eyes made such an act totally impossible. They were eyes she could drown in...making her feel weak...

For one long, endless moment she let herself gaze into those gold-flecked orbs, and felt her stomach churning like a cement mixer.

What was *happening* to her?

She'd *never* reacted this strongly to a man! Never! But this man—this complete stranger, whose name she didn't even know—was making the blood race in her veins, her face flush with heat...

Just by looking at her...

Their drinks arrived and she was grateful for the distraction. As the barman walked away she resisted the temptation to go back to gazing at the man opposite her, and instead forced herself to focus on what he had just said, not what he looked like.

'Stephanos asked you to seek me out?' she echoed dimly.

She sank back into gazing, riveted, into those magnetic, night-dark eyes.

They seemed to be looking into the heart of her. She felt herself go weak all over. All over again.

Nikos flashed another smile at her—and watched the girl's pupils flare.

'I hope you do not mind,' he said softly, 'that I have sought you out.'

His eyes rested on her and Janine felt her heart quicken. Oh, good grief, her bones were dissolving.... She just wanted to stare and stare.

Forcibly she dragged her mind back, fighting for composure. He seemed to be waiting for an answer.

'Oh—no. Of course not,' she managed to say. 'It's very good of you, Mr—er—?'

There was the slightest hesitation before Nikos spoke, but Janine did not notice it. Was quite incapable of noticing it.

'Kiriakis,' said Nikos smoothly. 'Nikos Kiriakis.'

Through veiled eyes he studied her for a reaction but saw none. The name meant nothing to her. He'd gambled that it wouldn't. Why should Stephanos talk about his brother-in-law to his mistress?

Nikos Kiriakis. Janine rolled the fluid syllables around in her head.

He was speaking again, and she brought her dazed attention back to what he was saying.

'Stephanos also had another suggestion,' Nikos went on, 'which for my part I would be very happy to comply with.' The lie rolled as smoothly as the first.

Janine stared. 'What suggestion?' Her voice still sounded totally abstracted.

Nikos was not offended. Usually he expected—and got— a hundred per cent attention from those he spoke to. But that Janine Fareham was incapable of bringing such focus to their conversation was only a good sign. A very good sign. He wanted her dazzled by him—lured by him.

'As you know, Stephanos is currently *en route* to the States,' began Nikos. He studied her reaction to this information—he calculated. Stephanos would have told her he was going to be abroad, although he doubted he would have told her that the reason for his sudden trip to New York was to take his wife to a fertility expert there.

'He is concerned that you may not have anything to do while he is away,' he continued. 'So he asked me if I would look after you while I am here—stop you getting bored.'

Janine's wandering thoughts snapped back. Suddenly the stomach-churning impact of Nikos Kiriakis's physical presence vanished. There was something far more important to focus on.

What had he just said to her? What was all that about Stephanos telling him she might be bored? Telling him to look after her? Surely, considering Stephanos's determination to keep her role in his life quiet, it was madness to send this Nikos Kiriakis to look her up?

Nikos saw the consternation in her face. It would not help his strategy.

'Perhaps I should tell you,' he said, his eyes resting on her, 'that, as a close friend of Stephanos Ephandrou, I am aware of the relationship between you, Ms Fareham—'

Her eyes widened, her consternation deepening.

'You *are*?'

CHAPTER TWO

OH, YES, thought Nikos savagely—that was good, Ms Fareham, that was very good! That little touch of surprise, and widening those big, beautiful eyes of yours. What the hell did you suppose everyone would think about your relationship with a fifty-two-year-old man? His mouth tightened.

She was sitting there, gazing at him, her eyes wide in her beautiful face. As if butter wouldn't melt in her mouth. As if neglected wives, heartbroken and despairing, had nothing to do with her. As if she were not responsible for his sister weeping in his arms.

The dark current of his anger surged dangerously near the surface. He forced it down. It had no part to play in his scheme now. The time for venting his anger on her would come later.

He made his mouth give a brief smile.

'Do not look so surprised. Such relationships are not unknown,' he remarked. For all his intentions, a sardonic tone was audible in his voice. He took a mouthful of coffee, then set back his cup with a click on the metal surface of the table.

Janine eyed him cautiously. Stephanos had urged such discretion that she was taken aback by this man calmly referring to it. But then, she reasoned, presumably such relationships were not unusual. Especially not with non-Greek women, with their more relaxed attitude to sexual behaviour. Clearly Nikos Kiriakis saw nothing exceptional about it.

Even so, it was disconcerting to hear this complete stranger refer to it. Although, of course, she realised belatedly, he wasn't a stranger to Stephanos. It was odd that they were friends, though—Nikos Kiriakis was easily a generation younger than Stephanos. He didn't look much over thirty, really. Thirty-five at the most. He was certainly in incredible physical condition…

'Please don't look so alarmed,' he went on, the smooth note back in his voice. 'I appreciate that Stephanos wishes to be discreet about your relationship. It is very understandable. You may be assured of my discretion.' He smiled again, a warm, reassuring smile, and she felt suddenly breathless.

'So,' said Nikos, knowing he had overcome that barrier successfully, 'would you care to undertake a little sightseeing? It would be very useful to me as, amongst other business matters, I am here to see whether this island would be suitable for a summer villa for myself.'

That was true enough, he thought. From what little he'd seen of the island firsthand so far, and from what Stephanos had already told him, it might well be suitable. The most southerly of the Ionian islands, Skarios was dryer and hotter than the others, and far less developed. The airport had recently been extended to allow tourist planes to land, but there was general agreement that any development should be both upmarket and sympathetic to the landscape—like his brother-in-law's luxury hotel, which had been designed to be low-rise and traditionally styled.

'Well,' he went on, 'what do you think?'

About what? thought Janine, trying to drag her mind back, because she had resumed gazing raptly at the incredible man sitting opposite her.

'Showing me the island?' he prompted, well aware of the reason for her vagueness, and well pleased by it. Her reaction was exactly what he'd hoped it would be.

Janine felt her breath catch. Those gold-flecked eyes were resting on her, making her feel…feel…

Breathless. Totally breathless….

'What do you say?' pursued Nikos. He was in no doubt as to her answer. Not in the slightest.

'It sounds wonderful!' said Janine, unable to stop herself sounding enthusiastic.

Suddenly Nikos Kiriakis's arrival could not have seemed more timely.

Stephanos had extracted a reluctant promise from her not to hire a car and explore the island herself—'The roads are far too dangerous!' he'd said anxiously—which had left only the not very appealing prospect of taking taxis or restricting herself to the very limited tour buses.

She'd be an idiot to turn down the opportunity of keeping company with the most breathtaking man she'd ever set eyes on…

Careful, a voice inside her cautioned. This Nikos Kiriakis might be gorgeous, but, believe me, he has the same effect on every female he comes across. Just because he eyed you up it doesn't mean you should start getting ideas.

She sobered. Anyway, this isn't a good time for getting ideas like that. This time should be devoted to Stephanos.

But Stephanos isn't here…and he's sent Nikos Kiriakis to me…

To show you around, stop you getting bored, she reminded herself acidly. Nothing else…

He was talking again, and she brought her mind back with a snap.

'Good. Then we are agreed. We shall make our first excursion tomorrow!' There was satisfaction in his voice. He had made contact, and got her agreement—incredibly easily!—to spend time with him alone. Now it was time for the next step in his carefully planned campaign.

'For today—' he shot back his cuff and glanced at the gold watch circling his wrist '—it is too late to make any kind of expedition. Besides—' the smile quirked again '—I have only just flown in from Athens, and that pool looks far too inviting to resist.' He frowned, as his gaze took in just how thronged with children it was. 'Perhaps it will get quieter later.'

'Yes, it empties out around six-ish,' confirmed Janine. Her spirits were zipping around in her, whooshing like crazy. 'The sea is a better bet right now. A path goes down to the beach just beyond the pool.' She indicated with her hand.

He nodded. 'The sea it shall be, then,' he said. His eyes swept over her once more. 'Perhaps you would care to join me there later when you have finished your sunbathing?'

Janine's eyes flickered. 'Thank you—yes.'

Her voice was still breathless, and she felt light-headed.

Nikos got to his feet. 'I'll see you down there,' he told her, and bestowed one last smile on her for good measure before he walked away towards the hotel.

Janine gazed after him until he disappeared from view.

Slowly, she bent her head to drink her frappe through the twin straws in the glass.

Her pulse was racing.

Nikos plugged his laptop cable into the wall-jack in his room and dialled into his e-mail. As he waited for his latest messages to download, the image of Janine Fareham floated enticingly in his mind. He let himself indulge in recollecting her charms, plentiful as they were, and replayed the exchange he had had with her.

Satisfaction filled him. Things were going exactly to plan. She was responding to him very satisfactorily.

And you are responding to her—definitely responding…

But that was good, he reasoned immediately. It was good that he should feel such desire for a woman he needed to seduce. It would lend great verisimilitude to the undertaking.

And danger?

He rebuffed the notion immediately. What danger was there for him in this enterprise? None. He would seduce

Janine Fareham, enjoy her—because she looked as if she were going to be very enjoyable indeed—and that would be that. She would not be returning to Stephanos.

Without conceit he knew that he had a lot more to offer than a man of Stephanos's age! And even if she thought she could go back she would discover otherwise. Once Stephanos knew of her defection there would be no way that he would take her back after she had fallen into his, Nikos's, bed!

No, his plan was entirely without danger—least of all to himself. Janine Fareham was a stunningly attractive female, and he would certainly enjoy taking her to bed—but then he always enjoyed taking beautiful women to bed.

And so many were so willing…

A caustic smile parted his lips. Demetria might volubly yearn for the day she saw him finally married, and berate him for his sexual lifestyle, but it was hardly a problem for him. The stream of women wanting him to desire them was endless, so even if he did tire of them—as he always did— it caused him no difficulty. He simply moved on to the next one.

There was always a next one.

And there would certainly be another one once he had finished with his brother-in-law's mistress.

Irritated with himself for giving form to such pointless musing, he stabbed at the mouse button to open the first e-mail his PA had forwarded as worthy of his attention. In an instant his mind was preoccupied, diverted totally on to business matters.

By the time he had surfaced from his business affairs, the sun was setting. The room temperature was pleasantly cool, thanks to the background air-conditioning, but when he stepped out onto the wide balcony of his room the afternoon warmth enveloped him. Even without his jacket he was far too hot.

Returning indoors, he stripped off and donned a pair of

swimming trunks, before reaching for a pair of crisply cut cotton shorts and a casual shirt. As he reached for a beach towel the image of Janine Fareham in her skimpy bikini wafted once more through his mind. She would be waiting for him by now, no doubt.

Time to go to work.

At the bottom of the flight of steps that cut into the rock between the gardens and the sea he paused, looking around him. To one side of the hotel beach and further out to sea the windsurfers were clearly in action, skimming and twisting over the surface of the water. Immediately in front of him were two rows of loungers and parasols, and a bar café was set back from the beach, to save guests having to go back up to the pool level.

Out to sea, the westering sun was turning the water to turquoise.

He could see no sign of the girl.

And then he spotted her.

She was out to sea, swimming offshore in a leisurely breast-stroke. Her hair, he could just tell at this distance, seemed to be knotted on her head, out of the water.

Casting around to see which lounger she had taken, he saw the beach bag she'd had up by the pool and walked across to toss his towel down on it. Then he undressed down to his trunks to wade into the water. It caressed him like silk, and, with a lithe movement, he dived forward, striking out to sea in a powerful, fast stroke.

He closed the distance between the shore and the girl in a few moments, and then went right on past her. He needed exercise after the inactivity of the day. Besides, the vigorous exercise would help to drain off that layer of submerged, persistent anger he had felt ever since Demetria had dropped her bombshell. It wouldn't drain out completely, of course. Nothing could make it do that until the cause of his anger was removed. But he knew he had to keep his feelings under tight control—he must not, *must not*, let it show. Janine Fareham must get no inkling of it—not until it was far, far too late for her.

Just thinking of her, of the pain she was causing Demetria, the damage she was doing to Stephanos's marriage, made the anger surge through him again. It flared through him, urging his muscles forward, pushing him past the pain barrier as he churned through the water at a punishing speed.

Only when he was several hundred metres out to sea did he finally slow, his burst of energy and aggression spent. He turned over onto his back, temporarily exhausted, floating on the swell of the sea for a while, letting his heart-rate slow and his muscles recover.

His anger seemed abstract now, far away. Demetria and her suffering seemed far away too. Another image formed in his mind. The image of a beautiful blonde with a sun-kissed body and softly rounded limbs.

The woman he was going to calculatedly and deliberately seduce—because she was his sister's husband's mistress.

For a few brief seconds another emotion surfaced. An alien one. Unwelcome.

Reluctance.

Reluctance at the task ahead of him.

And reluctance to question why he felt that way. What was wrong with what he was planning to do? The girl was threatening to destroy his sister's marriage—he was simply trying to help Demetria, who had quite enough torment in her life coping with her infertility. She did not need her husband cheating on her with a younger woman!

And just because, he reminded himself tightly, the younger woman in question had turned out to be so incredibly desirable, that was no reason to flinch from what he had promised Demetria he would do. No reason to feel reluctant to pursue his carefully-planned strategy of calculated seduction.

He put his reluctance aside. There was no reason why he

should not do what he was setting out to do. The girl had got her claws into his brother-in-law—he was going to remove them. End of story. He had set out on this course and he would pursue it to the end. He would accomplish what he had set out to do—what he knew he had to do.

And use whatever it took to achieve that goal.

There was nothing else to be done.

He flipped over and headed back to shore with a steady, unhurried stroke, making for the girl who was his target and his mission. She too had circled round to head back towards the beach, still kicking with her leisurely breast-stroke, head held high out of the water. As he neared her he dived and swam underwater for some metres, emerging just in front of her in a shower of spray.

Janine's breast-stroke stalled abruptly. She'd been miles away mentally, using the smooth, rhythmic movement of her body in the sea to let her mind drift miles away.

But not too many miles. Just as far as the memory of the man whose face had been burning into her retinas since she had laid eyes on him. Once he'd disappeared from view, heading back up to the hotel, she'd gone back to her pool lounger and scooped up her things, heading down to the beach.

She'd tried to sunbathe again, but it had been impossible. Impossible to relax. She'd been fizzing with electricity—electricity generated by Nikos Kiriakis.

She'd given up trying to relax and instead had knotted up her hair, retied her bikini straps firmly, and gone into the water. Here, cool blue satin slipping past her heated body, she had given herself to the indulgence of recalling every last detail of the most breathtaking man she'd ever laid eyes on.

And suddenly now here he was, in the flesh, beside her.

And such flesh…

They were both out of their depths, still treading water, but the translucent liquid did little to hide from her the power and perfection of his body. Broad, bare shoulders topped a muscled chest, fuzzed with hair, every ab and pec lovingly outlined. No wonder he'd been able to swim at speed! His body was in superb condition.

Just like the rest of him…

His dark, wet hair was slicked back from his face. Diamonds glittered on those lush, long lashes of his.

White teeth flashed in a grin.

'If you swam any slower you'd go backwards!' said Nikos Kiriakis to her teasingly.

Janine trod water, trying to regain her composure and trying not to stare open-mouthed at Nikos Kiriakis with hardly a stitch on him.

'You go ahead,' she managed. 'I'll catch you up.'

He gave a laugh and swam away. Janine watched him carve through the water.

Like a shark, she thought…

Lean, dark and dangerous…

Now, why should she think that? What was dangerous about Nikos Kiriakis? He was a fantastic-looking male, but that was the only dangerous thing about him—and it was a danger every female who set eyes on him would experience.

A danger that she would end up doing something totally stupid over him.

Her lips pressed together. Well, *she* was not stupid. She'd got this far in life by not being stupid—not in the way that the likes of Nikos Kiriakis made women stupid. Women like her mother. Always falling for a handsome face. Oh, her mother had thought it 'romantic' to have one fervid affair after another, but Janine had never seen it like that. And where had it got her mother? Louise's flitting butterfly existence, lover after lover, had been a gilded existence, filled with nothing but parties and self-indulgence. Filled with men like Nikos Kiriakis.

She knew what men like Nikos Kiriakis were like. They were too rich, too handsome, too damn sexy to be anything but bad. And Nikos Kiriakis was definitely bad. He would be used to women swooning at his feet in droves!

Well, she mustn't be one of them.

She made a face.

She didn't need to tell herself that! Didn't need to warn herself. Nikos Kiriakis had the seal of approval from Stephanos—he wasn't going to be any kind of danger. OK, so he'd eyed her up, but that didn't mean anything. And she'd eyed *him* up—it had been impossible not to. But that didn't mean anything either. She wouldn't let it.

Her impeccable logic as to her own state of safety from Nikos Kiriakis lasted as long as it took to follow him to shore. By the time she was wading out of the water he had already towelled himself dry and had calmly appropriated her lounger. Nikos lay back and let her look, hands behind his head, shoulders slightly raised by the adjustable headrest, and he was subjecting her to a long and thorough examination.

In the space of less than a second Janine felt more aware of her body than she had ever felt in her life. And of just how close to being totally naked she was.

Suddenly, from being a quite unexceptional item of swimwear, her bikini seemed to shrink on her body, clinging damply to her tautened breasts and barely concealing her pubis.

As for the rest of her, every inch of flesh was totally exposed to him.

And every inch of it tingled as if an electric current were passing through it.

Every step she made to her lounger, she felt that dark, gold-flecked gaze resting on her appraisingly.

Being able to seize her towel and wrap it around her like a cocoon was a moment of exquisite relief. And then, just like a switch being thrown, she realised that she had become the one doing the appraising.

He lay back and let her look.

Oh, she didn't do it as blatantly as he had her, he acknowledged. She made some pretence of unknotting her hair and shaking it loose. But he could see perfectly well that her eyes were fixed on him, covertly working over him through those long lashes of hers. Working over his body.

Well, that was good. That was very good. He wanted her to like what she saw. Wanted her to want him.

It made him want her too…

With a sudden movement he jack-knifed to his feet. It took a lot of control to make it look like an intentional movement.

Where the hell had that come from? The strength and immediacy of his reaction to her perusal shocked him.

With iron discipline he crushed his response. A public beach was not the place for it!

Immediately his imagination leapt to provide another venue—one where his reaction would be exactly what he wanted. A private beach—just the two of them—and Janine Fareham raising her arms to let the golden fall of her hair cascade over her bared breasts…

Again he crushed his response, forcing himself to regain control.

'Here,' he said, gesturing at the lounger he'd just vacated. 'This was yours. I'll use this one.'

He turned to the adjacent lounger, flicking his towel over it. But his gesture went unappreciated.

'I think I'll head back,' replied Janine. Her voice was not quite steady, she noticed, and it dismayed her. She mustn't react like this to this man. She just mustn't! 'I'll take a shower and wash off the salt.'

She flickered a smile at him, not meeting his eye, and grabbed her bag, stuffing her feet into her beach sandals haphazardly. She had to get out of here—fast.

Behind her, Nikos watched her hurry off, his eyes narrowing. Then, slowly, he lowered himself back down on the lounger, gazing blindly out to sea. OK, so she could turn him on. Fast.

Quite something for a man of his experience.

And very enjoyable…

And dangerous?

He frowned.

But it was good. That he was responding to her sexually like this. After all, he reasoned, he had to make this deliberate seduction of his look real. Convincing.

Convincing? He'd damn near convinced everyone on the entire beach!

With a rasp of irritation he pushed the mocking comment aside. It wasn't helpful. Instead he made a lightning review of the situation—the same as he would if this were a business deal he was pushing through. OK, so where was he on this?

Fact: he needed to get Janine Fareham into bed with him ASAP. The sooner she was in, the sooner she'd be out. And out of Stephanos's bed as well.

Fact: Janine Fareham turned him on.

Fact: that was good. Very good. Just as he could leverage *her* desire for *him*, so he could leverage *his* desire for *her*. The more leverage, the sooner he'd achieve his goal.

Saving Demetria's marriage.

Because that, and only that, was the object of this exercise. Enjoying Janine Fareham in bed was nothing more than incidental to that objective.

He'd better not forget it.

He closed his eyes. The westering sun was warm on his bare, damp skin.

Might as well catch some rays and chill out. Take a break before Act II of his fast-track seduction of Janine Fareham got underway.

He let his muscles relax.

It had been a long day. A long week. A long month. In fact it was a long time since he'd simply relaxed in the sun like this. Doing nothing. Letting the light breeze play over his body, the sun bathe his skin.

No one could contact him, no one could make demands on him. He didn't need to check e-mails, or stock prices, or take conference calls.

He could just stay totally out of touch and let the world outside take care of itself.

Time enough to pursue and put paid to Janine Fareham.

Right now he felt like relaxing.

Halfway up, the stone steps widened into a little parapet, affording a view down to the beach through the vegetation. Janine paused. She couldn't resist looking back.

Immediately she saw him. He'd occupied the other lounger and was lying there, hands behind his head, face tilted into the sun. She let her eyes move over his body. From here, at this safe distance, she could let herself do that. Let her eyes run over the smooth, bronzed, muscled torso, down over the taut, tight abs, and pick out the darker arrow that disappeared under the drawstring of his trunks. For a second her gaze lingered, then hastily moved on, down over the powerful hair-fuzzed thighs and down the long length of his legs.

He did not move—lay there completely motionless.

He looked, she thought, like a leopard drowsing in the sun.

The little shiver came again, that disturbing eddy that set her nerves tingling.

She wanted to go on gazing at him.

No! With an effort she pulled away, pushing back from the wooden railing that edged the pathway. Resolutely she twisted around and went on up the steps, not looking back.

The pool area was emptying now, much quieter. She did not linger but made her way indoors, her sandals flapping on the stone tiles, under the arching honeysuckle whose fragrance caught at her. Inside the hotel it was cooler, but only just. Her room was much colder, chilly even, with its background air-conditioning.

For the next hour she occupied herself showering, washing her hair, giving herself a facial and manicure, washing out her underwear, and finally pulling a sundress over her head. She phoned Room Service for coffee and watched an international news channel on television until it arrived. Then, tray in hand, she went out onto her balcony.

The sun was nearly setting now, licking the sea with gold. Janine sat herself down at the little table, stretching out her legs as she poured her coffee. Her still damp hair curled around her shoulders and she idly fingered it as she sipped her coffee, gazing out over the view.

It certainly was a fantastic setting for a hotel. From here the sea spread out before her as far as the eastern coast of Sicily. She sat and watched the sun slipping over the horizon, silhouetting the tall cypress trees, sure that she could see Pheobus's fiery chariot pulling the sun to its watery bed.

A strange, powerful feeling went through her. My first visit to Greece, she thought. All these years and I've never been here. Never known why it's so emotional a place for me.

Her thoughts slipped to Stephanos. If he wasn't in New York yet he must be very shortly, surely. He seemed very far away. Very distant from her.

Something—she did not know what—made her glance down, over the hotel gardens. Someone was strolling around the edge of the pool, shirt pulled on but unbuttoned, towel casually slung over his shoulder.

Nikos Kiriakis.

Hastily, lest he suddenly glance up and see her looking down at him, she dipped her head, pouring out more coffee. By the time she had lifted the cup to drink from it he had reached the hotel and she could see him no more.

The phone rang in her room some twenty minutes later. She was reading her book still out on the warm balcony, though she could hardly see to read any more. Already the lights in the gardens had been illuminated, including those in the pool, which glowed brilliantly. People had started to stroll out for the evening, making their way to the pool bar for a drink before dinner. Children's voices piped.

She would have an early dinner in the buffet dining room, where all the families ate with their children. Nikos Kiriakis would doubtless eat much later, and in the à la carte dining room reserved for adults.

The soft beeping of the phone interrupted her. Assuming it was Reception, she was completely unprepared for the dark, liquid tones of Nikos Kiriakis in her ear.

'I've reserved a table for nine. I'll meet you on the terrace at half past eight. Does that give you enough time to be ready?'

There was a note of humour in the voice, as though its owner were acknowledging that a woman needed a large amount of time to be ready to dine.

It took Janine a good few seconds to gather her wits. Even then she sounded no better than half-witted.

'Um—you don't have to reserve tables. You just wander in whenever you want. The buffet runs till ten.'

'We are not dining in the buffet restaurant.' The smile in his voice was even more pronounced now. 'Fond as I am of children, I prefer something a little more peaceful for dinner.'

'Please—you don't have to ask me to dinner.' The words blurted from her.

'But I would like very much to dine with you, Janine,' replied Nikos. 'So I look forward to seeing you at half past eight, *ne*?'

He rang off, giving her no chance to argue the point any more. For a moment she stood there, receiver in hand. Feeling dazed.

She bit her lip. The way he had looked at her as she

came out of the water sprang vivid in her mind. The way he had looked at her when she'd been lying by the pool. The way he had looked at her at the pool bar.

It doesn't mean squat! He's the kind of male who does that to every female. And every female does it back to him. I bet you every single female head will turn when he walks into the dining room tonight—and so what? He's only having dinner with you because of Stephanos. Got it?

She drew in her breath and felt better.

Promptly, a different cause for anxiety assailed her. She hurried over to her wardrobe and flung it open, staring at the contents.

She didn't have a thing to wear! Not for dinner in the à la carte restaurant! When Stephanos had been here she hadn't really bothered much with anything other than the expensive beachwear he'd bought her from the hotel's boutique. It had been perfectly OK to wear a long hibiscus-print wrap-around skirt and matching bolero top when she'd spent time in his suite.

But the à la carte restaurant was sophisticated and glitzy—and her wardrobe definitely wasn't!

For a moment it seemed like fate. No suitable clothes, therefore a sign that she should not dine with Nikos Kiriakis. She would dial Reception and get them to put her through to his room, and she would make her excuses.

Or, of course, she could simply go down to the hotel boutique and buy something that *would* pass muster...

The boutique certainly did stock evening wear. Very expensive evening wear too. But then those who could afford to stay here could afford those prices. Not that she would have to pay—Stephanos had made it clear she could get anything she wanted from the hotel's select collection of shops and simply charge it to her room.

With sudden decision, she fetched her room key and set off for the boutique.

* * *

Nikos glanced at his watch. She was late. Well, that was no surprise. Women usually were. He sipped his beer contemplatively, eyes scanning the gardens, artfully spotlit here and there, and splashed with light from the pool's underwater lighting.

There was a swish of skirts, and someone hurried up to the table.

'I'm sorry I'm late!' The voice sounded slightly breathless.

He turned his head.

Slowly, very slowly, he drank her in. He felt his gut kick as if in slow motion.

She looked—breathtaking!

And as he slowly, very slowly, exhaled he realised that that was exactly what she had done. Taken his breath away.

She was wearing saffron. It shouldn't have gone with her fair hair and golden looks. It was a colour meant for a Greek complexion, dark hair, dark eyes.

Yet on this particular blonde it looked, quite simply, ravishing.

It was chiffon, layers of it, and it seemed to float, skimming over that beautiful body of hers like a kiss. Her hair was caught up—not in a rough-and-ready knot, the way it had been when she was swimming—but in an elegant, flawless style that lent her height and grace. A few tendrils whispered at her face, the nape of her neck.

He felt himself relax back in his seat as he drank her in.

Tiny earrings glinted at her lobes. Gold, like the delicate chain that encircled her neck, and each wrist. Her waist was very slender—he could have spanned it with his hands. The bones of her shoulders were exquisitely sculpted. Her neck was graceful, holding her head poised, erect.

Her eyes were deepened by make-up, her mouth accentuated with lipstick, the colours toning with the saffron. Her cheekbones seemed higher than they had been—more artful make-up, he surmised. A scent came from her—a light, haunting fragrance.

It caught at him.

She caught at him.

Slowly, he got to his feet.

'Won't you sit down?'

Janine took her place. Her breathing was quick, and shallow. It was because she'd been rushing, she told herself. Rushing ever since she'd realised that she'd taken ages and ages in the boutique, trying on just about every evening dress they'd had in her size. The assistant had been very patient, assuring her that the shop would not close until late that night, and that she could take all the time she wanted.

Choosing had been impossible—she didn't know why, but it had. In the end she'd followed her instinct, not her reason, and gone for the saffron. Her reason had told her that it should be worn by someone with much darker, more dramatic colouring than she possessed, but there had been something about the way the dress felt on her, whispered over her flesh, that had made her know that this was the one she wanted. So eventually, having tried on everything else again, she'd gone back to the saffron.

And now she was getting proof that she'd made the right choice!

With that same quick breathing she settled into her chair. Her dining partner was not wearing a suit, but his open-necked shirt was clearly not off the peg. It clung with tailored perfection to his broad shoulders, smoothing down over his torso, exposing the strong column of his throat.

She dragged her eyes away and let herself meet his gaze. He was sitting looking at her, and appreciating everything he saw!

'Hi,' she said idiotically. She had to recover her composure. She had to appear normal. Right now she was having palpitations like some Victorian maiden!

'*Kalispera,*' replied Nikos, his voice soft with amusement.

He liked what he saw—he liked it a lot. Oh, not just the exquisite appearance of this extraordinarily beautiful girl, but the fact that she was so clearly responding to him, and the way he was looking at her.

A waiter was there, hovering discreetly, but attentively.

'What would you like to drink?' Nikos asked her.

For a moment she wanted to say *Something strong, to calm my nerves*, but then she realised that strong liquor was the last thing she should drink right now. So instead she murmured, 'Oh, orange juice, please.'

He raised a slight eyebrow at this, and she went on lightly, 'To go with my frock!'

A smile indented his mouth and he nodded, relaying the order to the waiter in Greek—unnecessary though it was, since the hotel staff all spoke English. The man disappeared.

'It's extremely beautiful.' Nikos indicated her dress with a slight inclination of his head.

'I got it from the boutique just now. That's why I'm running late!'

She could hear her own breathlessness in her voice. It annoyed her—alarmed her. She was sounding like some wet-behind-the-ears teenage girl on her first date! It was ridiculous.

But the thing was she *did* feel like a teenager again! Excitement was running through her, and it was because of the man sitting opposite her. She could tell herself all she liked that Stephanos had simply sent him to babysit her, but her body wasn't taking that on board. Her body was shimmering like a fairy light on a Christmas tree!

'It was worth the wait,' said Nikos. He let his eyes wash over her again, to confirm his words.

The waiter's arrival with her glass of freshly squeezed orange juice was a reprieve, and she sipped eagerly. Then the *maître d'* arrived with two large leatherbound menus, bowing copiously to Nikos and running through the speci- alities of the day in rapid Greek.

Janine gazed down virtually blindly at the menu, forcing herself to read the words. As the *maître d'* bowed one last time, and glided away, Nikos listed the day's catch.

'Oh, not calamari!' Janine exclaimed. 'It's the suckers on the tentacles. They're disgusting!'

Nikos laughed. 'It can be served without those append- ages,' he assured her. 'Have you not eaten squid yet?'

Janine gave an exaggerated shudder.

'I'll stick to real fish, please.'

She settled on red mullet, with a seafood terrine to start, and closed the menu. She gazed out at the gardens.

'Isn't it the most beautiful place?' she sighed. A won- derful feeling of well-being was suffusing her. It was ev- erything—the beautiful gardens, the soft Mediterranean night and, above all, the presence of Nikos Kiriakis sitting opposite her, drawing her eye inexorably to him.

'The view is certainly quite stunning,' her companion murmured.

She glanced back to smile at him—and saw that he was not looking out over the gardens at all. Instead, his dark eyes were fixed on her face, and there was an expression in them she'd have had to be blind not to recognise...

She felt the colour run again, and hastily took a drink.

Nikos watched her reach for her glass. For a woman who made her living out of the touch of wealthy men, she really was remarkably unflirtatious. Perhaps, he found himself thinking, that was her allure. That she did not come on to her targets—she let them come on to her.

After all, she was so very much worth coming on to...

Emotions twisted inside him.

She might be sitting there, with a beauty as breathtaking as it was alluring, but it did not—could not—take away what she did, what she used that beauty for. That was what he had to remember. And her looks were of interest to him for one reason only—they would make his seduction of her palatable to him. He would get his revenge for the pain she was causing his sister.

He let his gaze rest on her, with the eyes of a connoisseur. She really was extraordiny. Some women couldn't make the transition from bikini to evening gown—but she could. By the pool and on the beach, she had looked sexy and sun-kissed. Now she looked graceful and soft, like a gazelle—her slender neck, her parted lips, the soft swell of her breasts beneath the chiffon of her dress.

As he watched he could see her nipples just graze against the filmy material, each one outlined for him.

All he had to do was reach out his hand, and touch with the tips of his fingers. Close his palm over their sweet ripeness…

Like a sheet of flame, desire sucked at him. Wanting to be sated. Now. Right now.

With visible effort he slammed down on his reaction.

He felt shaken.

Just as on the beach, his reaction had come out of nowhere, like a flashflood, thundering suddenly through his veins. Desire—hot, tearing, urgent. And out of control.

With gritted teeth he dragged back control over his body, his reaction. What the hell was he doing?

He was acting like a man besotted, and with some foxy little piece like Janine Fareham.

Yes, that was what he had to remember! That Janine Fareham used men's desires for her own ends—to buy gowns like the one she was displaying her body in tonight! He let his anger at her, deep and unrelenting and unforgiving, seep back, filling him like a dark tide. That was the only response he should be having to her. Oh, sexual desire, yes—but at *his* bidding, not hers. Under *his* control, not hers.

He relaxed again, back in control of his reaction to her.

He would take Janine Fareham, possess her and enjoy her.

And then get rid of her from his life—and Stephanos's life.

A line from Shakespeare snaked into his mind—'I'll have her, but I'll not keep her long.'

It would do very well for Janine Fareham.

Janine carefully removed some bones from her fish and took a forkful of the delicious dish. It was weird. She seemed hyper-aware of every movement she made. Aware of everything.

Especially Nikos Kiriakis. In its own disturbing way, dining with him was nerve-racking. She wanted to do nothing more than just sit there and stare at him open-mouthed. But she knew she could not. Must not. Instead she had to make conversation, or rather let him make conversation, and she had to respond as if she had her brain in place, instead of just wanting to gaze and gaze at him. She had to chat away—talking about innocuous subjects, like what there was to see on Skarios, and what kind of villa he was interested in buying, and things like snorkelling and windsurfing.

Not that she wasn't grateful for the ordinariness of the conversation. She didn't think she could deal with anything more.

Windsurfing was nice and safe, and since it was something she knew nothing about it meant she didn't really have to do anything other than prompt with a question and Nikos Kiriakis would do all the talking. So she could sit there, chin on her hand, and indulge herself wondering just what it was about his eyes that were so compelling, watching how his mouth moved when he talked, and how his dark, silky hair shaped his beautiful face...

Anyway, windsurfing wasn't something she'd ever had a go at. It seemed very strenuous, and everyone she saw doing it seemed to be very good—which was pretty off-putting, considering how useless she knew she would be. She was bound to spend most of her time falling off the board in a very undignified way. Nikos Kiriakis, it seemed, judging by his enthusiasm and knowledge, was a keen exponent. She was not surprised. He hadn't got that muscle tone from sitting behind an executive desk all his life!

Thinking about Nikos Kiriakis's body was not a good idea—it brought too many images vividly to mind. Instead, she watched his lean, strong hands move salt cellars and cutlery into position on the white damask tablecloth as he explained the mysteries of tacks and gybes, wind speed and board directions.

He paused and looked at her expectantly. She sighed and shook her head.

'It's no good. I'm totally lost. I think I'd rather just waft along on a boat, really.'

He gave a laugh. 'You don't do much wafting when you're crewing on a yacht!'

'I was thinking of something that had an engine and didn't require any work on my part,' she responded lightly.

'You enjoy not working?' There was nothing in his voice, his expression, to indicate anything more than a light-hearted riposte, yet there was something…perhaps in his eyes…

'Who doesn't?' she answered, just as lightly. 'And right now,' she went on, 'I definitely don't feel like working. I'm on holiday!'

For a second that fleeting look was in his eye again, and then he went on smoothly, so smoothly that she was sure she must have been imagining it, 'So, what do you do when you *do* work?' he asked.

He was pretty sure he knew the answer. It was predictable. She would probably say that she modelled a bit, or flitted from job to job, or dabbled in something to do with the fashion world. Something that gave a thin veneer of respectability to her true career—leeching off rich men.

'It depends what you mean by work,' she countered. She didn't want to talk about her life before she met Stephanos. That era was over now.

'Earning money?' he suggested dryly.

'Oh, that kind of work,' she answered, with deliberate lightness. 'Well, I'm fortunate enough not to have to do that. Especially now, of course. Thanks to Stephanos. He's made everything so much easier.'

It was true. Stephanos's generosity had been fantastic, more than filling the gap left by her coming out to Greece.

Silent white rage filled Nikos. She had the audacity, the sheer, unashamed gall, to sit there and tell him that Stephanos provided all the money she needed—and that even before, when he hadn't, there had been some other man to do so!

'So, life is one long holiday for you, then?' He made himself smile. Forced himself.

Had something of his underlying fury come through? There was a momentary flickering, an uncertain expression in her eyes. She opened her mouth, about to say something, but before she could speak the *maître d'* was gliding up to them, asking whether everything was to their liking.

They nodded their assent, and he bowed and took his leave again, and the moment had gone. It was just as well. She must not get the slightest suspicion of what he felt about her.

He changed the subject, telling her of his itinerary for the following day. A general tour of the island, to get the feel of the place, and then see what was already available, should he wish to buy something immediately. There had been some villas built along the coast, and conversions made of old Venetian merchant houses around the harbour at Skarios Town, or farms and village houses in the interior.

Whether or not he found something he wanted to buy,

he would definitely need something to rent for the next week or two. He wanted Janine Fareham to himself, in his company 24/7. A tucked-away villa would be ideal.

A perfect little love-nest…

He suppressed a mocking smile.

Love wasn't a currency Janine Fareham dealt in.

She wouldn't know the meaning of the word.

CHAPTER THREE

JANINE stood on her balcony, her eyes dreamy. The soft night wind played in her hair; the scent of jasmine and honeysuckle wafted from the gardens below. She should go indoors, she knew, and take off the beautiful dress, and all her make-up, brush out her hair and slip into bed, go to sleep...

And dream of Nikos Kiriakis...dream about every moment she had spent with him.

Confusion filled her. What was he doing to her, making her think about him like this? Making her want to dream about him? Making her want to think about nothing and no one except him.

What was it about Nikos Kiriakis that filled her with yearning like this? Feelings she had never felt before.

Never let herself feel before. Never wanted to feel before.

She'd always been so wary of falling for men—all her life. Always on her guard. She'd grown up watching her mother flit from one affair to another, one man to another, like a butterfly sipping nectar from an endless procession of flowers. At first, at the beginning of every affair, her mother would be ecstatic, devoting herself totally to whoever her latest lover was, and then it would always fall flat, and she would mope and be miserable—until the next man came along.

And there had always been a next man. One had never been enough, whoever he was. She had never looked for commitment, or any kind of permanent relationship—had said it was stifling, claustrophobic. She had always wanted to be free—free to have another affair, and another...

Janine's eyes shadowed. She could not live her life like that. She had more sense.

And the life she'd chosen to lead had made it easy to be sensible about men. Very easy. She'd had other things to occupy her mind.

But now you haven't—and till now you've never met a man like Nikos Kiriakis...

The voice whispered in her ear—enticing, insidious.

The image of his face swam before her eyes.

For a few precious moments she let it linger, luxuriating in delineating every superb feature, recalling every look in his gold-flecked eyes, every smile of that beautiful, sensual mouth.

For once, just for *once*, she wanted to forget everything else, ignore everything else except thinking, *feeling* about the man she could not get out of her head. Who was simply sweeping her away...

She wasn't her mother. Wasn't going to become like her. Hadn't her life so far proved that? Hadn't she followed a completely different path from the one her mother had taken? Surely for once she could indulge in going weak at the knees over a man? A man who took the breath from her body.

She sighed. Oh, yes, falling for Nikos Kiriakis would be so very, very easy.

And totally insane!

Don't do it! Just—don't do it!

She sighed again. And went to bed.

She dreamt of him all night. She tried desperately not to. Kept waking and trying to dream of something else—anything else. Anything! But still he came back in every dream. She could not banish him.

And in the morning, when she finally awoke, she found her heart was filled with a lightness, an eagerness for which there was only one explanation.

She was going to spend the day with Nikos Kiriakis.

And she didn't care that she should want to. The sun was shining down like gold on the world outside, the crimson bougainvillea was vivid on the white, white stone of the buildings, and the blue of the sea and the sky and the pool almost blinded her with their brilliance. Everything seemed brighter, more vivid, more vibrant—and she knew why, and didn't care. Excitement filled her, and anticipation, and her heart skittered, missing little beats as she got herself ready. Ready for Nikos Kiriakis.

Getting dressed took for ever. She discarded at least six outfits. Too casual, too overdressed, too beachy, too stuffy, too revealing, too concealing…

In the end she settled for a short pale green flared skirt and a white tank-top that rode up a fraction over her tummy, but not much. It was sleeveless, but not too décolleté. With it she wore a bead necklace and bangle, and flat, strappy sandals. She pulled her hair back into a long ponytail, clipped on a pair of looped earrings, and stared critically at her reflection.

It would have to do. She put on some lip gloss, a twist of mascara—that was enough. This was a daytime expedition on a holiday island. Anything more by way of make-up would look ridiculous. She grabbed a floppy white sun-hat, her dark glasses and her bag. Then, without looking any further in the mirror, she set off downstairs.

Her heart was beating faster already.

He was waiting for her in the lobby, as they'd agreed the night before. He was casually dressed himself, in polo shirt and chinos, and even though they were obviously designer they gave him a relaxed air. Not that he looked relaxed, she thought suddenly. He'd tensed as she'd approached, and his eyes had narrowed slightly.

Or had they flared?

She could tell. Tell he was reacting to her. Was suddenly excruciatingly self-conscious about it. About herself. The way he was looking at her. The way she wanted to look at him. She had to force herself to keep walking up to him, putting a natural-looking smile on her face.

'Hi,' she said. Her voice sounded breathy.

'Kalimera,' said Nikos Kiriakis. His eyes were doing that rapid, totalising flicker over her face, her figure, and she could feel the moment her pulse started to race as he did so. Then his eyes came to rest on hers.

Whoosh! She just about heard the rocket go off in her head.

How could she have forgotten—in the few short hours since her last vivid, oh, so vivid dream of Nikos Kiriakis— just what it was like to have those night-dark gold-flecked eyes looking into hers?

'Are you ready?'

His voice was deep, accented. She wanted him to speak again, to go on speaking, so she could hear that beautiful dark voice talking to her. Wanted to go on staring into those beautiful dark eyes...

'Janine?'

There was no tension in his face now, only a thread of amusement in his voice, as though he well understood her reason for standing there and staring at him like an idiot. She started, and tried to collect herself.

'Yes. Thanks. Um—shall we go?'

A smile tugged at his lips. She tried not to look. Her pulse was shooting all over the place.

She shifted her weight to her other leg and tightened her grip on her shoulder bag.

'Then let us be off.'

He guided her from the hotel. The heat hit her like a hammer the moment she stepped out from the air-conditioned interior into the shaded portico. A car was drawn up, a large, expensive German-marque four-door saloon—obviously the best the hire car company possessed, she surmised. Nikos opened the door for her and she climbed in, sinking down low in the passenger seat, grateful for the air-conditioning which was already taking effect. He crossed around the front of the car and got in on his side, folding his long limbs beside her. Suddenly the car, which had seemed huge, seemed very small.

'Seat belt,' he prompted. Hastily Janine fumbled with the belt and drew it down across her. It seemed to slide very tightly between her breasts, tautening the material of her tank top so that each globe was conspicuously outlined.

She saw his eyes hover on them and dipped her head, feeling flustered, trying to get the buckle of the seat belt into its socket.

'Allow me,' said Nikos, and twisted slightly to complete the task for her.

She yanked her hands away as soon as she could, but not before she felt the touch of his fingers against hers as he guided in the buckle.

It felt like an electric shock.

She buried her hands in her lap, gazing resolutely out through the windscreen as he gunned the engine and eased out of the parking slot. Even more resolutely she did not let her eyes glance down and sideways, to where his hand had curved over the gear lever.

'Where did you want to go first?' she said with determined brightness, as he moved the car forward and down the hotel's driveway towards the road.

She'd gone into hyper-aware mode again; she could tell. It was as if he were radiating some incredibly powerful forcefield that held her motionless in position, all her molecules charged, taken up into a higher energy level. Everything seemed more vivid, more real, than it had ever done before.

He gained the road, swung out onto the right-hand side, and stepped on the accelerator. The powerful car moved forward effortlessly.

'I'm going to follow the coast road south, then drop

down to Lethoni and take a look round there. Then rejoin the road and circle round to Skarios Town. Have you been there yet?'

He turned his head to glance at her, and she felt she needed to give him an answering look.

He'd slid a pair of sunglasses on, and she was grateful. It meant she wasn't exposed to that dark gold-flecked gaze directly. On the other hand, Nikos Kiriakis in a pair of dark glasses took her breath away...

'Er—no. Not yet,' she managed to get out. 'I've not really left the hotel. Stephanos wasn't too keen on me going out and about on my own.'

Nikos felt his mouth tighten. Smart guy, Stephanos. Letting Janine Fareham wander around looking the way she did would be an open invitation to have her snapped up by the first passing predatory male.

Did the girl have any idea what she looked like?

Emotions conflicted within him. She'd sauntered up to him, looking so breathakingly lovely, even in that simple outfit, that he'd felt his whole body respond. Her figure was perfection. Legs not too long, breasts not too slight—not too thin, and certainly not too fat. Some slim girls simply ended up looking like a bag of bones—but not Janine Fareham! There was a softness about her, but a fitness—in both senses of the word!—too. Yet she didn't look like some muscular athletic type. She just looked—

Beautiful. That was the word that kept thumping back into his mind. Beautiful. Nothing more, nothing less. Beautiful.

Natural.

Breathtaking.

Desirable.

Beautiful.

She wasn't wearing any perfume—she knew enough not to wear scent in the sun—yet there was her own scent about

her. Shampoo, maybe, or skin cream, or just—just Janine.
He wanted to inhale it, breathe it in.

He wanted to taste it…

Taste her.

No! He slammed a lid down on his reaction.

Not yet. He might want Janine Fareham, want to feel that
soft body in his arms, want to feel her breasts tighten
against him, want to taste that sweet, honeyed mouth, taste
all of her, every inch—but not yet. He had to play this
carefully. Very carefully. If he came on to her too strong
she might get nervous.

Worse than nervous.

Suspicious.

She seemed to have swallowed it whole, that Stephanos
had asked him to look after her…

Theos! He smothered a savage laugh. What lover in his
right sense would send another man to look after his mistress? Let alone a man with the kind of reputation that
Nikos enjoyed in Athens!

Yet she had believed it. Believed him.

A slight frown threatened between his eyes. As before—
yesterday, in the sea—he felt a thread of reluctance take
shape within him. Reluctance to do to Janine Fareham what
he knew he was going to do. What he had to do.

As before, he put it aside. It didn't matter that he was
deceiving her, was following his own private agenda with
her. She was threatening his sister—his sister who had
enough troubles in her life without the added anguish of a
husband besotted with another woman.

A woman any man could so easily become besotted
with…

His eyes narrowed.

Well, not him. Definitely not him.

He was here to do a job. Complete a task. Help his sister.

His expression lightened again. He did not need to feel
any compunction about what he was going to do. Janine

Fareham had made a mistake when she'd selected his brother-in-law for her next protector. His face hardened when he thought of the damage she was so thoughtlessly doing by having this affair with Stephanos. No, he told himself reassuringly, he did not need to feel anything for the girl except desire. And it wasn't, he went on, as if she wouldn't get a great deal of pleasure from what he intended for her. He knew he would.

That sense of satisfaction filled him again. He was here to seduce Janine Fareham, save his sister's marriage, and, into the bargain, have a very enjoyable brief affair with a very lovely woman. How could he feel bad about that?

He revved the engine, changed gear with a fast, fluent movement, and stepped on the accelerator, pulling out sharply. Two seconds later the camper van that had been slowing him down was far behind.

Janine smothered a sharp gasp of fear. Nikos had pulled out to overtake so abruptly she hadn't realised what he intended, and for a second she had been staring out of the windscreen on the wrong side of the road, with a blind corner coming up in what had seemed nothing more than a handful of yards ahead. Then, just as abruptly, Nikos had swung the car back onto the right side of the road, and taken the corner in a smooth, powerful movement.

Her nails, she discovered, were digging into the palms of her hands, and her spine ached from where she'd had to exert all her muscles not to sway precipitously.

He turned to her and grinned as he sped the car up the ascending slope of the road towards yet another hairpin. Thankfully, this time there were no other cars in the way for him to overtake.

'Frightened I'll crash?' he asked, his mouth tugging back.

She felt her heart crunch again as she took in the full impact of his smile.

'You wouldn't like to slow down a bit, would you?' she asked faintly.

His grin deepened. He changed gear again, glancing briefly back at the road, then at her again, and then finally—thankfully—the road, curling around the next hairpin in a tight, engine-revving manoeuvre.

'I've never had an accident yet,' he assured her, 'and I don't intend to.'

No, she thought, he wouldn't crash. Nikos Kiriakis would speed through life, foot down on the accelerator, and other cars—everything else—would get out of his way. He was a man who would get where he wanted. Get what he wanted.

Especially women.

She bit her lip. When Nikos Kiriakis wanted a woman he'd just go and get her. Help himself.

And what woman would say no?

What woman in their right mind would say no?

Would I? Would I say no?

A warm, shivery languor stole through her. In her mind's eye she saw herself, saw Nikos Kiriakis walking up to her, purpose in his eye, walking up to her and taking her hand, leading her to his bed and helping himself to her. Making her his own...

She felt the warmth of her blood, felt the soft, persistent vibration of the car beneath her thighs, felt her breath quicken. The vision seemed so real, the fantasy so tangible, she could hardly believe it existed only in her own imagination.

The fantasy of Nikos Kiriakis helping himself to her. Would she say no? *Could* she say no?

The question teased at her. The answer crushed her.

He hasn't asked you yet...and what makes you think he's going to?

She risked another glance at him.

In profile he was even more fantastic than full-on—if that were possible. His cheekbones were high, his nose strong and straight, his jaw clearly defined. And then there was that mouth—so beautifully sculpted.

She had a sudden vivid vision of that mouth moving over her skin…

Determinedly she dragged her gaze away, and looked out over the countryside instead.

That was what she must focus on. Nikos Kiriakis might be looking for a villa, but she—she was looking for Greece. At Greece.

Stephanos's country.

And now hers. Thanks to Stephanos, who had brought her here. To his home.

That was to be her home now.

A strangeness went through her. Her eyes stole back to Nikos Kiriakis. His land too. His home. His country.

All around—from islands to mountains, from seas to forests—this ancient, timeless country was his. The country that had been the cradle of western civilisation, whose art and thought still illuminated the world, twenty-five centuries later.

She looked around her. The ancient landscape was bathed in the light of the sun, unchanged, it seemed to her, for thousands of years. The olive groves, trees with their clusters of ripening fruits, their silvery leaves so carefully pruned and tended. A tethered donkey, grazing in the shade of a tree. Vineyards, low and lush, and, where there was space, the dark splash of purple on the ground, where rich grapes spread out to dry into sweet raisins.

As he drove the expensive, powerful car along this road, which wound and meandered as it had done for centuries, even when nothing more than an unmetalled track, she watched him. They closed in on a tractor drawing a cart. She could see the back of the farmer driving it. Nikos slowed down. Unlike the camper van, he did not pass it immediately, did not roar past in his expensive car. Instead he waited patiently, until the tractor turned off into a field, before speeding up. It was a small gesture, but illuminating.

She found it reassuring.

They had climbed over a spur of the land as it headed down towards the most southerly promontory of the island. The hairpins were done now, and Janine felt herself relax more as they cruised through this fertile landscape.

'What are those trees?' she asked. 'They're not olives.'

'Citrus. Orange or lemon,' he answered. 'The Ionian islands are very fertile—even Skarios, though it is further south than the others, and drier. Historically, their main importance was strategic—they were coveted by the Venetians, who ruled the islands on and off, and then later the British, of course. Now their main contribution is tourism. Some would say they have been over-developed, especially Corfu, though it is still perfectly possible to find quieter parts away from the resorts. But that is why there is such concern that Skarios should be developed carefully, without repeating the mistakes made on other islands.'

She gazed around. 'It's so beautiful as it is—the last thing you'd want is high-rise resorts and so on.'

He nodded. 'Stephanos has got it right with his hotel here—it melds into the natural landscape. He will, I hope, have considerable influence on what happens to the island.'

She glanced at him. 'Do you really want to buy a villa here?'

He was silent a moment. 'If I find something suitable,' he said at last. 'But I want to get a feel for the place first. The turning for Lethoni is just coming up—its main claim to fame is the Venetian fortress.'

She frowned. 'What were the Venetians doing in Greece?' she asked.

'Conquering it,' he answered dryly, swinging the car off the main coast road and down towards the promontory on which the little town of Lethoni sat, dominated by its Venetian fort. 'Greece is a crossroads,' he went on. 'Not wealthy in its own right—we are still a relatively poor country for Europe—but useful. The Venetians coming from the west, like the Ottoman Turks coming from the East, coveted the riches of the Byzantine empire. Greece—just got in the way.'

They wound down the narrow road into the small village, dwarfed by its huge stone fortress, standing four-square against all comers, by land or sea. There was a shingly beach beside the fortress, and some shops and restaurants and bars, and some old seventeenth-century Venetian houses, looking slightly strange here, with their Italianate style of archicture. Nikos parked the car and they got out. Again, the heat hit like a furnace.

Janine stood staring at the dark mass of the fortress, bag over her shoulder, sunhat in her hand. Nikos came round to her.

'The day is heating. You must put your hat on or you will burn.'

Without asking he took the hat from her suddenly nerveless fingers and placed it on her head, smoothing away loose strands of hair. He smiled down at her.

'There,' he said. His hands slid to her shoulders, resting there a moment. 'Now you are protected.'

Protected? The word mocked in her brain. She stood there, quite motionless, while Nikos Kiriakis rested his hands on her shoulders and smiled down at her. His hands were warm on her skin, closing over the curves of her shoulders, where her bare arms met the tank top she was wearing. His thumbs brushed close to her throat.

She felt as if every nerve in her body were firing at once. Simultaneously.

Her lips parted, eyes hanging helplessly on his, even though she could not see them, even though the black, glittering surface of his dark lenses looked down at her unreadably.

Protected? She had never felt less protected in her life. Never in more danger!

He dropped his hands away.

'Would you like to have a coffee? The bar over there seems pleasant enough.'

He pointed to where a café sat, by the edge of the little beach on which some local children were playing, and they wandered across, taking a table in the shade of a large striped awning. Janine gazed across the beach to the fortress beyond.

'Can one go round it?' she asked, for something to say—something to try and sound normal.

Nikos said something in Greek to the waiter who had come out to take their orders. Then he turned back to Janine.

'Apparently it is closed, awaiting renovation. Parts of it are in such disrepair it is dangerous. In the early years of the last century it was used as a prison. The plan now is to open it as a tourist attraction, possibly using the main court-yard as a concert venue. But nothing has yet been decided for certain. As you can see—' he gestured around '—this is a sleepy place.'

Janine followed Nikos's gaze. On closer inspection the buildings, though pretty, were peeling, and one or two obviously were closed up, with boarded windows.

'It could be lovely!' she exclaimed.

'Indeed, yes. But it must be carefully done. One of my interests here, apart from searching for a villa for myself, is to see what investment can be made to restore such places as Lethoni.'

He gave the order for coffee, watched the waiter depart, then turned back to Janine.

'It's an interest I have in many such communities across Greece. Investments must be carefully made, so that any restoration or development is in keeping with the traditional style and way of life. The idea is to revive communities so that they may thrive once more in a new economy. In rural or remote areas, such as here, too many people have to leave to seek employment in larger centres. Only the old people are left. But there is also a danger that too much development will not only ruin these places, but also attract entrepreneurs from the cities, who simply arrive to take over any opportunities for profit from local people, who are left out of the loop.'

She looked troubled. 'Is that what Stephanos is doing?' She did not like to think of him profiting from this beautiful island at the expense of the islanders.

Nikos gave a wry smile. 'On the contrary. His hotel is a joint venture with Skariot business partners, plus all the staff are local, and a good percentage of the profits will be reinvested in the island's infrastructure. Stephanos owns hotels all over the world, but those in Greece are very special to him.'

She smiled. 'I'm glad. He's such a lovely man—he doesn't seem like a ruthless businessman at all!'

Nikos's smile became yet more wry. 'He can be very tough, when necessary, in business. I learnt a lot from him!'

Her eyes widened. 'You? But you seem loads tougher than Stephanos! He's such a total pussycat!'

'To you he is indulgent,' responded Nikos. She would have had to be deaf not to hear the cynical note in his voice.

Her chin lifted. 'Is it so surprising? In the circumstances?'

Again, as she had last night over dinner, she felt a sudden frisson of unease go through her.

If Lethoni was so sleepy it seemed to be in permanent siesta, Skarios Town, the main town on the island, was by contrast a hive of bustling activity. Though it wasn't unbearably crowded, it was certainly busy, with a good proportion of shops dedicated to the influx of holidaymakers who had already discovered this off-the-beaten-track island.

Janine sat dutifully while Nikos made clear his requirements to the town's two estate agents. The entire conversation was in Greek, obviously, and though Janine glanced curiously at some of the details of villas which were presented with great deference to their clearly very wealthy prospective client, only the pictures made sense, not the Greek writing. For the most part she simply sat and watched Nikos.

It was a joy simply to be able to watch him while he was busy doing something else. It was incredible, she found herself thinking in amazement. She had seen good-looking men before—they had been no strangers to her when she was growing up with her mother, in her rootless, purposeless existence—yet no one had ever had the kind of impact this man was having on her now.

It was everything about him—not just his looks, but the way he talked, moved. The way his hand slashed when he didn't like something; the way his palm opened expansively when he did. The way he held his head, with that slightly arrogant tilt to it, and the way he talked, even though she could not understand what he said, that spoke of a man who knew exactly what he wanted and expected to get it.

And was *she* on that list of things he wanted and expected to get?

He folded the last of the presentations away and got to his feet, drawing out one of the sets of details. Presumably, thought Janine, as she got to her feet too, one of them had found possible favour.

'Anything interesting?' she asked, as they walked out onto the cobbled street.

He gave a shrug. 'Possibly. But I took this to be polite more than anything.' He indicated the brochure he'd been given. He changed the subject. 'Now, you are a woman, and here are some shops—time for some retail therapy! As for me, I shall suffer in silence—and simply be on hand to do my masculine duty and pay for everything!'

There was resigned humour in his voice, as though he knew indeed that it was his lot in life to pay for what women purchased.

She gave an outraged laugh. 'You will not!' she exclaimed. 'I'll buy my own souvenirs, thank you! You don't have to pay for me.'

He glanced at her. 'I thought that was Stephanos's privilege,' he said dryly.

Her face stiffened suddenly. 'I do have money of my own,' she answered. 'Stephanos has been incredibly generous, yes—how could I possibly deny that?—but I'm not dependent on him.'

'No?' The doubt in his voice made her feel uncomfortable.

'No,' she answered firmly. 'And I'm not dependent on you, Mr Kiriakis, to buy my souvenirs!'

'Nikos.' He took her arm, his hand closing over her flesh, stopping her in the street. 'My name is Nikos.'

He was looking down at her. Too close. She could not see his expression, could not see his eyes, but she felt her heart suddenly give a little thrill.

'Nikos,' he repeated softly, and then with humour in his voice, real humour now, he let her go. 'And you may, with my blessing, buy all your own souvenirs!'

Her heart gave another little thrill—for a quite different reason this time. Nikos Kiriakis amused was just as capable of sending her heart-rate haywire as Nikos being formidable!

In the end she only bought one souvenir, a pretty little embroidered pouch that could keep jewellery in. She paid for it herself.

'Is that all?' Nikos frowned.

She nodded.

Was that her appeal? he found himself thinking cynically. That she was cheap to run? Even as he framed the question he mocked it. Oh, no. Janine Fareham had an appeal that was nothing, absolutely nothing to do with whether she was cheap to keep or not!

He watched her walk out of the shop ahead of him. The flared skirt was made of soft material, and moulded enticingly around the roundness of her bottom. Drawing his eyes to it.

And not his alone. He was not the only male present to be aware, very aware, of her blonde beauty. He intercepted one tourist looking lustingly after her, and found himself glaring at him aggressively. The man got the message and flicked his eyes away hurriedly.

Nikos followed Janine out of the shop. He did not like other men looking at her like that. He closed up on her. Without thinking about it, he realised he was reaching his arm to drape it around her shoulder and draw her closer to him.

Her head twisted, eyes flaring to his, and he could distinctly feel her tense under the hand that was over the curve of her shoulder.

He smiled down at her.

'Lunch?' he suggested. 'Let's try down by the harbour.'

For a moment she just stayed frozen. He wished he could see her eyes, but she'd replaced her dark glasses in the glare of the sun. But he didn't need to see her pupils to know that they were flaring.

Satisfaction went through him. He liked the idea of Janine Fareham responding to him. He liked it a lot.

He walked her down to the harbour, his arm still around her shoulder. He told himself it was to keep other tourists at bay, both physically and visually, as they threaded through the crowded narrow street. That it was part of his careful campaign to move in on her, stage by stage, until he could make his final move on her.

But there was another reason, too, he knew, why he kept his arm around her.

Because it felt good. It felt the right place for his arm to be.

And because Janine Fareham felt good pulled against him, very good. Very good indeed.

'Red or blue?'

His voice was genial as he indicated, with his free hand, the two restaurants with seating areas across the roadway right beside the harbour. One had a red awning covering the tables, the other a blue.

'I don't mind.'

Was there something a little odd about her voice? he wondered. A little strained?

He smiled. 'What is it you say in English, when you are trying to choose? *Any, many, many more*?'

Janine gave a laugh. It helped to break the strain that had engulfed her ever since Nikos had walked out of the souvenir shop and casually, as if it was the most obvious thing in the world to do, put his arm around her.

Her stomach had dropped to the ground and her heart-rate had gone crazy! For a moment she had simply stalled, unable to do anything except register the 'whoosh' that had gone off inside her again. Then, frantically, she'd tried to regain control of her reactions. She mustn't make anything out of what he'd done. It had been a casual gesture on his part, to guide her through the crowds. Nothing more!

'It's *eeny-meeny-miny-mo*,' she corrected him. 'And, no, I haven't the faintest idea what it means. Um—how about that one?' She pointed to the restaurant with the blue awning. 'There's a table free right by the water's edge.'

They made their way over to it, the shade of the awning taking away some of the heat. Janine sat down, slipped off her sunglasses and scraped off her sunhat, then untied her hair and shook it loose with a feeling of relief. As her head stilled she realised Nikos was looking at her.

He'd taken his dark glasses off at last, and she reeled under the full impact of his power-on gaze.

Weakness washed down through her. She could feel her lips parting wordlessly, her pupils dilating. Colour flaring along her cheekbones.

Then abruptly, like a light turned off, the moment ended. Nikos had turned his head as the waiter approached, placing menus down on the table and hovering attentively.

Janine reached fumblingly for one of the menus, but as she stared at it uncomprehendingly it was not only because she was staring at the Greek pages. It was because she was completely incapable of thinking.

Desire. Naked, blatant desire. That was what she'd seen in those intense gold-flecked eyes. Nothing more and, dear God alive, nothing less!

As if reaching for a shield she fumbled on the table surface, lighting on her dark glasses, and shoved them back on her nose as quickly as her trembling hands could manage. Then and only then did she feel safe. Safe enough to answer Nikos's enquiry as to what she would like to drink.

Her breathing felt ragged, and yet she managed to get out, 'Oh, just mineral water, please—sparkling,' before taking refuge once again in the menu. After another moment she realised she was still looking at the Greek pages, and hurriedly turned over to the pages which repeated the menu in both English and German, for the tourists.

Slowly she got control back over her body.

With real effort of mind, she focused on the menu.

'I think I'll just have a Greek salad,' she said at last. 'I can't face anything hot in this heat!'

'You're not tempted by the squid, then?' Nikos's voice was lightly baiting.

That powerful intensity had gone from his eyes, his face. It made it easier. Easier for her to try and be normal. She pulled an expression of exaggerated disgust.

'No sale! Not while they have wiggly tentacles with suckers on them!'

Nikos laughed. 'Fried in batter, you don't see the suckers.'

She waved her hands in horrified negation and he laughed again, then gave his order to the hovering waiter. Janine listened to the rapid Greek and caught not a word. She sighed. It was a tough language to learn. She couldn't even read a menu unless it was translated.

I'm going to have to try and learn, she thought. For Stephanos's sake.

The waiter took his leave, scurrying away, and Nikos's gaze came back to Janine.

He found his eyes softening. That moment, just now, when she'd shaken her hair loose, revealing her eyes from behind those shades, had kicked him—hard. The combination of that fabulous golden hair tumbling over her near naked shoulders and those beautiful chestnut eyes had riveted him. And when he'd seen her lips part, her pupils dilate like that as he'd looked at her, then it had been even more potent.

She'd been helpless, it was obvious. Helpless to do anything except let him look at her. She couldn't fight it, couldn't deny it. She'd just had to sit there and let him make it very, very clear to her just what he felt about her.

Now he wanted to reach out and touch her, stroke her bare arm as it lay on the blue and white paper tablecloth, close his hand over hers, wind his fingers with hers...

A strange feeling went through him. Desire, yes, but something more. He wanted to touch her, but not with desire, not just now. Now he just wanted to touch her...well, because. That was all. Because he did. Just as he'd wanted to put his arm around her as they'd left the souvenir shop.

To show her, and all the world, that she was his.

His body stilled. How could he be feeling possessive about Janine Fareham? He couldn't care less about her! He simply needed to remove her from Stephanos, get her out of his sister's marriage!

His mouth tightened. There was nothing *personal* about what he was doing. Janine Fareham was simply an obstacle, an impediment, a problem that had to be neutralised.

He'd better make sure he remembered that.

'Seen enough?'

Nikos's voice was lazy and amused. Janine turned round and felt her heart give that familiar skip it gave every time she set eyes on him again. He was leaning against a half-ruined wall, arms crossed, looking very relaxed.

He also looked quite untroubled by the afternoon heat, which even in this elevated position, which caught what little breeze there was, was still punishing. For herself, she felt hot and sticky, her feet chalky with dust. But Nikos Kiriakis just went on looking cool—in both senses of the word.

'Just about,' she answered. 'Sorry to have spent so long,' she went on, as she threaded her way towards him carefully amongst the broken masonry. 'But I've never seen a Greek temple before.'

'Never?' Nikos's voice was mildly enquiring.

'I've never been to Greece before,' she explained.

Was there something strange about her voice? he wondered. If so, he could not imagine why there should be.

Then she was speaking again. 'It's not really my end of the Med.'

'Spain?'

She shook her head, negotiating a tricky step.

'The South of France, more.'

Nikos's mouth thinned fractionally. The Côte d'Azur— the glittering French Riviera—oozing money and wealth and rich living. The traditional stamping ground of the adventuress. He was not surprised she was familiar with it.

She had paused by the broken base of a column, gazing around. It was, conceded Nikos, a beautiful place for a temple. He'd spotted the brown archaeological site notice along the road back from the northern extremity of the island, where they'd headed after lunch, and suggested a brief diversion. There wasn't a great deal left of the temple—much of the stone had been taken away over the centuries to build houses—but the views down to the sea were still spectacular. It was a high and lonely place. Just right for communing with the gods.

He'd been surprised at her interest. The site had been open, with no entrance ticket required, but the tourist authorities had set up explanatory noticeboards describing the site and mapping it out as it must once have stood. Janine had pored over them.

She must have spent a good twenty minutes trawling over the site. She seemed excessively taken with it. Nikos had left her to it. There were no other visitors at that time of day, and they were well off the beaten track. He'd watched her wandering around. She had an extraordinary natural grace, he'd found himself thinking—there was great pleasure in watching her.

She didn't look in the least what she was, he realised. He had called her a foxy piece last night, to remind himself just what kind of female she was. He frowned. But the description didn't fit. She was simply beautiful; that was all. With a natural, unforced loveliness in every line of her body, every turn of her head. And her behaviour was not that of a gold-digging mistress either. She'd cast out no lures to him—other than her own natural beauty!—made no attempt to flirt with him or attract him. Oh, she was highly self-conscious of him, that much was obvious, but there had been no deliberate come-on from her—nor any deliberate invitation.

His frown deepened. He should not be surprised that it had taken an exceptional woman to snare Stephanos away from his wife. As a rich man, Stephanos had all his life been pursued by women, just as he was himself. As Nikos was doing now, so Stephanos had enjoyed a good selection of them when he was younger. Then, of course, he had fallen in love with Demetria, and from then on no other woman had existed for him. He'd laid siege to her, determined to wait it out until she found the courage to divorce her first husband.

Nikos's eyes flickered. Love was a quite alien concept to him. He could not imagine falling in love with a woman. Desiring her, yes. But not loving her. As for going to any lengths to win her—well, that was beyond him as well. Yet not Stephanos, apparently. Stephanos had endured the wrath of his beloved's father, who hadn't wanted his daughter's marriage overturned, had stood by her when she did finally find the courage to end her marriage, and had married her the moment she was legally free to do so.

That was devotion indeed!

Nikos's mouth tightened. And yet it looked as if he was risking all that for a hole-and-corner adulterous affair with a twenty-five-year-old girl!

He watched her now, as she took a careful step down the ancient stairs. As her weight shifted, suddenly the cracked paving wobbled precariously. He was there in an instant, hands closing around her slender waist, steadying her.

For a moment, timeless and motionless, he felt her soft body pliant in his arms, her breasts crushed against his chest. Then, slowly, he lowered her to the ground and eased back from her, still touching her waist with his hands.

'OK?' he asked.

Janine caught her breath. Her heart was skidding away.

'Fine. Yes. Thanks.' Her answer was totally distracted. She could do nothing except gaze helplessly up at him.

His hands fell away from her waist. Immediately she felt bereft.

He smiled down at her.

'Time to go?'

She followed meekly after him, back to the little car park

down an unmade track from the road. She fought hard to regain her composure.

Nikos, however, she realised, was totally relaxed. Had it meant nothing to him, then, that unintentional embrace? Her eyes flickered to him as he drove off. Sexy as those dark glasses were, they were very frustrating. She could not see his eyes, or tell their expression.

His thoughts were veiled from her.

Hers, however, were all too transparent.

CHAPTER FOUR

THE silky water of the swimming pool slid over Janine's body, soothing the ragged edges of her mind. Her thoughts were going round and round in her head. Had been doing so ever since that moment in the temple.

Now, as she glided slowly up and down the pool in the early evening, she tried to confront them.

She was in danger, serious danger, of falling for a man it would be madness to fall for under any circumstances. Let alone these. She was here in Greece for Stephanos, that was all! For no other reason. There was no room in her life for falling for a man like Nikos. Outside Greece her life was so completely different from what Stephanos had given her—and here in Greece her focus had to be Stephanos. It had to be! Nikos Kiriakis was a complication she could do without.

A dangerous complication.

She did a sudden dive, as if she could escape her thoughts.

She surfaced in a shower of water drops and took a lungful of air, reaching with her toes for the bottom of the pool, which was just in her depth still.

Across on the other side, she saw that one of the male hotel guests was playing with his children in the pool, while his wife sunned herself. He punched an inflatable ball through the air and his children plunged after it like a school of baby dolphins, squealing delightedly. He looked after them, smiling broadly.

Something gave Janine a pang. One of the children, a little girl about ten years old, she thought, came paddling triumphantly back to her father, pushing the ball in front of her and calling out in a soft, piping Greek voice, *'Vava, Vava!'*—Papa! Papa!

The man held out his arms to his daughter.

'Ela!'

It was a word Janine had become familiar with. She wasn't sure what it meant, but the parents here often used it to respond to their children's calls. She watched the little girl swim up to her father, present him with the ball, and wrap him in a big hug. He laughed, and kissed her wet hair affectionately before tossing the ball to his other children.

Lucky little girl.

The words were in Janine's mind before she could stop them.

Lucky little girl to have a father to play with her, dote on her...

She had not been so fortunate.

She'd sometimes wondered if her mother even *knew* who had fathered her. She'd been so evasive, so completely indifferent all Janine's childhood, that she'd given up trying to find out. When she was a teenager she'd realised just how impossible it was for a woman to tell who had fathered her child if she slept with more than one man during a menstrual cycle. So perhaps her mother simply didn't know, she'd concluded chillingly.

She hadn't even had any clues from her own appearance. She was blonde, just like her mother, and apart from her chestnut-coloured eyes, physically very similar. So much so that as her mother had gotten older it had become obvious that she found it increasingly painful to have a grown up daughter hanging around, like a younger version of herself. The self that her mother's unforgiving mirror no longer showed.

It had been a kindness to her mother when Janine had taken herself off—and a relief to herself to be away from the world her mother adored, making a new life for herself. She hadn't missed the world she'd grown up in—the endless partying, the obsession with appearance, her mother's constant need to have men around her. It was all so superficial, so pointless, so purposeless. That was why she'd made her own life so different.

But it had still been a shock when she'd heard of her mother's death three years ago, even if she *had* died the way she'd lived. In a smashed-up sports car with another woman's husband in the driving seat. The post-mortems had shown that both of them were well over the limit for alcohol.

With her mother gone she'd had no other relatives in the world, so far as she knew. No one to whom she meant anything more than friendship.

Her face shadowed. Then Stephanos had come, like a gift from heaven, into her life. Her gratitude to him was boundless. She would make the very most of him she could, however little that could be.

As for Nikos Kiriakis, she wouldn't think about him.

He was dangerous. And he was unnecessary.

And she was better off without him.

Nikos strolled out onto his balcony. The setting sun streamed over the gardens, silhouetting the slender pointed cypress trees that framed the vista. Stephanos had chosen well, he thought. The site was superb. And his architects had done him proud. He had selected the best.

A frown furrowed between his eyes. Down in the pool he could see Janine, swimming slowly up and down.

He'd selected the best for his mistress, too. The day he'd just spend with Janine Fareham had made him realise just what it was about her that so beguiled his brother-in-law. It wasn't just her beauty, outstanding though that was. It was the way she moved, the way she smiled and laughed, the way she brushed her hair back off her face—every gesture caught at him. Captivated him.

He stilled. That was a dangerous word—captivated.

He put it aside. It had no place in what he wanted of the girl who was causing his sister so much anguish.

All I have to do is take her to bed. Nothing else.

That, surely, he thought with cynical self-mockery, would not be too hard a task! He only had to think of Janine to want her.

Deliberately he recalled the way she'd felt in his arms as he'd caught her in that ruined temple. Her body had felt so soft, so rounded, so enticing. He'd been hardening against her when he'd put her away from him.

And so had she. He had felt her breasts swelling against him.

It had been intoxicating.

Captivating…

His mouth thinned. What was wrong with him? Janine Fareham was a beauty, and he enjoyed taking beautiful women to bed. They enjoyed it too. He saw to that. He didn't have to be captivated by them to bed them!

And he certainly wasn't about to be captivated by the likes of Stephanos's young mistress. On the contrary, it was *she* who was going to be captivated by *him*. And he was making good progress on that score, he knew. Throughout the day her response to him had been growing—he'd seen to that, cultivated it carefully, step by step—and that final episode in the temple, when she'd pressed against him, had been the most expressive yet.

The way she'd gazed up at him as he'd held her in his arms. Her lips had been parted, her eyes wide…

Captivating. Quite captivating…

With a jerk of impatience with himself he pulled away from the balcony, striding indoors.

He headed for the phone. Time for stage two in his programme of seduction.

Stage one had been to cultivate Janine Fareham, make her responsive to him. Arouse her appetite.

Stage two was to starve it.

*   *   *

Janine sat at her breakfast table and crumbled tiny pieces of bread for the sparrows that hopped around on the paved terrace, eager for their breakfast too. She fed them in a desultory fashion, but her real attention was focused on looking out for Nikos Kiriakis.

She knew she was, and knew she should not be, but she couldn't help it. She wanted to see him.

She hadn't seen him since he'd dropped her off in the hotel portico the day before and told her he had some phone calls to make. She'd told herself she was glad he hadn't joined her in the pool, that she had no intention of spending any more time with him—no intention of letting him come anywhere near her again—but if that was so then why had she waited in her room until the last possible moment before the buffet stopped serving, just in case he might phone through to her and suggest they dine together again?

And why was she now watching everyone who came and went, longing for each one to be Nikos Kiriakis?

And why was there a dull churning in her stomach as she waited and watched for him though he never came?

A thought struck her like a knife. Had he gone? Left the hotel?

Dismay plunged through her. Dismay at the thought of never seeing Nikos Kiriakis again.

She scraped her chair back abruptly and stood up.

This was bad. She had to stop this. Now. She had to put a lid on this ridiculous reaction she was having. She had to get a grip. Control herself.

Determinedly, she picked up her book and her bag and headed indoors, up to her room. She would keep herself busy today. Take her mind off Nikos Kiriakis. Stop herself recalling in Technicolor detail every last minute of yesterday, and the night before over dinner.

I'll do the windsurfing course, she thought decisively.

Trying to stop myself falling in the water should take my mind off Nikos Kiriakis!

Immediately, like a traitor, came a vivid memory of how he'd moved the salt cellar and cutlery into position with those beautiful long fingers of his, to show her the effects of wind direction on board direction...

She pushed it aside and walked up to Reception to book herself on the course.

She saw him at once, her eyes flying to him, heart leaping like a traitor. He was standing, his back to her, talking to one of the reception desk staff, and he was wearing a hand-tailored business suit again. He looked tall, and dark, and devastating. Her heart leapt again, and then plunged. He had a black leather briefcase on the floor beside him, and she could see car keys in his hand. He said something to the receptionist, who smiled and nodded, and then picked up his briefcase.

He saw her the moment he turned. She was poised, immobile, just past the double doors that opened onto the reception area. He walked towards her with his lithe, rapid stride.

'Good morning. You look ready for the sun.' His voice was pleasant, his manner amiable. And there was nothing in it, nothing at all, to indicate that to him she was anything more than a woman he had babysat yesterday for the sake of his business associate and friend Stephanos Ephandrou.

She gave an uncertain smile in return, hiding the constriction in her throat that had suddenly tightened. 'You look ready for work,' she countered.

He gave a wry smile back. 'As you can see. I have several business appointments today, one of which is in Patra, on the mainland. And what have you planned for today?'

There was no suggestion that she might accompany him. She took her cue, fighting the wave of desolation that was sweeping through her.

'Oh,' she answered brightly—too brightly, 'I've decided

I'm going to give the windsurfing a go. I'm just going to see if there are any lessons free this morning.' She nodded towards the reception desk.

He smiled. 'Very energetic.' He shot the cuff back on his sleeve and glanced at his watch. 'Well, do please excuse me. I must set off.'

'Yes. Of course. Please don't let me keep you.' She kept her composure with iron nerve. Then suddenly, as his body language told her he was about to turn away, she said, 'Thank you so much for taking me out and about yesterday, Mr Kiriakis—'

He stilled. Then, with the slightest pull of his mouth, he replied, 'Nikos.' His voice dropped. 'Nikos,' he repeated. His voice was low, his lashes sweeping down over his cheeks. Briefly, so briefly she thought she must have imagined it, he touched the backs of his fingertips to her cheek.

'Enjoy your windsurfing…'

He smiled, and walked away.

Her eyes followed him all the way out of the hotel, her heart beating like a hammer.

Despite her windsurfing lesson, the day seemed to last for ever. So did the evening. A restlessness filled her, making every minute seem an hour, every hour a tedious eternity. And the windsurfing had left her with muscles aching in unaccustomed places and a severe loss of dignity—she had, as she had known she would, fallen a depressing number of times.

For the rest of the over-long day, the rest of the lonely, tedious evening, she idled the time away fretfully. Whereas she had once revelled in the laziness of being pampered at a five star hotel, now she was discontented. Restless.

Would she ever see Nikos again?

Stop it! she told herself fiercely, over and over again. Be glad he's gone. Grateful. He was the last thing you needed.

But Nikos had done something to her, and it could not

be undone. He had woken something in her that had never been woken before. And it was alive in her—and hungry.

Hungry for him.

She couldn't get Nikos Kiriakis out of her mind. Her thoughts. Her skin. She knew she was being a fool, an idiot—but she couldn't help herself. Endless arguments went round and round in her head as she paraded every reason, every *good* reason, why she should put Nikos Kiriakis out of her mind. And not one of them had the slightest effect on her.

She wanted him.

It was so very, very simple. She wanted him. Wanted to see him, hear him, be near him, feast her eyes on him. Wanted to be in his company, wanted to feel that wonderful, heady sense of intoxication that fired through her whenever she thought of him, remembered him. Remembered those beautiful, dark gold-flecked eyes, that sculpted mouth, the way his silky black hair made her yearn to play her fingers through it, smooth along those high-planed cheekbones, edge along the line of his jaw...

And above all—above all she wanted him to want her—to desire her, to make love to her.

Nikos. Nikos Kiriakis...

His name sang in her head, in her blood. Heating it like a fever. Filling her with a wanting that left her weak, sick.

Please let me see him again—please!

The litany sounded in her head. Relentless. Hopeless.

The next day was even worse. She couldn't face breakfast downstairs, couldn't face another windsurfing lesson. Couldn't face anything. She wanted to be brave and ask Reception if Nikos Kiriakis had checked out, but she didn't dare. Didn't dare admit to herself that if he had she would be desolate.

She tried to think about Stephanos. Think about where he was right now, what time it would be in New York, what he was likely to be doing. She wished she could phone him, speak to him, make him real for her again. To remind her why she was here in Greece. Not to ache for a man who had set her blood on fire but to make the most, the very most, of what she had been given so unexpectedly, so miraculously. Stephanos. Not Nikos. Stephanos.

But it was Nikos she wanted. Nikos she craved.

And Nikos she did not have.

He'd gone. He had to have gone. There was no point hoping otherwise. He must have left, and that was that. Why bother to leave a message for her? He'd done what Stephanos had asked him to do and then got on with his own life.

He'd have a woman somewhere, anyway, in his life. Of course he would! Someone poised and sophisticated and mega-glamorous. A man like that would never be on his own for a second!

Her heart churned as she thought of Nikos Kiriakis with that faceless, poised, sophisticated, mega-glamorous woman at his side. In his arms. His bed.

No! She pushed the tormenting thought aside, shifting restlessly on her lounger beside the pool.

Someone hunkered down beside her.

'So,' said Nikos Kiriakis, 'what happened to the wind-surfing?'

As her eyes flew open, as she heard his voice, her face lit like the dazzle of sunshine after rain. For a second Nikos reeled. Something shot through him, he didn't know what. Then he got his sense back.

Her response was just what he wanted. Confirming that he'd played his hand in exactly the right manner. Whetted her appetite for him—then withdrawn from the scene. Letting her hunger for him.

And she was hungry all right. He saw it leap in her eyes, in the way they lit up, her gaze fastening on his as though she could hardly believe it. He let her gaze feast greedily on him—all of him. Her eyes moved down from his face, widening as they skimmed down over his naked torso, and lower still. The squat he was in made his quads stand out, his forearms resting on them for balance. For a moment he let her go on gazing at him, then he straightened.

'Windsurfing,' he said. 'Let's see what you can do.' He held his hand down to her commandingly.

She took it like a lamb, getting up off the lounger. He frowned. 'You'll need a T-shirt—you'll burn on the water otherwise.'

Wordlessly she groped in her beachbag and drew out a loose white top. For his part he flicked out the dark blue T-shirt he'd had draped over one shoulder and put it on. She did likewise with hers.

He stood in front of her, smiling down at her.

'Ready?'

She nodded, still wordless. Incapable of speech. He took her hand, and they headed down to the windsurf station.

Bliss, thought Janine, her head a haze of delight. Bliss—oh, bliss! She felt her hand in his, warm and strong, and felt faint with it. She couldn't speak, could only go along with him, her feet wading through the hot sand beside him.

He went up to the attendant and chatted to him. They discussed various boards, and then he selected two. A beginner's board for her, and something very racy-looking for him.

'The wind's too light in the morning for anyone but beginners, but I haven't been out for a while,' he told her. 'So let's see how you're doing.' He held her board out to her, then turned to lift down the sails from their racks.

'Um, I'm not very good yet,' she managed to get out, as he fixed the sails onto the boards and checked they were stable.

He flashed a grin at her. 'After one lesson? How could you be? OK, let's go.'

The next hour passed in a blur of dazed, incandescent bliss. She was still totally useless at windsurfing, but she didn't care. Didn't care in the slightest. Because this time— this time Nikos Kiriakis was teaching her.

And the bliss of that was indescribable.

There were just so many opportunities for him to be fantastically, excitingly, intoxicatingly close to her. Running through the sail-raising manoeuvre on the sand and in the shallows. Helping her get her balance. Helping her back on her board when she fell off—several times. Helping her raise her sail again.

Today she made better progress. Not much, but a bit. He said as much as they finally headed to shore.

'You just need more practice,' he told her.

'About a million years of it!' She laughed ruefully.

'Maybe not quite that long.' He paused. 'But close…'

She laughed, not caring, and then suddenly she became aware that he was looking not at her face but at the way her wet T-shirt was clinging to her breasts.

And suddenly, quite suddenly, the humour vanished from her face.

She felt her breasts tighten. Felt it as distinctly, as clearly, as if a bell had rung. Felt her nipples puckering, visibly standing out through the clinging material of her bikini top and the T-shirt.

And then his eyes were being dragged away from her breasts—and up to her eyes.

For a long, helpless moment she gazed at him, while her body bloomed for him.

'Nikos—' Her voice was a thread.

He gave a small, minute smile, and she felt her breath still.

Then, with a flicker of his eyes, he was hefting up the board and carrying it to the rack. He came back to repeat the action for hers, and when everything was restored he turned to her and said, 'Lunch.'

They ate at the beach bar that did lunchtime snacks. He drank a beer, she a glass of white wine. It went to her head like champagne.

And so did Nikos Kiriakis.

It was heaven to have him again. Heaven to watch his eyes, his face, the strong column of his throat, the broad strength of his shoulders. Heaven to gaze at him, listen to his deep, accented voice, hear his laugh, watch his smile. Heaven to feel his eyes caress her...

Heaven, heaven, heaven.

Her heart sang like an uncaged bird.

If I have nothing else, she thought, I have this!

And then, as he pushed his coffee cup away from him, his eyes lifted to hers. There was no caress in them. His voice as he spoke sounded brisk and businesslike.

As if he'd just moved a million miles away from her.

'I'm afraid I have to go now, Janine. I've sorted out my business here. The estate agents know what I want by way of a villa, and will keep me informed, and all my business appointments are complete. I have to get back to Athens. I'm flying out this afternoon.'

It was like a dagger. A dagger plunging right inside her. She swallowed. It was like swallowing fire.

'Of...of course...'

His eyes flickered over her. 'It's been good knowing you, Janine.' The way his voice slid over the initial J, softening it to a 'zh', made her heart contract. He got to his feet. He seemed very tall. Very far away already. The dagger was sliding deeper inside. He looked down at her a moment. Then lightly, very lightly, he bent and let his lips just brush hers.

'Goodbye.' His voice was soft. He straightened. His mouth tugged in a little smile as he looked down at her. 'Don't forget your windsurfing.'

She shook her head wordlessly. He beckoned to the barman, signing the chit with rapid scrawl.

For one last time he looked at her. Was there anything in his eyes? Anything at all? She couldn't see. Could only know that hers were straining up at him, that her skin felt cold and clammy in the heat. That something was happening to her that she could not bear.

He raised a hand. The game was just getting interesting. 'Take care.'

Was there a husk in his voice? The slightest sign of regret?

He gave her one last brief smile and headed off.

She watched him go until she could see him no longer.

It was bad. It was worse than bad. She paced on her balcony. Above her, the cold stars blazed, giving no comfort. There was none to give.

She pressed her fingers to her mouth, as if she could keep all her feelings pressed down inside her.

She should be grateful. Grateful he'd gone. Removed temptation. The terrible, overpowering temptation to fall for him.

She tried desperately to rationalise it. She'd been here, in a foreign land, in an emotionally charged state after encountering Stephanos, and then a man like Nikos Kiriakis had walked in, looking like every woman's fantasy male. Sex on legs. The most devastating man she'd ever seen, oozing sex appeal from every pore, totally and effortlessly gorgeous! No wonder she had reacted to him! She'd spent her adult life avoiding any chance of such entanglements.

And she'd succeeded. Succeeded completely—till now. Nikos Kiriakis had simply knocked away her defences as if they had been made of paper!

She stared out over the dark mass of the gardens. Starlight gleamed dimly on the surface of the pool.

Wanting Nikos Kiriakis.

For the first time in her life she wanted a man, wanted *him*, Nikos Kiriakis. Only him, only him—and she didn't have him.

She was woken by the phone ringing. It was scarcely dawn. She groped for the receiver, feeling bleary and disoriented. For one terrible yearning moment she thought it was Nikos.

It was Stephanos.

He was brief—agitatedly brief. It was late night in New York. They would be going to stay with friends on Long Island in a few days—the wedding he'd told her about. He couldn't speak long—he was snatching a few stolen moments. Was she all right? That was all he wanted to know. All he had time to ask. He had to go. She was in his thoughts, his darling girl. She must take care... He had to go...

The line went dead.

She lay back, receiver slack on her chest. She'd hardly been able to say a word. Just get out the assurance he needed. She felt bruised, dazed.

Slowly, dully, she replaced the receiver. She had wanted it to be Nikos. So, so much. She wanted anything she could get of him—anything, on any terms. Even if it was nothing more than a single night in his arms...

She rolled over, hugging herself in misery.

You aren't even going to get that! Hasn't he made it clear enough? He voted with his feet. He said goodbye and left. You are simply unimportant to him.

The knowledge ached through her. Ached all the way through the next few sleepless hours until at last, with slow dreariness, she got up. An early-morning swim, a long shower, washing her hair, her underwear, hanging it dripping on her balcony, gazing out blindly over the sea. Then finally, drearily, getting dressed in the first things that came to hand, and going downstairs to breakfast, to pick at food that tasted like sawdust, drink coffee that tasted like dishwater—all with that same slow, dull dreariness, that same slow, dull ache all the way through her.

Nikos had gone. She wanted him, and he had gone.

She stared down blindly into her coffee cup.

A pair of dark glasses landed on the tablecloth beside her. Someone sat down opposite her.

Her head started up.

She froze, not believing her eyes. Just not believing.

Dark gold-flecked eyes rested on her. Burning through her.

'I couldn't stay away from you,' said Nikos Kiriakis.

The motor yacht at anchor in the harbour at Skarios Town gleamed like a sleek white monster. A Greek flag fluttered from its stern, flapping blue and white.

'Not a sail to set or a tiller to pull. And a crew to turn on the engine and steer!'

'It's my kind of boat!' said Janine with a laugh.

Not a word had been spoken about Nikos's return. Not one. He had simply said, 'After breakfast I've got a surprise for you.'

He wouldn't tell her what, had just let a smile play around his mouth.

She'd gone with him in a dream. Floating off the ground. Her heart had been singing. Soaring. In her room she'd ripped off the T-shirt and shorts she'd put on so listlessly an hour ago and riffled through everything in her wardrobe. In the end she'd grabbed a sleeveless white sundress, completely impractical for the beach, but now, as he ushered her aboard this millionaire's monster, she knew it was ideal. The breeze winnowed her hair, floating it around her head like a maenad's.

She stared, wide-eyed, at the luxury on board as he led the way up to the sundeck above the cabin. Two loungers were set out beneath a stretched white awning, and Nikos settled her in one as if he had been handing her to a throne.

Janine sat down and gazed around her. A mix of fishing boats and sailing yachts bobbed about in the harbour, but there was nothing to compare with this floating monster. She felt the deck start to vibrate and saw the swirl of water that indicated the propeller was turning. One of the crew loosened the moorings and then jumped lightly aboard, gangplank already retracted. The boat started to nose away from the quayside.

As they gained the open sea and the yacht started to speed up she turned to Nikos.

'This is fantastic!'

He flashed a smile at her. He'd known she would be impressed. Who wouldn't be? He had chartered the cruiser in Patra and had her sailed over for this morning. Ready for his return from Athens.

It had been a nuisance having to detour to Athens yesterday, even though it had allowed him to drop in at his office and catch up with various business matters in person. But leaving Skarios—and Janine Fareham—had been a necessary part of his carefully calculated blow hot/blow cold strategy. And it had worked perfectly, he could see. As he'd walked up to her at breakfast she'd been sitting there like a forlorn, wilted flower, dejection and rejection in every line of her slender body.

The transformation as he announced his presence had been total.

She'd revived instantly, immediately. Incandescently. A glow of wonder had lit her face, her eyes, parted her lips. Shining from her like the sun.

Dazzling him.

He'd felt a kick go through him like a blow to his solar plexus.

Theos mou, but she was so beautiful! Her eyes alight, glowing with pleasure, her smile so radiant it all but knocked him over.

Satisfaction filled him. She was ready for him now.

And he, oh, he was more than ready for her.

It had been hard, much harder than he'd envisaged, to walk out on her yesterday. He'd had to force himself to his feet, force himself to smile down at her and tell her that he had to go back to Athens. And as for kissing her…

That had been hardest of all—to confine himself to nothing more than the most fleeting brush of his lips when he'd wanted to haul her up against him and ravish her warm, honeyed mouth with his…

Instead he'd had to straighten and saunter off, as if he hadn't got a single thought in his head except getting to the airport.

But now, ah, now it was a different story. He would not be leaving Janine Fareham again—not until he had tasted every ounce of honey she had to give.

And she would have so much! His eyes washed over her as she lay back in the lounger, lifting her face to the sunlight filtering through the awning, her long, beautiful hair flowing in the wind. His gaze stroked her, taking in the little details of her beauty—the delicate arch of her narrow feet in their strappy sandals, the elegant ankles, slender calves, honeyed thighs, and her wand-like waist, and those two sweet, gently swelling breasts, and her sculpted shoulders, her graceful neck, delicate jawline, tender earlobes and the long sweep of her eyelashes…

Why the hell did she have to be mixed up with Stephanos?

The thought came out of nowhere, hitting him like a blow as he realised how he had phrased that question. It should be the other way round. It should be *Why the hell did Stephanos have to be mixed up with her?*

But it hadn't come to him like that. Suddenly it had been Stephanos he resented, not Janine Fareham.

Janine.

He felt a smile hover at his mouth. Janine. Zhanine.

He liked saying her name, liked the way her name

sounded. And he liked the way *she* liked him saying it, with that soft 'zh' pronunciation that Greek gave it. The English pronunciation was harsh and ugly in comparison. Zhanine…

Much better. Much, much better…

His eyes flickered over her blonde loveliness again. Though her skin was tanned, she was completely un-Greek in appearance. He let his gaze rest on her. There was something familiar about her, he felt, with a strange flickering of memory. Who was it? It was not obvious, but every now and then there was something about her that made him think she looked like someone he knew.

He shook his head minutely. No, it was simply that he hadn't seen her in thirty-six hours and her beauty was stunning his senses again. That was all. It was just because he wanted to have her. Not because she resembled anyone he knew.

A sound of footsteps behind him made him turn. One of the crew was coming up to the sundeck, carrying a silver tray bearing two long-stemmed flutes and a bottle of freshly opened champagne nestling in an ice bucket. He set it down on a table between the loungers. Nikos nodded his thanks and the man took his leave.

Janine half sat up.

'Oh, I adore champagne!' she cried, her face lighting.

'I thought you might,' murmured Nikos, and poured her out a glass, and one for him, handing her the former. She took it with a grateful smile.

The chill, gently fizzing golden liquid iced beautifully down her throat, and Janine sighed with pleasure as she tasted the distinctive biscuity dryness of vintage champagne. It went perfectly with the bliss she was feeling. Had been feeling ever since Nikos had returned. She heard again, singing in her head, those blissful words—*I couldn't stay away from you…*

They had made her decision for her. She knew it, and she accepted it.

I couldn't stay away from you...

The words circled in her mind, making her heart swell.

I couldn't stay away from you...

Well, she couldn't stay away from him either. Whatever was happening, whatever was lifting her heart like this, whatever was making her breathless—heart racing, giddy with intoxication—whatever it was, she would go with it.

She would not be sensible.

It was far, far too late for that.

I can't think about anything else. Or anyone else.

Just Nikos.

Just Nikos.

She wouldn't question, wouldn't ask, wouldn't doubt or fear.

She would simply accept—and be glad, so glad.

She would go with him wherever he took her. Because she was helpless to do anything else.

She wanted only one thing—to be with Nikos Kiriakis.

Whatever happened.

CHAPTER FIVE

THE cruiser made its way northwards, leaving the shoreline of the island to port. Janine lay back and enjoyed the sensation, just as she enjoyed the exquisite flavour of the vintage champagne in her glass—and the even more exquisite pleasure of having Nikos Kiriakis beside her.

Sailing away with her.

He was watching her, she knew. She could feel it. It was almost tangible, the way his gaze set her nerve-ends quivering, vibrating finely in a way that was far more than the resonant vibration of the cruiser's engine. She wanted to turn her head and meet his eyes, knew that if she did the quivering would leap, sending her heart-rate skittering away. She felt breathless, intoxicated. And it was not the champagne—it was him, *him*, Nikos Kiriakis, pulling her towards him, drawing her inexorably towards him, and she could not hold back, could not resist him.

As the cruiser headed onwards, its sleek lines propelled by its powerful, throbbing engine, she felt that that was what Nikos was doing to her. Propelling her onwards, taking her with him. And she could not say no. Could not resist.

Where was he taking her? Where would their journey end?

She did not know, did not want to ask, was content to be swept along wherever he wanted her to go.

She had put herself in his hands.

She glanced back to the island across the churning of the wake. It seemed very far away.

Just like the rest of her life.

The only reality was here, now, with Nikos.

She tried to think of Stephanos, but he was so far away too. He slipped away from her mind, fading, dwindling.

She had longed so much for Nikos, dreamt of him, yearned for him and ached for him.

And he had come back to her.

She took another sip of champagne and let intoxication take her. The wind streamed over her face; the sun dazzled her eyes. She felt the cruiser alter direction subtly, felt the helm going a few points to port. Then they were rounding the island, starting to curve back south again, with the sun shifting direction.

'Are we going to go back around to the hotel?' Janine asked.

She looked across at Nikos and felt the now-familiar lurch of her heart at setting eyes on him. He was wearing his dark glasses, and glamour just oozed from him. What was it about dark glasses that made a man look so damn sexy? she found herself thinking. And on a man as sexy as Nikos in the first place the effect was devastating!

She hardly heard his answer, so rapt she was by gazing at his gorgeousness.

'Not quite that far,' he answered.

'So where, then?' she pressed.

But he would not answer, only let an enigmatic smile play around his mouth in a way that made her more riveted than ever, and quite took her mind off the mystery of where they were going to have lunch. So far as she knew there were no villages along that north-west shore—nothing until you reached Stephanos's hotel complex, which was just north of a tiny fishing village.

But it wasn't a village they were heading for—or even a hotel.

After following the dramatically rocky shoreline of the north-west coast, the cruiser suddenly veered inshore. For a while Janine could not see where on earth they might be heading. Apart from a rocky death upon the sea-washed cliffs. But then as they got closer and cleared another head-land she saw, nestling in its shelter, a tiny cove, gleaming with sand in a tiny half-moon, bordered by a simple stony quay running out from a track that wound up the cliffside. And as her eyes lifted she saw a sight that made her gasp.

A villa was perched on the crest of the cliff, so cunningly landscaped into the contours that it hardly showed from the sea. Only the sunshine dazzling on its windows gave away its existence.

Janine turned to Nikos.

'We're heading *there*?'

Nikos nodded. 'The agent sent me details—it sounded intriguing.'

It also, he thought, but did not say, sounded ideal for his purpose. Its remoteness was perfect.

There was a strange look in her eyes suddenly.

'Is—is that why you came back?' she asked. 'Just to view this villa?'

He heard the catch of doubt in her voice.

His eyelids drooped.

'No,' he said softly.

For a long moment he held her eyes, and he saw the colour stain out across those high, beautiful cheekbones un-til she looked away in confusion.

More than confusion.

Relief.

They drew nearer the shore, into the lee of the cliff, until they were able to moor along the quayside. As Janine walked down the short gangplank she felt the swell of the sea against the stone quay unbalance her slightly. She had nearly two glasses of champagne inside her, and had not yet eaten, and she swayed, catching at the guidebars on either side.

Hands steadied her at her waist, warm through the thin cotton of her sundress. Her heart gave a flutter and she paused, regaining her balance, then glanced back over her shoulder.

'Thanks.'

Her breath caught. Nikos—towering over her, his height accentuated by the slope of the gangplank—seemed over-whelming. His eyes were still shielded by his dark glasses, making her focus on that beautiful sculpted mouth of his, the lean outline of his jaw. For a second time stilled, and she felt as if she were drowning, unable to draw breath. She could feel the imprint of his hands on her, holding her still. He seemed so close to her—so close...

Oh, dear God, what is happening to me?

Emotion surged in her, sweeping through her like a wave. She felt herself sway again, and this time it had nothing to do with the sea, with the champagne. This was emotion trembling through her.

But what emotion?

Desperately she tried to give it a name. Intoxication? Wonder? Wanting?

Whatever it was it surged through her, unstoppable, making her weak, so weak...

A crewman was standing on the quay, dutifully holding out a hand to her to help her off. She stepped forward. Nikos's hands released her. The moment passed and she forced herself to recover some semblance of composure.

But as she fell into step beside Nikos she could feel her heart racing.

She glanced ahead of her. Judging by the way the rough track led off the shore end of the quay, winding up the lowest portion of the cliff to the right of the villa, it was going to be a steep climb. There seemed to be a stone hut of some description at the base of the track, with double doors like a garage. Maybe there was a Jeep inside or something? Janine wondered.

She didn't get to find out.

'Come,' said Nikos, and led the way forward. Not to the

unmetalled track, but across the head of the tiny cove beyond the quay.

Janine gazed about her. It was exquisitely lovely, a perfect, tiny jewel of a beach, with golden sand and azure sea, backed by limestone cliffs tumbling with greenery, and tiny wavelets breaking in miniature foam. At the far end of the beach, where the cliff was sheer, she realised there was a kind of glass pod set against vertical rails, soaring upwards. It was, she realised, amazed, a lift.

Her lips parted in wonder as, after she was ushered inside by Nikos, they soared upwards. As they gained the villa level her lips stayed parted in wonder. A fantastic expanse of glittering blue water greeted her—an infinity pool set so cunningly into the terraced rock that as she looked it seemed to merge with the sea and the sky.

'Come,' said Nikos again. He led the way around the head of the pool, lightly ascending a shallow flight of steps that led to the villa itself.

It was very low and modern. Built in gleaming white stone, its wide expanse of sea-fronting windows dazzled in the sunlight.

Janine gazed about her, open-mouthed.

'Let me show you around,' said Nikos.

He slid open one of the vast pairs of windows and she walked inside. Again, the décor was startlingly modern—white and low and totally minimalist—and totally stunning. Polished wooden floors offset the white walls and furniture, and a pair of huge stone *pithoi* stood like sentinels at the far end.

Her sandals clacking noisily on the wooden floor, she followed him, still open-mouthed, as he showed her round the rest of the villa. It was all on one level, and from every room the same incredible view out over the sea greeted her. The huge bedroom had its own terrace and she wandered out, gazing at the spectacular view all around.

'This is an incredible place!'

'It is, is it not? And now that we are here let us enjoy what it has to offer. Beginning—' he smiled down at her '—with lunch.'

Her eyes widened. 'Is that allowed?'

'The villa is at my disposal,' he answered, as if the very idea that Nikos Kiriakis should not be allowed to do something he wanted to do was absurd. 'Now, would you care to freshen up?' He indicated the *en suite* bathroom off the main bedroom.

'Well, if you say it's OK,' she said doubtfully.

'Of course.' He smiled again.

She went off to make the most of the palatial facilities. When she emerged she headed down the little flight of steps that led from the bedroom terrace down to the main terrace, beside the infinity pool. As she descended she saw that the crew had set out a table with a huge canvas sunshade overhead, and were now busy unloading what looked to be half a dozen picnic hampers. Nikos was lounging against a stone balustrade, gazing out over the incredible view of the sea.

For a moment she just stood, gazing at him. Her heart seemed to still.

He turned and smiled at her, and held out his hand.

She went to join him.

The food was exquisite—delicate trifles that melted in the mouth, morsel after morsel, tempting and irresistible. Dessert was even more delicious, and Janine did not even try and say no to the iced almond parfait in its crystal bowl. Spoonful by tiny spoonful she consumed it, sighing with pleasure.

Nikos sat back and watched her through half-closed enigmatic eyes.

She felt his gaze on her, heavy and sensual.

'I can't eat another mouthful—'

Reluctantly Janine set down her dessert spoon, pushing the half-finished dessert away from her and leaning back in her director's chair, tilting back the rest, stretching out her legs. She reached for her glass of sweet Sauternes wine. On top of the glass of Chablis Nikos had persuaded her to drink, and the champagne earlier, she could feel the wine soothing through her body.

Her limbs felt heavy, languorous. Heat licked at her skin. A tiny breeze toyed with the tendrils of her hair, playing over her bare shoulders, her bare arms. The Sauternes slipped down her throat like honey, and she sighed again with pleasure.

She felt replete. The combination of wine and heat made her feel dreamy, indolent. She didn't want to move. Not for a long time. Perhaps not for ever. She wanted time to hold still, the way it was doing now. So she could go on being here, now, with this man, beneath the azure sky, heat beating over her like a slow pulse.

She gave another long, pleasurable sigh, and relaxed back even more in her chair.

'I could stay here for ever,' she murmured. 'It's so peaceful. So beautiful.' She turned her head to smile sleepily at Nikos. 'Thank you for bringing me here,' she said softly. Then, even more softly, 'Thank you for coming back...'

He gave a half-smile back, that same enigmatic look in his eyes. She let him look at her, let his gaze entwine with hers. There was silence all around them. Silence and the sweet scent of white jasmine drifting through the air. She was holding his eyes still, and they seemed very dark. She could see the flecks of gold deep within.

He reached and stroked her arm. It felt like the drift of swansdown on her skin.

She ought to move her arm. Ought to tell him not to do what he was doing. But the drift of his fingers was too lovely.

She saw his eyelids droop, saw the enigmatic half-smile pull at his mouth—that beautiful, sensual, sculpted mouth.

'Nikos...' She breathed his name.

His fingers went on drifting over her skin.

Her eyes twined with his.

'I came back,' he said softly, 'because I could not stay away.'

She said nothing, could say nothing, though her eyes were wide and wondering.

His fingers went on drifting, stroking. They slid over her wrist, holding her. His thumb circled slowly over the delicate skin over her veins. His eyes held hers, slow-burning coals, flecked with golden flame.

He got to his feet, drawing her up with him. She came with him, helpless to resist. The wine sang in her blood, low and sweet. The warmth caressed her skin. The sun beat down on her, making her weak.

His hands slipped over her shoulders, warm and heavy.

He lowered his head to her mouth.

His kiss was everything she had dreamt it would be. Slow, and sensuous, tasting her like wine.

And she gave herself to it.

The world slowed. Time stopped. His mouth moved on hers and she was drowning, drowning. Bliss ran in her veins like slow, sweet honey.

Weakness washed over her, wave after wave. Her muscles had no strength. Her will had no strength. She was caught in his arms, her hands touching the contours of his shoulders, her breasts pillowed on his chest. She could feel her nipples prickling, feel the little shivers of arousal teasing through her veins. His hands moved across her back, stroking her, as his mouth moved softly, so softly, over hers. The wave of weakness washed through her again.

I can't resist him, she thought. I can't, I can't.

It's too late for resistance, too late for regrets. I thought he had gone, that he did not want me. But he came back to me and I cannot, cannot, say no to him. Not now, not now. Madness it may be, but it's too late, too late.

'Nikos…'

She breathed his name into his mouth and the world slid away. Her hands slipped upwards, winding around his neck, holding his head to hers as her mouth opened to his and his tongue eased within.

The flush of desire coursed through her body; the sun beat on her back. Her swollen breasts felt heavy, ripening against him. His hands slipped down to her hips and then, as if she were no more than a feather, he gathered her up.

He took her indoors. Her head hung bowed, heavy, upon his shoulder as he carried her, her body limp and weak in his arms. Inside was cooler, the shaded bedroom cooler still, and he laid her down upon the wide bed.

She lay, her sundress riding up her thighs, one strap half-descended from her shoulder. Her heart was slewing in thick, heavy beats.

For one long, endless moment she lay there as he stood quite still and looked down at her. In the shadows of the room she could not read his eyes. His face was taut. Only the pulse at his throat betrayed his condition.

He reached a hand down to her. But it was not to touch her body. Only the thin, strappy sandals. He slid them off her bare feet and tossed them away. Then he stood back again.

'Perfect,' he said softly. 'Quite, quite perfect.'

His gaze laced over her, just as it had done the first time he had ever set eyes on her, she knew. But now—now he would do more than look. He had set her body alight that very first time he had stood looking down at her, so near naked in her bikini. And that same hot flame shimmered within her now.

'Nikos,' she breathed again, helpless in desire.

She wanted him so much. Wanted that lean, hard, male strength pressing on her, possessing her.

A smile curved at his mouth and she felt her breath catch. He plunged his hand into his trouser pocket with slow deliberation and took out a handful of silvery packets. With

the same carelessness with which he had treated her unnecessary sandals, he tossed them down on the bedside table.

He smiled down at her again. Her eyes had widened. He
started to unbutton his shirt. She lay there, watching him
undress, watching his beautiful, lean body emerge, her eyes
feasting on him with helpless desire. As he removed the
last of his clothing she saw just how very, very aroused he
was.

He paused, reaching for one of the packets, and sheathed
himself. Then, with that same slow deliberation, he came
towards her.

A smile was playing around his mouth.

So this, thought Janine, in as much as she was capable of
thinking, as her body melted around her, was what it was
like to be seduced by Nikos Kiriakis.

Because that was what he was doing. Seducing her.

Touch by touch by touch.

How could she have thought he didn't want her? How
could she possibly have thought that?

He stroked her limbs, hands gliding like silk along her
bare arms, mouth lowering to graze along the fine ridge of
her collarbone, before moving softly, exquisitely, across her
throat, to nuzzle at her tender earlobes. She sighed with
pleasure, feeling herself melting beneath his silken caresses.
He teased her lips with his, easing them open, stroking her
tongue with his as she opened beneath him.

And as he did so he slid the half-fallen strap from her
shoulder and softly peeled the fine material of her dress
away from her swelling breast.

His fingers played with her a little, skimming the delicate
underswell, grazing the aching tip, until she moaned, neck
arching. His lips left hers and his head bowed, mouth closing over her straining nipple instead. He suckled her softly,

oh, so softly, and the little moans in her throat came again and again.

'Do you like that?' he murmured, smiling as his mouth left her breast and then, his gold-flecked eyes holding hers, which gazed up at him, wide and dilated, he moved his hand to her other shoulder, lifting away her other strap and taking it down her arm to expose her other breast.

He paused a moment, his eyes breaking with hers to gaze down upon her nakedness, edged with the white material of her half-removed sundress.

'Such beautiful breasts,' he breathed, and his head lowered again.

Her fingers twisted in the bedclothes, and her spine strained upwards as he suckled her again.

Desire was dissolving her, dissolving her into a soft, boneless mass of sensation—such sweet, sweet sensation.

He went on suckling her, his tongue making soft circles around her nipple, each circle more blissful than the next. And as he laved her breasts his hand glided like silk along her leg, sliding under the rucked hem of her sundress, fingers hooking around the low-slung waistband of her panties.

He eased them down, lifting her hips enough to free them from the rounded globes of her bottom, and slid her legs free of them. And then his hand returned to her.

If she had thought she could know no further bliss, she discovered with a breathless parting of her lips just how much bliss was yet to come. With the delicate, skilful tips of his fingers he played with her a while, exploring each delicate fold, loosening her, dewing her, readying her for his possession. And all the while his mouth worked its magic upon her breasts.

She was quivering with desire—aching with it, melting with it.

'Nikos—'

His name was an exhalation. An invocation. A plea.

He lifted his head and looked into her eyes. In the dim light they were deep, dilated pools. He smoothed his hand over her forehead. She gazed up at him, helpless with her desire. For one long, long moment he looked down at her.

She could not see his eyes. His face was shadowed, only the contours of his features visible.

He was the most beautiful man in the world.

'Nikos...' She breathed his name again, whispering it. Her thighs slackened as his hand moved from her, easing her legs apart.

He lifted himself and slowly, teasingly slow, glided into her, so smooth, so powerful that he filled her absolutely, completely.

For a moment, a brief, timeless moment, he stilled, and she could feel her muscles strain around him, enclosing him. Her fingers hovered on the smooth, warm skin of his shoulders.

Then with absolute control he moved within her.

She felt the exquisite pleasure of his movement within her, stroking her, caressing her with the most intimate part of himself.

She sighed, sweet and susurrating.

Her eyes fluttered shut and she gave herself to the sensation. Her hands folded over his shoulders, feeling their strength, the smoothness of his skin, the muscles layered beneath.

So beautiful. He was so sublime, so male. And what he was doing to her was beyond words.

She breathed again, exhaling slowly, then breathing in again, taking him with her as she did so.

He went on stroking her, caressing her, and her body became one single point of sensation, just there, *there*, where her sensitivity was greatest, her arousal most exquisite.

She breathed his name again, her head moving slowly, as if submerged, and then, as if a slow underwater wave were welling through her, her body undulated. The sweetest honey was oozing through every vein, every nerve, reaching up, and up, and up—and releasing, out, out into her skin, her flesh, suffusing her body with one long, endless welling of sensation so exquisite she exhaled in a long, endless sighing.

And then, just as she felt the sensation begin to ebb, making her ache with the loss of it, he moved once more within her, and then again, in one slow, final, releasing surge, and the sensation was released in him, so it came again in her, again and again, over and over, wave after wave, sweetness after sweetness, until her body was a fusion of it, and nothing existed, could exist, would ever exist again. Her whole body was one exquisite, endless wave of sensation.

To the end, the very end, she let the sweet, honeyed wave carry her, oblivious to everything else, existing only in her own exquisite bliss. Until at last, at last it was no more, no last drop of honey remained.

She gave a long, languorous sigh, limbs slackening, muscles releasing.

Her eyelids fluttered. She should open her eyes, she thought dimly, vaguely. But her eyelids were too heavy, her limbs were too heavy.

'Nikos?' Her voice was a sigh.

A hand smoothed over her forehead.

'Shh…' he murmured.

'It was so beautiful…'

She felt his mouth on hers, soft and tender. Then he was coming down beside her, folding her to him, enclosing her.

'Nikos…' she breathed again.

His hand smoothed her thigh.

'So beautiful…'

Her eyes were heavy, limbs weak. Her breathing slowed, her heart rate calmed, and the warm peace of sleep crept over her.

* * *

Nikos watched her sleep, a smile curving his mouth. Her breasts rose and fell gently. They were soft again, soft and very beautiful, their skin paler than the surrounding flesh. His smile deepened. She could sunbathe nude here. There would be no one to see. The villa was his. He had bought it the day before yesterday, fully furnished, at the asking price. The agent had not been able to believe his luck. Nikos hadn't cared. One of the business appointments that he had used as an excuse to stay away from Janine that second day had been to take a helicopter trip here, to check it out. He had bought it on the spot.

It was too beautiful not to possess.

His hand reached to smooth Janine's golden hair. Just as she was too beautiful not to possess.

A deep satisfaction filled him. He tried to remember the anger he'd felt about her, but it seemed impossible to recall. And it was irrelevant now, anyway. Janine would never go back to Demetria's husband—he had seen to that, irrevocably. His satisfaction deepened.

He curled a thread of hair around his finger. She really was so very, very lovely. Her body had melted around his, taking him with her in a fusion of the senses.

It had been good. Quite extraordinarily good.

He gave a soft, silent laugh. He had intended the experience to be incredible for her, not for him. That was, after all, the whole purpose of the exercise. To seduce her.

But she had made it incredible for him too.

He still wasn't really sure how. She had done nothing except accept everything he did to her. Absorb every sensation he aroused in her. Absorb it deep, deep within her. Then radiate it out again, as if she were molten in his arms.

It had been the intensity of her responsiveness that had aroused him so much, he realised. No other woman had ever responded to him like that.

He wanted to feel that response again.

He shifted position. He could feel his body reacting to that thought. He eased further back. Whatever he might want to do, first he must visit the bathroom. Then, when he returned, it would be time—oh, yes, time to rouse Janine from her slumber.

'Do you mean it? Do you really mean it?'

Janine's eyes were like stars.

Nikos raised his hand in a very Greek gesture. 'Of course. Why else should I have said we would stay here?'

'But your work—don't you have to be back in Athens?'

He shrugged. 'The villa is fully equipped—I can be on-line to my office whenever I choose. It will do perfectly well for a while. And I didn't buy this villa so that I would never get to spend time here!'

She shook her head. 'I still can't believe you bought a place like this just like that!'

He looked surprised. 'Why not? The villa is spectacular—and as an asset it will only increase in value. Property prices on Skarios are rising steadily as the island opens up for more tourism. It is a good investment. And—' his eyes washed purposefully over Janine '—it affords the privacy we need.'

He lowered his head to kiss her again. They were leaning, side by side, on the balustrade overlooking the pool. The sun had set. Above their heads the stars were pricking out, one by one. Ahead, the darkening sky was faintly tinged with a golden streak along the horizon.

A light wind was winnowing their faces.

As Nikos's mouth moved softly on hers Janine dared not think, only feel. This was bliss. When Nikos had told her just now about the villa, told her that it was his, that they were to stay here together, she had scarce dared believe it.

'I told you,' he had said, kissing her softly, 'that I could not stay away from you.'

She had searched his eyes. His expression had been full.

'I want you very much,' he had said, as softly as his kiss.

And he did want her—she'd had proof of that all the long, hot afternoon. Even now, as they stood here, his arm around her, she could feel the afterglow of his desire for her—of hers for him—in every part of her body.

Wonder filled her. Wonder that what she had wanted so much had come to her! That Nikos had swept her away to this beautiful private place to make love to her.

The outer world ceased to exist. Had ceased to exist since the moment when he had first kissed her here, and she had known there was but one destination for her. His bed.

She had gone gladly, rapturously, putting everything aside except this—this consummation of her desire for him. He had cast a glamour over her, woven a spell to enchant her, captivate her. And she could not resist him.

She leant against him, feeling his strength, his warmth. His arm tightened around her shoulder. Around her the world stilled, the moment captured. Time had stopped. She never wanted it to start again.

Nikos leant back in the wooden-slatted padded steamer chair set out on the terrace above the pool, sipping his beer and watching Janine swim slowly up and down. Her naked body parted the water, gliding forward, her blonde hair streaming behind her like a mermaid's tresses, iridescent in the submerged lighting of the pool, which turned every brush of water to champagne and limned her body with gold.

A near full moon was riding in the sky. Crickets clicked in the vegetation. Down below, on the beach, he could hear the low murmur of the sea. The faint wash from Janine's breast-stroke was the only other sound.

They had the world to themselves.

It felt good. Very good.

He took another mouthful of beer. When he'd first come here the moon had been nothing but a silver sliver. Since then the days had passed, timeless, measured only by the sun and the moon, by the intervals between making love to Janine.

Janine...

He let her name play on his lips.

In the water her body moved with sensuous grace. He watched her, feeling desire germinate yet again deep in his being. When she emerged he would take her again. So many times now...and each coming together had been unforgettable. Sensual, incredibly sensual, and her extraordinary responsiveness to him, which had so amazed him that very first time, had never abated, never ebbed. Every, *every* time he took her it was there, intensifying the experience beyond words, beyond rational thought.

But it was more than her responsiveness. He searched for a word that would fit, but it was elusive. Then it came to him.

There was a *sweetness* about possessing Janine that he had never expected. How could he have? She was a woman who had attached herself to a wealthy, married and older man, who was threatening his sister's marriage. There was nothing of *sweetness* in such an activity!

A faint frown crossed his forehead. The woman he held in his arms each night seemed so very different from how such a woman should be. A woman who took rich married men for her lovers! Such a woman as that he might feel desire for, yes, but other than that, nothing but contempt and anger... Yet those two last emotions were not there any longer, he realised, wonderingly. His frown deepened, How could that be? Where had those dark emotions about Janine Fareham gone? Where was his anger at what she had done to Demetria? Where was his contempt for her affair with Stephanos?

Why was the only feeling he now had towards her simply...desire? Pure, burning, incandescent desire. More overwhelming than he had ever known for any woman. All consuming, all powerful.

Why? Why was the woman in his arms, his bed, so different from what he had expected her to be as Stephanos's mistress? Here, with him, she simply didn't seem to connect with such a female.

His brow furrowed again. What was going on? And worse, why did he trouble himself with it? Trying to discover why it was that he felt now only desire for Janine Fareham—a woman he should hate, should despise, for the way she lived her life. A thread of unease ran through him, disturbing him.

He didn't want to think about her affair with Stephanos. He wanted to blot it out. Once again, as on the cruiser, he found himself wanting to think of Janine as if she were not another man's mistress.

As if she were simply *his*.

A slow smile curved his mouth. Well, she was his now, all right. He had brought her here and made her his own.

His eyes rested on her as she glided silently, steadily, through the silken waters, beneath the silver light of the moon.

So very beautiful…a timeless image to remember.

That was all he had to focus on. The simple fact that he wanted Janine Fareham—desired her more than any woman he could remember—and that he had got her.

He took another sip of beer. As he moved his hand moonlight glinted on his watch. Time, he thought, was marching inexorably on. Bringing Stephanos back to Greece, to the moment of inevitable confrontation.

He was not looking forward to it. It would be messy, and unpleasant—but it had to be done. For Demetria's sake.

And when it was over? What then? What would he do with Janine Fareham?

His smile turned mocking. Self-mocking. He already knew very well what he would do with her.

He was going to keep her. He wanted her far, far too much to let her go.

He was captivated by her. Captivated by her beauty, her

sensuality, her sweetness. He admitted it. He hadn't wanted to be, but he was.

And he didn't want to fight it any more. Why should he?

He had achieved exactly what he'd set out to do—seduced Stephanos's mistress away from him and taken her himself. Whatever her reasons for having become his brother-in-law's mistress, she was finished with Stephanos now. He'd seen to that.

A stab of fierce, hard satisfaction went through him. Primitive, atavistic—and too powerful to deny. It might have been for Demetria's sake that he had started out on this course—but now he had a reason all of his own.

He wanted Janine for himself—and he didn't want Stephanos to have her.

The knowledge mocked him, but he didn't care. She had captivated him and that was that.

And where was the problem? There was no problem— Janine Fareham had been a problem only when she'd been a threat to his sister's happiness. That threat was over now—and he, *he* was free to enjoy her.

Desire her.

Sate himself on her.

Make her honeyed sweetness his own.

A sense of well-being eased through him. For as long as he wanted he would have Janine to himself. She was his, only his, from now on.

Nothing—and no one—could take her from him.

Janine walked along the sand. This early it felt cool to the touch, still shaded by the cliff from the morning light. Nikos was at his laptop, ensconced in the high-tech office, touching base with his affairs. For herself, she had time to wander on this beautiful, perfect gem of a private beach, letting the water wash around her feet as she walked slowly along, wondering at the happiness she felt. The air was clear, with not a breath of wind. The cruiser was gone from the quay, out on its daily journey to Skarios Town, where the crew picked up the provisions needed for the villa. Apart from when the chef came up to cook dinner, she and Nikos hardly saw them.

It was almost as if they were the only people in the world.

Like Adam and Eve, in a world new-made for them, and them alone.

She felt her heart squeeze. Something was happening to her, here in this beautiful, magical place. Something that overwhelmed her. That she could not deny, could not prevent. She halted, staring out to sea. The morning sun was pouring down upon its surface, making it too bright to look at. Little wavelets flowed over her bare feet.

Emotion welled through her.

An emotion she would not name. Dared not.

She didn't want to give it a name. Didn't want to admit it. Because what was the point of admitting it? She had given herself to Nikos because she could not have done otherwise. Because he desired her as intensely, as irresistibly as she desired him.

But there could be no future in it. None. She knew that. Knew it with a deep, deep pain that made her refuse to name the emotion that welled through her. He wanted her for now, that was all. He was as caught up with her as she with him, but for him, she knew with bleak certainty there would come a moment when it would be over.

And what was the point? Oh, what was the point of dreaming of something that could never be? Not for a man like Nikos Kiriakis, for whom women were an endless stream.

For a second—a brief, tantalising, excruciating moment—she allowed herself to dream. Dream of a happiness so great that it would make her current state of bliss negligible in comparison!

Supposing—oh, just supposing Nikos felt the same emotion she felt. That same emotion that must not speak its name...

Supposing—oh, just supposing Nikos should turn to her

and take her hand, tell her he wanted her to be part of his life…

For just a few precious moments she let herself imagine such a thing.

Then, with a sigh, she went on walking.

She would have this time with Nikos, this precious time—the days of exploring each other's minds, the nights their bodies. And no one could take it away from her. Nothing could spoil it. It would be a precious, beautiful memory. Nothing could destroy it.

Cradling a glass of cold, fresh orange juice in one hand, Janine slid back the huge glass doors of the living room and stepped out onto the terrace. Nikos was already there, sitting at the shaded table, drinking coffee and reading the morning's paper. It had been delivered a short time ago, when the cruiser had returned from Skarios Town. She drifted up to him, feeling warm and languorous, her silky robe wafting around her. When she had come up from the beach Nikos had finished with his e-mails—and he'd been hungry.

But not for breakfast. He'd gathered her up in his arms, peeling off the strap-tied suntop and shorts she'd worn down to the beach to walk along the sand. He'd led her back to bed. Desire had lit his eyes.

An eternity later he'd shaved and showered while she slept in the aftermath of their passion, and now she was finally emerging herself, her body honeyed and replete.

She kissed his hair, and he lifted his eyes briefly from the paper to smile fleetingly at her, then took her seat opposite him. The day was heating, and she felt the strength of the sun even through the parasol.

It would be another hot day.

She smiled to herself. Every day was hot. Every day sunny, cloudless. Every day a day in paradise. Like glowing pearls she gathered them on her rope of memory.

They would not last for ever, she knew that, but while

they lasted she would distil every last ounce of happiness she could, full and overflowing.

She sipped her orange juice, bringing her gaze back from the breathtaking vista all around, of sea and sky and dazzling white cliffs, of splashing green vegetation, the brilliant azure of the pool almost at her feet.

All my life, she thought. All my life I'll remember this. Sitting here like this, in the morning heat, with Nikos beside me.

Her eyes swept back to the paper Nikos was reading. In Greek, it was indecipherable. She gazed at the picture of the politician on the front cover as Nikos perused the report of some football match on the back page. She could read nothing—nothing except the date, written in numerals.

As the numbers swam in front of her eyes and resolved themselves she felt her heart plummet. How could it be that date already? How could the days have passed so quickly?

Foolish question! Time had seemed to stop here, in this beautiful, magical place, but in the rest of the world the clocks had kept on ticking.

Remorselessly.

She bit her lip. She might have wanted time to stop, but it hadn't. She might have wanted the outside world to disappear, but it hadn't.

And now it had returned. Stephanos had been due back yesterday.

She felt her heart contract. With Nikos she forgot everything but him! Everything—even Stephanos.

But Stephanos was her priority—he had to be. He could spend so little time with her, and she had to place him first. However magical this time with Nikos had been, she owed it to Stephanos to be there for him when he returned.

As for herself and Nikos?

Well, she'd answered that question already, down on the beach.

Resignation filled her. There could be no future for them. Nikos would move on to another woman, and she... Well, she would be left with bittersweet memories. And an emotion she would not name, which would surely, if it were left unfed, wither and die all on its own?

It would have to. Her time with Nikos was over. Suddenly, without her realising it, the hourglass had run its course and the sand was all gone. Her time with him was all gone.

All gone.

A sense of loss flooded through her.

Would she ever see Nikos again? He knew about her and Stephanos, so perhaps there might be a chance of encountering him again...

Yes, with his next woman on his arm.

She pressed her lips together, accepting that reality. She had had her time with Nikos. Now it was over.

And it was time to go back to Stephanos and be grateful, oh, so grateful, that she had him in her life now!

Nikos was folding the paper away, paying her some attention again. As his eyes lit on her he paused, seeing the strained expression on her face.

He frowned, concerned.

'What is it?'

She reached automatically for the coffeepot, jerkily.

'I've just seen the date.' She lifted her eyes to Nikos. She swallowed. 'Stephanos was due back yesterday.'

She poured out her coffee. Reality was crashing back. 'I've got to go back to the hotel. To be there for him. He can spend so little time with me—'

She looked at him, her expression troubled, then the words burst from her.

'I know I shouldn't have had this affair with you, Nikos. But you made it impossible for me to resist! I took one look at you and everything else just went out the window.' She gave a faint, rueful smile, trying so hard to be brave, though she felt like howling, weeping, crying, keening.

'This...this time with you has been magical, Nikos—truly magical! I'll never forget it—and I'll never regret it!'

He was looking at her. His expression was closed. She could not read it.

'But clearly,' he said, 'it meant very little to you.'

She stared. 'How can you think that? How *can* you?'

'What else am I to think?'

His voice was cold. A chill went through her. What was happening?

'What else am I to think?' he demanded again. 'You sit there and calmly tell me you are returning to the hotel to wait for Stephanos.'

She was bewildered, dismayed. 'But…but of course I must. You *must* know how much he means to me!'

His eyes were like gold chips. Hard. Anger was lashing through him. It had come out of nowhere, like a summer storm at sea, brought on by her words. Her serenely uttered words that told him, oh, so calmly, that she was returning to her protector.

'I had thought that you *must* know how much you mean to *me*!' His voice mocked her intonation.

She stilled. 'Do I? Do I, Nikos? Do I know what I mean to you? We've spent this time here—and it's been magical for me—magical!—like nothing else in my life! But what was it for you?'

Her eyes were wide, pained. And suddenly Nikos understood. She had no idea what he intended for her. The storm vanished from his eyes.

He got to his feet and came round to her. He drew her up, taking her hands in his. He looked down into her face. Her beautiful, captivating face. He was quite resolved now. Her talk of returning to Stephanos had made it crystal-clear in his mind. He wanted Janine still, and he would keep her. Even had her protector been anyone else he would still have wanted her, would still have kept her. His desire for her was as overpowering now as it had been when he had first taken her.

He was going to keep her, and nothing was going to stop him. Nothing and no one.

'I don't want to part with you, Janine,' he said softly, his eyes lambent. 'I want us to be together. I want to take you back to Athens with me and make you mine. Recognised by all the world as mine.'

She gazed up at him. The breath had frozen in her throat.

Was she hearing right? Was she really, really hearing right?

Of all the words in all the world, those were the ones she had most longed to hear—the ones that she had never, never thought she would.

The emotion that she so feared to name leapt in her heart.

Her face lit like sunlight within.

'Do you really mean that?'

Her voice was a whisper. Dared she believe him. Dared she?

Her heart was full, so full...

'Do you doubt me?' he countered. 'You've swept me away, Janine. Captivated me!' He gazed down at her. Her eyes were shining again, like stars. He liked that. He liked that a lot. He liked Janine gazing up at him with stars in her eyes. He lifted her hands to his mouth and kissed each one softly, tenderly. 'I don't care who you are. It doesn't matter to me. You are mine now, and that is all that I care about. And I want you to be my—'

He paused, listening. He could hear something. A faint, distinctive thudding. It came from the land.

She drew back a little. What had made him stop—and at such a moment?

Then she heard it too.

'What is that?' She sounded alarmed.

The noise was getting louder. Closer.

Nikos glanced at her, then up to the sky. The noise was getting almost intolerable now. 'It's a helicopter,' he said. 'It's coming in to land. There's a helipad behind the villa.'

'But who on earth—?' Her words were inaudible. The racket of the rotors was deafening this close, as the machine descended.

Nikos didn't bother to answer her. He knew with every instinct just who was in that helicopter. But no purpose would be served by telling Janine. She would find out in a moment anyway.

He steeled himself. This had come too soon. He'd wanted more time. But he should have known it would happen. If it had been him coming back to find that Janine had gone from him, been taken, he, too, would have been in the first helicopter here.

The noise of the rotors increased. So did the tension stealing through him.

This was not going to be pleasant. But it had to be done. Janine was his—his completely. There was no doubt of it in his mind. Not a shadow. Her reaction just now, to his telling her that he was taking her back to Athens with him, showed him that.

Stephanos was finished—and Nikos had his revenge and had saved his sister's marriage.

His mouth tightened in a grim line. All he had to do now was convince his sister's husband of that.

Convince him that his young mistress had taken a new lover—that he, Nikos, had taken her. And was keeping her.

His eyes glanced over Janine. She looked perfect. Just the way he wanted her to look. Ideal for his purpose. Hair tousled, wearing only a loose silk robe, skimming her beautiful body, her lips beestung from passion. No guesses as to how she had spent the night. Or—he closed his arm around her shoulders, pulling her tightly, intimately against his body—who with.

The change in the pitch of the rotors told him the helicopter had landed. The infernal racket cut out any other noise. He felt tension tighten all the way through him. He had to get through this ordeal, however ugly it proved. He had to convince Stephanos that Janine was finished with him.

'Nikos—what's happening? I don't understand?'

There was bewilderment in her voice. Did she really have

no clue who was about to storm in here like a SWAT team? Well, he thought grimly, it was too late to mount a rescue for her. Much, much too late.

And the lady didn't even *want* rescuing! Was perfectly happy right where she was. Had chosen *him*, Nikos. Was *his*. There was no going back for her. Not now.

Footsteps pounded on the stairs leading down from the helipad past the villa. Then suddenly he was there. He was breathing heavily, Nikos could see.

His eyes fell on the pair of them immediately, and he stopped dead. At his side Nikos could feel Janine freeze totally.

'Stephanos—' he greeted the other man smoothly in his own language. 'I thought it might be you. You really shouldn't have left such a delectable creature on her own the way you did. You have arrived too late. Much, much too late. Janine is with me now.' He swapped to English suddenly. He wanted Janine to get this message too. 'She's staying with me, Stephanos. I'm taking her back to Athens.'

He brushed his lips across the top of Janine's hair, caressing her shoulder as he smiled at the other man. It was like sticking a knife into Stephanos's gut. His brother-in-law's face had gone completely white.

Then another face swam in his mind. Demetria—gaunt, desperate, despairing. His heart hardened. Stephanos should never have caused her so much pain and grief. His hand tightened around Janine's shoulder.

'She was very easy to seduce, Stephanos…' he taunted softly. 'And so very rewarding.'

For an endless moment the tableau held. Then, with a roar, Stephanos launched himself forward.

'You dare,' he yelled, his face contorted with rage, 'you *dare* to stand there and boast to me of seducing my daughter?'

CHAPTER SIX

His fist flew forward, ramming right at Nikos's face. Janine screamed. Instinctively Nikos blocked, letting go of Janine as he did so and seizing Stephanos's forearm before his fist could impact.

'Daughter?' Nikos's voice was a hiss. 'Do you take me for a fool? Do you take your *wife* for a fool? My *sister*! My poor, wretched sister! Who begged me from her hospital bed to help her. Who wept in my arms because her husband was infatuated with a twenty-five-year-old girl he'd picked up at an airport! You took one look at her and she was in your bed the same day!'

There was a low moan from beside him. He ignored it. His face was contorted, as he still exerted all his force to hold Stephanos's striking arm away from him.

Abruptly Stephanos's fist dropped. He took a step back. The expression on his face was ghastly.

'You don't understand.' His voice was a hoarse rasp. 'Janine is my daughter. The daughter I never knew I had. I saw her at Heathrow. She's...she's the image of her mother. I knew her...her mother...so many years ago. Long before I knew Demetria. When I saw Janine I thought I was seeing Louise—her mother. It was uncanny—the likeness. I had to speak to her—we got talking. And then—' His voice broke with emotion. 'I realised...the dates fit—everything fits. Nine months before Janine was born I had an affair with Louise, her mother. Louise never told me—I never knew that she was pregnant with my child. I never knew I had a daughter. Until now.'

Nikos was still. Completely still. In his cheek a muscle worked.

'Your daughter? You're telling me that Janine is your daughter?'

His voice was flat. Disbelieving.

Janine spoke in a low, faint voice. She felt sick, ill.

'You said you knew. You said you knew about Stephanos and me.'

Nikos turned his head. Janine was hanging on to the edge of the table as if it was the only thing that was keeping her upright.

'I knew you were his mistress.' His voice still had that same flat, dead tone.

'Oh, God!' Janine choked, covering her mouth with her hand. 'How could you think such a thing?'

'Very easily,' he replied. There was a grimness now when he spoke. 'My sister told me. How should I doubt her?'

Janine lifted her eyes to him. He was still the same man she had embraced so short a time ago.

But he was a totally different man.

One she had never known.

'All along...' Her voice was a thread. 'You thought I was Stephanos's... Stephanos's...' The word choked her. 'His mistress—'

She felt the pressure building up in her, up and up, unbearably.

'Oh, God! Oh, God!' Her hand flew to her mouth again and she lurched away from the table.

With wide, distraught eyes, she stared for a moment at the hideous tableau in front of her.

'Janine! My dearest child! *Pethi mou!*' Stephanos held out his hands to her.

She ignored them. Slowly, as if she were drowning, she shook her head from side to side. Then, with a cry of anguish, she ran indoors, to gain the blessed, solitary sanctuary of the bathroom.

*   *   *

The world heaved around her. Heaved, inverted, turned the wrong way up. It was like some hideous jumbled nightmare, where the floors became ceilings, the ceilings floors.

And there was no way out—none. No way to wake and find it all a horrible, terrible nightmare.

She felt sick—so nauseous that she longed for the ability to purge herself.

Purge every last day and night of this vile, hideous nightmare.

The scene on the terrace replayed itself over and over, churning through her in cold, sickening waves. She sat on the floor, on the cold marble tiles, backed into a corner as if she could bury herself in the wall. Her hands were pressed over her mouth, her knees hunched to her chest.

She was shivering—shivering with shock, and horror, and disbelief.

But believe it she must. She had no choice. Out there on the terrace two realities had crashed into each other, and she had been sucked, as if down into a vortex, into that other vile reality that Nikos Kiriakis inhabited.

She gagged in her throat.

He thought she had been Stephanos's mistress. Had thought it all along. From the moment he had laid eyes on her—from before then. And he had believed it right until the truth had been forced in front of his disbelieving eyes.

He had not wanted to believe the truth. Had wanted—*wanted*—to stick with his own sickening reality—that she was Stephanos's mistress.

Stephanos's mistress—

The vile words stabbed at her again.

That was what he thought her.

A married man's mistress. His sister's husband's mistress...

Shock buckled through her again.

Shock upon shock.

He was Demetria's brother. Nikos Kiriakis was Stephanos's brother-in-law.

And a man on a mission. A mission to get rid of the threat to his sister's marriage. By a method that could not fail. By seducing Stephanos's mistress away from him.

And that was exactly what he'd done. Calculatingly, deliberately, cold-bloodedly.

He'd come to the hotel with no other purpose than to seek her out—and seduce her.

She lifted her head, lowering her hands. She had to face up to this. Had to.

She said the words. Said them clear and incontestably.

'Nikos Kiriakis seduced me deliberately. He thought I was Stephanos's mistress. There was no other reason he had an affair with me.'

It was like a knife going into her. A knife so deep she gasped aloud with the pain of it.

'And that means that everything—everything that ever happened between us—was a lie. Everything.'

She said the words. Took them into her. Squeezed them tight to wring every last drop from them. Every last pain.

Everything.

Even that most precious moment of all just now, before her dreams had been destroyed before her eyes, that precious moment when for a few brief seconds she had believed, had actually believed, that Nikos had asked her to marry him...

Her face buckled again as the agony of it knifed through and through her, again and again.

There were voices in the bedroom beyond. Shouting, yelling. In Greek. One was Stephanos's—his gruff tones dominated, excoriating in their fury. The other voice was lower—biting out in terse, grim tones. She could understand not a word of what was said. There was a final volley of fury, one last grim reply. Then she heard footsteps, heavy, receding. Then silence.

There came a low, urgent rapping on the bathroom door.

'Janine!' It was Stephanos.

She made no reply.

'Janine—my child—my dearest girl—I must speak to you! I must! Come out, please!'

She could hear the emotion in her father's voice.

Her father.

All her life she had wondered about her father, questioned her mother and got no answers. None.

'Oh, darling, don't ask! It's all so long ago.' That was all she had ever had got out of her mother. At first she had grown up thinking there was something terrible about her father—or that she did not deserve to have one. Then, eventually, as she had come to understand her mother's lifestyle—the endless parade of men, the endless houses they'd gone to live in, apartments they'd occupied for a brief time, nothing more, the ceaseless restlessness of her mother, her pointless, idle, butterfly existence—she had arrived at a bitter conclusion. Her mother had simply had no idea which of her lovers had fathered her.

Sometimes, when she was an adolescent, on holiday from the boarding school she'd been packed off to as soon as her mother could get away with it, she had searched the faces of her mother's myriad acquaintances, trying to see if there was any resemblance to herself in them.

But how could she have seen any when she herself was the image of her own mother? Only her brown eyes were a clue—and hardly a helpful one. Her mother had seldom fallen for blonds.

So slowly, bitterly, she had come to accept that she would never know who her father was, or what nationality, or even if he was still alive.

Until a chance encounter—whose statistical improbability still made her feel terrified at how easy it would have been for it never to have taken place—had changed her life for ever.

The moment was engraved on her memory. She, arriving back in London, heading down to Baggage Reclaim, had seen a man pause by the entrance to the first-class lounge, pause and stare, as if he were seeing a ghost.

She might have taken no notice, intent on collecting her luggage, had the man not said, in a stunned, disbelieving voice, 'Louise?'

He'd put a hand out, saying something in a language she had not at first recognised, and repeated her mother's name. She'd stopped then.

She knew that her physical resemblance to her mother sometimes caused confusion, and this man was about the right age to have known her. And since he was clearly a habitué of first-class lounges, looked to be wearing a hand-tailored suit and was, moreover, good-looking with silvering hair, he was just the type.

She'd shaken her head, pausing fleetingly. 'No, I'm Louise's daughter.' She'd spoken in English, knowing that, despite his clearly non-English appearance, a cosmopolitan man like him would be bound to speak it himself.

'Ah, yes,' he answered. 'Even Louise, with her incredible beauty, could not have defied time so much!'

He rested his eyes on her. They were kind eyes, she thought, and just a touch familiar somehow. She wondered at it. Had she ever met him before?

'And you have very clearly inherited her beauty—I hope you will not mind my saying so?'

She smiled back. 'Not at all.'

He nodded, and then said, as if it were something he ought to say, 'And how is Louise these days? If you are her daughter, then she must have married at some point. She was very against marriage when I knew her!'

Her face stilled. 'Louise died three years ago. A car crash.'

His sympathy was immediate. 'I'm sorry. Please accept my condolences. And to your father.'

She gave a little shake of her head. 'Louise never did marry—her aversion to the institution remained to the end.'

The man looked very slightly shocked, then he looked rueful. 'I remember her being very vehement on the subject, but I put it down to her youth. She was very young—so was I, for that matter! It must have been—' he visibly cast his mind back '—oh, twenty-six years ago now. I remember I met her at the Monaco Grand Prix, so it must have been May. We were together six weeks. She... What is the English expression? She bowled me over! Quite the most beautiful woman I'd ever—'

He stopped. She'd taken a sharp inhalation of breath.

'What is it?' the man asked immediately, concern in his voice.

She stared at him, spoke before she could halt the words, forming them even as her brain registered what he'd just said.

'I'm twenty-five,' she blurted. 'My birthday is in February.'

For a moment he just looked at her, nonplussed. Then, his expression still arrested, he said something in his own language. Staccato. Shocked.

It's Greek, she registered finally. He's Greek.

And he could be... He could be...my...my...

She went on staring at him, her face draining. How often—how often in the night over the years—had she lain awake trying to work when she must have been conceived? May was right on the button. May, twenty-six years ago...

Her fingers pressed against her lips, the unimaginable thought leaping in her brain. For one long, endless moment she still stared at this foreign, middle-aged stranger. Who had had an affair with her mother the month she must have been conceived.

No! This was insane, absurd! She turned away, almost stumbling.

His arm shot out, strong and halting.

'Wait!' He turned her back towards him. 'Wait,' he said again.

His eyes were searching her face. Then, abruptly, he spoke.

'Who is your father?'

She shook her head. 'I...I don't know.'

Her voice was thin. As shocked as his.

'My mother...my mother never told me. I...I don't think she knew...'

A look of total grimness possessed the man's face.

'Oh, she did! I think she did indeed! I might only have been a temporary *affaire* to her, but while I was her lover she had no one else! I would not share her with anyone!'

Suddenly his expression changed. He looked at her—and she could see the shock in his eyes. More than shock. Suddenly, like a blow, she realised why it was he seemed familiar. It was his eyes. They were darker than hers—but they were hers.

And he was seeing the same in her face.

'I think...' he said, and there was something very strange in his voice—something that gave her the strangest feeling in the world. 'I think we need to talk.'

And that was all it had taken. All it had taken for Stephanos to accept her as his daughter. The daughter he'd never even known he had. He'd demanded no other proof from her, accepted her completely, taken her into his heart, his life, without question, without doubt. With strong and immediate love.

But with miracles there came a price, and it was one that Janine had known she would pay, and had not begrudged a penny of it. He'd been flying back to Athens because his wife was due to go into hospital and finally be medically investigated for the cause of her long infertility.

She had understood completely, and without resentment, that Stephanos had felt he could not present her as his daughter at such a moment. It would have been too cruel to Demetria to parade a daughter in front of her when she was trying so desperately to give him a child of her own. So she had accepted what had to happen—that she had to remain, for now, a secret, hidden part of his life.

But not as secret as he'd thought...

The low, urgent rapping came again, and her father's voice called, anxiety and concern twisting in his words.

'Janine—please—Please, I have to talk to you. Please—'

Slowly, very slowly, feeling as if death had washed through her and left her a living corpse, she got to her feet. The tie of her robe was almost undone, revealing half her body. With a deathly shudder she refastened it.

Then she went out to face her father—the man Nikos had thought her lover and taken such ruthless steps to part her from.

Stephanos stood uncertainly, a little way back. He looked old, Janine thought, stricken. Her heart went out to him.

'Janine—' His voiced sounded broken. 'I'm so sorry...so sorry.'

A choke sounded in her throat, and then, in a strangled whisper, she said, 'Vava—'

He opened his arms.

'Ela—'

With a heartbreaking cry, she threw herself into his paternal embrace.

He let her cry. Let her cry and cry and cry.

It was ludicrous, she thought, somewhere in the middle of all her tears, ludicrous to be like this. She was a twenty-five-year-old woman, not a little girl, and her life had taken her to places she would not wish on her worst enemy. Yet she felt like a child again. A child being comforted by her father.

He held her wrapped around him, his hands gently patting her back, speaking to her comfortingly in the language she had grown up not even knowing was her birthright.

Gradually, very gradually, the storm of weeping abated. Gradually, very gradually, her father eased her from him. He stroked her hair.

'If I could undo what has happened to you I would give my life's blood,' he told her, and the pain in his voice was terrible to hear. 'I will bear the guilt of this for ever.'

She shook her head, the pain dulled to a heavy ache. 'It wasn't your fault. It wasn't your fault.' She shuddered. 'I should never have…never have…'

She halted suddenly and looked around, fearful.

'Where—where is—?' She stopped, unable to say his name.

'Gone.' Her father's voice was tight. 'He didn't need me to tell him to get out! He's taken off in that cruiser of his.' His voice softened. 'Get your things, my child—we are leaving too.'

She wiped away the last of her drying tears, taking a breath. 'I'll get dressed. Then I'll pack. Am I…am I going back to the hotel?'

There was a tremor in her voice. She didn't want to go there—not ever again.

'No. You are coming to Athens. With me.' Stephanos's voice was decisive.

Janine looked at him. 'But I thought…Demetria?'

She said the name of her father's wife, for whose sake she had accepted that she could not be openly acknowledged as Stephanos's daughter.

'I cannot do it to her,' he had told her, and she had accepted it. 'For ten long, agonising years Demetria has hoped against hope that she will be able to give me the child she knows I long for. I cannot…*cannot*…tell her that I already have a child…she would be devastated. Think herself useless. Already she punishes herself endlessly! Calls herself barren!'

Janine's heart had gone out to her father's wife. She already knew the story of her unhappy first marriage, so she had accepted that, for the time being at least, her existence would have to be kept secret from Demetria.

And because of that...

Her mind veered away. No. She would not let herself think, feel what that secrecy had caused—

Stephanos's face tensed. Taut with guilt.

'I will have to be honest with Demetria. I thought I could keep you hidden entirely from her. That she would never know about you—at least, not until—until...' He took a deep breath. 'Until we might be blessed with a child of our own! Had I thought...for an instant that she might discover your existence and make...' He sighed heavily. '...such an appalling assumption, I would never, never have taken the risk!'

His expression became bleak. 'But now I must try and undo the harm my silence has caused. To my wife—and my daughter.'

He turned to go. 'I will leave you to your packing. Let me know when you are ready, and we can go. Forgive me, but I must phone Demetria. She has no idea I am here. When I called the hotel yesterday, after landing from New York, and was told you had left, I was scared. As soon as I had tracked you down I flew here. I cannot cause Demetria any more anxiety than I have already.'

He bowed his head and left the room. Alone, Janine got on with the bleak, numbing task of packing.

The helicopter flew them back to Skarios airport, and there the executive jet that Stephanos had chartered was ready for takeoff.

As Janine had emerged, finally, from the villa, numb from head to toe, the dazzling view of sea and sky had nearly undone her. Biting hard on her lip, she'd turned her back and walked up the stone steps to the helipad on the flat land above the villa. The rotors had churned idly. All around, the wild landscape had stretched beneath the azure sky.

As they had taken off she'd looked down. The villa had fallen away from them—the terraces and the spectacular pool, the white limestone cliffs and the tiny crescent beach with its little stone quay. No cruiser moored there. Gone.

Gone, gone, gone.

She had shut her eyes, feeling sick.

The flight to Athens took scarcely an hour. A haze of smog sat over the city in the summer heat. Janine sat in the chauffeured car, still feeling numb.

The numbness lasted all the way to the quiet suburb of Kifissia, where the rich of Athens lived, through the security gates of Stephanos's villa, and into the house itself. Servants greeted her father's arrival, not even blinking as he arrived with a beautiful young blonde, ushering her protectingly inside.

Stephanos's face was drawn as he turned to speak to her.

'I must see Demetria,' he said quietly. He gestured to one of the staff, waiting discreetly in the background. 'Will you show *Kyria* Fareham to her room?'

She was taken upstairs, to what was obviously one of the guest suites. It was beautifully furnished. A maid came up to unpack for her. Janine almost told her not to bother. She could not stay here. She could not stay in Greece. She must go—go.

Back to London. Back to work. She could see Stephanos when he came to England. It would be enough. It would have to be.

Her throat tightened dangerously. She went to stand by the window, looking down into the gardens. They were immaculately kept.

The maid closed the closet doors, murmured something, and left. The room was very quiet.

I'm going to have to think about it, she thought. I'm going to have to think about what happened.

I'm going to have to think about Nikos.

Her throat constricted. Her nails clenched in the palm of her hands.

Nikos. Nikos Kiriakis.

Her father's wife's brother.

Well, you always did tell yourself it was a bad idea to fall for him. And it certainly was. Oh, it certainly was.

The enormity of what he had thought swept over her again.

How could I not have noticed? Her question was savage. How could I not have noticed that he thought I was Stephanos's mistress?

The answer was even more savage. Because he thought you already knew you were!

She was back in the nightmare again, the one where everything shifted round, and floors became ceilings, and up became down. She tried to make sense of it—terrible sense of terrible things.

It was, after all, once you had turned the floor to the ceiling, very simple.

He thought you were Stephanos's mistress. That's why he seduced you. To take you away from Stephanos. So you wouldn't threaten his marriage any more. So he started an affair with you himself.

And if Stephanos hadn't come storming down out of the sky, looking for his missing daughter, what then? What would have happened?

Her nails dug into her palms. She heard his voice, soft in her ear. The devil's voice.

I don't want to part with you, Janine. I want us to be together. I want to take you back to Athens with me and make you mine. Recognised by all the world as mine.

Pain lacerated her, and she swayed with it.

A few short hours ago and those words had opened the door of heaven for her.

Now they ushered her to the mouth of hell.

She wrapped her arms around herself to stanch the pain.

A soft knock sounded on the door. She stiffened. The door opened and Janine turned, arms still wrapped around herself.

A woman stood uncertainly in the doorway. She was thin, very thin, but she was beautifully dressed, with the kind of effortless elegance that Janine was used to seeing in wealthy women in the South of France. She looked to be about fifteen years older than Janine.

'May—may I come in?'

The woman's diffidence was painful to see. Slowly Janine nodded.

'This…this is your house,' she answered. Her eyes were riveted on the other woman's face. Her features were strained, and yet Janine could see the stamp that Kiriakis blood had made on them. She felt the knife stab at her again.

The woman closed the door behind her and advanced a little way across the thick carpet. She held out a hand. 'I am Demetria Ephandrou. Stephanos has told me the truth about you. I…I wish we could have met under happier circumstances.'

Janine swallowed. 'Whatever you think of Stephanos now, he never meant you to know about my existence. He knew it would hurt you too much.'

A strange look passed over Demetria's face. 'Hurt me? How could it hurt me?'

'Because…because… To flaunt me in your face, your husband's daughter. When you…when you could not bear a child yourself…'

There was a little choking sound from Demetria. 'So he thought it better that I should believe he had taken a mistress?'

Janine clenched her hands. 'He didn't want you to know anything at all!'

Abruptly, Demetria lifted her hands 'Did he really think his own wife wouldn't tell that something was going on? Did he really think I wouldn't *notice*?' She came forward further. 'Did he think I would rather believe he was unfaithful to me?' Her expression changing, she reached out her hands to Janine again. 'And instead he was hiding a secret I would have rejoiced at learning!'

Janine stared. 'Rejoiced?'

Demetria slipped Janine's nerveless fingers into her own. 'Don't you see?' she said, and there was a crack in her voice. 'You are living proof that Stephanos can father a child. I was frightened, so frightened, that it might be him, not me, who was infertile. Oh, I know the doctors did their tests—but tests can go wrong, can be misleading, give false hope. But to see you here, strong and well and so very, very alive! Stephanos's child!'

Janine looked into Demetria's shining eyes. 'You're *glad* to know about me?'

The world was turning on its head again.

'How can I not be? How can I not be glad that Stephanos has found you after all these years?' She gave a poignant smile that suddenly lit her thin face with beauty. 'It will not stop me moving heaven and earth to give him a child myself, but knowing that he is already a father gives me more hope than ever!'

The smile faded. She let Janine's hands fall. 'I should have had faith in Stephanos. I should have trusted him. He has loved me so faithfully for so many years—even when I was most unhappy, trapped in a loveless marriage. How could I think that he would betray me? And because I did think that, what has happened now is my fault. All my fault!'

Her eyes lifted to Janine, filled with remorse. 'I sent my brother after you. I turned to him because I was desperate and terrified. I do not ask you to forgive me—' Her voice broke off.

Janine's hands twisted. What could she say? Demetria had acted to save her marriage. And so had Nikos. Her throat thickened. It was like some ghastly Greek tragedy— one misunderstanding, one error, bringing with it a wealth of destruction…

'It's…it's all right,' she got out. 'Please—'

She took a constricted breath. She could not take much more of this. The situation was impossible. *Impossible.*

'Do you think,' she went on, speaking jerkily, 'it might be possible for me to lie down for a little while? I feel… I feel…'

Immediately Demetria was all concern. She hurried to the bed, drawing down the damask cover.

'I will send up coffee. Or do you prefer tea? Something to eat?'

Janine shook her head. 'Thank you, no. I just need to rest a little.'

Demetria nodded. 'Of course. I…I will leave you, then. For now.'

Face still troubled, she took her leave.

Slowly, Janine sat down on the bed.

Her head was swimming. She let her body fold down onto the bed, lifting up her legs. They felt very heavy. Her whole body felt heavy, numb. Her eyes closed. The cotton pillowcase was cool on her cheek. She reached to pull the damask coverlet back over her.

I want to sleep, she thought. Sleep, but not to dream…

She dreamt. Instantly, immediately.

She was there, at the villa, on the terrace. Nikos was beside her, his arm around her. She leant into him, feeling his strength, his solidity. Joy filled her. Joy and relief. She had had such a terrible nightmare, but now she had woken from it. A nightmare so awful she did not want to think about it. But it was over. She was here, with Nikos, and he was holding her and everything was wonderful and beautiful and blissful...

He was making love to her, moving over her body, whispering to her, murmuring, his hands gliding over her skin, his mouth caressing her... She was on fire, on sweet fire, her limbs dissolving. The fire was burning through her, and through him, and she cried out, cried out...

Her eyes flew open.

To an empty room.

Misery enfolded her, wrapping around her like weed, drowning her.

She curled in on herself against the misery, against the pain lancing and lancing through her.

It was a lie—everything was a lie! I meant nothing to him, nothing. Less than nothing—I was just something to be picked up, manipulated, and disposed of. Whatever it took. A problem to be sorted. A threat to be disarmed, demolished, removed.

And what had it taken? A look, a day, a kiss, a smile. She had gone down at the first fence, willingly going with him, putting up not the slightest resistance. She had melted at his feet.

He didn't have to break a sweat to seduce me...

A chill went through her. Demetria had known what she was doing when she sent Nikos to deal with her...

She had sent a master to do the job. The job of seducing the woman she thought was stealing her husband.

Except that I wasn't that woman. I was just—

What was the word the military used? When unintended targets got hit?

Collateral damage.

That was what she had been. Collateral damage.

The target hadn't existed at all.

Her stomach iced.

But the damage was real.

Horribly, horribly real.

She gave a smothered cry, flinging back her arm across the pillow, staring up at the ceiling with wide, pained eyes.

CHAPTER SEVEN

SHE dined that night with Stephanos and Demetria. The strain was all but unbearable. It was an awkward, painful meal, and Janine could hardly eat. The delicious food tasted like straw. Conversation was minimal, stilted. They talked only of innocuous things, like the weather and the wedding they'd been to on Long Island.

What made it worse was that it should have been a joyful meal, thought Janine anguishedly. After all Stephanos's fears Demetria had accepted her; she would have a recognised place in her father's family. She could be her father's daughter for all the world to see. She could love him openly, freely. Without hiding or secrecy or worry about hurting Demetria. She should be glad, rejoicing. And so she would have been...

She would have to go, she knew. She could not stay here, however much she wanted to spend precious time with Stephanos, get to know him, the father she had never known. The father she had never been told about.

Demetria found it very hard to accept Louise's actions.

'How could she not have told Stephanos she was pregnant?' she asked uncomprehendingly.

'I think Louise simply didn't want any hassle,' Janine answered. 'She must have known Stephanos would insist on marrying her. And she would have refused—she always hated the idea of marriage. She saw it as a shackle for women. Constricting their freedom. So she never told him, just went ahead and had me.'

She didn't look at Stephanos as she spoke, but she could feel his pain—because it was her pain too. Her mother had denied them both the chance to know each other, love each other.

'And yet,' she said, saying what must be said, 'if it had been otherwise then Stephanos would have married Louise, and not you.'

Pain went through Demetria's eyes.

'Stephanos would have had a child,' she said in a low, anguished voice.

'I want only you, Demetria! With or without children, I want only you!'

Her husband caught her hand, holding it hard. Between them, tangible in its power, Janine could sense the strength of their love, holding them together against their mutual grief. What must it be like, she thought, to be loved like that?

No! Don't think, don't think!

Instead she awknowledged the painful irony that she should have been born to a woman with so few maternal feelings when Demetria yearned for a child with all her being. She found herself giving a small prayer that her father's wife should be granted the blessing she so longed for.

She has a generous heart, thought Janine. She could so easily have bitterly resented my existence, and instead she has welcomed it, rejoiced in it. Yes, perhaps there is an element of what she told me, that I am proof that Stephanos can father a child, but for all that she could so easily have seen me as a taunt to her own infertility.

She felt a silent shiver go through her. Had Stephanos only realised how large Demetria's heart was then he would never have thought to keep his new-found daughter's existence a secret—arousing his wife's suspicions and making her act so swiftly, so devastatingly, to protect her marriage…

Misery filled her. None of this would have happened. This vile, sick situation would never have arisen.

Another thought pierced her, even more anguished.

Supposing Stephanos had introduced her into his family life straight away, the moment they arrived in Greece? Supposing she had come here, to his own house, had met Demetria—and her brother? An image leapt in her mind so painful she could not bear it—Nikos coming here, Demetria's brother, being introduced to his brother-in-law's long-lost daughter, knowing who she really was right from the beginning...

She saw him as vividly as if he had been real, looking at her with those night-dark eyes, taking her hand, welcoming her—

The beeping of the house phone sounded and she blinked. Nikos was gone.

Well, that much was true. Nikos was gone. Gone from her life for ever. And she must go too. She could never meet him again. *Never.*

And she didn't want to see him. The very thought of him made her buckle with nausea. After what he had done to her...

The instinct to run, run and lick her wounds, was overpowering.

Tomorrow. I'll go tomorrow. After breakfast. I must find out about flights and all that. She would ask her father as soon as he'd finished speaking on the phone.

He'd answered in Greek, his face tightening slightly, then nodded, said something more in Greek, and hung up.

She opened her mouth to speak, but her father forestalled her.

'Janine—will you come with me a moment, *pethi mou*?'

There was tension in his voice; she could hear it.

He got to his feet and waited for her to do likewise. Puzzled, she did so. The atmosphere seemed strained somehow—and yet expectant.

She saw Demetria look at her, then glance to meet her husband's eye in silent communication. The look in the other woman's eyes was tense as well. Then she got to her feet too and came across to Janine. She took her hands in hers.

'I caused you great harm,' she told her. 'I never meant to, but I did. The harm cannot be undone—but what can be done will be done.' She leant forward to place a kiss on each of Janine's cheeks.

Janine's eyes widened. The moment seemed so solemn suddenly. Then, just as suddenly, Demetria's face suddenly lit. 'Yet I am happy as well as sad—I cannot help it!' Her hands squeezed Janine's. 'You do not know how much I have longed for this day! Oh, it should not have been like this, I know—but all the same I cannot stop my happiness! And that it should be you of all people fills my heart with joy!'

Janine just stared at her. Demetria's words were inexplicable.

Then her father was touching her shoulder, drawing her away. He said something to Demetria, and she nodded. The tension was back in the room, yet Demetria's face still was lit from within.

Bemused, Janine went meekly with her father. Perhaps she needed to sign documents or something—to do with the transfer of money he was making over to her.

They went out of the large, ornate salon, across the wide marbled hallway to a door set off a small lobby towards the rear of the huge house. Janine could hear her footsteps echo off the marble floor.

Stephanos went ahead of her and opened the door. She stepped through into the room beyond.

And stopped dead.

Nikos was inside.

Blindly, instinctively, she turned to run, bolt, flee. But her father was there, catching her shoulders.

'My child, my child—I know, I know. But this must be done. It must.'

There was grimness beneath the softness, the sympathy. Gently but inexorably he turned her around, ushering her forward a little so he could close the door behind him.

She wanted to shut her eyes, wanted to cover her face, but she could not. Nikos was standing there, across the room. It was a kind of study, she noticed with the tiny fragment of her brain that was still registering the existence of anything that was not Nikos. There was a large desk, a computer on it, leather chairs, shelves with books, massive tomes and business journals. A masculine place. A place of business and financial transaction, of legal documents, contracts and commerce.

Nikos looked completely at home in it.

He was wearing a suit. Dark this time, not the lightweight suit she'd first laid eyes on him in. Whereas in the light grey suit he'd looked elegant and devastating, now he looked sombre.

And just as devastating.

That was the worst thing, she thought, as her mind fragmented into a thousand shards, each one needle-sharp, piercing her flesh like knives. That she could feel her heart jolt as her eyes took him in, took in those broad shoulders, the long, lean body, that beautifully planed and sculpted face, those dark gold-flecked eyes.

Veiled eyes.

Eyes that saw her but did not look at her.

Eyes that were shuttered, had no expression in them.

Her nails dug into the palms of her hands. As they did so she saw that a muscle was working in his cheek. He looked grim, and tense.

Why? Why was Stephanos doing this to her? Why this hideous ordeal? How could he be so cruel to her?

The silence stretched endlessly, it seemed. But it could

only have been a few seconds—though they seemed to last for ever, Janine felt.

Stephanos spoke. Though she could understand none of the words, Janine could hear the heaviness in them. As he spoke Nikos's face tensed even more. His eyes moved from her to look at her father.

Then, abruptly, as Stephanos fell silent, they snapped back to her.

For a second something blazed in them, something that made her flinch with shock. Then it was gone. The veil was back over those dark and gold eyes, a veil she could not see past.

Stephanos placed a hand on her shoulder, turning her slightly towards him.

'My daughter.' His voice was solemn now, as Demetria's had been. 'Great wrong has been done to you. Now it shall be righted.' He placed his other hand upon her other shoulder, leant forward and dropped a kiss upon her forehead. It was almost like a ritual, a paternal blessing.

Then, exchanging one long last, level look with Nikos, he left the room.

She wanted to run, bolt, flee from the room. But her feet were rooted to the ground, her body frozen.

Nikos looked at her. As before, the moment seemed to last for all eternity, not the few fleeting seconds that was all its true duration.

Her nails dug deeper into the palms of her hands.

What was he going to say? What could he say?

That he'd made a mistake? An error?

Collateral damage.

The chill euphemism echoed in her mind.

She looked at the man who up until this moment had never set eyes on her without thinking that she was a woman who had taken the financial protection of a married man—a rich, married man—a man—and the irony of it bit so deep she had to stop herself crying out—a man old enough to be her father.

For one long, ghastly moment he went on looking at her, not speaking. Then, abruptly, his voice broke the unendurable silence between them.

'Janine—'

Just her name. The softness of his pronunciation, the familiarity, undid her. Her nails seemed to pierce her skin, so deep did she dig them into her palms. For one terrifying moment she felt she was going to burst into tears, sob with pain and despair, break down entirely.

She wouldn't do it. She would *not*. She would not break down. For some horrible reason her father thought she should endure the ordeal of facing Nikos again—why, she could not tell. She didn't want an apology, didn't want an expression of regret, didn't want any awkward, stilted voicing of contrition.

With immense effort she schooled herself.

'Yes?' Her voice was cool, unemotional.

Something flashed in his eyes. For a moment she thought it was anger. But that could not be. It was so totally inappropriate that she must have imagined it.

'This is a difficult situation for us both,' he said tightly. 'Let us try and get through it with as much grace as we can muster.'

He looked, she thought suddenly, very formidable. Every inch a man of wealth and consequence, a man born to riches, a powerful man. Like a shot to the heart she remembered that first frisson she had felt as he towered over her in his business suit at the poolside, making her feel so exposed, so vulnerable in her skimpy bikini.

No, she mustn't remember that. Mustn't remember anything as dangerous as that.

He was speaking again.

'The arrangements have been set in motion. From my meeting with Stephanos this afternoon I understand that he has already taken steps to settle an appropriate sum on you, as capital. That will, of course, remain yours. He and I have also agreed a separate sum, from my own resources, that will be settled on you as income. As for the ceremony itself, I know that Demetria is very keen to make a splendid occasion of it. Whether you are happy with that, or would prefer something quieter, I leave entirely to you. Whichever you choose, you will, of course, have my support—whatever Demetria's feelings on the subject.'

He spoke briskly, as if running through the key points of a business deal. As he finished he looked at her questioningly, as if affording her the opportunity to input her comments, if any, before he moved on.

She stared at him blankly.

'I haven't the faintest idea what you're talking about,' she said.

A frown creased between his eyes.

'I appreciate, Janine, that your background means you are unfamiliar with the concept of settlements and the disposition of property on such an occasion, but be assured that Stephanos is obviously ensuring that your interests are safeguarded to the utmost. You may safely leave everything to him. As for the other matter...' His voice became dry. 'You may, if you prefer, leave that equally safely to Demetria. She will, I know, be in her element.' His mouth tightened minutely. 'It is, after all, something she has longed for on my behalf.'

'What is?' She was lost—completely lost. Nikos looked at her.

'To see me married,' he said tightly.

She drew her breath sharply. It was like a blow coming out of the blue. And it hurt. Over everything that had happened, all her pain and misery, this smote at her with lethal force.

'You're getting married?' Her voice was faint. Her nails spasmed in her palms.

He was looking at her as if she was deranged.

'Have you not listened to anything I have told you?' he demanded. He could have been speaking to an underling, a recalcitrant employee. 'Stephanos and I have agreed the settlement—you are, it goes without saying, extremely well provided for. Demetria will undertake the organisation of whatever form of ceremony you prefer. Unless you feel strongly, I would suggest a civil ceremony—but of course if you wish I can arrange for you to receive whatever instruction is necessary so that you may participate in an Orthodox service. Our wedding can be as large or as small, as public or private as you wish. Demetria will make all the arrangements necessary.'

Faintness was washing through her. Faintness and disbelief.

'Our wedding...'

Her voice trailed off.

He took a step forward. 'Our wedding,' he repeated. He took a breath. 'Janine, we must be married. It is obvious. Surely you understand that?' There was tension suddenly in his voice.

Slowly, her head shook from side to side.

'No. I don't understand.' Her voice was still faint.

Something changed in his eyes. And in his voice.

'Don't you?'

She felt her breath catch. There was a caress in his words as tangible as if he had stroked her arm.

Pain squeezed through her.

'Don't you, Janine?'

He reached towards her. The gold in his eyes was molten suddenly.

She backed away. Blocking. Rejecting.

'No! I don't understand.' Her voice was hectic. 'I don't understand in the slightest! It's ridiculous, absurd!'

The flash of anger in his eyes came again. 'Try saying that to Stephanos! To Demetria!' His mouth thinned.

'They're consumed with guilt. Each of them feels that this…débâcle…is their fault. Stephanos's for not confiding in Demetria about your existence. And Demetria's—' his voice became grimmer yet '—Demetria's for coming to such a disastrous conclusion about your identity!' His eyes held Janine's. 'Our marriage is the only way they can accept what has happened. The only remedy.'

She shook her head. It felt heavy, muzzy.

'If you love your father as I love my sister then we must do what they so desperately need us to do. Only marriage will recover the situation.' His face tensed even more, and then in a heavy, hard voice he said, 'They feel you have been dishonoured.'

'Dishonoured?' Her voice was incredulous.

That emotion flashed in his eyes again.

'This is Greece, Janine. In Greece a father protects his child. In Greece a family holds together, is the most sacred part of society. Stephanos feels that he has failed to protect you. That his failure has resulted in…what has happened. And Demetria—Demetria is punishing herself for having sent me to…deal with you. For her, for Stephanos, the only way that this…dishonour…can be undone is by our marriage. Then and only then will our families be united once more.'

She looked at him. Looked at him long, and hard. Then, in a brittle, taut voice, she said, 'I have never heard anything so sick in all my life.'

She reached for the door, pulled it open, and walked out.

She crossed the marble hallway. Her footsteps were jerky, her body stiff as a board. She headed for the staircase.

She had not gained the lowest step before the double doors to the drawing room were flung open.

Demetria hurried out.

'So! Is it done?' Her face was alight with hope. It shone

like a beacon from her eyes. But behind the hope Janine could see another emotion.

Guilt. Haunting her eyes, bringing tension to her thin body.

Her father came up behind his wife, his hand at her back. Expectancy was in his face. Guilt shadowing his eyes.

Janine looked from one to the other. A cold, horrible numbness started to creep over her. They meant it. They really meant it. They wanted her and Nikos to marry.

Were desperate for it.

'Janine. *Pethi mou*—'

The anxiety in her father's voice was audible.

'My dear...' Demetria's voice was faltering.

She looked at Demetria, tormented by guilt and by her infertility. Haunted by the damage her unfounded suspicions of her husband had done to his daughter. Looked at her father, who had taken her into his arms, his life, without question, without doubt, with only joy and gratitude. Now tormented by what had happened to her. What his silence had caused.

Footsteps sounded behind her, heavy on the marble floor, issuing from the room she had just bolted from. They approached steadily.

Nikos came to stand at her side.

She stood, frozen, beside him.

She wanted to move, step away from him. But the numbness was spreading all through her. Like heavy, dulling anaesthetic.

Stephanos said something in Greek. Sharp. Enquiring.

Nikos answered. His voice level.

She heard her name—that was all she could make out. Two pairs of eyes flew to her. Her father's and his wife's. Tension radiated from them like cold waves. Numbing her even more.

'Janine?'

It was Nikos. Nikos saying her name. Asking her a question she did not need spelt out.

The numbness reached her brain. She could feel nothing—nothing at all.

Nothing.

Nothing except an inescapable inevitability.

She yielded to what she knew, in her bleak heart of hearts, she had to do.

She bowed her head.

'Yes.'

It was all she said. All she had to say.

Before her eyes, her father's face broke into a smile. Relief shone from him. Demetria's eyes took on the shining look that they had held just before Janine had left the drawing room, so short a while ago. Her father's wife's strange words then made sense now. Horrible, hideous sense.

But it was too late. All too, too late.

Demetria surged forward. She caught Janine's hands, bestowing a kiss on either cheek. Her father came behind her, hugging her. Then Demetria was kissing her brother. Her father's hand was stretching out to Nikos. Slowly, through the numbness that was complete now, Janine saw Nikos hesitate. Then he took Stephanos's hand, clasping it. He said something. Her father nodded. Something was exchanged between them. Between the man whose daughter had been dishonoured, however unintentionally, and the man who was now making due reparation for that dishonouring.

It was like something out of the Middle Ages. Not something that had anything to do with her. It could not be. It could not.

Then Demetria was clapping her hands.

'Champagne! We must have some champagne!' She hurried off eagerly to summon one of her staff.

Stephanos was ushering the happy couple back into the drawing room. His face was wreathed in smiles.

It was a nightmare. As Demetria returned, and a bottle of chilled vintage champagne arrived, Janine could only stand there. The numbness kept her going, kept her upright. Nikos stood beside her.

Stephanos gave her a glass of champagne. She took it in nerveless fingers. Her father gave a toast. She could understand not a word, but it was clearly a toast.

Their glasses were raised.

She drank.

The liquid, chill and effervescent, slipped down her throat.

Just as the champagne had slipped down her throat when Nikos had borne her away on his cruiser to the fate he'd intended for her...

But in her worst nightmares she had never expected this.

Someone else was living in her body. She could tell. It seemed to be moving, walking and talking, and she was smiling. Smiling when her father kissed her, smiling when Demetria chattered away. Smiling when visitors came to call and she was introduced.

'Stephanos's English daughter,' Demetria called her, and whatever people thought they kept it to themselves. 'And my sister-in-law to be!'

There was more astonishment over that announcement than over the unexpected production of Demetria's twenty-five-year-old stepdaughter.

'My dear, you will be envied to death! What *is* your secret? How on earth did you manage to catch our handsome Nikos?'

The enquiry was friendly, but Janine could hear the barb in the voice of this designer-clad matron who was clearly one of Demetria's good friends.

Well, she felt like answering, it was like this...

But even as the vicious thought formed in her mind she

knew that Demetria was rewriting history for public consumption.

'It was a *coup de foudre*!' she exclaimed, clapping her hands as if it really were thundering. 'Janine came out to visit us, and as soon as Nikos set eyes on her he was lost!'

'Wonderful!' cooed her friend. 'But then she is a beauty, and only the most beautiful will do for our handsome, handsome Nikos!'

There was definitely a barb in her voice now.

When she had gone—surely, Demetria said with a gleam in her eyes, to spread the word as fast as possible—her sister-in-law-to-be whispered conspiratorially, 'She wanted an affair with Nikos herself! He turned her down! Mind you...' Her voice became even more conspiratorial '...she was one of the few he did. My darling brother has a reputation that—'

She stopped dead.

'It's all right,' said Janine.

The haunted look was back in Demetria's face. 'It's why I sent him,' she said in a low voice. 'I knew if anyone could entice a woman away from another man it would be Nikos.' Guilt resonated in her voice.

'It's all right,' said Janine again. What else could she say?

She was moving in a daze, a haze of numbness. She had no will left of her own.

Apart from introducing her as her sister-in-law-to-be to all her extensive social acquaintance, Demetria was whisking her around the most expensive shops in Kolonaki, the chic shopping district of Athens. Money burned through her fingers in amounts that Janine could not bear to watch. At first she tried to stop her, but Demetria didn't listen. And she didn't listen when Janine said she did not want a religious wedding.

'I know it will seem strange to you, but you are Greek—

you are Stephanos's daughter—and to be Greek is to be Orthodox—' Demetria began.

But Janine held fast. She might let Demetria go crazy in clothes shops, but she would not make a mockery of religion—any religion—with this travesty she was engaged upon.

But she must not think about that. Must not think about what she was doing. She must not. Or she might break down and shatter.

And she must not do that. Stephanos and Demetria needed to see her married. She had to go through with it. She had to.

Her feelings didn't matter.

Besides, she had none. She was quite, quite numb.

As for Nikos, she never set eyes on him.

It was her only mercy.

'My wretched brother!' Demetria lamented. 'What a time to go haring off to Australia! Business—always business. But—' she sighed '—at least he is getting it all out of the way. He has promised me that you will honeymoon for a month!'

Her eyes gleamed, though there was a brightness in them that was almost desperate, Janine thought. 'And you will have a trousseau to die for!' She glanced at the diamond-studded watch on her wrist, and tut-tutted. 'Oh, we have scarcely time for lunch before your next fitting.' She gave a laugh. There was a feverish note in it. 'How can we possibly get everything done in time?'

The days slipped by, one by one. August slipped into September. The heat hardly slackened. Janine stayed in the air-conditioned interiors, still feeling numb.

Two days before the wedding Nikos returned to Athens.

'He is coming to dinner tonight,' announced Stephanos at breakfast.

Janine's fingers clenched on her cutlery.

Demetria exclaimed volubly at the short notice, but rallied immediately. She spent all day preparing the house. Bouquets arrived, heavy and scented, lavished all over the house. Demetria spent time closeted with her chef. Servants polished the house till it shone. Stephanos, Janine noted, kept to his office in the city.

In mid-afternoon Demetria banished her upstairs. 'Rest, then bathe. I will send Maria to dress you at eight, and the hairdresser and stylist come at half-past seven.'

Numbly, Janine did what she was told.

'Oh, my dear, you look wonderful!'

Demetria clapped her hands together, clasping them to her bosom. She herself looked incredibly slim and elegant in dark blue. Janine was in emerald-green.

The dress was a masterpiece—a couturier number— wrapped around her in tiny overlapping plissé tissue from breasts to ankles. Her shoulders and arms were bare, her hair swept up into a complicated pleat that had taken nearly an hour to dry and style and pin. Her make-up was immaculate—the professional stylist had applied it.

She wore no jewellery. Not a scrap.

'No—nothing,' Demetria had insisted when her maid remonstrated, and had said something in a whisper to Maria that had brought a conspiratorial smile to the older woman's face.

Demetria held up a hand. From downstairs, quite audible, came the sound of the front door admitting someone. Voices murmured.

'I will check on Stephanos,' Demetria said to Janine. 'Five minutes,' she instructed Maria.

The maid nodded, and set about fussing one last time over Janine.

Janine stood staring at her reflection in the long glass.

She did indeed look spectacular. The dress moulded her figure revealingly, but without the slightest trace of vulgarity. She looked what she was supposed to look—the rich daughter of a rich man.

About to marry another rich man.

A man who was marrying her because he had dishonoured her and who had, quite accidentally, taken her for the mistress of a married man...

I can't do this. I can't. I can't go through with it. I can't endure it. I can't face it.

Her breath froze in her throat.

I can't face him.

She felt the numbness start to crack—tiny, filigree cracks that began to radiate out across her consciousness. They spread rapidly, terrifyingly, and underneath was seeping something so painful she could not deny its existence. It forced itself upon her, welling up through every crack...

There was the lightest touch on her hand. Maria was looking at her questioningly.

'*Kyria*, I think it is time to go down now.'

Janine nodded. Walking carefully in her high heels and long dress, she crossed the room and headed down the wide staircase. There was no one in the hall, but she could hear voices in the drawing room.

She swept across the hall and one of the staff opened the double doors for her. She nodded her thanks and walked in.

Stephanos and Demetria were there, already seated. Nikos was standing. He was dressed like Stephanos, in a tuxedo. Janine felt her insides hollow.

As she came in, he turned.

His eyes focused on her with an expression of absolute arrest. He didn't move, not a muscle, just looked at her.

For a moment, a long, terrifying moment, she felt as if she were standing on the very edge of a cliff. As if one single movement of her body would send her hurtling over the precipice to be destroyed on the rocks below.

Then, like a saviour, her father walked up to her and took her hands.

'My beautiful daughter.'

There was such pride in his voice, such love. Such gratitude.

She felt her heart squeeze.

Then Nikos was speaking. His voice was deep. Oppressively formal.

'Janine.'

That was all. Then he was slipping a hand inside the jacket of his tuxedo. He drew out a slim, oblong box.

'Demetria told me you would be wearing green tonight.' He flicked open the box, his voice quite impersonal.

The lamplight made the emeralds within gleam with green fire. Nikos took out the necklace, discarding the case. Taking an end in each hand, he approached Janine.

'Turn around.'

Wordlessly, she turned.

She felt his fingers at her nape. Faintness drummed through her and she fought it off. This was part of the charade. This hollow, meaningless, bitter charade that she had to endure for the sake of her father, who loved her, for Demetria, who loved Stephanos...

His fingertips touched the delicate hairs at the back of her head as he fastened the necklace around her. The stones felt cold to her skin. Then he stepped away, returning to his original position in the room.

His sister gave a little gasp.

'Nik, they are exquisite!' She said something else in Greek. He nodded, glancing at Stephanos. Then he slipped his hand inside his breast pocket again and drew out a smaller jewel case. A ring case, square and bulbous. As before, he flicked it open.

The ring—diamonds set with emeralds—drew another gasp from Demetria. Janine watched in silence, as if she were far outside her body, and waited while he removed the ring, came forward, lifted her nerveless hand and slid the engagement ring on her finger. Then he raised her hand to his lips and kissed it.

He might have been a stranger.

He is a stranger—a man you do not know. You thought you did, but you didn't.

But you've got to marry him all the same…

'Thank you,' she murmured, as a fiancée *should* thank the man who had offered to marry her, to restore the honour lost so accidentally, so unintentionally. Her eyes slid away.

Then one of the staff entered, bearing a tray of champagne.

All through dinner, through each of the long and complicated courses with which Demetria's chef had excelled himself, Janine saw the ring winking on her finger. It seemed to drag her hand down, making it feel heavy, clumsy.

She sat opposite Nikos, letting her eyes constantly slip past him to focus on a painting on the wall of the dining room. It looked like a Dutch landscape. Seventeenth-century. By the end of dinner she was acquainted with the position of every lowering cloud, every sail of the passing barge, every feature of every distant peasant.

What was talked about she had no idea. The evening was a blur. She seemed to pass the time answering questions put to her and sipping from her wine glass. There was a lot of wine. The champagne, then white, then red, and sweet. As she sipped her dessert wine she remembered the bouquet of the Sauternes she had drunk that first lunchtime on the terrace of the villa, hot in the summer sun, with the scent of the dry earth, the heat of the air.

The languor of desire.

Of their own volition her eyes slid to Nikos. She could not help it. She had to look at him. Had to.

She let herself go back. Let time wash her away. Sweep

her back to where she once had been, gazing at the man she had so desired. Possessing him.

Weakness hollowed through her, and an ache so great she felt it fill her every atom. She sat across the table from him and poured out her desire.

He was talking to Stephanos. It was something to do with property and prices, location. She was not paying attention—hadn't been at all. They'd slipped back into Greek, and she welcomed it. Now all she had to do was sit here and give herself to the wonder, the breathtaking wonder, of gazing at him, feeling her heart fill and fill and fill...

Suddenly, without warning, without any pause in what he was saying to her father, Nikos's eyes flicked to hers.

They caught her gaze as a hunter snared game, seizing and holding her so fast she could not even breathe. For the long, timeless moment he held her she could not not move, transfixed by his regard.

The world disappeared. Simply disappeared. Stephanos's voice faded, the softly playing baroque background music faded, Demetria faded, the room faded, blurred. There was nothing left, and no one. No one except Nikos, holding her with his eyes, those dark and gold eyes. Holding her...

Just holding her...

Nikos, holding her...

Then his head turned back to Stephanos and he let her go.

The room surged back around her. There was her father, talking, music playing from the recessed speakers, the wine winking in her glass, the scent of Demetria's perfume, the flowers on the table.

Her heart was beating. Beating so rapidly she felt it racing inside her, pulsing with a strength that made her feel weak.

She reached for her wine again.

Demetria said something and she turned to her, fixing a

polite smile on her face, trying to make her brain work again, function.

She started to talk about something quite innocuous. It might have been flowers. Or food. Janine couldn't really tell. She murmured, and nodded, and smiled politely.

Trying to stop her eyes stealing back to where they yearned to go.

To Nikos.

Who had taken her to heaven. And left her in hell.

CHAPTER EIGHT

FOR a second, as Stephanos drew his attention again and Demetria diverted Janine's, Nikos felt a surge of some powerful emotion he recognised as rage. Rage that he had been interrupted.

He had got her! For the first time since she had run from him, as white as milk, on that gut-twisting morning at the villa, he had got her! She had been responding to him—helplessly, totally. Had they been on their own he would have hesitated not a second—he'd have come around the table, swept her up into her arms and made her his own again!

Frustration seethed through him. She was so incredibly, fantastically beautiful! She'd walked into the room and his breath had simply stopped in his lungs. Never, *never* had she been more beautiful!

Or so untouchable.

Totally untouchable.

But then he'd known that from the moment when, like an icy deluge down his spine, Stephanos's words had sunk in. The girl he'd thought his brother-in-law's mistress was his daughter.

He could still feel now the shock that had buckled through him as the world inverted around him and black had turned to white before his very eyes. The hideous scene in the villa when truth—blazing, self-evident, convincing truth—had dissolved in his hands. And new truth, a truth that had hollowed him out like a knife eviscerating his guts, had stared at him out of Stephanos's eyes.

Janine's eyes.

The two had blurred.

Like something in a nightmare.

And like something in a nightmare his emotions had blazed in total conflict with each other. Horror that he had taken Stephanos's daughter for his mistress. Realisation that that meant Stephanos didn't *have* a mistress—had never had a mistress—that his sister's marriage was not in danger.

And above all, overriding everything, the realisation that Janine had been taken away from him. Janine—the woman he desired beyond anything. Anyone. The woman he had to possess again—*had to*. His whole being was focused on her—on Janine.

Who had been taken away from him—when he wanted her so much, so much.

Taken away and walled up, here in her father's house. And there had been only one way to get to her. Only one.

He hadn't needed the excruciatingly painful interview in Stephanos's office the afternoon he'd got back to Athens, or the even more painful telephone conversation with a sobbing Demetria, to tell him that.

Marriage. Stephanos demanded it. Demetria begged it.

As for Janine—

His face darkened. He had tried to make her see why they must marry—not for their family, but for themselves. She was trying to deny what they had. What they still had. What they would always have. Couldn't she see that?

Well, he thought, she'd seen it now. Seen it blaze in his eyes, just as he'd seen it blaze in her eyes.

He had to get her to accept it. He had to!

Frustration ate at him. Stephanos had all but ordered him to take himself off while Demetria got on with organising his daughter's wedding. He'd had no choice but to agree. Stephanos had made it totally, absolutely clear that Janine was out of his reach. Out of his reach totally until she had his ring on her finger.

Nikos's mouth tightened. He'd accepted Stephanos's edict, had been in no position to object, but every day in

Australia had been a torment. Even tonight he was under stringent scrutiny, forced to behave with a formality towards Janine that was excruciating. He would be allowed no time with her alone. Stephanos had made that clear. No chance to speak to her—no chance to touch her, to break through her denial. No time to break through that wall she had put up around herself.

Slowly he let himself exhale, trying to breathe out the frustration that choked him.

It would not be long now. He had to cling on to that. Soon he would have Janine in bed with him again.

He would count every hour.

Janine closed her eyes and leant her head back against the cool leather headrest. Through her body hummed the low vibration of the twin engines of an executive jet. Her hands rested on the wide leather armrests at either side. On her finger a band of gold glinted.

Her wedding ring.

It was done. It was over. She had married the man who had sought her out to get her into bed with him, out of the bed of the man he had assumed was her rich, married lover.

She heard her own voice echo in her mind, after he'd told her that it was 'obvious' that they must marry—'I have never heard anything so sick in all my life!' But she had gone and done it all the same.

No, she wouldn't think about her wedding. Wouldn't think about marrying Nikos. Wouldn't think about Nikos period.

It was much too dangerous to think about him.

Instead she pulled the numbness back over her, like a blanket, and settled down under its reassuring folds.

'Would you care for something to drink, *Kyria* Kiriakis?'

The soft voice of the flight attendant murmured at her side.

She shook her head. Then promptly changed her mind

and asked for a gin and tonic. She'd drunk no alcohol at all at the opulent reception at one of Athens's top hotels. The champagne in her glass had scarcely touched her lips. She didn't think she could have swallowed. She'd made a pretence of eating, but hadn't been able to force the food down. She'd tried desperately not to look as sick as she'd felt.

The reception had gone on and on, a babble of Greek voices. Everyone had been looking at her, she knew, but she had simply stood there, as tall and immobile as a Greek column, in her ivory satin gown with its narrow skirt and long train. She hoped, for her father's sake and for Demetria's sake, that she had simply looked as if she were suffering from bridal nerves. Certainly she'd been on the receiving end of a few envious looks and remarks from a considerable number of the female guests. She'd smiled a pale smile and said nothing. Feeling numb. Endlessly numb.

Her numbness was a blessed relief.

The only time it had come near to cracking—the way it had that evening when she'd stared at her reflection the night Nikos had come to dinner—had been when they had taken their leave. Her father had taken her in his arms and kissed her on her forehead.

'Remember, my darling girl, that I love you very much.'

That was all he had said, and it had nearly undone her. Then Demetria had been kissing her on both cheeks, clutching at her. Her eyes had been fevered. Janine hadn't been able to bring herself to meet them. For their sakes she had gone through this travesty.

Louise's image floated in front of her eyes. How scornful she would have been! Her daughter's travesty of a marriage would have confirmed all the contempt she had ever felt for the institution.

Her drink arrived and she sipped it. The gin kicked in her throat. She took another sip—more of a gulp this time.

A hand reached over from the seat across the aisle and removed her glass.

'Drinking on an empty stomach is not wise.'

She darted her eyes venomously to where Nikos sat, engrossed in the current issue of the *Harvard Business Review*.

'Give that back!'

He levelled a glance at her.

'You ate almost nothing at the reception. The alcohol will go straight to your head.'

She pulled her eyes away. They had the power to pierce her numbness, and she didn't want that. Her numbness was all that was keeping her going.

She turned her head. Below, the dark mass of the Balkans was relieved only by the occasional gleam of moonlight on a lake or river.

At least it would be cooler in Austria, thought Janine. She had taken no interest whatsoever in the choice of honeymoon destination. She vaguely remembered Demetria asking her whether she liked the Alps, and that was about it.

She went on staring out of the window, seeing nothing.

Across the aisle, Nikos rested his dark eyes on her. The wedding had proved more difficult than he'd anticipated. Demetria must have invited everyone she knew.

He understood why. The wedding had been a statement, a very public statement, that he was making the appropriate reparation to Stephanos's daughter. Only Demetria and Stephanos knew that, of course, which was what had made the wedding so hard. Amongst his male acquaintance there was a general consensus that this was, in effect, a dynastic marriage, drawing the families of Ephandrou and Kiriakis even more closely together. That Stephanos Ephandrou's daughter happened to be a total knockout was considered a bonus for him, whatever the financial advantage and the mutual exchange of corporate cross-holdings that must inevitably be the main commercial driver for the marriage. His female acquaintance had been less generous about his motives.

'Nikos, darling, so you've finally met a woman you've had to marry to get into bed!' one ex-lover had murmured to his face that evening, with a malicious expression in her eyes.

She didn't know it, of course, he thought, as he flicked his eyes over an article on corporate governance, but she'd omitted one vital word from her analysis.

Back.

Back into bed.

That was what his marriage meant to him. The only way to get Janine back in his bed.

The hotel in the beautiful Austrian spa town had once been the summer residence of a Hapsburg prince. Its baroque splendour had been restored to its former glory, and now catered to the most expensive clientele.

Idly, Janine wondered if it was one of her father's.

She walked silently beside Nikos as they were ushered to their suite, and looked about her as she entered. Gilded furniture and heavy drapes made it seem palatial. Their luggage was carried through to the bedroom, and a maid arrived to unpack for them. Janine smiled vaguely at her, avoided looking at the vast four-poster bed, and went into the bathroom, converted from the dressing room it had once been. She locked the door and started to run a bath. The room filled with billowing steam as the huge claw-footed bath began to fill.

With the same numb composure that had got her through since she had gone back to Athens with her father, she took off her suit. It was ivory white, very tight-fitting, and as elegant as it was expensive. She draped it carefully over a gilded chair. Her hair was still in its elaborate coiffeur, and she unpinned it, shaking it loose, then knotting it loosely back up on top of her head. Then she set about removing her make-up. There was an armoury of toiletries supplied at the vanity unit.

When her face had been stripped clean of every last speck of make-up, she took off her underwear and stepped into the bath. She sank into its foaming depths, lying back and gazing up at the ceiling.

She felt tired. Tired all the way through to her bones. A deep, deep exhaustion.

She went on lying in the hot water.

There seemed nothing else to do.

The light above the vanity unit seemed to be pulsing slowly, going in and out of focus. In and out...

After a while, she did not know how long, she got out, dried herself, and wrapped her body in a large bath towel, letting her hair tumble down over her shoulders.

She felt so tired. She needed sleep.

Probably for ever.

The numbness seemed to be wrapping her more tightly.

She walked out of the bathroom into the bedroom.

And stopped dead.

Nikos was getting undressed.

He was down to his shirt and his underpants. His shirt was already open down the front and he was concentrating on slipping off his gold cufflinks.

She stared, transfixed. The tanned, powerful sinews of his thighs drew her eyes inexorably. By effort of will she hauled them away.

It was little improvement. As she raised her gaze it collided head-on with Nikos's. He was sweeping his eyes over her, taking in her tumbled hair, the tightly wound towel around her body, her bare legs and shoulders.

Time seemed to stand still. Then Nikos was strolling towards her and time started again.

He stood in front of her. The expression on his face was

strange—a mix of absolute tension and exultation. He looked down on her, his eyes like powerful searchlights.

'You have absolutely no idea,' he told her slowly, in a deep, throbbing voice, 'none whatsoever, how I have *ached* for this moment...'

His fingers touched her face, just grazing along her cheek.

'*Theos mou*, but you are so beautiful. So beautiful—and mine at last.'

His voice was a husk, low and rasping.

She simply stood there.

This wasn't happening. This couldn't be happening. It couldn't.

'Are you insane?'

The words croaked from her.

But he wasn't listening to her. He was reaching for her, letting his hands slide down her bare arms, then back again, as if he was smoothing lustrous marble.

'Nikos!' Her voice was a faint breath now.

His eyes were half closed. Some emotion seemed to be working in him, powerful, inexorable. 'Yes—Nikos,' he breathed. 'At last you say my name. And at last, at *last*, this hell is over and we can be together again.' His eyes were washing over her, as if he were reminding himself of every curve, every inch of her.

'*Theos*, but I want you so much...'

He began to pull her against him.

She threw him off. A violent, jerking movement convulsed her.

'Get off me!'

Her voice was shrill. Disbelieving. Panicked.

She took a stumbling step backwards. 'Get out!' The pitch of her voice was higher yet.

He stilled. His tanned chest showed dark against the brilliant white of his open shirtfront.

'*Out?*' He spoke as if she had slapped him.

'Yes—out! Out as in out that door—out! As in get the hell out—as in out! *Out*!'

'You cannot mean that.' His voice was flat. Irrefutable.

As if a note had been struck that hit a resonant frequency the numbness that had wrapped itself around her shattered.

Emotion poured through her as if a dam had burst. Pouring through her like a deluge in her veins.

Her eyes flared.

'What do you mean, I can't mean that? What else should I mean!' She stared at him, transfixed. Her heart had started to beat in huge, ghastly thuds. 'You can't possibly,' she said slowly, her voice strangled, 'you can't *possibly* have thought that this was going to be a marriage in anything other than name only?'

'In name only?' he echoed. He looked at her as if she were the one who was insane. 'Is that what you thought?'

Her face worked. 'Of course it's what I thought! You told me! You told me that it was for Stephanos's and Demetria's sake—because they felt so guilty!'

His eyes flashed with incredulity. 'That did not mean I intended this marriage to be an empty charade! *Theos mou*! It's the only thing that has been keeping me sane! I have been just *aching* to get you back—to take you in my arms again. Make you mine once more!'

He stepped towards her, purpose in his eyes.

'Make love to you again,' he said softly.

She threw her head back. 'Make love?' she bit out. 'We've never made love in our lives!'

He cocked an eyebrow. 'Your memory is so short?' he queried mockingly. He reached for her again. 'Then I must remind you—remind you of each sweet, passionate encounter—each and every time we made love…'

Her face contorted. 'We never made *love*, Nikos! We had sex, that's all. Sex under totally false assumptions—me about you and you about me. That means we never made love—we had sex! When I make love with a man I want him to know who I am! And I want to know who *he* is too. Both those conditions were sickeningly absent!'

He dismissed her words as irrelevant sophistry.

'Those conditions no longer apply. And if you think I *wanted* you to be the woman I thought you were you must be mad! Don't you think I rejoiced to discover you weren't Stephanos's mistress?'

His dark eyes were black, not a speck of gold in them.

Her bosom heaved. 'Of course you rejoiced—it meant there was no threat to your sister's marriage after all!'

He looked at her, his eyes narrowing dangerously. 'You really think that was the only reason for my rejoicing?'

'Well, there wasn't much else, was there?' she threw back at him. 'My God, out of this vile, vile mess that's the only up side there is!'

She was breathing heavily now; her heart-rate had soared, her pulse was pounding.

He shook his head. 'Oh, no, Janine. There is another one too.' He levelled his gaze at her, lambent, sable. 'I get you back. Back where you belong. In my arms. My bed. I told you—I have ached and ached for you since you were ripped from me. Stephanos kept me away from you, and I knew why and accepted it, even as it drove me mad with frustration—counting, just counting the days, the hours, to this moment—now. It's been the only thing I've hung on to.'

He took a step towards her. She backed away and found the wall behind her. Panic was mounting in her. Panic and another emotion. Stronger, more powerful.

'And now,' said Nikos, as he closed in on her, 'now I have got you back—'

'No,' she answered, and there was a deadness in her voice that had not been there a moment ago. 'You won't lay a finger on me. I couldn't bear you to touch me. Ever again.'

He stilled.

A long, slow shudder of revulsion passed through her.

'Everything you did to me, everything you said to me was a lie. Right from the start. From the first time you saw me everything was a lie. There was nothing that you did or said to me that was honest! You manipulated me, controlled me, deceived me—*lied* to me from beginning to end! And it was worse than a lie. It was abuse. You deliberately and calculatedly sought my seduction. And I know, with my brain, that you did so in the belief that I was what you and Demetria believed me to be, and that that, to you, justified your actions—but it doesn't make any difference. I feel abused—I *was* abused. It happened.'

'It wasn't like that—' His voice was harsh.

Her face convulsed. Emotion was churning in her. Sick and angry and poisoned.

'It was exactly like that! I know—I was *there*, Nikos! I look back now and I see that every single time you touched me it wasn't *me*. It was a woman you thought capable of having an affair with a married man! A rich married man twenty years older than me! Do you know what that real-isation does to me. *Do you?* It makes me want to be sick! Physically sick! And for you to stand there and actually tell me that you want to have sex with me again—that you've been dying for it—makes me feel even sicker!'

Her face convulsed again. 'I'm just a body, aren't I? Just a body! Not a person. You didn't care that I was someone having an affair with a married man—and you don't care that I'm not! You just don't care! Whichever woman I was—or am—doesn't matter to you!'

His hand slashed down through the air.

'That isn't true. I've told you I rejoiced to discover you were never Stephanos's mistress! That you are his daugh-ter.'

'You don't care which one I am. You're perfectly pre-pared to have sex with either of them!'

He wheeled away from her. 'I don't believe I'm having this conversation.' Emotion stormed through him. What the hell had gone wrong? How the hell had it exploded in his face like this? He turned back to her. 'Listen to me. Out of everything that happened only one thing was true—only one!' His eyes blazed gold. 'This.'

He reached out. His fingers brushed her cheek.

'This.' His other hand slipped around the nape of her neck, stroking with the tips of his fingers.

'This.' He tilted her chin and lowered his mouth to hers.

'This.' He brushed her mouth with his.

For a moment so brief it was less than the space of a single heartbeat she felt the world still.

'*This* was true!' His voice was soft. As soft as velvet. He brushed her lips again with his. As soft as velvet. 'This was always true. That we took one look at each other and wanted each other. That's what we have to remember— only that. Nothing else.'

He was drawing her closer to him. Or moving closer to her. She could not tell. Could only feel herself being pulled into his orbit, powerfully, inexorably. She looked into his eyes. They were glazing over with the blindness of desire. She'd seen it happen so often before, as he became absorbed in a world where only touch existed, only sensation.

It had been the same for her. Every time. *Every time.* She had ceased to think, ceased all mental activity except that of focusing with all her being on the sensations, the exquisite, arousing sensations, of Nikos making love to her…

Ice trickled down her spine.

But he hadn't been making love to her. He'd been having sex with the woman he'd thought was the mistress of a married man. Every time.

That, *that* had been the truth of it. The vile, hideous truth behind the soft words, the softer touch…

Slowly she pulled away.

'Do you know,' she heard herself saying, and her voice was strange—very strange, 'that when you told me just before…just before Stephanos arrived, that you wanted to take me back to Athens with you...do you know what I thought, Nikos?'

She lowered his hands away from her.

'I thought you were asking me to marry you. Isn't that amusing? I thought you were asking me to be your wife. But you weren't, were you? You were taking me to Athens to be your mistress—to make sure I never went back to Stephanos. You were prepared to do that, weren't you Nikos? Prepared to go that far to save your sister's marriage.'

He looked down at her. His face was very strange.

'No,' he said. 'I was prepared to go that far to keep you for myself. I wanted you so much. I want you still so much. I will always want you.'

Her eyes shadowed. 'Whichever woman I am—Stephanos's mistress or his daughter—it doesn't matter. It's just the body that you want.'

A nerve ticked in his cheek.

'I told you that is not true.'

'It has to be!' she hissed. 'It had to be just my body that you wanted—want still. How could you possibly have *made love* to a woman you'd been sent to seduce, deliberately and calculatedly, and then dispose of? Mission complete! Sister's marriage saved!'

'No!' He ran his fingers roughly through his hair. 'No.'

He turned away suddenly. There was tension in every line of his body. He crossed the room, flinging open the wardrobe door and yanking out a cashmere dressing gown. Without looking back he ripped off his shirt, tossing it at a chair, and then dragged on the gown. He belted it with sharp, vicious movements. Then abruptly he turned back to Janine.

For one long, long moment he just looked at her as she stood there across the room, hand clutching the knot of her towel, eyes flashing with hatred for the man who had taken her to bed thinking she was the mistress of a married man, a woman he had been sent to detach from her married lover by any means possible.

Whatever it took.

Including heartbreak.

A sob choked in her throat.

No! Don't think that. Don't. Or you might say it—admit it—and the torment would kill you.

But it was too late. The last, terrible emotion poured from her. The one she had been so desperately, desperately trying to deny—trying to numb as it lay writhing in agony, deep within her wounded self.

Love.

Love for Nikos Kiriakis.

Love for a man who had never looked at her, never touched her, never kissed her or caressed her without seeing her as the woman destroying his sister's marriage, ensnaring his sister's husband. The woman he had been sent to dispose of.

He didn't intend you to fall in love with him...

But she had all the same. She hadn't wanted to, had been fearful of falling for a man like Nikos Kiriakis. But she had embraced it after all, knowing as she did that whatever happened, however brief a time they had, she would be able to treasure her memories of him all her life. Her dreams might never come true, but her memories would always be there.

A laugh bit in her throat. It had no humour in it. Only gall—bitter, bitter gall.

Her memories were false. Each and every one of them.

'I haven't even got my memories,' she said accusingly 'They're false memories. In my every single memory of you you're wearing a mask—hiding from what you saw, a married man's mistress, hiding what you felt—'

'No.' His voice was low, intense. 'It wasn't like that. I wanted you from the moment I laid eyes on you.'

She gave a harsh laugh. 'Well, just as well, I'd say—

wouldn't you? Would have been a bit of a tough challenge having to seduce a woman you didn't fancy!'

The glimmer, the merest glimmer of a mocking smile haunted his mouth. 'That's what I thought.' The smile vanished. 'But it came back to curse me.'

She looked blank. For a long moment he just looked at her, then with a violent gesture ran his hands through his hair. His hands fell to his sides and he rested his eyes on her.

'Your hell started when Stephanos's helicopter landed. Mine started a lot earlier.' He took a deep breath.

Truth time. She wanted truth.

It was all on a knife-edge now. He felt he was standing at the edge of a precipice. And it was going to be her call as to whether she pushed him off the edge or not.

He looked at her. Despite the enveloping towel he could see so much of her. The gentle swell of her breasts. Her slender figure. Her hair tumbling around her beautiful shoulders. The smooth skin of her thighs.

With sheer effort of will he tore his mind away.

It was hard.

Excruciatingly so.

And he knew why. Ever since Stephanos's arrival had turned his world upside down and inside out, sending him hurtling out into the abyss, only one thought had sustained him. That he had to get Janine back.

Because he wanted her, desired her. Whoever she was, whatever she was—mistress, lover, bride.

If he could just get her back everything would be all right. If he could just possess her again everything would be all right. In bed everything would be all right.

Getting her there had become the entire focus of his existence.

I told myself that it was the only truth that had been there all along—the only thing we had emerged with. The only thing that counted.

But he'd been fooling himself.

He went and sat down on the edge of the bed, elbows resting on his knees, and ran his hands through his hair once more. Then he looked up.

Truth time.

For her.

And for him.

His eyes rested on her. She looked so beautiful, so achingly beautiful.

Something churned in him, grinding down through him. The memory of the first moment he'd laid eyes on her leapt in his mind. He saw it—vivid, real.

He'd thought her delectable. So lovely. Spread out there, displaying that soft, sun-kissed body. It had stirred him even then. He remembered his feeling of satisfaction that the mission he'd been sent on would have its compensations. That it would be more than his duty to seduce Janine Fareham—it would his pleasure too.

But it had become much, much more than either.

It had become something he had never, ever before felt for a woman. Women had been for pleasure, that was all. He'd enjoyed them and kissed them goodbye, moved on to the next one.

But Janine—

He had felt the danger. He couldn't even deny that, whatever else he denied. From the moment he'd set eyes on her! Felt it and dismissed it! He remembered standing on the balcony of Stephanos's hotel on Skarios, thinking how captivating she was. The word had made him alarmed, he realised. He'd argued around it mentally and had applied it to Janine instead. That *she'd* be captivated. That way he'd felt safe.

Fool! Fool to think that he could just reassign words—feelings—to other people!

Fool to simply ignore what had been happening to him.

Ignore everything about Janine Fareham except the need to seduce her.

Ignore everything except his desire for her.

Fool.

Psychologists had a phrase for it. Displacement activity.

Something you did instead of doing what you wanted to do. Because there was such a block against doing what you wanted to do that you couldn't do it. So you did something else instead.

Well, that was what he had done. He had done something else instead. He'd focused totally and absolutely on the one thing that he'd known he could do with Janine Fareham. He could desire her, and he could seduce her, and he could get her into bed with him and possess her utterly.

And once he had possessed her he would keep her.

Whatever happened he would keep her.

He would do anything, but he would keep her.

And when she was taken away from him, as Stephanos had taken her, then he would do anything to get her back.

And that was just what he'd done. He'd married her.

But he hadn't got her back.

He looked across at her. She stood there so beautiful. Achingly beautiful.

And as remote as a shining, distant star.

Hell closed over him. The same hell that had started the moment he had first laid eyes on her. He hadn't known it—couldn't possibly have known it. But he had walked into it all the same. Step by step.

He had been seducing her. Step by step. And all the while—all the while she had been seducing him. Not his senses, but a far, far more powerful part of his being.

His heart.

His eyes rested on her still. She hadn't spoken, hadn't moved. How long had he been silent? He didn't know. Couldn't tell.

'My hell...' he said, and his voice was very strange. 'My hell started when I fell in love with the woman who was breaking up my sister's marriage.'

CHAPTER NINE

HE HAD said it. Said a word that had come out of nowhere. Shocking him to the core. Shocking him because he had known the moment it came out of his mouth that it was true.

He hadn't known he was going to say it. Any more than he'd known he was going to do it.

Or realised that it had happened.

Why? he thought, with a weird, dissociated sense of strangeness. Why had it happened? It was an alien word to him—totally alien. It had never been part of his life, not with any of his partners. He'd never wanted it to be and he'd never even entertained the idea of falling in love.

It had been unnecessary and he'd never even thought about it.

And so, he realised, with a sinking, deadly hollowness, he had not recognised it.

I called it desire.

But it was love.

Love all along.

The shock of it buckled through him.

And in the wake of shock, in the slipstream left behind it, pain lanced him like a spear thrown with lethal, mortal accuracy.

Unrequited love.

Because what else could it be? Hadn't she made it clear? After what he'd done to her—even though he hadn't meant to—how could she feel anything for him but loathing?

'I can't bear your touch!' He'd heard her say it—her voice shuddering with revulsion.

He'd tried to sweep it aside. Wanted only to push past

175

her defences and dissolve her resistance to him, make her see, feel, that the only thing they must focus on was on the one good thing that had come out of this sorry, sordid mess. That in each other's arms nothing else mattered. Not whether or not she was Stephanos's mistress. Not whether or not he had been sent to ensure her defection from his sister's husband.

Just each other.

But she hadn't seen it that way.

She had been revolted by what had happened between them. Revolted by the lie, revolted by what he had thought her then.

Slowly his head sank into his hands.

Despair took him over.

There was a soft footfall on the carpet, a shadow falling over him. A scent of soap and body cream—and Janine. Her own scent, that sweet bouquet that he would have recognised anywhere—in the dark, on the moon…anywhere.

Fingers smoothed his hair.

'Oh, Nikos.'

Her voice was soft. As soft as her silken skin. As soft as her sweet breasts.

She knelt down beside him, her hand slipping from his head to rest on his knee.

He turned his bowed head towards her.

She was so close, so *close*. Her lips were parted, her eyes wide and luminous.

He couldn't help himself. Dear God, but he could not help himself.

His mouth reached for hers blindly, instinctively.

She let him kiss her, let his mouth move and taste hers. And then slowly, oh, so slowly, she started to kiss him back.

He gathered her up to him, drawing her down on the bed beside him. The towel had loosened and he felt her breasts pressing against him. His eyes had shut. He did not want to see, only to feel. To feel the bliss, the sheer bliss, of having Janine in his arms again.

He had ached for her. With his body. With his heart.

His hands stroked over her as his mouth went on and on, kissing and kissing her. If he died now, this moment, it would be enough.

Her fingers were at his waist, loosening the tie of his robe, smoothing over his chest, his flanks. He laid her down on the bed, his hands slipping to her breasts, shaping and caressing them. He could feel the beat of her heart, the soft rise and fall of her lungs.

'Janine—'

His voice was a husk. A plea.

She placed her fingers over his lips.

'Shh—no words. No words.'

She slipped her fingers away to let her lips graze along his jaw, his neck, arching her spine towards him. Her legs were easing along his, her other hand smoothing over his back, along each muscled ridge.

He felt himself surge against her, and realised, feeling the exquisite, arousing *frottage*, that he was still in his shorts.

He groaned, and he felt her smile against his throat.

Wordlessly she eased them from him, her hands coming back to cup over the tensing muscles of his buttocks. He surged again, his flesh seeking hers. Blindly, instinctively.

Sinking within her was paradise. Paradise, and heaven, and home.

Such paradise that he did it again, and again, and yet again.

He felt her head begin to thresh, felt her mouth leave his, her neck arch. Heard, felt all the way through him, the low, vibrating moan that started in her throat and built all through her body, all through his, building and building until his whole body was resonating with hers in one perfect, endless harmony.

She came as he did. He could feel her peak, pulse all around him, slow and deep and heavy and endless. As endless as the rush that came as his seed filled her and filled her.

He gathered her close to him, as close as his heart, enfolding her even as he finished surging within her, even as she still softly pulsed around him. His arms wrapped around her, his cheek was against hers, and he lifted her from the bed to embrace her, so close to him, so close.

A great lassitude filled him. Slackening all his limbs, loosening all his muscles. She slipped from him, her weight pressing heavy against him. Heavy and warm and soft, so soft. He pillowed his head upon her breasts and felt her stroke his hair, her fingers sifting, soothing.

Peace filled him. A peace so profound, so absolute, that it stilled him utterly as he lay there, enfolded and enfolding. His mouth formed one more soft kiss against her breast, and then sleep, sweet sleep, came at last and took him in.

For a long, long time she held him, tears seeping through her lashes.

And in the morning she was gone.

He woke, instantly knowing something was wrong. Desperately, appallingly wrong.

Janine was not there.

Like a terrible yawning chasm her absence swallowed him, devouring him. He clawed around him, as if he might feel her suddenly there, back again.

But she was gone. Gone.

Pain clutched at him.

I thought I had her back! I thought I had her back!

Black agony sawed through him.

He forced his eyes open. Forced himself to see her absence. See her not there. Not there.

Not her, nor her bag, nor her shoes or her clothes, nor any part of her.

Nothing of her. Nothing.

The emptiness of the room was everywhere, inside him and outside him. She had left him. She had gone. He had not won her back. Could never win her back.

No hope. None.

With eyes like death he got out of bed, groping for the bathrobe that she had peeled from his body when she had taken him back—back to that paradise that came only in her arms. Only hers.

Pain scissored through him. A lifetime of pain waiting to devour him, day by day. Without her. Without Janine. The woman he loved—and could not win back.

He slid his arms down into the robe's sleeves, yanking the belt across him.

And froze.

There on the chest of drawers, propped up against the wall, was a piece of folded paper. Dread filled him. This was it, then. This was the final moment when he would see, in words, her absolute rejection of him.

He crossed the space in a second, seizing up the paper, opening it with rapid fumbling fingers. The words blurred, resolved, and blurred again.

Then cleared.

And as he read them a gratitude so profound went through him that he wanted to fall to his knees.

She had not left him.

The paper shook in his hands but the words held steady. Shining true and faithful. Filling him with the one thing he craved above all now.

Hope.

He stared again at what she had written.

'In our end is our beginning.'

He set down the paper, looking up. His eyes saw far. Very far. As far as the woman he loved. Words moved on his lips. Silently. Lovingly.

I am coming to you, my beloved. I am coming to you.

*   *   *

Janine eased herself over onto her stomach and sighed languorously, giving her body to the sun. In front of her the sunlight danced dazzlingly off the azure swimming pool. Beyond, slender cypresses pierced the cerulean sky.

The sound of children splashing and calling in the pool was the only noise. She felt the warmth of the sun like a blessing on her naked back.

A shadow fell over her.

'*Kyria* Fareham?'

She looked up, twisting her head round.

Her breath caught.

She was looking at the most devastating male she had ever seen in her life.

Sable hair feathered across a broad brow, strong and straight, with deep lines curving from it to the edges of his mouth.

His mouth—

Sculpted. That was the only word for it. With a sensuous lower lip she had to drag her eyes from, forcing herself to meet his eyes instead. Dark eyes, flecked with gold. And blazing down at her with an emotion that made her feel weak with its strength.

She felt the world shift around her, then resettle.

As if something had changed for ever.

He had asked her a question, she realised, and she must answer it. But she must be cautious. So much, so very, very much, was at stake.

'Who wants to know?' she asked softly.

That same overpowering, overwhelming emotion blazed from those dark, devastating eyes.

'The man who loves her,' answered Nikos Kiriakis. 'The man who loves her and will always love her, to the end of our days.'

He held out a hand for her and she placed hers in it. It closed over hers, warm and safe. He drew her up.

'Why did you come here?' she asked, in that same soft voice.

His eyes rested on her.

'*"In our end is our beginning."*'

A smile parted her lips. It lit her face.

'You understood—?'

He nodded. 'Yes. When I woke to find you gone my first thought was despair. You had left me. And then...' His voice changed. 'Then I saw the note that you had left behind. "In our end is our beginning." And I knew what you were trying to tell me.'

He took a deep breath, gazing down at her. 'You wanted us to start again. To undo, unmake all that had gone before and make it again. Just you and I. Meeting, desiring, loving. Nothing else. The way it should have been.' He lowered his head, gently grazing her mouth with his. 'The way it always will be now.'

A deep, deep joy filled her. A happiness so profound it made her weak with the wonder of it. She felt the tears start in her eyes.

'Nikos. Oh, Nikos!'

He held her tight, so very tight, crushing her against him. But for a few, brief seconds only. Then, carefully, he set her back. She gazed up at him. Love blazed in her eyes.

He smiled down at her. Something moved in his eyes, blazed forth like her love, and then, with long lashes sweeping down, veiled itself.

'I wonder, *Kyria* Fareham,' he said in a courteous voice, 'whether you might like to take a little cruise? Not far. Just along the coast. I've a villa there you might like to see.'

She tilted her head slightly. 'Does it have an infinity pool?'

'It does.'

'And wonderful sea views?'

'Indeed.'

'Sunsets?'

'Fabulous sunsets.'

'Is it very private?'

'Completely private.'

She paused a moment. 'How many bedrooms?'

A smile quirked at his mouth. 'I never bothered to count. But we,' he told her, 'shall be using only one.'

He took her hand. 'And it hasn't,' he told her, 'got twin beds.'

She slid her fingers into his.

'Sounds irresistible.'

His free hand cupped her cheek.

'Then don't resist. Don't resist anything.' The flecks of gold in his eyes burned molten. 'Especially,' he murmured, 'me.'

She felt her body melt against him.

'Never,' she answered. 'For the rest of our lives.'

'Good,' said Nikos Kiriakis. And kissed her.

As their bodies moved and fused in the dim light of the shuttered room, the cool air playing over their skin, and they took each other to that one private paradise which only they inhabited, it was as if nothing that had gone before had ever happened. It was all made new between them.

And afterwards, in the peace that came only after loving, she spoke, cradled safe in his arms. At last so safe.

'It hurt so much that you could think such a thing of me. Something so vile and horrible. For the first time since Stephanos had taken me into his heart as his daughter the reality of my Greek heritage was starting to take root. And you were part of it! Part of the country I was trying to feel a part of. You had swept me away, made me feel so wonderful! I had woven such dreams about you, such longing fantasies—that you would take me back to Athens, declare your love for me to Stephanos, and we would all live happily ever after.... And then to find out, like that, what you really thought of me. Had thought of me all along.'

Her voice gave a little choke and he crushed her to him even closer, anguished at her anguish. She went on speaking, draining the poison from her.

'I couldn't bear it. Just couldn't bear it. I knew with my head that you had had every reason to think ill of me—that everything had been a hideous, terrible misunderstanding! And neither of us had realised! You talked about my relationship with Stephanos and I thought it meant you knew I was his daughter! And all along you thought I was…I was his mistress! You thought I lived off his money, that I didn't even work for a living and never had! And that wasn't true either. I mean, I did work. But not for money.'

She took a deep, shuddering breath. 'You see, when my mother died I inherited her money. She was never poor— she always had a private income—but she used her money simply to flit around on the Côte d'Azur, wasting her life away in one long, endless holiday. I vowed I would never lead such a pointless life. So I went to the opposite extreme and went to work for a Third World agency. Louise—my mother—thought I was mad, but she was glad to see the back of me. She didn't want a grown-up daughter making her look old. When I inherited her money I could work for the agency for free. And for the last three years I've been working for them abroad. It was gruelling, but so incredibly worthwhile! I chose to work abroad, in some terrible, heart-breaking places, but in the end I reached burnout. I'd just arrived back in London, feeling guilty for not having been able to cope any more, and that's when I met Stephanos.

'It was a miracle! A complete miracle! My mother had never told me about my father. Hadn't been in the least interested. And since she'd died I'd accepted—I'd had to accept!—that I'd never, ever know. But Stephanos—he simply took me to him. Took me into his life, into his heart. Without question. And him being rich was another miracle. He's settled so much money on me that I can support the aid agency I used to work for so much better than I could before. But…' She hesistated, then went on. 'But I know that the life I led sheltered me from…from men. The kind of men that Louise surrounded herself with. Rich and glamorous. Like you.' She closed her eyes. 'I didn't want to be tempted by you. But I was. I couldn't resist you. I just couldn't! So—so I gave in to you. I fell for you totally. Completely. Then…then when Stephanos arrived it was like a nightmare. And I felt…I felt I was being punished—rightfully—for having been such a prize idiot as to fall for a man like you.'

She gave a long, shuddering sigh. 'I hated you. I hated you for thinking such vile things about me—that I was Stephanos's mistress—the kind of woman my mother was, who thought nothing of having an affair with a married man!—and I hated you because I'd fallen in love with you.'

He smoothed her hair tenderly, with a hand that was not quite steady.

She lifted her head from where it had lain on his chest, his heart beating beneath her cheek. She looked at him suddenly, urgently.

'But it's all right now—it's all right now, isn't it, Nikos? Isn't it?'

He kissed her softly, cradling her head.

'Yes,' he breathed. 'It's all right now. It's all right—and from now on it will always, always be all right. Because we are together. We've found each other—the people we truly are. No more lies.' He kissed each eyelid, each corner of her mouth. 'We've made our new beginning.'

She smiled into his mouth, deep, deep peace filling her. *'In our beginning is our end?'*

'Yes,' said Nikos. 'Oh, yes.'

And he kissed her, slow and deep and full of love.

EPILOGUE

'SMILE! One more time! All four of you!'

Nikos raised the camera and focused through the lens once more.

His sister made a face. 'They're too young to smile! They don't smile until at least three months!'

'And then the books say it's usually wind!' added her stepdaughter for good measure.

'Then you two smile!' ordered Nikos.

Demetria sat up a little straighter and fussed over her son's magnificent christening robe. Beside her, on the sofa, Janine smoothed the head of *her* son—and rearranged him slightly in her arms. The two women glanced at each other, sudden tears filling their eyes.

Tears of happiness. Sheer happiness.

Demetria took Janine's hand.

'I beat you to it,' she said in a low voice. 'I was determined to do so!'

Janine pressed the other woman's hand, feeling her joy, her relief. Demetria had longed so much, and so long, for a child of her own.

When she'd first realised she was pregnant, less than six months into her marriage, Janine had been torn between joy and anguish. For close on two months she and Nikos had kept it a closely guarded secret, dreading the time when Demetria would have to know that her sister-in-law was to bear her brother a child, a grandchild to her own husband.

And then, during the Easter celebrations, Stephanos had drawn his wife to her feet.

'We have something to tell you,' he had said to his daughter and his son-in-law—his brother-in-law.

He placed a proud, protective hand over Demetria's stomach.

'Our child is growing here,' he said. 'Through the miracle of science he lives and grows.'

'We didn't want to say anything,' said Demetria, her voice full with emotion, 'not until the first trimester was over and we knew the pregnancy was secure.'

Janine rushed to embrace her, and as her arms folded around her sister-in-law—her stepmother—she heard Demetria say, 'And now, my dearest Janine, you can tell me why you will drink no wine, and have a glow about you that I see only in my own mirror!'

It had been a race from then on. A race that Demetria had been determined to win.

'I have a secret advantage,' she'd told Janine smugly. 'One of the nicest things about assisted conception is that you know exactly what day your baby is conceived! That means my due date is as accurate as it can be! As for you…' She'd looked with mock resignation at her brother's wife. 'If you can know which night Nikos gave you your child, then all that billing and cooing you do all the time will have been a most unlikely lie!'

Janine had coloured, and Nikos had looked even more smug than his sister.

Now, with both babies successfully delivered, both mothers recovered from childbed, the two women sat, posing themselves and their offspring while yet more photos were taken.

On the other side of the room Stephanos sat back in his comfortable chair. Champagne beaded in his glass. His eyes were suspiciously wet.

As his brother-in-law, his son-in-law, finally lowered his camera, Stephanos raised his glass again.

'One more toast!' he cried.

Nikos set down his camera and picked up his glass. The

two men raised their glasses. Two pairs of eyes rested on the women sitting on the sofa, their babies on their laps.

'To happiness,' said Stephanos. His voice was thick with emotion. 'To my daughter and my wife. My son and my grandson. May this day be blessed.'

'I think,' said Nikos, as his eyes rested on Janine and hers on him, and the lovelight blazed from both of them, 'it already is.'

And then, quite suddenly, his eyes were suspiciously wet too.

THE ITALIAN PLAYBOY'S PROPOSITION

Kim Lawrence

Kim Lawrence lives on a farm in rural Anglesey. She runs two miles daily and finds this an excellent opportunity to unwind and seek inspiration for her writing! It also helps her keep up with her husband, two active sons, and the various stray animals which have adopted them. Always a fanatical consumer of fiction, she is now equally enthusiastic about writing. She loves a happy ending!

CHAPTER ONE

REFERRING to his notes occasionally, Tom Trent spoke at length. He knew the man who had had him flown back from his Stateside holiday on Concorde for this meeting well enough to know he wouldn't want him to pull his punches, and he didn't.

Elbows set on the mahogany desktop, long brown fingers steepled, the figure behind the desk listened Tom out in silence. Tom could only imagine how he was feeling, for his dark patrician features gave no clue whatsoever of what was going on in his mind—a mind that was the sharpest that Tom, who was no intellectual slouch himself, had ever encountered.

'So that's about it, then,' Tom concluded leaning back in his seat.

Luca didn't respond immediately; instead he rose to his feet in one fluid motion. At six feet five fit inches of solid bone and muscle he made an imposing figure. His dark, contemplative gaze rested on his friend for several moments before he sighed and began to pace the room.

As he watched the languid, loose-limbed tread of the tall man Tom, not a person renown for his imaginative flights, found the image of a sleek panther, its natural instincts confined within cage bars, appear in his head.

After a second circuit of the room Luca came to halt by the big desk and, placing his hands palm down on the gleaming surface, he leant towards the other man. The thick curling eyelashes, which Tom's own wife had declared to be sinfully sexy, lifted from sharp, jutting cheekbones and

Tom found himself on the receiving end of the famous Di Rossi stare. It wasn't a comfortable place to be.

'So what you're saying is the only foolproof way to avoid a custody battle would be for me to find a wife, preferably one who has a child of her own?'

Tom shook his head. It was typical of Luca to condense thirty minutes' worth of complicated legal explanation in one sentence, but then Gianluca Di Rossi was not a man who used two words when one would do. Like his words, his actions too were always focused and to the point.

Small talk was not Luca's thing!

The flip side of this was that when other people wrote memos and had endless meetings Luca acted. Making decisions was not something that Luca agonised about; he didn't feel the need for other people to validate his actions or anyone else to blame when those actions had consequences. So the fact that some people called him reckless and others called him inspired did not matter to him.

So far his supreme self-belief had been more than justified by the spectacular success of the empire he had carved out of nothing.

'Well, I hadn't thought of it that way, but a ready-made family would really damage their case, if not kill it stone-dead. If you're going to interview for the job, a couple of kids, one of each would be good.'

His humour produced no lightening of the sombre, brooding expression in the dark penetrating eyes fixed unblinking on his face, nor any relaxation of the taut lines in Luca's lean, hard face. But then, Tom conceded, feeling inexcusably insensitive, I wouldn't feel inclined to laugh at my pathetic witticisms if someone were trying to take my kid off me.

'A ready-made family...' Luca repeated slowly.

'Bad joke, but it's not like I'm telling you anything you didn't already know.'

'Sometimes it takes someone else to point out the obvious before you see what's staring you straight in the face,' Luca observed somewhat enigmatically before folding his long, lean length into his chair once more.

Hands rested lightly on the leather arm-rests, he tilted the head-rest back and stared up at the high ceiling. The London office of Di Rossi International having recently moved from its cramped modern offices to this Georgian terrace, which had been restored with meticulous attention being paid to period detail and very little to cost, he found himself looking at some pretty fine plaster mouldings.

The shadow cast by the downward sweep of Luca's lashes effectively concealed his deep-set eyes and expression from the other man. To all intents and purposes he appeared relaxed, but as people over the years had learnt, frequently to their cost, with Luca appearances could be deceptive.

'Di Rossi is at his most dangerous when cornered!' a shrewd economic analyst had once written. This went tenfold for his personal life, which he guarded jealously. And at that moment his personal life was under attack.

'You could always put an advert in the personal column. All right,' Tom conceded quickly with a grimace, 'that wasn't funny either. 'But lighten up, it's not like I'm actually suggesting you go out and get married! For one thing they don't stand a chance in hell of winning the case.'

'But they will make sure my name is dragged through the mud.'

'The negative effect on the company will only be temporary Luca,' Tom was quick to point out soothingly. 'And that's not just spin, I promise you. Di Rossi is far too solid in the market-place to suffer any long-term damage from a court case.'

One sardonic brow arched. 'Your concern for my financial interests is laudable.' The accented drawl became diamond-hard as he added, 'However, the damage on Valentina might not be so temporary.'

Tom winced. 'Ah, God, yes, what was I thinking about? Sorry, Luca.'

Luca lifted his head. 'Why?'

Tom blinked and looked nonplussed by this abrupt question. 'Why what?' he queried, his manner guarded.

'Why should I not get married?'

'You're not serious!' Again he received the look. 'Well, other than the odd hundred or so reasons that spring to mind, it would be totally—'

'Necessary, according to you,' Luca interjected seamlessly. 'If I want to kill off the case before it gets to court. And I'd do anything it takes to protect Valentina from being dragged through that. Being exposed to those vultures.'

Looking into those implacable eyes, Tom realised this was no figure of speech. In a world where people frequently said things they didn't mean for effect, it had taken him some time to catch onto the fact that when Luca said something that was exactly what he meant!

It was the lawyer who felt the need to break the ensuing heavy silence.

'To them it must seem you moved her to England to deliberately make it harder for them to have access...' he suggested tentatively.

Luca ran a hand over his smooth shaven chiselled jaw and gave a wolfish smile. 'I did.'

'Then when you refused to give them unaccompanied access—' Tom shrugged '—you *must* have known how they'd react. Natalia Corradi hates you, Luca, and Valentina is her granddaughter.'

'And *my* daughter,' Luca flashed back, a lick of flame in his glittering eyes that made his friend draw back in his seat.

'Don't kill the messenger, mate,' he pleaded, holding out his hands palm upwards in pacific gesture.

The muscles in Luca's brown throat worked as he swallowed. The strong lines of his face were set in stone by the time he had regained his composure.

'Did I tell you what I heard her saying to Valentina?' he asked in a soft voice.

'No, Luca.'

'Her *loving* grandmother was telling her what a shame it was she is not as beautiful and talented as her mother was. Telling her that if she had never been born her mother would not be dead.' He drew a deep breath that expanded his powerful chest. '*Dio*…Tom, what was I to do?'

Tom, who was deeply shocked by these revelations, shrugged weakly.

'Who knows how long she has been dropping this poison in Valentina's ears? I will not let it happen to my daughter. I will not permit history to repeat itself,' he added half to himself. 'The woman, she has no feelings for the child,' he stated emphatically, adding the wry rider, 'at least not as you or I understand it. For her Valentina is a weapon to punish me.'

Once more he rose to his feet, grim determination in every line of his tall and vital figure. 'I have taken her contempt and vitriol over the years—it is of no matter to me.' He shrugged. 'But she has overstepped the mark this time. Valentina's needs must be considered above all else.'

'They'll say it is in Valentina's interests to be brought

up within a loving family,' his friend pointed out gently. 'They will try and paint you as a...'

'Work-obsessed womaniser, I know.' His tight smile held self-mockery. 'I suppose the Erica factor is going to come into it?'

Tom nodded unhappily.

'And if I had sued the newspaper for libel as you, my friend, suggested at the time...?'

'Considering you had Erica admitting on tape that the bruise was nothing but clever make-up I still think you should have exposed her publicly at the very least, but then I don't have your gentlemanly code,' he admitted drily. 'Don't beat yourself up over that, Luca, it's easy to be wise in hindsight, but, yes, your refusal to defend yourself against those ludicrous accusations is going to look bad.'

'Oh, but you forget there were no accusations—in fact the beautiful victim bravely denied I had laid a finger on her, if you recall—'

Tom looked uncomfortable. 'Let's concentrate on things we *can* do something about,' he suggested. 'It's the male household factor that is a major stumbling block. The fact there is no female role model except for your...' He paused, looking awkward.

'My *women*?' Luca bit back with a hard, satirical smile.

The other man sighed. 'You can forget about your personal life being sacrosanct if this thing comes to court, Luca. You'll have to be prepared to have your love life dissected.'

'I am not a monk,' he admitted calmly. 'However, my love life is not nearly as interesting as the press would have you believe.'

A laugh was wrenched from the lawyer. 'If I don't believe you, Luca, how do you expect to convince a court? And have you thought how Carlo is going to look to a judge? I mean, *I* know he's a great chap but, let's face it, he's not most people's idea of a nanny. And then there's the matter of his record.'

'Carlo stays.' There was no room for negotiation in Luca's flat response and Tom, who knew personally of Luca's unswerving loyalty to his friends, did not argue the point. 'But I can—' The intercom on his desk buzzed and Luca's dark brows drew together in a frown. When he spoke into the offending machine his tone was terse and impatient.

'I thought,' he intoned coldly, 'that I said I didn't want—' He stopped and listened to whatever was being said and sighed. 'All right, tell him I'll ring back in five minutes.' He turned to the lawyer. 'Sorry about this, Tom, but it's Marco. He's got a problem.'

And when Marco had a problem he always turned to his half-brother. Tom couldn't prevent the look of disapproval that spread across his face. It was inexplicable to him that Luca, who did not tolerate fools gladly, should have such a fondness for his charming but feckless half-brother.

Luca saw the play of expression on his friend's face. 'You don't like Marco do you?'

'Anyone *normal* would resent a half-brother who is favoured so unfairly, Luca.'

Luca's severe features relaxed slightly as a thoughtful expression slid into his silver-shot dark eyes. 'Has it ever occurred to you that being considered incapable of doing anything wrong and supremely talented in all things by one's parents is not an easy role to fill for anyone with the normal degree of human weaknesses?'

'Well, Marco's got his fair share of those,' Tom conceded with a dry laugh. 'But to be honest, Luca, I think it's more of a *burden* to have your achievements, not only go totally unrecognised by your family, but resented,' he added, unable to repress his indignation on his friend's behalf.

'I do not seek anyone's approval,' Luca declared with chilling hauteur, which would have repressed nine men out of ten.

Tom, the tenth, shook his head. 'God, but you're an arrogant beggar!'

An unexpected grin of immense charm totally transformed the billionaire's dark features. 'That's seemed to be the general consensus,' Luca agreed drily. 'I'll ring you later,' he added as the other man moved towards the door.

'Are you going back to the house tonight? The renovations are completed?'

'They are, but we're staying in Marco's apartment for a few nights. I didn't say, Tom, but I am sorry to drag you away from Cape Cod.'

'I forgive you, but Alice might not.' Tom smiled. 'Luca, is there anything you want me to do in the meantime?'

'You could make up a list of possible brides.'

This comment made the other man pause as he reached for the door handle. 'I've known you ten years, Luca, and I still can't tell when you're joking.'

'I've never been more serious in my life, Thomas.'

'Mum, you've *got* to help me!'

'You expect me to drop everything, Jude?' There was a note of laboured incredulity in Lyn Lucas's husky voice that didn't quite ring true. 'Just like that!'

Appealing to her mother's maternal instincts always had been a long shot. 'There's a first time for everything,' Jude muttered, rueful affection in her stressed voice.

'What was that, Jude?'

'Nothing.' She took a deep breath and swallowed her pride. If begging was what it took she was prepared to beg;

things were really that desperate. 'Listen, Mum, I wouldn't ask unless this was an emergency.'

'And if it were an emergency I would quite naturally be there for you,' Lyn returned serenely. 'But really, Jude, don't you think you're just a tad over the top with the drama, darling? They're only three little children...just how much trouble can they be?'

'How much? How *much*?' Jude standing in the middle of her open-plan living room, *once* a tribute to tasteful minimalism, took a deep steadying breath. 'Where,' she asked as the weight of her failure oppressed her, 'shall I start? Oh, God, Mum, it's not *them*, it's *me*!'

The logical part of her knew she was wasting her breath. How could you explain to someone whose idea of hands-on parenting was giving her teenage daughter charge accounts and a car?

When they'd been younger a long series of nannies had made sure she and David had only ever been produced for parental inspection when they'd been freshly scrubbed and on their best behaviour. As soon as it had been possible they had been shipped off to boarding-school. That, she mused, was probably why they'd ended up being so close.

'The children need someone who knows what they're doing,' she began in a frustrated tone when from the corner of her eye she caught movement. 'Hold on a minute, Mum,' she grunted, diving to retrieve a bottle of hair conditioner before the five-year-old could apply it to the blond curls of her sleeping baby sister.

'No, Sophia, that's Aunty Jude's.' Jude was frustrated to see her firm but reasonable remonstration had no visible effect on the five-year-old. Maybe it's not what I say but the way I say it.

'No!'

'Don't shout, Sophia, you'll wake Amy,' Jude pleaded, giving an anguished glance at the baby who stirred sleepily.

The little girl finally relinquished the bottle upon being offered a chocolate biscuit in exchange. You didn't have to be a trained clinical psychologist like herself to know bribery wasn't generally recommended as a method of child discipline, but Jude was frankly past caring about such niceties.

David, a dentist, would have been horrified by her breaking his draconian 'no sweeties or chocolate' edict; a great tide of sadness that had physical heaviness washed over her as she thought of her brother. David wasn't here to protect his children's teeth and neither was his wife, Sam. They had been killed the previous month when their car had gone through the central reservation on the motorway and collided head-on with a lorry.

When no other explanation for the accident had been forthcoming the inquest into the tragic deaths had concluded it was most likely the driver had fallen asleep at the wheel. The driver—*David*, her brother.

She knew all about the stages of the grieving process. Should that be helping? Jude didn't know. She just knew that she didn't have time to grieve, not yet. Right now her priority had to be three little children who needed a lot of love and understanding and the best way to do that seemed to be not trying to look more than a day ahead. If she did, the sense of her total inadequacy for the task that had been thrust upon her paralysed her.

She had loved being *Aunty* Jude, who could spoil and indulge them before handing them back at the end of the day. Having total responsibility was quite another matter, as she was learning!

She wanted to make the children feel safe and secure after their little world had been blown apart, but it was hard when she was scared herself. Scared because for the first time in her life something wasn't coming easy. She was failing at something, and this *something* wasn't an exam or a job. You could resit an exam or change a job, but where children's lives were concerned you didn't get to go back and try again.

Lately she'd begun to wonder if children, like animals, could smell fear. Well, whatever the reason, this brood had decided about ten seconds after they'd arrived that they didn't have to do as she asked.

I have to face it my mothering instincts are dreadful, she decided dully. Somewhat ironic, not to mention embarrassing, for the author of the catchily entitled *Parenting Skills for Beginners*.

With a token, 'Don't do that, sweetheart,' to Sophia, who was smearing chocolatey fingerprints all over her new cream sofa, she wearily raised the receiver to her ear in time to hear her mother say—

'What can they have done that is so bad? The twins are only three—'

'Five, Mum. The twins are five and Amy is eighteen months,' Jude reminded her mother wearily. 'And *they've* not done anything.' How could she explain to her literally minded mother that it wasn't the paintwork or the broken items she was worried about? That she hardly ever thought about the time when she had enjoyed coming back to her flat, kicking off her shoes and shutting the rest of the world out. 'Amy cries for her mum, and Sophia has nightmares, and Joseph—he *doesn't* cry.'

'Well, they've just lost their parents, Jude, what do you expect?'

'I know…I know, but it's not just that. It's this place, it's really hard to contain and amuse three children under

six in a one-bedroomed apartment, Mum. I need somewhere with a garden?' she ended on a hopeful note.

Her mother had stayed in the family home after the divorce, a rambling Edwardian house on the edge of a pic-
ture-postcard village set in two acres of child-friendly gardens.

'Five is a delightful age, Jude,' replied the children's
doting but absent grandmother with a catch in her voice.
'And I'd *love* for you all to come and stay here—'

'You don't know how glad I—'

'But unfortunately I have a meeting in New York this
Friday and then guests next week. David,' she recalled huskily, 'was so sweet when he was five, so bright, so enquiring and so innocent...' Her voice dissolved into tears. 'I
don't know how you can ask me to help when I'm suffering
so much,' she reproached. 'And work is my only solace,
you know that, Jude.

'They were such a lovely couple,' Lyn Lucas continued
with a sigh. 'With everything to look forward to. 'Why
them?'

Jude could only shake her head; her throat ached with
unshed tears as she thought of her brother and his wife.

'I can't do this, Mum,' she whispered miserably down
the phone. 'I'm messing up big time.'

'Well, David must have thought you could or he
wouldn't have named you as the children's guardian,' came
the bracing response.

'I doubt he expected I'd ever be put to the test,' Jude
retorted sadly.

'Well, you have, and you'll just have to get on with it.
It'll be a lot easier when you've sold the flat and bought
something more sensible,' her mother continued. 'A nice
little place in the country somewhere,' she mused as she
conjured a picture of domestic bliss.

'I hate to ruin the roses-around-the-door scenario, but I have to live where the work is, Mum.' Thankfully they were being really good about giving her time off at the university where she lectured, so that was one less thing for her to worry about right now.

'Is all this about your job, Jude? I must say I'm disappointed in you, but not surprised.' Lyn sighed. 'You always have had a selfish streak. I mean, there's nothing *wrong* with a women having a career, but I would have thought under the circumstances that you would have been prepared to make a little sacrifice.'

This breathtaking piece of hypocrisy coming from a mother who had never made a parents' evening or sports day in her life left Jude momentarily speechless.

'This isn't about my job, Mum,' she managed finally. 'Though financially I do have to work,' she added drily. 'I'm good at my job. I'm not good at—'

'There's no such thing as the perfect parent, Jude,' her mother interrupted. 'Your problem is you're a perfectionist; you always have been. You don't like situations you can't control, or people. Just look at your boyfriends.'

'Must we?'

'Not a single one of them had an opinion of his own.'

'That's a gross exaggeration, Mother,' Jude retorted indignantly. 'I'm just not attracted to men who order dinner for me.'

For a liberated woman her mother had some very old-fashioned views of men. After her father had gone to live abroad she and David had found a new 'uncle' in residence every holiday they'd come home. The only thing they'd had in common beside their short shelf-lives had been their overbearing personalities.

'I've lost track,' she said, pressing her fingers to the pulse spots on her temple where the throbbing headache was building. 'Why exactly is my taste in men relevant to you refusing to help me?'

'Children are not predictable, Jude.'

'I'd noticed.'

'You have to be flexible and compromise.'

Jude was just too tired to fight. 'I'll try,' she promised.

'Good girl. It's just a pity that you haven't got a husband yet, because, let's face it, no man's going to look twice at a girl who comes with a ready-made family of three.' And on that cheery note, Jude thought, shaking her head slowly from side to side. My mum really is a one-off, which is probably just as well!

'Now, if there's anything you need just ask.'

And you'll be there for me so long as it doesn't interfere with a bridge game. 'Thanks, Mum.'

CHAPTER TWO

JUDE put down the phone and slumped down on the sofa amongst the biscuit crumbs and building blocks. The appeal to her mother had not had the outcome she had hoped for but Lyn's rather abrasive style had helped her get things back in perspective.

If I could have the last five minutes back, she reflected, I wouldn't have made that phone call. She gave a philosophical shrug. So I wimped out! This is not really that surprising, all things considered. I'm exhausted, I've lost my brother and I've become a mother of three almost overnight. Maybe I shouldn't be so tough on me?

Mum's right, she thought, squaring her shoulders, I need to stop bleating and get on with it. After all, there are plenty of single mothers out there who have it a lot worse than me and actually, Jude, girl, you're not doing so bad.

Her natural optimism and strength of character began to reassert itself as she sat there making the most of the moment of peace. Soon enough bedlam would break out once more; best to enjoy the moment whilst it lasted. Her affectionate glance slid to where Amy was sleeping—they really were delicious when then were asleep—and Sophia was sitting cross-legged on the rug crayoning and Joseph was…?

Where was Joseph?

When had she last seen Joseph, or heard his voice…?

Suddenly the silence seemed ominous. The mega dose of adrenaline suddenly introduced into her bloodstream wiped away the last dregs of tiredness. Revitalised and terrified, she levered herself up and ran into her bedroom, which had been transformed for the duration into a nursery. It was empty. The bathroom produced similar results. There weren't many places in the bijou flat that would conceal even a small child.

Heart racing, a sick feeling of dread curdling in the pit of her churning stomach, Jude raced back into the living room.

'Do you know where Joseph is, Sophia?' Don't scare her, don't scare her, Jude, she told herself, trying hard to keep the panicky tremor from her voice as she appealed to his twin.

'Yes,' the little girl replied without looking up.

Jude fought hard not to scream with frustration. She was about one heartbeat away from total panic. 'Where is he, Sophia? Where is Joseph?'

The little girl lifted her head and brushed a soft curl from her grubby forehead with her equally chubby forearm. 'He's gone to see the nice man with the computer game.'

Jude dropped to her knees beside the child. 'He's gone to see Marco?' she repeated with a note of hope in her voice.

Sophia nodded, her attention on the picture she was drawing. 'We like Marco, he's nice.'

Jude nodded, her thoughts racing. Illogically she was sure her nephew would be safe with Marco, even if the handsome occupant of the impossibly plush penthouse apartment upstairs did seem a little feckless at times.

Actually most of the apartments were plush to a greater or lesser extent—she occupied one of the token modestly priced apartments the builders had been forced to include in their project to satisfy local planning restrictions.

If only Joseph had got to Marco's apartment safely.

She couldn't let herself think about him not doing so.

She couldn't bear to think about the little boy lost and alone. You heard such terrible stories...no, don't go there, Jude...focus, girl!

God! When she found that boy she was never going to let him out of her sight for a single second! If necessary she was going to superglue him to her side. Silently praying it actually would be that simple, she began to unstrap the sleeping baby from her reclining rocker seat.

'Come on, Sophia,' she said, turning to the little girl. 'We'll go and get Joseph for his lunch,' she added brightly. Her mental barriers were keeping the nightmare 'what ifs' at bay...just!

'That's it, Amy, we're going to take a little walk,' she told the drowsy baby as she lifted her into her arms.

'I don't want to go...' The little girl's mutinous response was almost drowned out by Amy, who had begun to loudly protest at being so rudely woken from her nap.

'Now!' Jude was as much surprised as relieved when the little girl responded without any further argument to her forceful command.

She was halfway to the door, her free hand tightly wrapped about the child's, when there was a loud, imperative knock on the door.

Jude ran across the room and flung the door wide.

'Aunty Jude!'

'Joseph!' To her relief her nephew looked none the worse for his experience, in fact he looked pretty pleased with himself.

Thank you, God and thank you, Marco! The closer her gaze got to the face of the man upon whose strong shoulders her nephew was perched, the more strained her beaming smile of gratitude became.

They had to travel a long way to get there, which may have accounted for the falling-off-a-tall-building suicide dive her stomach went into. At a conservative estimate he was six four, with a hard, athletically lean body under the superbly cut suit he wore. The jacket hung open to reveal a washboard-flat belly and lean, snaky hips. He had legs that went on forever to perfectly balance the magnificent shoulders.

When she had finally worked her way up to his face her exploration stalled and her smile vanished as her gaze locked onto a pair of spectacular midnight eyes.

This is more than surreal!

Of course she knew who he was—only someone who had spent the last few years in a coma or a convent would not have instantly recognised those dark, classically proportioned features.

It was easy to see why the camera loved the enigmatic, impenetrable deep-set eyes, sculpted, razor-sharp cheekbones, strong, mobile mouth and that glorious golden Mediterranean colouring. Unlike normal mortals, the closer you got, the better he looked. This guy didn't have a bad angle or need special lighting, he was about as close to flawless as you got.

Strangely, faced with this flesh and blood Adonis what hit Jude most forcibly was not his incredible face or scrumptious body, but what the lens had not been able to capture—the man exuded his own personal force field of raw, undiluted sexuality!

Jude, standing up close and personal, not *literally* obviously—now there was a thought—felt her stomach muscles quiver as she got a full dose of what he had in abundance. The impact was like walking into a solid wall. Staring up at him too dazed to hide her shock, Jude realised that what he exuded actually had little to do with his perfect bone structure, eyelashes long enough to make a girl weep or his wide, sensual mouth—though they naturally didn't do any harm!—but the innate sexuality of a virile male animal at the peak of his powers.

And, my God, doesn't he know it? she thought, her nose wrinkled slightly with distaste. She found this brand of self-assurance not only disconcerting, but unattractive. He was the visual equivalent for her of someone scraping a nail down a blackboard.

She couldn't think of one reason, but there was probably a perfectly simple one, to explain why her nephew was sitting on the shoulders of The World's Most Notorious Playboy. One tabloid had stuck him with the title a couple of years back when it had run the personal story, complete with the obligatory salacious details, of a supermodel girlfriend he had ignominiously dumped.

The nickname had stuck and if half the things the girl had claimed were true it was well deserved she thought disapprovingly. She was no prude but *really*...! Jude felt heat travel over her skin as she recalled claims of his insatiable nature...did people really do things like that?

The stories of his sordid sexual exploits had actually done him no real harm—when had it done a man harm to be labelled a superstud? she thought cynically. What had actually done the damage to his reputation had been the dramatic black eye the model had been sporting in front of the cameras when interviewed. When asked she had instantly disclaimed that darling Luca had done it, but very few had believed her and suddenly people had been popping out of the woodwork with stories that seemed to give credence to his allegedly violent nature. Though significantly none of those stories had originated from previous lovers, who rubbished the reports.

Her protective instincts came on full alert.

'You're not Marco!' she heard herself exclaim accusingly.

Marco, with his bold eyes and warm smile, was handsome, and until she'd met this man she'd had him in her mental file marked 'attractive, predatory and dangerous.' Meeting this man had Jude rapidly redefining her definitions of predatory and dangerous!

'He's Luca!' Joseph announced importantly.

He's devastating! *Please let me not have said that out loud.*

'Are you all right, Joseph? You're not hurt or anything?' If she could have reached she would have yanked him down from those broad shoulders, but Amy was still nestled in her arms.

The man turned his head slightly, giving Jude a view of his perfect profile, and said something to the child that made the little boy laugh and ruffle the man's sleek hair with chubby fingers.

Jude, who was trying so hard to act as if she were totally cool about discovering a billionaire playboy on her doorstep that she was basically dumb, envied the child his naturalness.

A dreamy, unfocused expression slid into her wide-spaced eyes as she found herself speculating about what it might feel like to slide her own fingers into that thick, glossy... Without warning the muscles of her stomach tightened, making her gasp.

This was not a man a girl could let her imagination run wild around; fortunately she was not a girl who had any trouble keeping her imagination under control. And I thought I was too tired ever to even think of sex again. I guess we all have our breaking-point.

He turned his head suddenly and Jude froze.

'The child is, as you can see, unharmed.'

There was no evidence of the warmth she thought she

had seen in his face as he'd spoken to Joseph; his eyes were drilled into her like knives.

'Thank you for returning him safely.'

Luca slipped Joseph off his shoulders in one smooth motion. She noticed that the expensive fabric of his perfectly cut dark grey suit fell back into place without a crease across his back as he straightened up.

She dropped on her knees beside the boy and hugged him with her one free arm, juggling Amy in the other. Blinking away the tears that filled her eyes, she rose to her feet. 'Go along inside, Joseph,' she bade huskily, all thoughts of remonstrance washed away by relief.

'Right then, thanks again,' Jude mumbled, guiltily avoiding contact with those unnerving dark eyes. He probably took being lusted after as no more than his due, but she was deeply embarrassed by her wayward imagination.

The awkward silence stretched, at least awkward on her part—she doubted this man had ever felt awkward in his life. He was assured down to his fingertips, one set of which was at that moment impatiently brushing a strand of dark hair from his broad, intelligent brow. As she followed the gesture with her eyes Jude discovered that his elegant, shapely hands with their long, tapering fingers exerted a strange fascination that made it difficult for her to drag her gaze away.

When she finally did so she could feel the dampness of nervous perspiration sticking her tee shirt to her back.

'I'd ask you to come in but—'

'You are a—*friend* of my brother's?' Mingled with the suspicion there was a note of cynical resignation in his voice, which passed Jude, who couldn't think about much beyond her overriding desire to get rid of this disturbing man, clear by.

He clearly expected her to say something; she wanted to

say something, something that would draw a firm line under this incident. Unfortunately her brain chose that moment to disconnect with her vocal cords.

One strongly defined ebony brow arched when she remained dumb. The longer the silence stretched, the harder it was to fill. Frustration welled inside her as she stood there as if she were some tongue-tied, awestruck teenager rather than a responsible, mature career woman.

His deep, sexily accented voice was part of the problem. Even after he'd stopped speaking it continued to vibrate in a strange way through her body. Despising her susceptibility to his sexy vibes, she forced herself to concentrate.

'Marco?' she finally managed.

Marco was a Di Rossi? Well, of course she knew he was, but she hadn't previously made the connection with the incredibly wealthy Gianluca Di Rossi. For starters Marco, like many Italians of Northern extract was blond and secondly he didn't go around acting as if he had been born into one of the oldest Italian families, unlike his brother, who seemed very conscious of his blue blood not to mention his own importance.

The Di Rossis had been born with everything except money: impeccable lineage, enviable connections, a crumbling historic *palazzo* in Venice and a second home in Umbria surrounded by a neglected estate. Now thanks to Luca they had the money too—pots of the stuff. Or at least Luca did, but if the sort of clothes Marco wore and car he drove were anything to go by the elder brother's wealth was enjoyed by the entire family.

There were numerous theories, the darker even hinting at underworld connections, about how he'd made his first million before he was twenty-two, but nobody seemed to know for sure. There was no mystery about the source of his wealth these days—his international interests were diverse, ranging from a string of hotels to his own airline. Luca had an ability to read the market that some financial observers considered to border on the supernatural.

Being left standing on a doorstep was a first for Luca, who had decided it was concern for the child that stopped him from turning around. He was beginning to think the brunette was not only the owner of the most sultry mouth he had ever seen, but stupid.

With a less vacant expression on her face she would probably be quite attractive. Actually almost beautiful, he mentally corrected, re-evaluating the small, appealing face with its tip-tilted nose, luminous eyes and wilful mouth upturned to him—if, that was, you were prepared to overlook the slight irregularity of the features and the angularity of her small, determined chin.

The evidence that she had recently shed tears—she had the sort of pale, almost translucent complexion that showed such things—did not stir his pity. In Luca's considered opinion it was the children some parent had unwisely committed to her care that deserved his sympathy.

Doubtless her attention had been divided between her charges, watching daytime television and talking to her boyfriend on the phone—the children coming a poor second, he thought scornfully.

As he visualised the likely scenario that had led to a small, defenceless child wandering alone in the building his contempt for the girl and the persons who had left their children in the charge of the youthful incompetent escalated.

'You are a *friend* of my brother?' Luca disliked repeating himself almost as much as he disliked the idea of this girl knowing his brother, who was renown for his inability to see beyond a pretty face and was, despite some very severe lessons on what *not* considering the consequences of his actions resulted in, painfully impulsive.

'Friend…?' Even as she echoed the word the not-so-subtle emphasis he placed on the word and the contemptuous curl of his lip belatedly hit her. *Friend* in this instance was clearly a euphemism for lover and from his expression it was equally clear that Luca Di Rossi didn't much like the idea of his brother slumming it.

Angry spots of colour appeared on her cheeks as Jude felt a surge of anger. She lifted her chin. Marco, with his easy charm and pleasing manner, had made it plain that he was interested, but she wasn't, and now it was academic— as her mum had said, no man wanted a woman who came with three small children.

Actually, now she came to think of it the one time she had seen Marco since the children had arrived he hadn't asked her out, whereas previously he had never let an opportunity pass. Clearly his alleged devotion had limits, Jude thought in amusement, but she was prepared to forgive him this lack of staying power because he had been so nice to the kids, but then Italians were reputed to be dotty about children. Though, she thought, angling a glance up at the dark, arrogant features of the man looking down his nose at her, there had to be exceptions.

So no need whatever for Marco's autocratic, stuck-up brother to know that the chances of her developing the sort of *friendship* he was talking about with the younger Di Rossi was nil—let him worry a little.

She pretended to consider the matter. 'I think that would be overstating it…' she lowered her eyes and looked up at him through her lashes with a coy smile '…for the moment…'

Luca watched with narrowed eyes as she gave a complacent toss of her head that sent the glossy curls dancing.

The action completed the message in her words, namely that it would only take a click of her fingers to change that situation.

Not stupid after all, or beautiful, but she had something more dangerous than beauty—she oozed sex appeal. A man looked at her mouth and wanted to kiss it, at her body and imagined it minus clothes. Maybe there was not a world-class intellect lurking behind those gold-shot eyes, but, he thought cynically, when you combined a face and body like hers with a degree of animal cunning you didn't need to be a genius to get what you wanted.

The question was did she want Marco? Not that this was a scenario he would countenance.

Her confidence was, he conceded as his eyes slid slowly over the firm curves of her taut, youthful body, most probably justified. Her body might not be lush enough for some men's taste, but they would be in the minority. Luca had come across this sort of female before, the sort that possessed a sensuality that drew men like the proverbial moths to the flame, the sort that liked to control a man with sex.

During the few moments it took him to draw these conclusions the subject of his conjecture, oblivious to the opinion he had formed of her, was occupied with trying to soothe Amy who, having apparently been almost as gobsmacked by the sight of Luca Di Rossi on the doorstep as her aunt, had recovered her voice.

Amy, who was clearly destined to be a future diva, had a staggering vocal range.

When Jude looked up she found the not-so-friendly neighbourhood billionaire playboy was watching her with a peculiar intensity. There was absolutely no discernible expression in those heavy-lidded midnight eyes, but Jude was suddenly painfully conscious of her dishevelled appearance.

Wild hair—her smooth blow-dried bob was fast becoming a dim and distant memory—not a trace of make-up and last year's joggers that hung loosely about her slender hips teamed with the cut-off tee shirt that she only normally wore in the gym. Face it, Jude, he's probably seen bag ladies who looked more attractive.

Well, there's news, Jude, you don't meet the fastidious Luca Di Rossi's high standards!

She shifted Amy's weight and hitched her top up over the bare shoulder that had been exposed by the restless baby. It promptly fell off the other shoulder. She began to repeat the process.

'Save it,' a bored I've-seen-it-all-before drawl softly advised. 'I am not my brother.'

The reason he'd chosen to remind her of the one thing she *didn't* need reminding of passed Jude by. A perplexed frown knitting her smooth brow, she gave up on the overstretched tee shirt. As her eyes collided with his she had several fresh reminders of why she didn't need reminding!

Marco did not make her feel jittery or uncomfortable in her own skin. When he was around her pulse rate behaved beautifully and she could string more than three words together without breaking out in a sweat.

'The helpless act and a little flesh on show will not have me panting!' His eyes narrowed suspiciously.

'Panting…?' she echoed in genuine bewilderment.

'Or did you plant the idea of visiting Marco in the boy's head?'

He was suggesting she would actually…? No, he couldn't be; she must have misheard. Then she saw his contemptuous expression and realised there was no mistake. It took about ten seconds for her temper to reach boiling-point, during which time her complexion went through several dramatic colour changes, settling finally for deathly pale.

'Thanks for that insight, but actually I think I've already got a pretty good idea of what makes you pant.' You and every other man, she thought, watching with satisfaction the bands of dark colour across the twin crests of his high slashing cheekbones.

He scanned her through eyes narrowed to slits. 'And what might that be?' he enquired in a dangerous voice that was as smooth as silk.

'Let me see…' she murmured, raising her eyes to the ceiling in an attitude of deep concentration. 'No, don't tell me,' she begged. 'It's on the tip of my tongue. Blonde hair, long legs…oh, *lots* of flesh on show. Am I warm?' she asked, flashing him an innocent look of enquiry. The icy stare encountered was not encouraging, but Jude found herself in the grip of a strange recklessness and ignored the danger signals. 'Oh, I almost forgot—an ability to treat everything you say as a pearl of wisdom would be a vital ingredient…' Her angry gold-shot eyes clashed with scorching black.

Vile, vile man, she thought, making no attempt to hide her contempt for men like him, the shallow ones who were all gloss and no substance, the ones who could take their pick and inevitably opted for trophy girlfriends.

'Oh, and just for the record I am not helpless!'

'I never imagined you were,' a distracted expression slid into his dark eyes as they slid over rigid outrage. '…but it is a convenient ploy when you require male attention.'

'Why on earth would I require male attention?' she demanded with a contemptuous sniff, before Amy started to whimper again and wriggle.

Luca watched her struggle for a moment. 'That child is tired.'

As he delivered this judgement in a manner that suggested his words were inscribed in stone Amy threw her head back and let out a loud wail. Suddenly everyone's the child-care expert, Jude thought, fast approaching the end of her tether. Except me!

'I'm aware of that,' she snapped. 'If you think you can do better...' she added, glaring at his perfect profile with dislike that seemed to be growing at an alarming rate.

'Dio mio!' he ejaculated scornfully as he watched her clumsy attempts to calm the child. 'A moderately well-trained Labrador could do better.'

Jude gave a gasp of outrage and, ready to do battle, threw out her chin, an action that he totally ignored as he looked over her head—an easy thing to do as she barely topped his shoulder. Well, if he was hoping to see a responsible adult he wasn't hoping nearly as much as she was!

'I find it increasingly hard to believe that Joseph's parents have left these children in your care...'

I find it increasingly difficult to believe you are human. Jude gritted her teeth and forced her lips into a smile. The man had brought Joseph safely home—she had to be at least civil, even if he wasn't.

'Well, they have.'

He looked at her face and shook his dark head slowly from side to side in an attitude of insulting disbelief.

'Listen, I really am very grateful to you for returning Joseph.' One of them had to act like a grown-up, she thought, gritting her teeth and thrusting out her hand in an olive-branch fashion.

He looked at her small outstretched hand, but didn't take it. 'Then you had noticed he was missing,' he said in a voice that was all the more deadly for its softness. 'I suppose that's something.'

Her outstretched hand fell to her side as her cheeks

burned with angry colour. The caustic, cutting comment was made worse by the fact she couldn't, with a clear conscience, deny it. *As if I needed reminding I'm not fit to look after a goldfish!* Grimly she pushed aside the negative thought. *I'm going to get better at it—even if it kills me!*

'He was only out of my sight for a minute...' Jude cringed inwardly to hear an unattractive whining note of self-justification enter her voice. She buried her face in Amy's soft curls and inhaled the sweet baby smell. 'Hush, darling,' she pleaded raggedly.

Luca gave an exasperated sigh—the quiver in her voice was audible. The girl sounded and looked at the end of her tether. When another child appeared clinging to her leg he gave vent to a hissing sound of exasperation.

This isn't my business, he told himself, glancing at the metal-banded watch on his wrist. The action brought his eyes in line with the innocent, trusting gaze of the little girl peeking out from behind the brunette—her eyes were blue, not brown, but they reminded him very much of Valentina.

CHAPTER THREE

'THIS is an untenable situation,' Luca declared abruptly.

Tell me about it.

The vehemence of his declaration made Sophia, who had crept up behind Jude to get a look at what was going on, grab handfuls of joggers in her chubby hands and duck back behind her aunt, yanking the pants embarrassingly low over Jude's hips in the process.

'I don't know what you're talking about,' Jude said, lifting her head from her efforts to anchor the drawstring waist of her joggers before it revealed more than it already had.

She discovered that his dark gaze was fixed on the expanse of her flat stomach and midriff. Something electrifying and scary rushed through her body. Her bare skin tingled as if he had touched her.

'Admiring my appendix scar?'

If she'd thought to discompose him, Jude was disappointed. However, her own composure fled when the heavy screen of dark lashes lifted, revealing the glitter of dark eyes beneath.

There was nothing covert about the smouldering sexual appraisal. The breath snagged in her throat as she tried to swallow past the occlusion in her dry throat. She wrenched her eyes from his, horribly conscious of the heavy dragging sensation low in her belly and her pinched nipples burning as they rubbed against her tight, constricting top.

Head bent, she hastily yanked the joggers around her waist and cinched the cord tight. She didn't look up until the dizziness that had made her head spin had lessened.

Jude was furious with her body for betraying her this way. Anyone would think a man had never looked at her before!

'I'm sorry to have taken so much of your time.' Her cold words were as clear an invitation for him to leave as you could get without saying get lost.

'Just how many children are you meant to be looking after?' he demanded, striding decisively into the room. 'Are there any more hiding anywhere?'

Jude clenched her teeth as he stepped past her. Obviously she'd been too subtle. Maybe she should have stuck with get lost.

As his dark eyes scanned the untidy room she repressed a ridiculous impulse to apologise for the mess.

'Mr Di Rossi, I'm really very grateful to you for returning Joseph safe and sound but—'

He cut in without even looking at her. 'You have the telephone number of the children's parents?'

The unexpected question hit her like a physical blow. 'No.'

It was the sharp inhalation and not the brief reply that followed that brought his attention zeroing back to her face. A perplexed frown drew his dark brows together as he encountered the inexplicable shimmer of unshed tears in her wide, luminous eyes. Her soft lips definitely trembled before she caught her full lower lip between her teeth.

'What sort of parents would not leave a contact number?'

'You leave them alone!' she snapped.

Luca looked from her flushed face to the small white-knuckled fist she had pressed to her mouth. 'I am not leaving anyone alone until I have satisfied myself that these children are safe.'

'Of course they're safe.'

His dark glance slid significantly to Joseph, who was playing with his sister at the opposite end of the room, and

Jude flushed. He smiled—it was not a nice smile. She hit back instinctively.

'At least I don't go around bashing—' The silence that followed her abbreviated accusation simply simmered with tension.

One dark brow lifted as he replied in a slow, measured, conversational tone. 'You were saying…?' Like black ice, his stunning eyes rested unblinkingly on her burning face. Jude, already slightly ashamed of her below-the-belt jibe, squirmed.

'Sensitive subject?' she threw back recklessly.

It was nothing short of amazing, she reflected, unable to tear her eyes from his extraordinary face, that such extremes of emotions could be conveyed with little more than a quiver of a nostril and a twitch of an eyebrow. Although he had done nothing more than this, it was pretty clear that Luca Di Rossi was in the grip of *extremely* extreme emotion at that moment.

'As someone who clearly believes I am indeed a man who vents his anger on anyone who can't hit back, you must be hoping it isn't a sensitive subject,' he observed softly.

He's right, she thought. I'm standing in the presence of just about the most physically intimidating male I have ever met, who, just to make life interesting, has a well-rumoured inability to control his temper, and I'm winding him up. Either I'm very stupid or I don't believe the stories.

The former was debatable, but, rather to her own surprise, Jude found that the latter was true. Luca Di Rossi might well be The World's Most Notorious Playboy, but she didn't believe for one minute he went around hitting women—he might wish he could right now, but he didn't.

'What makes you think I can't hit back?'

His look of amused condescension made her wish she'd

attended more than two of the judo classes she'd begun with such enthusiasm. I would most likely be a black belt at least by now—the man did say I showed promise. Then, she thought viciously, I could wipe that smile right off his face. For a moment she allowed herself to wistfully visualise herself victoriously astride his prone body, completely at her mercy—*completely*!

Jude blinked and gave her head a tiny shake as her imagination, a little overexcited by the image, began to embellish the scene dangerously. Clearing her throat, she turned her attention to the real thing—he wasn't at her mercy. He had probably never been at anyone's mercy in his life; he was your original in-control man.

'You're not going to go away, are you?' she said, a note of dull resignation in her voice.

'Not until I am sure there is someone capable to take care of these children.'

'Do you *always* get what you want?'

'Eventually,' he admitted factually. 'There is actually nothing more I would like to do than walk out of that door,' he added with an expressive shrug of his shoulders. 'However, I feel it is my duty under the circumstances to inform these children's parents that they have left them in the care of someone who is clearly not up to the task,' he explained formally.

That's what I've been trying to tell everyone. The irony of finally finding someone who agreed with her brought a bitter smile to Jude's lips.

'Duty?'

His lip curled contemptuously. 'A foreign concept to you?'

You pompous…prig. A man who dumped girlfriends the way other men changed their socks knew a lot about duty.

'I'm familiar with it,' she admitted. 'I'm just surprised someone like you is.'

He sucked in his breath nosily and fixed her with a cold and unforgiving knife-edged stare. 'I don't know what these people expect, leaving their children in the care of an irresponsible teenager.'

Jude was so absorbed with scoring points in the battle of insults that the significance of what he'd said didn't sink in for several seconds. She scanned his face incredulously. He was serious—he actually thought she was a teenage babysitter! The incredulous laugh that was wrenched from her throat brought his dark, frowning disapproval.

Considering that she felt as though she'd aged twenty years over the past four weeks, it was almost flattering—*almost*!

'I'm not the babysitter,' she stated, placing Amy on the floor. The toddler crawled a couple of feet before grabbing a coffee-table to haul herself to her feet. 'Neither,' she added, flexing her wrist to ease the ache where she'd been carrying the baby, 'am I a teenager.'

Jude didn't have opportunity to savour him looking nonplussed by her response as the twins chose that precise moment to begin to squabble over a toy.

'Can you do nothing about this racket?' Luca demanded, raising his voice above the din.

'Children make noise; it's what they do.' On this score at least she felt qualified to give an opinion. It was actually something of a confidence boost to encounter someone who knew *less* about the practicalities of child care than she did. 'And actually,' honesty impelled her to add, 'it's pointless me trying to make them stop—they won't listen to me.'

He responded to her frank admission by snorting something in rapid Italian, which, if the look of unqualified contempt that accompanied it was any indicator, was not complimentary!

'Fine—you think you can do better,' she choked, 'feel free!'

To judge by their expressions the children were just as amazed as she was to see the authoritative figure of Luca Di Rossi take up her challenge. A stunned silence fell as he bent over and calmly confiscated the item they were fighting over.

'If you are unable to share, perhaps it is better that I keep this,' he told them repressively.

'*But...*'

Joseph's half-hearted protest was stilled by a single look from the tall man. Even whilst she resented the way he was usurping her role, Jude secretly envied his ability to inspire unquestioning obedience in the children.

'Do you have a box for these toys?' Two blond heads gave an affirmative nod. 'Then I suggest you put them in it before someone breaks their neck.'

'You can't speak to the children like that,' she hissed, catching his arm.

His eyes touched the hand she had laid on his arm to get his attention before shifting to her face. 'Like what?'

'So harshly,' she explained, rubbing her palm against her thigh. 'They're...they've had a lot of...upset in their lives lately—they need tender loving care, not being bawled at by a big bully.' She could no longer resist sliding a furtive peek at his upper arm; her stomach dipped as she recalled how hard it had felt. Even more inexplicable had been the strange reluctance she had felt to remove her hand.

'I was not harsh,' he denied. 'I was firm, and children need to know the boundaries; it makes them feel secure. This is *especially* important during times of upheaval—children need continuity.'

Jude stared at him in frustration. She could hardly denounce what he was saying when she had a string of letters after her name that said *she* was the one who ought to be saying it. It was after all pretty basic stuff, but as she'd discovered the gap between theory and practice was pretty big, especially when you were thinking with your heart not your head.

She pushed an unsteady hand through her hair. I'm just too involved to be objective, she concluded unhappily.

'You didn't have to be so...so brutal,' she denounced stubbornly.

One eloquent brow lifted. He inclined his head towards the children. 'Do they look crushed or traumatised?'

Jude normally had no problem with admitting when she was wrong, but on this occasion— 'You can't always tell with children.'

The look he directed at her made Jude flush and turn away.

It would be very easy to hate someone who made it look so easy, she thought, watching the twins doing as he had instructed and acting as though it was an enormous treat. It didn't help knowing full well that if *she* had suggested they pick up their toys they would have given her an exhaustive argument before ignoring her.

Jude didn't know what was more difficult to believe: their co-operative behaviour or the inescapable fact that The World's Most Notorious Playboy knew about children. He was the very last man in the world she would have had down as being comfortable with children.

'If this baby has a cot,' he said, switching his attention to Amy, 'I suggest you put her in it.'

And the hell of it is, Jude thought as she tucked Amy in, I did exactly what I was told. It was mortifying.

To compensate for her meek compliance Jude returned

to the living room with a combative tilt to her chin and a
determined gleam in her eyes. She was going to get rid of
Mr Child Expert Di Rossi after she had told him exactly
what she thought of him. It was one thing for her to say
that she was not up to the job, it was quite another for a
perfect stranger to point it out!

He looked up as she entered. The room, she immediately
noticed, was already looking less like a disaster area and
the twins were contentedly playing like model children in
a corner.

Joseph smiled as he caught sight of her. 'Aunty Jude, do
they have phones in heaven?'

Jude froze, aghast at this evidence their low-voiced conversation had been overheard. 'No, darling, I'm afraid they
don't. Mr Di Rossi can't call heaven,' she said huskily.

Joseph gave a sigh that broke her heart and returned to
his quiet game.

'Would you two like to go and play on the computer for
half an hour?' she asked, a tell-tale quiver in her painfully
bright voice.

The twins responded eagerly to the offer and ran off to
the study, which was a rather grand name for something
that was little more than a cupboard. As they slammed the
door behind them Jude released a deep sigh and covered
her face with her hands.

Since the funeral she'd imagined that she'd wake up one
morning and find it had all been a bad dream. The little
boy's question had brought it home; she was living the bad
dream and they weren't coming home—ever!

The brutal pain of loss was physical as she made herself
think of them in the past tense. David and Sam had been
the original odd couple. Many had shaken their heads and
said it would never last when they'd married, but they'd
proved the critics wrong.

It had been a classic case of opposites attracting. Her brother had been to patience what his wife had been to organisation. Ironically David, with his obsessive need for punctuality, had got married to a woman who'd been late for everything.

Jude could remember asking her sister-in-law once if she didn't mind always putting her own needs last.

'I've never been this happy in my life,' Sam had replied simply. 'You just wait until it happens to you, Jude, and you'll see what I mean.'

'Oh, it's not going to happen to me,' Jude had replied confidently. 'I'm never going to give up my freedom to be at the beck and call of some man, and I'm just not the maternal type.'

Sam had just laughed and said, 'We'll see.' In that enigmatic, irritating way that married people did with singles.

Jude's opinion of marriage and motherhood hadn't changed, but after a month of trying to fill her sister-in-law's shoes she was beginning to appreciate just how hard it was to be even a mediocre mother, let alone a brilliant one as Sam had been.

'I didn't realise they were listening to us.'

Luca looked at the down-bent head of the young woman and his severe expression softened. 'Children have a habit of hearing more than you imagine,' he told her with the voice of experience. 'Both parents?' he added abruptly.

With a shuddering sigh Jude lowered her hands. 'Yes, both,' she confirmed bleakly. 'It was a car accident last month.'

'Last month? *Madre di Dio!* What a tragedy.' His eyes went to the door behind which the children's laughter could be heard. 'Why didn't you simply tell me the children's parents were dead?'

Jude shook her head. 'I don't know.'

A hiss of exasperation escaped his clenched teeth at her weak reply. 'And this is you? Dr Judith Lucas…?'

Jude saw for the first time that he was holding a paperback copy of her book. The photo on the flyleaf was turned to her and he appeared to be scanning the bio on the inner page.

'Yes,' she admitted. Not much point denying it; the photo was not a good likeness but it was still recognisably her, even if the powers that be had decided to opt for a sexy look as opposed to studious.

'*You* wrote a book on child care?' Luca drawled, closing the book and running his index finger down the spine before replacing the book on the shelf he had removed it from. His eyes touched her face and Jude nodded. 'And people *read* it?'

She flushed at the heavily satiric note in his voice. 'I've had a lot of letters from parents who found it very useful,' she gritted defiantly.

'Is that so?'

'Are you calling me a liar?'

'I was merely thinking that if this is such a good book it might be a good idea if you read it yourself.' His smooth, hateful drawl brought a flush to her cheeks. 'I'm sure you offered your services to the children's guardian from the best motives,' he conceded stiffly, 'but it was hardly prudent considering—'

'Considering what?' Conscious that her raised voice might be able to be heard in the next room, Jude made an effort to moderate her tone. But it was hard to be moderate when you were talking to a man who had a first-class honours degree in patronising, a man who insulted you every time he opened his mouth and treated you as if you were a total fool. 'That I'm totally clueless?' she hissed.

'The facts speak for themselves,' he told her bluntly.

'I'm sure you're just great chairing a group therapy session.' Though frankly he couldn't see it. 'But you don't know the first thing about children…'

His condescension grated on her almost as much as his accuracy. 'I don't actually practice, I lecture at the university and I never claimed that I had hands-on experience,' she snapped.

'Some things are taken as read. You writing a book on child care is like a virgin writing a sex manual. You're not one of those too, are you?'

'Of course not, don't be stupid!'

He shot her a strange look. 'I wasn't actually being serious.'

Jude didn't like his calculating expression. 'I know that…' she retorted quickly.

After all, you couldn't tell by *looking* at a person, and the surest way to make people suspect was to start acting weird every time someone said virgin.

'What exactly is your relationship to the children? I'm assuming that Aunty is a courtesy title?'

'No, it isn't. David, their father, was my brother.'

A nerve beside his expressive mouth jumped; you could almost see his brain making the necessary links and coming up with the unlikely conclusion. '*You* are their guardian?'

Dark eyes scanned her face, interpreting the over-prominent cheekbones, the lines of strain around her mouth and the violet bruises beneath her eyes in the light of this astounding information. 'This cannot be.'

'Why, because *you* say so?' His face darkened with displeasure at her sarcastic jibe. *Tough*, Jude thought, her jaw tightening. In some corner of her mind, where a professionally trained part of herself lurked, she knew that she was focusing all her pent-up frustration and aggression on him—but what the hell? He looked big enough to take it!

'*Because*,' he contradicted in a driven voice, 'I think it's a formula for disaster to leave children in the care of someone who will probably reach adolescence at the same time as them. I suppose you thought it was very amusing to deceive me?'

It was the extraordinary addition rather than the insult that preceded it that made Jude's eyes fly open. How did he have the barefaced cheek to say that? This man was totally unbelievable.

'What are you on?' she quivered. 'I hate to be the one to break this to you but some people have more important things on their mind than making you look silly. I didn't do any deceiving!' she yelled. 'It was you, you couldn't wait to jump to conclusions,' she accused—even if, barring the teenage thing, they were essentially correct.

'What was I meant to think?' Luca demanded. 'You have no control over the children in your care. Your manner, your dress is not that of a woman.' His furious eyes flicked scornfully over her rigid figure. 'Everything about you suggests adolescence and immaturity. If it was not your intention to deceive then I must conclude that you have a lot of growing up to do,' he delivered scornfully.

As she listened to this ruthless character assessment his features swam out of focus as hot, angry tears of humiliation filled her eyes. Jude pressed one clenched fist against her mouth before she had enough control of her temper to speak. It was not in her nature to take such treatment lying down.

Luca caught the shimmer of tears in the beautiful eyes before she turned her head away. The fine quiver of muscles just below the surface in her pale throat suggested she was fighting for control.

In business dealings he never allowed the opposition to provoke him into using unconsidered language; this was a philosophy that he carried through to his personal life. As the heat of anger dissipated Luca became dismayed by his failure to follow his own golden rule. As infuriating as he found her sharp-tongued antagonism and total lack of respect, he found the young woman's dejected demeanour and bowed head infinitely harder to endure.

He admired spirit and would no more have wanted to extinguish the characteristic in this infuriating female than he would have crushed the spirit of the fine Arabian horses he bred on the Umbrian estate where he spent most of his leisure time.

Luca admired spirit.

The moment her head lifted he realised his lament for her fire and spirit had been premature.

'If we're going to get into character analysis I'd say a man over thirty who mentally strips a woman he thinks is a teenager stands some examination!'

'*Dio!*'

The dark stain of colour that accentuated his cheekbones was proof her jibe had found its mark. A muscle clenched in his lean cheek as he looked down at her from his superior height as if she were a sub species not fit to grovel at his feet.

'Men look, it is their nature,' he framed with a shrug.

Jude got the impression, despite his cool contention, her remark had really got to him. 'Well, it's not my nature to stand there and take it.'

'Oh, was that not the reaction you wanted?' he returned, sounding surprised.

Now wasn't that just like a man to blame the woman? 'Sure, I just *love* being drooled over by some oversexed, lecherous pig! It sets me up beautifully for the rest of the day.'

He froze and looked at her as if he couldn't believe what

she had said. His entire body was rigid with a combination of outrage and disbelief.

'Your problem is you're just not *man* enough to admit you're in the wrong.' A person would be excused for thinking I *wanted* to see him flip. Whatever his expression he was beautiful, but wanting to strangle her really gave him an extra edge, she admitted, suppressing a little shiver of excitement as she covertly admired the strong lines of his impassioned face.

'*Dio!*' His nostrils flared as he inhaled deeply, fighting an uphill battle to contain his feelings. 'Calling a man's masculinity into question is a dangerous tactic, Dr Lucas…'

'Oh, spare me the macho demonstrations. Besides, if you can't take a few home truths you shouldn't have been so free with your opinions.' It was totally irrational and it wasn't as if she suffered from low self-esteem or anything, but his words had hurt—not that she had any intention of letting him see that.

He looked at her, no trace of comprehension on his drop-dead gorgeous features.

'You felt at liberty to insult me,' she reminded him. He continued to look blank. 'You said I wasn't a woman.' To her horror Jude was unable to control the noisy sob that rose convulsively in her throat, then another and another. They shook her slender frame, gathering force with each successive one.

'Are you crying?'

Not here, not now, *please*!

'What does it look like I'm doing?'

Even as she was in the process of delivering her acid retort Luca could almost hear the sound of her control snapping. He blamed himself for being too distracted to register that she had been on the brink of this breakdown. All the signs had been there. He was naturally sympathetic to her loss, but he had enough problems of his own without getting caught up in someone else's trauma.

'You said I'm hopeless with children,' she began in a low, impassioned voice, 'and you're right!' she declared with a bitter laugh. 'I am, I'm a total, complete failure. If it hadn't been for you goodness knows what would have happened to Joseph…' She turned horror-drenched eyes to him.

'There is absolutely no point going down the road of what-if scenarios. The point is Joseph is well and safe.'

Jude shook her head, refusing to be comforted. 'Despite me, not because of me. But I'm all they've got, you see, and I've got to g…get it right!' she cried, her voice rising to a teary crescendo of seismic self-pity.

The sound made Luca, who was standing stock-still, wince.

Jude wiped her hands across her damp face and tried to get her breath, which was emerging as a series of uneven gulps. 'I never cry,' she explained just before she released another shocking wail.

She never lost sight of the fact that she was going to regret this display, but this knowledge had no power to stem the unbridled misery that seeped out of her. For so long she had been unable to cry and now she couldn't stop. *What terrible timing I have!*

Luca glanced towards the closed door behind which the loud noises of a computer game could be heard as the slender, hunched figure gave way once more to sobs.

'I'm terrible at all this, you know!' *What am I saying? Of course he knows.* 'And,' she wailed, lifting her tragic red-rimmed eyes to his and delivering a bitter pronouncement, 'I'll never have sex again! It's not funny,' she yelled when he callously smiled.

'*Per amor di Dio!*' Luca muttered softly under his breath

as, sobbing helplessly, she pulled a tissue from her sleeve and blew her nose noisily. 'Come here,' he instructed, a note of exasperation in his deep voice.

There was no resistance in the pliant body he drew against his. She felt cold, incredibly fragile and strangely the essence of everything that was female. A deep sigh vibrated through her slender frame as he smoothed down her hair in a distracted fashion. She burrowed into him with a soft, trusting sigh and Luca, who could have identified any number of expensive perfumes, found himself unable to place the disturbing scent that filled his nostrils.

They stood that way for some time. Luca felt the exact moment she stopped reacting like a hurt animal seeking comfort and became aware of where she was and who he was—the enemy. Her body jackknifed away from him.

Jude pushed her hair from her face and raised aghast eyes to his. 'I don't know why that happened.' She blinked in a bewildered fashion.

'Perhaps because you haven't let it happen before.'

He might have a point, she admitted, blotting the tear stains with the back of her hand. Luca seemed to be taking being cried all over by a hysterical woman rather better than she would have imagined, she thought, casting a wary glance at his criminally handsome face.

Maybe this sort of stuff happened to him a lot, women flinging themselves on his manly chest? A more worrying thought was him thinking she went around doing this sort of thing on a regular basis!

'Maybe, but I'm really sorry about subjecting you to that.' She sniffed. She sensed she was going to be even sorrier at some stage now that she knew what it felt like to be in his arms.

'Why do the English feel the need to apologise for displays of emotion?' he wondered drily. 'If you let go of your emotions once in a while people like you might be out of a job.'

His ironic words passed over her head. 'Pardon?' She found it hard to look at him and not recall how hard his body had been or how good it had felt—so don't look at him, idiot! She inhaled and discovered the warm, musky male scent of him was still in her nostrils. She lowered her eyes quickly.

Luca placed a finger under her chin and firmly tilted her face upwards. He scanned her tear-stained face critically. 'When did you last have any sleep?' he demanded.

'I'm fine.' He was looking at her much the way he had Joseph when he'd considered defying him. There was nothing *remotely* childlike about the way she was feeling.

'I am not considered to be a patient man.'

This drew a weak laugh from her. 'Now there's a surprise.'

'When?'

She frowned in concentration. 'I think I had a couple of hours last night.'

'You know, the world might look less bleak if you had a decent night's sleep. Is there no one who could help you out with the children to let you get some sleep? Your mother, maybe?'

This suggestion produced a bitter laugh. It had been David who had pointed out the obvious to her when they'd been in their teens.

'Of course Mum's keen on us being self-reliant, Judy. It makes life easier for her if we're not expecting to be bailed out of trouble every five minutes.' David had developed a philosophical attitude to their mother's brutal sink-or-swim approach earlier than she had.

'My mother has a meeting.' Could I sound more bitter and twisted?

'That sounds like an unresolved issue—is that the correct psycho-babble speak?'

'It works,' she agreed.

'In that case I won't go there.'

'That's a pretty good call.'

'As for having sex, I do not think you should totally give up on that, *cara*.'

Jude froze at the sex bit; by the time he'd completed his sentence her respiratory muscles had stopped working. For a little while there she'd convinced herself she either hadn't said what she thought she had, or he hadn't heard it. It hardly seemed possible you could be this embarrassed and not die!

'Easy for you to say,' she croaked.

Jude's eyes widened with alarm as he framed her face between his hands, his thumb stroking the delicate but firm line of her jaw as he studied her. Jude trembled, totally mesmerised by the hungry expression that slid into his dark eyes. Luca's breathing quickened as he watched the pupils of her eyes dilate.

When his hands abruptly fell away Jude was left with knees of cotton wool and a terrible sense of anticlimax.

'Trust me on this one,' he suggested in a strangely grim manner.

CHAPTER FOUR

JUDE never knew where she got the nerve and plain reckless insanity to do what she did next.

Conceivably some residual effects of Luca's touch had something to do with it, or maybe it was the depressing vision of the enforced celibacy of her future she saw stretching before her that made her a little crazy.

At least this way I'll have something to remember.

Boldly she took hold of Luca's dark head. As her fingers sank into the sleek, glossy pelt that covered his head she realised that she'd actually been wondering what this would feel like from the moment she'd opened the door and found him standing there.

As she dragged him down to her level she stretched upwards on tiptoe until their faces were almost level. In the nanosecond just before she placed her lips against his she looked directly into his eyes; what she saw smouldering in his gave her the courage to take the last step.

After all the build-up it was a bit of an anticlimax. Almost before she even started kissing him a persistent voice in her head put a damper on things by saying, You thought this was a good idea because…?

It was probably just as well because actually things weren't going well; kissing someone who was taking no active part was no more fun than she remembered kissing the back of her hand to practise her technique had been when she was twelve.

She began to pull back, she *would have* pulled back had not Luca suddenly murmured something harsh and uneven against her mouth in his native tongue. Out of nowhere the chemistry materialised; the air around crackled with the energy looking for an outlet.

Her face was framed between his big hands as she stood there rigid, her enormous eyes shadowy smudges in her pale face, feeling his tongue trace the outline of her lips.

'*Oh, my God!*' Her insides melted. She made a final total protest before giving into the heat coursing through her veins. 'This isn't a good idea.'

'You thought it was a minute ago,' Luca, whose thoughts had also been running very much along those lines, rebuked her throatily.

'I've stopped thinking.' It was true—gone was the inhibiting voice-over she had never been able to silence before when she'd been kissed. It had always been as if part of her had remained separate from what had been happening. '*That's* never happened before.'

He laughed at her husky confidence, but it didn't lessen the tension she felt emanating from his big body as he turned her face between his hands, examining her flushed features in a manner that suggested compulsion rather than curiosity.

'Maybe you should stop talking too,' he observed, sliding his tongue between her invitingly parted lips.

At the first stabbing incursion a wave of extreme lethargy rolled over Jude, and as the air was snatched from her lungs in one breathy gasp she went totally limp.

Instead of catching her Luca controlled her stumble, allowing the impetus to take them both the several feet to the wall.

A disorientated Jude found herself standing with her back pressed against the wall, her hands pinioned either side of her head. She gasped and stopped moving; the fric-

tion created as her breasts pressed against Luca's chest sent
darts of painful pleasure through her body.

'This isn't happening!'

'You're in denial, Doctor,' he diagnosed, transferring
both her hands to one of his and using his freed hand to
caress her face.

I'm in deep trouble, she thought, running the tip of her
tongue across her swollen, tender lips as his hand lightly
skimmed across her middle, then slid more firmly down her
thigh.

'*Dio, cara*, kiss me!' he instructed, releasing her hands
and taking a step back from her.

Her response to the sound of his voice was so extreme
she didn't want to think about what would happen if he did
more than talk. Of course, inevitably she *did* think about
it. Jude had no control over the low feral moan that issued
from deep in her throat as she wound her arms around his
neck. Strong arms circled her waist as he effortlessly lifted
her face up to his level.

Their lips touched and there simply wasn't anything else.
His competence in the kissing department was only to be
expected, but it was the raw desperation that laced his expertise that enchanted her.

When they finally broke apart they were both panting as
their eyes reconnected. The need stamped on his dark, tense
features excited her almost beyond endurance.

She hadn't known that wanting someone could physically hurt.

Luca's eyes had followed every flicker of emotion across
her expressive face. It was fascinating to watch; he had
never seen anyone whose emotions were so close to the
surface. Her ability to respond and react as though everything she was experiencing was a first-time thing was
amazing.

As her eyelashes began to settle protectively against waxily pale cheeks he shook his head. 'No, I want to see your face.' As her chin lifted he pressed the lower half of his body to hers until their bodies were sealed thigh to thigh.

Jude's eyes flew open to their fullest extent as she felt the brazen pressure of his erection grind into the softness of her lower belly. His eyes burned into hers so hot she felt the prickle of tears sting the back of her eyelids. Everything about him was hot and she just wanted to be part of that heat, to lose herself in it and him. It never even occurred to her to pull back in protest; instead, back arched, she pressed herself into his heat and hardness, striving to seal their bodies even more intimately together.

He kissed her again and again, deep, searing kisses, as though he couldn't get enough of her. It took Jude longer to respond to the sound of the door opening than Luca.

When the children ran into the room Jude was banging the TV remote on her thigh, babbling in a high-pitched voice, 'It must need new batteries and I really wanted to watch that documentary.'

Luca adjusted his jacket and smoothed down his tousled hair, no trace of the paralysing embarrassment she was feeling evident in his relaxed manner. 'Which documentary would that be?'

Jude's reproachful gaze flickered to his face.

Oh, God, how could I?

'I...I forget.'

'Aunty Jude, have you been crying?' Joseph's voice shattered the tense atmosphere.

With a bright smile on her face, Jude turned to the little boy. 'No, of course not, darling.' But she felt like it now. Her entire body burned with humiliation. It was a nightmare—the one where you were in the supermarket when you realised you were only wearing your undies, and they weren't the nice glamorous ones but the ones that had seen too many wash cycles.

She couldn't look at him, but she was overpoweringly conscious of his scrutiny. Right from the off her reaction to him had been pretty schizophrenic, but to kiss him…? God, it had gone way beyond kissing.

'She *was* crying before cos you were lost,' Sophia announced.

'I wasn't lost,' Joseph denied indignantly. 'I knew exactly where I was. I have Daddy's sense of direction,' he explained proudly.

He sounded so like his father that Jude could hardly keep the tears in check. 'That,' she said in a shaking voice, 'is as maybe, but you must never, *ever* go anywhere without asking me first. Is that understood?'

To Jude's immense frustration the little boy glanced almost imperceptibly to the masculine figure beside her before coming up with a suitably contrite, 'Yes, Aunty Jude.'

All she needed was for Joseph, starved of a male role model, to decide to put Luca in that part. It was a very worrying development, because Mr Di Rossi was going to disappear off their horizon for ever any second now.

'Now I think we should all say a big thank-you to Mr Di Rossi,' she said brightly. What should I thank him for? Turning me into a sex-starved idiot, maybe? 'Especially you, Joseph, for being such a bother.'

'I wasn't a bother, was I, Luca? You like me, don't you?' he suggested with a guileless smile.

'And me,' his twin piped up, giving her brother a shove.

'You're both revolting.'

To Jude's total amazement this growled response appeared to delight the children, who both began to giggle helplessly.

'See, Aunty Jude, he likes us,' Joseph told her complacently.

Jude's eyes suddenly filled. She turned away, but not before Luca had seen the shimmer. A little bit of hero worship was harmless, but it concerned her that they were so hungry for love.

Maybe it's not *their* hunger for love you're worried about?

'Of course he likes you.' She smiled mechanically as memories of her wanton behaviour flashed kaleidoscope-fashion before her eyes.

'Can Luca stay for tea?'

'I'm afraid that isn't possible, children.'

Jude hated to see their little faces fall, but in the long run it was better for them not to nurse false hopes.

'Mr Di Rossi is a very busy man.'

Luca squatted down to child height. 'Perhaps one day you could come and have tea with me at my house in the country. I have a little girl who is only a little older than you two.'

'Wow, can we, Aunty Jude?'

'We'll see.'

Once she had reached the front door with Luca she allowed her anger to boil over. With a quick glance over her shoulder, she followed him into the corridor, leaving the door behind her ajar so that she could hear should the children need her.

Her hair lashed across her face as she spun around, eyes blazing, to face him. 'How dare you fob the children off with false promises?' she demanded in a furious whisper. 'It was cruel and unnecessary, but I don't suppose you thought beyond getting away without a fuss and remaining the nice guy,' she sneered, pausing to catch her breath.

'Well, congratulations, they think you're a hero, but it's

me who will see their faces when they don't get an invite
to tea.' She rubbed her nose vigorously with the back of
her hand as her feelings threatened to overcome her. 'You
can walk away and never think of them again—' she
frowned to hear the quivery note in her voice '—but *I'm*
the one who will have to come up with an explanation,'
she finished with breathless resentment.

Luca appeared to listen attentively but remained frustratingly unmoved by her recriminations. For several moments he just stood scanning her angry, tear-stained features with an enigmatic expression.

'*What?*' she demanded querulously when he just carried
on staring.

'You don't wish me to walk away? Is that the problem
here?'

Jude flushed at the sly insinuation in his amused voice.
'You walking away is the *solution*. You can vanish in a
puff of blue smoke for all I care.'

This childish declaration brought a sudden grin of quite
devastating charm to his lean face. 'You know, I suddenly
see the family resemblance. I think,' he decided, after peer-
ing at her through thoughtfully narrowed eyes, 'that it's the
pout.'

'I do not pout!' she denied crossly. Then she noticed his
eyes were still fixed on her lips and he wasn't smiling. Her
sensitive stomach flipped and she rushed into speech to fill
the dangerous silence developing. 'The problem is you lying to the children without thinking of the consequences. I
suppose the daughter doesn't exist either.'

'She does and her name is Valentina.'

'Oh!'

'And the only time I have not considered the consequences of my actions was when I kissed you.'

So fine, he regretted kissing her—she could live with

that. 'Forget it,' she suggested casually. 'I have. It was nothing.'

'It was many things, but we both know *nothing* is not one of them.'

'So what did you have in mind? Disgusting? Revolting? Well, let me tell you, for someone who didn't like it you seemed to be putting a lot of effort into it at the time!'

'Does frustration always make you this cranky?'

'Frustration?'

'That's the risk you take when you start something you can't finish.'

His meaning finally hit her. 'Good God, there was never any chance of…me…' She shook her head vigorously. 'None whatsoever!' she insisted.

His dark, implacable eyes drilled into her. 'You wanted me.'

More than I've ever wanted anything in my life.

'If we hadn't been interrupted we'd have ended up in bed, or, more realistically, on that nice rug. We wouldn't have made it as far as the bedroom.'

The erotic image his soft, insidious words conjured was so vivid that for a moment she could almost hear the hoarse pleas emerging from her mouth! She literally shook herself to expel the wanton images crowding into her brain.

'You're crude and disgusting!' she choked, pressing her trembling hands to her flaming cheeks.

His eyes brushed her face. 'And you are the most amazingly passionate woman I have ever met. It was like holding a flame in my arms.'

Me?

'We both know what I'm saying is so.'

Stubbornly she shook her head.

'And I did not lie to the children—I would like them to visit. We've just moved over from Italy and Valentina has no friends yet. It would be good for her to meet children near her own age. I could show you our new house—it is an old vicarage in the countryside. It had nine bedrooms—the housekeeper seems obsessed with keeping all those beds…?' He spread his hands in a very Latin gesture of appeal.

'Aired?'

'Thank you. I understand that sleeping in them is the best method of doing this. We could use them on a rotational basis.'

'I don't want to see your house, I don't want to sleep in your beds and I don't want to see you.'

'You would have me break my promise to the children?' he asked.

Jude literally ground her teeth in frustration. 'I would have you get lost,' she hissed ungrammatically. 'I don't want to sleep with you.'

'Don't you believe in fate? I do,' he revealed. 'And I think you and I are fated to be lovers.'

Luca looked out over the incredible vista of the city and didn't see a thing as he picked up the phone and dialled.

'Get me everything you can on a Judith Lucas—she lives in this building. *Dr* Lucas—she's a psychologist.'

'Finally getting therapy, are you? Good move. Listen, Luca, I know you pay me well, mate, but the private detective stuff really isn't in my remit.'

'I need someone I trust, Tom.'

There was a pause the other end. 'This isn't about what we were talking about earlier, is it?' There was a troubled note in the lawyer's voice.

'I think she might be my future wife,' Luca confirmed simply.

'You can't marry a total stranger, Luca.'

'Have you never heard of fate, my friend?'

'Fate! Have you been drinking, Luca?'

With a smile Luca poured a measure of brandy into a glass. 'Oh and, Tom, I'd like to know if she's slept with my brother.'

There was an even longer pause. 'And if she has would that make a difference?'

'Only to my tactics, not my intentions.'

'Remind me never to own anything you want, Luca,' the other man said wryly.

Luca replaced the receiver and took a swallow of the golden liquid, savouring the taste as it slid over his tongue.

CHAPTER FIVE

'CAN I have a kite?' the little boy asked wistfully, watching a child in the distance who was being taught the art of kite-flying by her father.

The response she'd always sworn as a child that she was never, ever going to say to *her* children sprang automatically to Jude's lips. 'Maybe.'

'Dad said I could have a kite.'

Jude bit her lip. 'I said we'll see, Joseph,' she said huskily. 'Now keep up, please, there's a good boy.'

'That's Luca!' Sophia suddenly shouted as she pointed to the path a little farther ahead.

'Luca! Luca!' Oblivious to Jude's remonstration not to run ahead, they both ran off.

Being a responsible adult meant she couldn't obey her own instincts, which were telling her to run too—in the opposite direction. Taking a deep breath and hoping that her knees would not fold under her at an inappropriate moment, she was left with no choice but to follow, but at a more sedate pace dictated by the buggy she was pushing.

It was possible to disguise the fact she was about two heartbeats away from total panic by the time she reached the group with a relaxed and confident smile. It was less easy to disguise the fact she could hardly breathe.

There was another man with Luca and a little girl who looked to be around seven or eight.

Pinning her glassy gaze at some point over Luca's shoulder, she hoped he'd put her raised colour down to her recent exertion, and *not* her inability to look at him and not imagine him wearing nothing at all! She let her stiff smile embrace all three, aiming for polite but distant.

The effort made beads of sweat break out across her upper lip. Moistening her dry lips with the tip of her tongue, she tucked her resilient curls behind her ears. Her racing heart was trying to batter its way out of her chest.

Her eyes skimmed over his tall, distinctive figure without focusing. It had taken her a sleepless night to reach an explanation she could live with—namely what she had felt and *done*, could all be attributed to her overwrought condition. A condition exacerbated by sleep deprivation, which everyone knew could make a person act peculiar.

A doctorate and all I can come up with is peculiar! If this whole scenario weren't so horrifying she'd have laughed.

'Dr Lucas…' Luca greeted her with his hand outstretched. One dark brow took on a satiric slant when she didn't make any effort to take his extended hand, but he didn't comment.

Touching him voluntarily was totally out of the question. A wave of heat washed over her as she looked at him—if she'd been overreacting last night, she still was.

Like her he was casually dressed, in a white tee shirt and black jeans, but, unlike her own faded denims that because of her recent weight loss fitted loosely over her hips, his clung lovingly to the well-developed lines of his long thighs.

She was suddenly neck-deep in a confused mess of high-octane excitement, sexual longing and fear.

'What a pleasant surprise.'

Speak for yourself.

Their eyes touched and she discovered he was lying. He'd known she was going to be here; maybe he'd even followed her. Oh, God! Now I think rich and powerful men are following me—I really have lost it!

Despite the fact she knew it made no sense, her gut feeling this was no accidental meeting persisted. Maybe the kiss had kept him awake all night too. Jude, who didn't number vanity amongst her faults, gave a self-derisive little grimace. He'd probably forgotten she existed before he'd returned to the luxury of his own apartment.

'Can I introduce my friend Carlo?'

Jude's eyes widened fractionally as she focused on the older man. The thick-set figure, who was almost as broad as he was tall, smiled. The action pulled at the puckered scar that ran from one corner of his mouth to his ear, making him look even more sinister. Jude saw that he had kind eyes and smiled back, wondering where someone who looked like a bouncer fitted into the set-up. Her first guess would have been that he was some sort of bodyguard, but Luca had called him 'friend' so that ruled that out.

'And this,' Luca began, urging the reluctant child forward, 'is Valentina, my daughter,' he explained, pride in his voice. 'Say hello to Signorina Lucas, Valentina.'

She did so in halting English, adding, 'I'm sorry my English is not so good.'

'It's a lot better than my Italian,' Jude said with a warm smile at the shy little girl. 'You have a very beautiful daughter, Mr Di Rossi.'

'Yes, I do.'

The little girl dimpled and blushed madly.

'Actually, Dr Lucas, it is fortuitous meeting you here. I was wanting to speak with you.'

'You did?' Whatever Luca wanted to say to her, Jude was sure she didn't want to hear it. 'I promised the children they could play on the swings,' she said quickly. 'Another time perhaps.'

As she turned away, calling the twins, strong fingers curled around her upper arm, cutting into her flesh through the cotton of her shirt.

'Now!'

Startled, she spun back. Her eyes collided with his and she could see the steely determination shining through his casual attitude.

'Valentina too is wanting to go to the playground. Carlo will take them whilst we have out little…chat.'

When he said it, 'chat' had a very sinister sound to it.

'You can have no fears about leaving the children in Carlo's care; he is more than capable. I would trust him with my Valentina's life.'

When Luca said something like that you got the impression he meant it quite literally.

'Well, after that recommendation what can I say?' she responded weakly. 'I'll keep Amy with me,' she told the big man when he approached her.

'Aunty Jude's going to get us a kite,' Jude heard Joseph boast to Valentina as they left under the watchful eye of the sinister-looking Carlo.

Despite Luca's reassurances Jude was still concerned. 'Does he work for you?'

'He worked for my father originally, but he has worked for me for some time.'

'Doing what?'

'He takes care of Valentina.'

'As a bodyguard?'

'That is part of his role, certainly. What is wrong now?' he asked, his impatient gaze fixed on her apprehensive face.

'Does he…is he…?' She lowered her voice to a confidential whisper. 'Does he carry a gun?'

'Several.'

Jude gave a gasp of alarm and then saw his expression. She coloured. 'You're joking.'

'I do not employ a private army who follow me around with bulging shoulder holsters—at least not in this country,' he delivered, straight-faced. 'Carlo,' Luca told her, 'is a gentleman in the true sense of the word. Now, shall we sit down?' he suggested, gesturing to a convenient park bench.

'I'd prefer to stand.'

Luca looked amused by her petty defiance. 'As you wish.'

'I didn't think my wishes came into it,' she remarked, rubbing her arm.

A frown formed on his formidably handsome features. 'I hurt you?'

'Don't worry, I'll survive.'

Their eyes locked. 'I am sorry,' he said stiffly. 'You are so tiny, delicate...' His glance flickered over her slender frame.

'But tough,' she promised him. Made uncomfortable by his intense scrutiny, she rushed into speech. 'Now, why don't you do us both a favour and say what you've got to? Though I really can't imagine what you want to talk to me about.'

He met her unfriendly and suspicious eyes. 'Are you always this prickly?'

'Prickly?'

'Touchy, irritable, belligerent...' he enumerated, ticking off these characteristics on the tanned fingers of his left hand.

'I am not—' she began, and then saw his expression. She bit her lip. 'I can just think of better things to do with my time.'

'Do I make you nervous?' he continued without giving her an opportunity to reply. 'You know what I think?'

Jude folded her arms across her chest. 'No, but I'm pretty sure I'm about to find out,' she observed with a long-suffering sigh.

'I think you are antagonistic towards me because I witnessed your loss of control. You allowed me to see your vulnerability and now you are embarrassed about it,' he concluded with chilling detachment.

'Who gave you the right to stand there and dissect my feelings like I'm a specimen in a jar?' she demanded furiously.

'Afraid I'm muscling in on your professional territory?'

'Do you have a problem with psychologists?' she asked grimly. This was just the latest in a long line of sarcastic jibes on the subject.

'No, I have a problem with someone who needs help but is too stubborn to admit it.'

'And that's your professional opinion, is it?' At least he hadn't brought the wretched kiss into it.

His expressive shoulders lifted infinitesimally as he slanted an expectant glance towards her. 'And of course there is our unfinished business.'

Jude dealt him a look of loathing. 'There's nothing to finish because nothing started, and if you don't mind I've been trying not to think about what happened all night long so the last thing I want is some long drawn-out post-mortem now. It's not something I'm exactly proud of!'

'You're ashamed of your appetites?'

Put like that it made her sound an uptight bundle of repressions. 'I didn't say that!'

'If you're not proud, surely that means you are ashamed. But I digress…now, to what we are here for…'

'You mean it's not to insult me?'

'You have been left with the care of your brother's children. Your brother was a spender not a saver, and with share prices being as depressed as they are the value of what investments he did have has been more than halved.' His eyes sought Jude's for confirmation but she was too shocked to respond.

'The rest of the money is tied up in trusts for the children's education. There is the house, of course...' he mused. 'After the mortgage is paid off, how much would you say will be left over?'

With a sick feeling of dread in the pit of her stomach, she looked at him, her eyes wary. 'You tell me,' she replied hoarsely. 'You seem to be pretty well informed. *How*?' she added. 'How do you know all of this?' And why, she thought silently, did he want to?

'The how is not important.' He brushed aside her angry question impatiently.

'It is to me,' she promised. Though not as much as the much more perplexing 'why'...?

'You are in a situation from which there seems no deliverance.'

'I happen to have a well-paid job—not by your standards, maybe, but—'

'Ah, yes, your job,' he derided softly. 'The one you enjoy so much. You want to work.'

Her eyes narrowed. 'Is that a crime?'

'Not at all, but you no longer have just yourself to consider. You are faced with the dilemma of a working mother. High-cost child care, the needs of the children balanced against your desire for a career?'

All true and very depressing, though until he'd so eloquently summarised it she had managed to put it to the back of her mind. 'Listen, where exactly is this going?' she interrupted, seriously alarmed to hear him calmly discussing things she'd avoided thinking about herself so far.

'I have a suggestion to put to you, a solution...'

'Why would you want to help me?'

'Marry me.'

A strangled laugh emerged from Jude's throat. She tried to walk away—she didn't exactly relish being the target of some sort of sick joke—but she appeared to have lost most of her voluntary motor function.

'The idea of marriage to me is so amusing?' He didn't sound particularly put out.

'I take it that is what passes as a joke where you come from?' she finally managed hoarsely. 'I suppose the next thing you'll be telling me is you have fallen desperately in love with me?' She gave a slightly wild laugh.

'I would not insult you by suggesting anything so absurd.'

'*Thank you,*' she returned drily.

'I,' he announced, 'am your way out of a difficult situation.'

'My white knight, in fact…' she suggested.

He watched sombrely as she smiled as if at a private joke. 'If you like,' he conceded with the air of a man willing to humour her. 'If you marry me you will be free to pursue your career untroubled by concerns for the children. They will be well provided for.'

'You mean you're going to give up your job and become a house-husband? How very modern,' she trilled admiringly. He looked serious, he sounded serious, but logic told her he couldn't possibly be.

Her frivolity caused his brows to draw into a dark line of disapproval. 'I am getting the feeling that you're not taking this seriously.'

'And that surprises you?' Jude buried her face in her hands and then slid her hands downwards until just her eyes were revealed. 'Tell me, Luca, do I look mad?'

He seemed to consider her satirical question an invitation

to search her face. 'No,' he pronounced after several uncomfortable moments of searching scrutiny. 'You look exhausted. Did the children not have a good night?'

'No, I…' She stopped; she could hardly explain that she'd spent the entire night reliving his kiss. It didn't matter how hard she'd tried to fill her head with other things, she hadn't been able to blank it out. 'Didn't sleep,' she ended abruptly.

'Neither did I,' he supplied surprisingly.

But not for the same reason as me, she thought despondently. It didn't seem fair that he was the picture of glowing health and vitality after his sleepless night whilst she, by his own mouth, looked terrible.

He bent and picked up a toy that Amy had thrown from the pushchair, giving Jude a view of the back of his head and neck. Her oversensitive stomach muscles clenched as she observed the way his dark hair curled into his nape. He straightened up and Jude quickly lowered her gaze.

From under her lashes she watched him smile and return the toy to the child. That smile held none of the sneering arrogance he reserved for her, and suddenly Jude was seized by an irrational desire for him to smile at her that way. Amy might not have understood a word of the Italian he spoke, but she was clearly charmed by it. Jude watched the interchange, marvelling at the alteration in the man when he was around children.

'Well, as you're not about to announce your undying love for me, perhaps we should get down to what this is really about.' She folded her arms across her chest and adopted what she hoped was a suitably hard boiled expression. 'What would you get from marrying me?'

'I get insurance.'

'Insurance?' she echoed blankly.

'My daughter's grandparents are trying to contest custody of Valentina, or, at least,' he corrected, 'their son and his wife are.'

'Why would they do that?' Jude asked, startled.

'Because they think I'm a bad father?'

'No!' Jude responded without thinking.

A look she couldn't quite analyse passed across his dark face. 'Thank you,' he said quietly.

Jude blushed. 'Well, you obviously love your daughter even if you are…'

'A womanising rat with a reputation for violence? That,' he continued smoothly before Jude could agree with or deny his analysis, 'is exactly my problem.'

'What about Valentina's mother? I assume you are not together?'

'We were *never* together.'

The peculiar emphasis in his voice made Jude frown. 'But surely she has some say.'

'She is dead.'

Jude's eyes softened with sympathy. 'Oh, I'm sorry. How? Sorry.' She shook her head with embarrassment. 'I didn't mean to pry.'

'I have just asked you to marry me, you are allowed to pry—a little.' This qualification made it clear there were limits to how far her curiosity would be tolerated. 'Maria killed herself just after Valentina was born. Apparently she was suffering from a severe form of post-natal depression.'

'Post-natal psychosis.'

He nodded. 'Unfortunately the condition went undiagnosed.'

Which would explain his antagonism towards her profession; many people lumped together psychiatry and psychology. 'That's terrible.'

'And in the past.'

Jude found herself wondering if he dismissed the past

because it held too many painful memories. Had he loved Valentina's mother so much that it hurt to recall what he had lost?

'You know, I really don't think you have anything to worry about,' she reflected, so caught up in the story he had told that for a moment she forgot why he was telling her.

'That's all right, then.'

Her lips tightened at his derisive tone. 'Unless the stories of your financial empire have been exaggerated?' Her brows lifted as she shot him an interrogative glare to which he responded with an almost amused shake of his head. 'Well, in that case I'm sure you can afford the best legal advice there is.'

'I can, and it agrees with you—I would most likely win a court battle. However a court battle would be a messy business and dredge up a number of things I'd prefer stayed buried.'

'I'm not surprised, under the circumstances,' she admitted thoughtlessly. 'It must be awful to read things like that about yourself in the newspapers.'

She heard his stark inhalation and looked up to find his piercing gaze of displeasure fixed upon her face.

'It isn't *my* embarrassment I'm concerned about,' he told her, continuing to regard her as though she were something unpleasant on his shoe. 'I would like to save Valentina from being the focus of speculation and unwanted media attention.'

'I agree it is terribly unfair that innocent members of the family suffer for the failings of one person. Perhaps you should have thought of that before you—'

'My *failings*?' His incredulous echo cut through her critical condemnation. 'So my daughter is suffering because of my sins?' he enquired, his glittering gaze fixed on her face.

Jude didn't see why she should back down. 'Well, I'm sorry if you don't like it, but it seems to me that for someone who complains about it you do seem to court publicity.'

His eyes narrowed. 'You may well be right. But think about this,' he suggested in a silky, lethal voice. 'I take a stroll in the park, I sit down and chat to a pretty girl with—' he paused to murmur something soft in Italian to Amy '—a baby,' he added, his eyes hardening as they swivelled to Jude.

'The next day I wake up to discover I have a love-child and you and your friends are being doorstepped by so-called journalists for details of your affair.'

Jude's eyes had widened to their fullest extent. 'You're not serious, they couldn't?' His dark brows lifted. 'Could they?' She couldn't help glancing over her shoulder. Then laughed nervously at her own foolishness. 'That would be dishonest.'

Her relieved comment caused Luca to throw back his head and laugh. 'Are you *really* that naïve?' he wondered, the amusement fading from his face.

'I'm not naïve,' she denied, stung by the accusation.

'Don't knock it, it's a rare quality.'

Jude, her thoughts still revolving around the life he had described, didn't register his response. The idea of a life where what you had for dinner was a story filled her with horror.

She shook her head. 'How do you live that way? I think I'd want to hide away behind tall walls patrolled by armed guards.'

'That is one solution, certainly,' he agreed.

'But not yours?'

His head moved fractionally in acknowledgement. 'I take security precautions.' He shrugged. 'I would be a fool not to, but the opinion of strangers has never been something which has kept me awake nights.' Again the inimical shrug. 'Life is too short.'

'Lucky you.'

He shot her a sharp look as if suspecting her of sarcasm, but he found only wistful envy in her face.

'You worry about what people think of you?'

'Everyone does…' she began, then with a wry smile corrected herself. 'Except you.'

'Do you worry what people will say when you marry me?'

She couldn't let him get away with that one. 'Don't you mean *if*?'

He bared his teeth in a wolfish smile and shook his head. 'No,' he replied simply.

What did a person do when faced with such impregnable self-belief? 'You just decide something's going to happen and assume that it will, don't you?'

'I have a positive attitude to life.'

Jude was torn between laughter and tears; the man was totally unbelievable. 'That's what I used to think about me, before I met you.' She hard the rising note of hysteria in her voice and took a deep, steadying breath before continuing. 'In answer to your question, people who know me know I have no intention of ever marrying. They would never believe it.'

'Well, if that concerns you, you will just have to convince them that falling desperately in love has altered your whole perception.'

The colour drained from Jude's face as she shook her head. 'That's ludicrous,' she responded faintly.

'It is,' he agreed. 'But I think you'll find that people generally accept *love* as being a perfectly valid excuse for aberrant behaviour that under normal circumstances would see you sectioned under the Mental Health Act,' he observed with a contemptuous sneer.

'Did I miss something here? Did I say yes to you and not notice?' She slanted a frustrated look at his bronzed chiselled face. 'Why me? Why marry me?'

'You have the children.'

This had gone beyond surreal. 'An instant family unit.'

Hearing the edge of hysteria creep in her shrill question, Luca shot a wary glance at her averted profile.

'Wouldn't it be more practical…?' Jude laughed and lifted a hand to her brow. What was she saying, *practical*…? Could there be a less appropriate term to use when describing such a totally insane proposition? She exhaled a gusty sigh and continued in a more composed tone. 'More…more rational,' she corrected, 'to marry someone you already know, someone you've…?'

A flicker of amusement crossed his dark features as her expressive face was suffused with colour. 'Slept with?'

Seeing him enjoying her embarrassment, Jude lifted her chin. 'Well, it would make a lot more sense.'

'The sort of qualities which make my lovers desirable companions are not those I am looking for in a wife.'

'I don't think I want to know what those are!' Jude exclaimed in an accent of outrage. Then almost immediately contradicted herself by demanding angrily, 'I suppose you think wives should be placid, undemanding creatures who don't mind their husbands seeking their excitement elsewhere!' she accused with disgust.

'You misunderstand me,' Luca replied, thinking he had rarely seen anything less placid than his proposed bride's impassioned face.

Jude snorted. 'My wife doesn't understand me—not very original! And we're not even married yet. Not,' she added hastily, 'that we're going to be.'

'We are,' he promised her. 'you just haven't admitted it yet.'

God, what did she have to do to get it through to him she wasn't going to say yes? Jude wondered helplessly. She suspected it would probably take a bomb to puncture his hermetically sealed confidence.

'When was the last time someone said no to you?'

A dangerous glint appeared in his dark eyes. 'Last night, as it happens.'

'Listen, I'm not going to marry you. There are no circumstances in this world that would make me say yes! *None!*' she yelled. 'I'm going to find the children and if you follow me I'll have you arrested for stalking,' she threatened him wildly.

CHAPTER SIX

JUDE picked up the phone for the fourth time in as many minutes, her face creased with indecision.

'This is stupid,' she told herself. 'I'm going to ring him.'

After all, what was the worst that could happen if she called out the doctor and it was a false alarm? He would think she was a time-wasting neurotic woman who couldn't distinguish a tummy bug from a life-threatening illness. If on the other hand it wasn't a tummy bug and she didn't seek medical help—well, when you thought about it that way there was no choice.

The doorbell rang just when the mechanical voice the other end was telling her that the surgery was closed and giving her an alternative number to ring if it was an emergency. Jude, who couldn't imagine why anyone would ring a doctor's surgery at this time of night if it weren't an emergency, repeated the number under her breath whilst she tried to find an elusive pen—the one she *always* kept by the phone.

The doorbell in the background kept on ringing. With an exclamation of irritation she ran across the room and flung it open, still repeating the numbers under her breath like a mantra.

'Go away,' she snapped at the tall figure, then added, catching hold of his arm, 'No, don't...'

'I wasn't going to,' Luca replied, his perceptive glance moving thoughtfully over her face.

'Have you got a pen?'

This terse demand made Luca blink. 'A pen?'

Jude ran her fingers through her hair in frustration. 'Yes, a pen, the thing you write with.' Closing her eyes to concentrate, she began repeating the number under her breath.

It was a few moments later, when she had the number written down, that she started to see how her behaviour might have seemed a little strange.

'Thank you,' she said, handing Luca his pen back.

'Keep it.'

Jude didn't lower her hand, their eyes touched, and though there was a flicker of irritation at the back of his eyes he shrugged and took it off her.

'I had thought you might enjoy a little adult company once the children had gone to bed,' he observed as he tucked the pen back into his inside pocket. His eyes lifted. 'But it looks as though I disturbed you,' he acknowledged, his eyes skimming the cotton nightdress she wore even though it was still only ten p.m.

'You always disturb me.' Jude didn't even register what she had said, let alone the effect her words had had upon Luca. 'Oh, my God, I don't believe this,' she groaned in frustration when she got an engaged signal. Receiver clutched to her chest, she ran a hand across her face and was surprised to discover the wetness of tears.

'What is the matter?'

She lifted her head. 'Are you still here?' She looked at the bottle of wine in his hand and gave a bitter smile. 'Sorry, it looks like I've ruined your seduction scene.'

Her attempts to redial were frustrated by a large hand that depressed all the keys.

'Tell me who you are ringing with such urgency.' His brows drew together in a straight line. 'A boyfriend?'

'A boyfriend?' she repeated as though he were mad. 'I'm ringing a doctor. At least,' she added wryly, 'I'm trying to.'

'A doctor! Are you ill?'

She shook her head. 'Not me, Joseph—at least, I think he is. It's probably nothing, but I—'

He closed the door and immediately his overpowering presence filled the tiny vestibule. 'Tell me.' When she showed reluctance he added, 'Sometimes it helps get things in perspective to have another person there as a sounding-board.'

Jude would have dearly loved to tell him to go to hell, but the fact was he was right and this was no time to be allowing personal animosity to dictate her actions.

Animosity…is that what you call it? She shook her head to silence the ironic laughter.

She sighed. 'All right, I suppose you'd better come through, but keep it down,' she added, nodding to the figure curled up under a duvet on the sofa. 'Sophia,' she explained. 'Joseph wanted to come in with me when he couldn't settle, but there wasn't much room so I popped Sophia on my bed.'

'You're sleeping on a sofa?' He sounded appalled.

'Only temporarily,' she gritted defensively. She perched on the arm of chair as far away from the sleeping child as possible and, eyes fixed on her bare feet, she began to recount the sequence of events over the past couple of hours.

'I went to bed after the children fell asleep about eight,' she explained. Ironically the idea had been to catch up on some lost sleep. 'Joseph woke me about half an hour later. He wanted to get into bed with me—they do sometimes. About half an hour later he started complaining of tummy pains and he was really hot. He seems to be drifting in and out of sleep now…I didn't know what to do, wait until morning or call out the doctor…'

Luca's response was immediate and straightforward. 'Well, if you have any doubts whatever obviously you must get a medical opinion.'

She gave a sigh, relieved to have her decision validated. 'What if the doctor won't come out?' she questioned, revealing another anxiety. 'It'll probably be hours before he gets here anyway. Perhaps I should take him straight to Casualty or one of those drop-in places?'

'Traipse a sick child across the city in the middle of the night?'

'You don't think it's a good idea, then? Has Valentina ever been sick in the middle of the night?'

'All children have been sick in the middle of the night— it is in their remit.' Luca looked at her pale, distressed face and then without a word withdrew a phone from his pocket. 'Another thing all children have in common is their recuperative powers,' he said before punching in a number.

The conversation was short and conducted in Italian. 'A doctor is coming.'

A wave of relief washed over her. 'Just like that?'

'He is a friend.' He stopped as Joseph's distressed cries rang out.

'I want my mummy!'

In that split second before she broke eye contact it had all been there in her eyes for Luca to see—the desperate pain and anguish. And then even before his brain had told him what he was seeing she was turning away, a hand pressed to her trembling lips.

Under the thin covering of cotton he could make out the shadowy curve of her spine and the feminine flare of her hips. He watched her hunched shoulders heave and was gripped by an overpowering desire to take away the problems that weighed her down. The strength of feeling astonished him.

For the first time he saw her as more than a means of solving his problem or a woman whom he had found himself strongly—*extremely* strongly—attracted to. He saw someone who was facing a bad time in her life with guts.

'It does get better, you know.'

His soft words made her lift her head. 'Oh, God, don't say anything nice to me,' she begged him, 'or I'll cry. I have to go to Joseph, he needs me...' She smiled awkwardly. 'And thank you for organising the doctor; it was—kind of you.' The perplexed frown that pleated her brow spoke volumes.

'Is there anything else I can do?'

'You can leave that if you like,' she said, nodding to the bottle in his hand.

Luca's own eyes drifted in the same direction; slowly he began to shake his head. 'Drinking alone is not a good habit to get into.' For a second she thought he was adding secret drinker to the list of faults he must have ticked off beside her name. Then he placed the bottle on the table and said. 'It stays, I stay.'

Jude, already halfway across the room, stopped and turned. 'That's really not—' Joseph cried out again and she bit her lip, threw one last confused look over her shoulder and hurried away.

By the time she had settled Joseph she could hear the soft, subdued sound of deep male voices in the other room.

'The doctor has come to see you, Joseph.'

'I don't want to see a doctor,' the child replied crankily just as two figures, preceded by a soft knock, entered the room. 'I don't like you,' he proceeded to tell the first figure, who Jude was astonished to see was magnificently attired in full black-tie glory. The significance of this outfit filled Jude with embarrassed dismay. Had Luca wielded the big stick and dragged the poor man away from a special occasion?

'Well, my first impressions of you are not all that favourable either,' she was amused to hear the man with slate-grey hair and dark eyes respond as he sat down on the edge of the bed. If he resented being dragged here he was hiding it well, she decided in relief.

'Though my friend, Luca here, tells me you are his friend also,' he added, casting a professional eye over the child's flushed face. 'So maybe we should try to get on.'

Jude saw the little boy flash a quick look at the second man; he received an almost imperceptible nod in return. 'All right, then. Where is Luca going?' he added, a note of panic in his shrill voice. 'I want Luca to stay.'

'I am going to make your aunt a cup of tea whilst the doctor here examines you. You must be a special patient because Dr Greco doesn't normally come to see people at home. I will see you a little later,' he promised as he made his exit.

Jude was impressed at how well the doctor handled the fretful little boy, and his eventual assessment, after a thorough but gentle examination, that there was nothing serious wrong beyond a mild stomach bug brought a relieved smile to her lips. She felt as though the weight of a small continent had been lifted from her shoulders.

'I could kiss you,' she admitted with a happy sigh as they left the room.

'I don't think Luca would like that,' the medic commented with an amused twinkle in his eyes.

'I wouldn't like what?'

Jude jumped and her heart started to thump a little faster.

'Me, kissing your bride to be.'

'Jude hasn't said yes yet, Alex,' Luca spelt out, a thread of annoyance in his deep voice. 'But you're right, I wouldn't like it, and neither I suspect would Sonia? Talking of whom, if you hurry you'll just make the second act.'

The other man rumbled something in Italian and turned

back to Jude, who hadn't moved a muscle since she'd heard
herself referred to as Luca's bride to be. Just how many
people had he shared this misinformation with?

'Just keep him on clear fluids,' she heard the doctor ad-
vise when she tuned back into the conversation.

She gave a tight little nod.

'And he'll bounce back in no time,' he added soothingly,
quite obviously attributing her rigidity to lingering concerns. 'But if you've got any worries,' he continued, 'don't
hesitate to call me. Luca has my number.' He nodded and
banged the taller man on the back.

'I feel terrible about bothering you over nothing,' Jude
admitted huskily. 'And I've obviously ruined your evening,' she said her pained gaze fixed upon his elegant outfit.

It was amazing how well Italian men wore clothes, she
reflected, sliding a secret sideways glance towards the other
Italian in the room. Now he would look simply magnificent
similarly clad, not that he looked half bad as he was, she
admitted, repressing an appreciative sigh.

'Actually you saved me from a interminable evening,'
he told her frankly. 'My wife,' he explained in response to
her sceptical expression, 'is the opera buff. I—according to
her—am the philistine. I usually disgrace myself by falling
asleep. Now is there somewhere I could wash my hands?'

Jude directed him to the bathroom. That left her alone
with Luca; the sleeping child's presence could be safely
discounted. And being alone with Luca scared her witless.

Did one piece of kindness cancel out the acres of unac-
ceptable behaviour that went before? Her most immediate
problem seemed to be what did she do first: thank Luca or
strongly protest him going around telling the world she was
going to marry him? There was a limit to the time you
could pretend someone wasn't there and she had already
exceeded it.

She took a deep breath, exhaled and turned her head.

It didn't take her long—long as in about five seconds of contact with those almost unbelievably seductive eyes—to figure out that she'd been totally wrong about her immediate problem. That status went to the charged atmosphere that was building up between them.

The build-up of tension in the air between them was almost palpable; the air, thick with it, crackled.

'I'm glad it's nothing serious. You were thinking appendicitis?'

'It crossed my mind. I suppose you think that's stupid of me?' We're talking, she thought, and everything sounds normal, but it's window dressing—just below the surface the tensions still seethe.

'Valentina had a headache and a gnat bite on her leg. I rushed her to a casualty department with suspected meningitis.'

A giggle was drawn from her. 'You didn't!'

One corner of his mouth lifted a sardonic half-smile. 'No,' he admitted, 'I didn't, but only because there was a consultant paediatrician staying to dinner.'

Her eyes widened. 'Dr Greco?'

He nodded. 'He is Valentina's godfather.'

'What did he say to you back there, when he spoke Italian?' she suddenly blurted out.

A veil came down over his expressive eyes. 'I'm sorry— we didn't mean to exclude you.'

'What did he say, Luca?'

'He said having to do the running for once might teach me a bit of humility. He seemed to like the idea of me running after a woman who wasn't interested. Only you are interested, aren't you, Jude?'

A surge of weakness washed over her. The sudden desire

to concede defeat and have the weight of responsibility lifted off her shoulders was enormous.

She was perfectly well aware that any number of women would equate what she was being offered with winning the jackpot on the lottery. She would be universally envied her wealthy, incredibly handsome husband. There was only one element in the happy-ever-after equation missing...

'I think, all things considered, you should look elsewhere for your insurance policy.'

A spasm of irritation crossed his face. 'I want a wife, not an insurance policy.'

'You want a wife who is an insurance policy,' she countered wearily.

'Semantics apart, what are these ''things'' you have considered?'

Something inside Jude snapped; she was just too tired to take part in this clever play on words any longer. 'You really want to know? Fine, I'll tell you. I'm interested in you, not marriage, and you're interested in marriage, not me. I'd say those differences are pretty irreconcilable.'

Ironically if she'd hadn't fallen in love with him it might have worked. In theory, acknowledging her feelings should have been an empowering experience; in reality she had rarely felt less in control of her fate in her life. It was easy to see why repressing was so popular!

'But whilst you're looking for someone more suitable, if you like we could...not when you find someone else, of course,' she added hastily. 'But until then...?'

'*While I am looking?*' An expression of total astonishment washed across his face. 'You are saying...?' He raked a hand through his sleek dark hair and gave a strange laugh before restarting in a slow, carefully measured tone. 'You are saying that you want to be my mistress but not my wife?'

'I wouldn't have put it exactly like that, but I suppose that about sums it up,' she admitted.

'*Dio!*' he ejaculated rawly as his glittering dark eyes raked her face. 'You never fail to surprise me, *cara*. You have given this matter some thought, it seems?'

Jude caught her full lower lip between her teeth and turned her attention to her bare feet. 'I haven't thought about much else but you since we met.' Had someone put a truth drug in her cocoa this evening?

The sound of his harsh inhalation brought her attention back to his face. 'You are tired and stressed.' His voice sounded oddly stilted.

'Oh, God, I've embarrassed you!' She gave a mortified groan. 'I'm so sorry, take no notice of what I say,' she begged. 'You're right, erratic mood swings, irrational behaviour—it's all classic signs of sleep deprivation.'

Her babble was cut off by a finger laid against her lips. 'I am not embarrassed, *cara*. I am…' He suddenly took her face between his hands. 'I am in a state of almost constant arousal since I met you. When you make an offer like that I do not feel embarrassment, I feel pain,' he revealed with an earthy laugh, which deepened as her eyes slid downwards over his lean male body.

A wave of scalding heat had engulfed her from head to toe by the time her wandering gaze settled back on his face.

'You see I wasn't exaggerating.' His face was wiped clean of mocking humour when he leaned towards her. The feathery touch of his warm breath lightly brushed her cheek; it sent tiny electric shocks skimming across her skin. When he added in a throbbing, throaty whisper, 'I want to make love to you right here, right now.' Her body swayed towards him as though their bodies were attached by some invisible thread. 'What wouldn't I give for a few hours alone with you to show you just how strong that need is?'

It was difficult to speak when you were burning up with lust and longing, but Jude forced the words out. Even the most desirable of situations—namely being lusted after by a man who turned you on just by breathing—had a downside.

'So you agree with my terms?' It wasn't necessary to speak above a whisper—the sides of their noses were almost grazing...their laboured breaths were intimately mingling.

'Hell, no!'

Jude's head jerked back. 'But you said—' she began to protest in agitation.

Luca slid a finger over the soft, full outline of her lips, effectively reducing her reasoning powers to nil. 'I said I want to make love to you. The only conditions that I abide by are my own.'

Jude had been crossing to the other side of the street to avoid men who liked to take charge and have it their own way all her life, and now she had fallen for a man whose arrogance was off the scale. Now *that* was irony!

'But you said...' she protested weakly.

'You think that I will take no for an answer now that I know you want me?'

'I thought you already knew that.'

He acknowledged her wry jibe with a tilt of his head. 'It's pleasing to hear you say it, *cara*. You will enjoy being my wife,' he promised. 'But,' he added, drawing himself upright, 'that is the last you will hear me say on the subject for the moment. You are tired, and nursing a sick child—it is not an atmosphere that lends itself to romance.'

So far it was lending itself pretty well. 'I can think of nothing less romantic than a marriage of convenience.'

His shoulders lifted in one of his elegant, peerless shrugs. 'A marriage of any sort is what two people make of it,' he claimed imperiously. 'Now to more immediate matters.' He picked up with a flourish a blanket that was draped over a threadbare overstuffed chair. 'I suggest you curl up in this chair and have a nap. I will wake you if Joseph needs you.'

'That's ludicrous.'

'Alex, Jude thinks it is ludicrous that she catches up on some sleep whilst I hold the fort. What is your professional opinion?'

Jude, who hadn't been aware of the doctor's entrance, gave him a quick smile and hoped he hadn't been standing there too long.

'My professional opinion is that you should take the opportunity to rest. My personal opinion,' he added, flashing a sly grin in the direction of the younger man, 'is that arguing with Luca is *always* a pointless and exhausting exercise. If argument fails he wears you down by attrition. Oh, and if you're worried about his welfare, don't,' he advised. 'Luca is one of those unnatural individuals who function perfectly well on a couple of hours' sleep.'

'Is this a conspiracy?' she asked, looking from one man to the other, her glance resting significantly longest on Luca. She was just too tired to resist or even think straight.

'Well, I'll go and check on Joseph and *maybe* I will take a short nap…' She stifled a yawn and pretended not to notice when the two men exchanged knowing glances. 'You promise you'll wake me if I'm needed.'

'You have my word.'

Jude awoke to the smell of coffee. She stretched, finding a number of painful knots in her spine.

'She's awake, she's awake!' a shrill voice carolled. 'Can I watch the cartoons now?'

Jude watched Sophia, a piece of toast in her hand, dance

around the room in her favourite bunny pyjamas whilst she waited for a response to her bellow.

Jude had just pushed aside the blanket when Luca appeared. The sight of his tall, vital figure jerked her from drowsiness to a full state of over-stimulated alert in two seconds flat!

Luca's jet eyes slid to hers and her oversensitive stomach went into a spiralling dive—my, God, but it wasn't fair that anyone could look that good on no sleep.

'Well, if she wasn't awake she is now. Do you mind?' he asked Jude. 'I did promise her.'

She gave a jerked abstracted, affirmative nod. 'You stayed all night,' she accused huskily.

Luca strolled over to the TV and turned it on with a firm, 'Half an hour only,' to the impatient child. 'I would have woken you, but Joseph settled well soon after you fell asleep. He woke up about half an hour ago asking for breakfast. He settled for juice and he's dozing again.'

'So you made a unilateral decision on my behalf.'

'It was hard to make any other sort when you were asleep.' He responded with maddening calm to her aggressive accusation. 'I can live with the snoring,' he added in a solemn aside.

'I do not snore, and it's not your job to look after my family.'

'I would like to make it my job.'

Jude couldn't think of a retort, cutting or otherwise, to this simple statement.

He gestured towards a laptop open on the table. 'I had some work to get through. I had it brought down, so you see I wouldn't have slept anyhow. It seemed more sensible for you to get some rest. I have not had time to bathe the baby…is something wrong?' he queried in response to the choking sound that emerged from her throat.

'The picture of The World's Most Notorious Playboy bathing a baby is kind of...surreal.'

He accepted her comment with a shrug. 'I had begun to think that maybe you were looking at me, not my public persona...'

'I am!' she protested unthinkingly as she stumbled sleepy-eyed to her feet. 'I think they give you a very hard time. If it was left to me I'd make sure those...' Belatedly becoming aware of his interested expression, she moderated her spirited defence and added awkwardly, 'It's just my father never had much to do with us...hands-on stuff, you know. You...Italian men seem more relaxed around children.'

My God, he stayed the night. I've spent the night with a gorgeous man and I'm still a virgin—this could only happen to me!

'Your father is alive? You should not keep coffee beans in the fridge,' he explained, planting a steaming mug on the occasional table beside her. 'It destroys the flavour.'

'Thank you,' she said quietly as she tried to smooth down her hair. 'My father lives overseas; my parents divorced when David and I were quite small. He has remarried, I have a half-brother and sister but I've never met them. We write...I write.' She gave a quick strained smile. 'He's not much of a writer.'

'When was the last time you saw him?'

'About five years ago. We speak on the telephone occasionally.' She gave a small brisk shrug and smiled to show that she was all right with the situation. 'Nice coffee,' she added, nursing the hot mug between her hands.

'Did he not come for your brother's funeral?'

'He wanted to, but apparently his wife was rushed into hospital just as he was about to board the plane. You were actually bang on when you said I was completely clueless about the hands-on stuff of parenting. I know all the theory, of course. I think being a decent parent is something you're born with.'

'I disagree. I think most people learn by a mixture of example and trial and error.'

'Well, I *definitely* didn't learn by example.'

'How so?'

She considered telling him to mind his own business and then thought—why not answer him? He was easy to talk to—maybe, she mused, it was because he gave the impression that he was actually listening, a rare quality in her experience. Most men she knew were much happier talking about themselves.

'My mother is a partner in a successful—*very* successful—PR firm. We, David and me, didn't exactly see a lot of her either. I used to resent the fact she never had any time for us, but later on I appreciated that her working was what paid for the lifestyle I enjoyed. I expect,' she added, looking at him over the rim of her mug, 'it seems a bit strange to you, that sort of dysfunctional family. I suppose you've got an enormous extended family and hundreds of brothers and sisters, aunts and uncles…?'

A wistful note entered her voice as she envisaged an idealised big, noisy family where everyone laughed, loved and argued loudly but presented a united front to the world.

'There is just Marco and myself; he is my half-brother. My own mother died when I was very young, and my father never stopped loving her. This was not a situation which made my stepmother feel secure or inclined her to be particularly fond of me. Once Marco was born she did everything she could to isolate me. She saw me as a rival for my father's affections, which was foolish because he never actually noticed I was there.'

Behind this prosaic declaration Jude saw the years of hurt beyond the protective wall he had built up. 'Oh, Luca.'

The soft sound of her voice brought Luca's attention back to her face. 'I'm sorry to spoil your image of a warm, loving family.'

Her tender heart ached for the unloved boy he had been. 'Well, you have your own family now.'

'Yes, *we* have?'

'Luca!'

He took her chin between his thumb and forefinger and smiled down into her flustered face. 'I have an early meeting I cannot miss, and breakfast to take with Valentina.' He placed a hand on his flat midriff. 'You must come live with me—my waistline will not survive two breakfasts on a regular basis. Think about the practicalities and we will speak later.'

Jude sat there disconsolately after he had left. Did he think saving money on fuel bills was going to swing her undecided vote? A hissing sound of frustration escaped through her clenched teeth. She didn't want to think about practicalities; she wanted to think about love!

'Stupid man!'

'Who's stupid, Aunty Jude?' Sophia asked, climbing up onto her lap.

Me for falling in love with someone who thinks marriage is a merger, she thought. 'Nobody, darling,' she replied, stroking the little girl's soft curls.

CHAPTER SEVEN

AFTER she had finally shut the door on the two women Jude allowed her fixed smile to fade. She was literally shaking with fury. The aftermath of shock made her feel as if she was going to be physically sick. She closed her eyes, leaned her back against the wall and waited for the waves of nausea to pass.

When he'd said he wouldn't take no for an answer it had not occurred to Jude that Luca would resort to this sort of scummy underhand tactics. Which makes me, she thought furiously, exactly what he accused me of being—ridiculously naïve. She ought to have realised what he was capable of—you only had to look at him to see that he was totally ruthless and without scruples.

It just went to show children and animals were not the benchmark of approval people claimed. Children loved him and he was a traitorous rat! Well, no more, the gloves were off and she was going to fight fire with fire. If he thought that he could scare and intimidate her...

A troubled expression settled over her pale features as she pressed her fingers to her drumming temples. A fine sweat broke out all over her body as she recalled the heart-stopping shock and apprehension she had felt when the two women had introduced themselves as representatives of social services.

A 'concerned neighbour'—they couldn't say who, of course—it transpired, had reported children's distressed crying all through the night. *Concerned neighbour*. Rage rushed through Jude as she looked back at that terrible half-hour. It hadn't taken the ladies from social services long to satisfy themselves that the children were fit and healthy.

They were actually extremely sympathetic about the situation, but did express concern about the cramped conditions, which Jude hastened to assure them were only a stopgap. Despite their assurances that they were more than happy with how she was coping, the spectre of being considered an unfit parent had raised itself in Jude's head. She was going to spend the next ten years looking over her shoulder, waiting for someone with an official-looking document to arrive and whisk the children away—because quite frankly you're not up to the job, she told herself.

A sudden knock on the door jolted her from her reverie. Her eyes narrowed as she drew herself to her full height— all five feet two inches of it—and shook back her hair. No doubt he just couldn't resist coming to gloat…she would give him gloat!

She wrenched back the door, her bosom heaving, her eyes blazing, and stopped, a taken-aback expression stealing over her face. '*Mother!* What are *you* doing here?'

Lyn Lucas, who had looked equally taken aback to be greeted by a blazing figure of retribution, recovered her composure as she stepped into the flat. 'Well, really, Jude, is that any way to greet your mother?' Delicately she kissed the air either side of her daughter's face. 'Especially as I've cancelled several meetings to be here.' Her brow wrinkled delicately, as though she was faintly mystified by her own actions. 'What,' she added in horror, 'have you done with your hair?'

Jude lifted a vague hand to her curly head. 'Oh, nothing, literally,' she replied absently. 'Listen, Mum, you couldn't just hold the fort for a few minutes, could you? Thank you, that's great, marvellous…they can watch a cartoon video.

Not the one in the machine—it scares Amy,' she yelled over her shoulder.

A look of total astonishment on her exquisitely made-up face, Lyn Lucas watched her daughter run off towards the lift.

'Granny Lyn!' a piercing young voice suddenly yelled. Squaring her narrow shoulders, Lyn Lucas stepped with fastidious care over the toys scattered across the wooden floor. 'Come and see what presents…Granny has for you, children,' she said, turning to her grandchildren with an attitude reminiscent of an early martyr.

Carlo opened the door. He took one look at Jude's stormy face and stepped aside to let her enter without asking for an explanation as to why she had presented herself unannounced.

'I will see if—' he began.

'Oh, he'll see me, all right!' Jude hissed, rounding like a spitting cat on the unfortunate retainer. She looked around the long hallway, her expression frustrated; there were at least a dozen doors leading off it. 'Where is he?'

'I believe he is in his bedroom, miss. Sixth door on the left, but—'

'Fine,' Jude flashed, baring her teeth in a savage grin as she turned on her heel and began counting off the doors under her breath as she passed them. 'One…*inevitable* I'll marry him! Two…the only *inevitable* thing is me strangling him with my own bare hands! Three, he's a manipulative, conniving rat!' By the time she had identified the correct door she had torn Luca's character to shreds and come to the conclusion that death was too good for him!

She took a deep breath and opened it without pause, not giving herself time to have second thoughts.

Luca lifted his head as the door banged against the wall

behind it, causing the lamps set either side of the king-sized bed to shudder. The incredulous frown that drew his dark brows in a straight line relaxed into a quizzical expression as an avenging goddess—of diminutive stature—hands set on curvy hips, strode aggressively into his bedroom.

He lowered the towel he had been about to dry his hair with and looped it around his neck. 'To what do I owe this pleasure?' He suddenly stopped what he was doing. 'Is it Joseph?'

'No, he's fine…I…I…' If Jude had considered the possibility, which she hadn't, she might have recognised that if you walked into a man's bedroom unannounced there was a very definite possibility you might see more than you wanted.

If you don't like it, don't look, the sarcastic voice in her head suggested. Jude carried on staring.

What was not to like? He was quite simply…*sublime*! The muscles in her calves and thighs began to twitch and quiver the way they did after a long run; her breathing went the same way.

Thirty seconds might seem a long time when you were waiting for your nail varnish to dry, but when your eyes were welded on the gleaming bronzed body of a half-naked man it seemed way longer. Especially when it was the same man you only had to think about to become a mindless mass of craving hormones. *Way longer!*

'Like you don't know why I'm here!' she sneered, finally recovering the power of speech. Cheeks burning, she turned her back on him—*about thirty seconds too late*! Thirty seconds during which her complexion had gone through several dramatic colour changes and she had struggled to remember what she was here for.

She stood there drawing air into her oxygen deprived lungs in great gulping gasps. Closing her eyes, she just prayed that the faint rustles she could hear indicated he was putting on some clothes. If he had it wouldn't be because he felt awkward at being caught semi-naked—unlike her, Luca had been totally unselfconscious.

Obviously he had stepped out of the shower literally seconds before she'd walked in. He'd still been wet—a glazed expression slid into her half-closed eyes and a voluptuous little shudder slid down her spine as she recalled the drops of moisture from his drenched hair streaming down his face. Besides the towel around his neck and the other tiny one wound loosely about his narrow hips, he hadn't been wearing a stitch.

Water droplets clung to each smooth inch and every hard angle of his taut, toned body emphasising the already clear definition of his perfectly developed muscles. There was not an ounce of surplus flesh on his greyhound-lean frame. Her greedy gaze had eaten up the details. He possessed incredibly long legs roughened over the thighs by a dusting of dark body hair. There was a similar but denser sprinkling across his broad chest that narrowed down to an arrow strip across his washboard-flat belly.

She couldn't even think about the way he looked without experiencing another sharp stab of immobilising lust.

Of course Jude had been aware that he was a impressively built man, that much was evident in the grace and controlled power of his slightest movement or gesture. Actually seeing with her own eyes *just how* impressive and powerful was something that it would take a very unusual woman not to be affected by, she told herself.

Despite Jude's stubborn efforts, it was hard to rationalise and impersonalise the effect Luca had upon her—there was something *extremely* personal about the knot of heat low in her belly.

'Tales of my omnipotence have been greatly exaggerated, so perhaps you'd like to fill me in... How is Joseph this afternoon?'

Even before he came into view the hairs on the back of her neck had informed her of his silent approach. As he walked past her Jude caught the clean male scent of him and experienced the pleasure-pain feeling again.

'Pretty rich to complain when it's the people you pay to promote you who most probably started the rumours of your omnipotence.'

He came to a halt a few feet in front of her wearing, to her immense relief, a robe in a silky black fabric.

A flicker of distaste passed over his lean features. 'I am not a commodity to be promoted.'

'Did I offend you? So sorry.' Her voice dripped malicious insincerity.

His eyes narrowed as he scanned her angry face. One dark brow lifted in sardonic enquiry. 'What is it I am meant to know, Judith?'

'Don't call me that,' she snapped. 'My name is Jude.'

He gave a very Latin shrug. 'I like Jude too.'

'*You* can call me Dr Lucas, and don't play the innocent with me.' Anything *less* innocent than the raw, earthy image of male virility he presented right now would be hard to imagine. 'You don't have a scruple in your entire body, do you? You'll do whatever it takes to get what you want and to hell with anyone else who gets hurt in the process...'

As he listened to her unflattering description of his character Luca's sardonic gaze continued to drift down to her passionately heaving bosom. He looks and I react, she thought, helpless to control the response of her own flesh to the brush of his lustrously lashed eyes.

'Finished?' he asked when she paused for breath.

'I've not even got warmed up yet,' she promised him grimly.

'Well, if this is going to be a long job why don't you make yourself more comfortable?' He inclined his head towards a sofa that was set against one wall. 'Or,' he added, a gleam appearing in his brooding, deep-set eyes, 'would you be more comfortable here?' he wondered, patting the opulent-looking bed.

Jude's eyes followed his gesture and a sharp thrill of excitement zapped through her body. The image that flashed through her head of tumbled bedclothes, and tangled limbs gleaming with sweat, made her throat close over. It was several moments before she trusted herself to respond.

'I think that you're comfortable enough for us both,' she choked, unable to control the movement of her eyes as they hungrily travelled down his long, lean, muscle-packed length.

'I'd have dressed,' he promised drily, 'if I'd known I was having a guest.'

She knew it was impossible, but when he looked at her *that* way… God, maybe he actually could read her mind! Even thinking the impossible made her stomach tie itself into terrified knots. What's wrong with me? The man's not a mind-reader, he's just a monster.

'Don't worry, I won't be staying long—I just came to tell you it didn't work.' She schooled her expression into something approaching boredom. 'The social workers could see that the children are well cared for—' she sniffed, her voice thickening emotionally '—*and loved*…'

He shook his head slightly with a look of blank incomprehension. He's very good, she marvelled bitterly. If I didn't know he was lying through his teeth I'd believe him myself.

'Social workers?'

An explosive sound of frustration escaped from between

her tightly pursed lips. 'Yes, the ones *you* reported me to. You have to be the lowest form of life ever to crawl out of the primeval slime and draw breath, and if you think you can frighten me…blackmail me into marrying you… Well, think again,' she declared defiantly. 'After your act last night and this morning I actually started thinking I hadn't been fair to you. I thought you were pretty heroic being so supportive and not taking advantage of me when you had the opportunity because I was vulnerable. That was a stroke of pure genius. I was *touched* by your restraint— how funny is that?'

'If it makes you feel any happier I spent most of the night regretting my…erm…*restraint*,' he interjected. 'I am a little confused—last night you revealed a desire to be my mistress?'

She saw his eyes were glittering and realised that underneath the sardonic mask he was not nearly so laid-back about this as he was pretending. Maybe he hadn't reckoned on her finding out. The irony was he hadn't needed the extra insurance; she'd been ready to say yes.

'Something,' she told him in a shaking voice, 'that I can't think about without being physically sick with shame! Are you listening to me?' she demanded as she wrathfully identified an expression in his face that suggested he had tuned her out. She raised her voice. 'Am I keeping you awake? I'm terribly sorry if I'm boring you.' Her lethal sarcasm appeared unappreciated.

'You have had a visit from social…what are these people called?' he demanded with a click of his fingers that suggested he was impatient that his extensive vocabulary had let him down on this occasion.

'Services,' she snapped, tapping her toe on the floor.

'Services…' With an air of purpose that created a draft he walked straight past her to the door, which he opened.

She noticed he left damp footprints on the waxed wooden surface.

Her eyes tracked upwards from his feet and hair-roughened calves over the areas barely concealed by the sexy black robe. Her stomach muscles cramped as imagining what the black silk concealed sent a flash of heat over her skin.

How, she wondered despairingly, was it possible to loathe someone and ache for them in every fibre of your body at the same time?

Watching him with an air of studied disinterest, she was struck once more by the incredible energy the man projected. He was like a force of nature—unstoppable—like a hurricane. Like the hurricane, when he ripped your life apart you couldn't help being fascinated by the sheer beauty of the elemental force that had inflicted the destruction.

Standing with one foot in the hallway and one in the room, he yelled something in Italian. Carlo's deep voice replied in the same language. He turned back to Jude.

She held up her hand. 'Don't waste your time or breath,' she advised cynically. 'I'm well aware that Carlo would swear on a stack of bibles he was the Prince of Wales if you asked him to. Though what the hell you've done to inspire such devotion in a decent man beats me.'

'Carlo is a deeply religious man. He would not lie with his hand on the bible. He likes you too, which is unusual,' he admitted with a thoughtful expression. 'Normally he does not care for my female friends.'

To be lumped together with his trophy girlfriends was just too much for Jude, who went a pretty shade of pink. 'I am *not* your friend!' she announced in a revolted tone. 'And,' she added, 'I am not a girl...that is, I am a girl, just not in this context.'

Luca stood there listening with an expression of polite

interest and showed no inclination to help her out as her garbled explanation became more fragmented.

'Oh, you know what I mean,' she finally concluded, wringing her hands in exasperation.

'Only for about fifty per cent of the time,' he admitted. Then added before she could respond, 'Mrs Montgomery.'

Jude gave an irritated shake of her head. 'I don't know any Mrs Montgomery.'

'I believe she lives in the apartment above you…?'

'She might do.' Jude shrugged. 'I've lived here twelve months and Marco is the only person I've had a conversation with and he only talked to me because he…' She stopped and blushed.

'You don't need to explain. You are female and have a pulse, that would qualify you.'

Jude's chin went up. 'I was going to say he found me attractive.'

'I suppose,' he conceded, 'that is not impossible.'

Jude folded her arms across her chest and issued an embittered, thin-lipped smile. 'You're *too* kind.'

'Did Marco invite you in here?' Despite his throw-away tone, the look he slanted her was strangely intent.

'This bedroom, you mean?'

His dark eyes flashed and Jude realised that she had unwittingly angered him, which was ironic because when she'd been trying she hadn't managed to. 'You are well aware of what I am asking—do not be obtuse.'

Jude could have quite legitimately claimed innocence because she didn't have a clue what he was getting at, but instead she shrugged and said, 'I'll be whatever I like.' And if you don't like it, all the better, she thought, in keeping with the childish theme as her unwillingly curious gaze swept around the large room for the first time.

Sunlight streamed in through three sets of patio doors

that led out onto a large roof terrace giving the room, despite the dark wood underfoot, an extremely pleasant, light, airy feel. Other than the bold original artwork on the walls, the rugs scattered over the gleaming floor were the only splashes of colour in an otherwise subdued-hued room. Equal restraint was evident in the furnishings of what was a sparingly, but expensively equipped room.

The splendid king sized *lit bateau* with its intricately carved frame was the one feature that didn't follow the 'less is more' rule. The decadent piece dominated the room, or it would have if the owner had not been present.

'You like?'

She looked up to discover his eyes on her face.

She shrugged but was unable to prevent her eyes straying back to the suggestive bed. A guilty flush mounted her cheeks.

'It says more about the bank balance than the man,' she offered nastily, 'but then that's always supposing there actually is any substance in the man—that he isn't just a pretty face and a set of well-developed pecs...?'

There was a moment's startled silence before Jude was frustrated to find her insults had fallen on unappreciative ears—nobody witnessing his burst of spontaneous laughter would have assumed he was cut to the quick!

Looking at him with his head thrown back to reveal the strong brown lines of his throat, it occurred to her that if any photographer had been in a position to capture that image it would have made his career. The human and *extremely* attractive image of a man famed for his iron control.

She might not possess the picture but Jude, experiencing a sudden flash of insight, knew that the image was indelibly imprinted into her brain. How many times at some future date will I remember this moment and think—I could have married him?

Would she regret the decision…?

What would David say if he knew that the incredibly famous and wealthy playboy had proposed to the little sister he'd called Judy? Would he have congratulated her on standing by her principles? Not likely, not David! He would have spotted her true feelings before she had.

You've had a better offer, have you, Judy? She could almost hear her brother's dry voice.

'Then this isn't a style you are comfortable with?' Luca's deeper voice, still tinged by the amusement, interrupted her moment of soul-searching.

'I find the minimalist look in a bedroom a little cold myself,' lied Jude, who knew that any room that held Luca and *that* bed was never going to feel cold to her!

Luca ran a hand through his dark hair, a hint of impatience creeping into his expression. 'I asked you a question,' he reminded her.

'I've forgotten what it was.'

'I asked has Marco ever invited you in here.'

'Why would Marco invite me into your bedroom?'

A hissing sound escaped through his clenched teeth. *'Have you slept with my brother?'* he rapped in a voice like a steel trap.

Jude's mouth fell open as slowly heat began to seep into her pale face until it was burning. 'I'd say that's none of your damned business.'

'On the contrary, as the man you're going to marry I'd say it is quite definitely my business,' he contradicted smoothly. 'You know,' he mused, 'for a psychologist you have a very uptight attitude to sex.'

Just when Jude had been about to rebut this outrageous claim—both of them!—he added in a honey-coated drawl that sent secret little shivers up and down her spine, 'There should be no secrets between us, *cara*.'

'Does that mean you're going to give me chapter and verse on all your mistresses?' She gave a caustic laugh and felt sick as her fevered imagination supplied images of Luca in that bed with one of the innumerable beauties she'd seen hanging on his arm in news articles. 'I really don't have the stomach, or for that matter the odd month to spare, for that!'

Dark eyes scanned her flushed face and abruptly the frown lifted. 'You are jealous,' he discovered.

CHAPTER EIGHT

BEFORE Jude could smack Luca's smug face, or hotly disclaim this preposterous claim—or both—he seamlessly picked up the theme he had dropped earlier. It made Jude dizzy just trying to keep pace with his thought processes.

'I mention Mrs Montgomery,' he explained, nothing in his manner suggesting he'd been interrogating her about her sex life seconds earlier, 'because apparently we had a visit from that lady earlier this week, or so Carlo tells me. I was not at home.'

Jude, who found the name conjured an image of a rather stern, hatchet-faced woman, thought he might have been lucky.

'I understand most of the other residents were treated to a visitation too.'

'Well, I wasn't, and I really don't see what this has got to do with—'

'She wanted us to sign a letter complaining about the noise issuing from one of the apartments.' He watched her freeze, then try very hard to hide her anxiety—a poker player this girl was not! 'Your apartment.' She gulped. 'I think she found Carlo's attitude perplexing. He couldn't understand why, if there were babies crying at all hours, she did not go and offer the mother her help. But then British restaurants which ban children are equally a mystery to him. Italian culture does not discriminate in this way,' he explained. 'Children are considered a gift, not something adults need to be shielded from.'

Whilst he had raised some very interesting points on cul-

106

tural differences, Jude's attention was not at that moment concentrated on the British attitude to children. She was totally humiliated. She'd bounced in, oozing moral superiority, so sure—so very sure—that Luca was the person responsible.

Of course, now it was too late she recognised that if she had actually stopped and thought, not leapt in with guns blazing, she would have realised that the time-scale didn't fit the facts. She had only met Luca two days before, whereas the younger of the two women had revealed that they had received the complaint several days earlier. To add insult to injury, she recalled that the horrid Mrs Montgomery had been involved in a similar dispute with another neighbour.

But she hadn't stopped or thought, which was why she was standing here with egg all over her face struggling to say sorry to the one person in the world she least wanted to grovel to.

'Mrs Montgomery reported the tenants in one of the ground-floor flats when they had a puppy—there was a clause in their lease,' she recounted unhappily.

'That seems in character.'

'Then it really wasn't you who reported me?' she whispered.

'I'm sorry, but no.'

Jude groaned.

'I have to assume that Mrs Montgomery didn't canvass the support she needed and chose an alternative course of action.'

'Oh, God!' She took a deep breath and lifted her chin. 'I suppose I owe you an apology,' she admitted grudgingly.

'Marry me and we will call it quits.'

A startled hiss was drawn from her throat as Jude's wide eyes meshed with his. Two of the very last things she had expected to see were humour and warmth, but both were there in those dark, liquid depths. Suddenly she was more confused than ever. She shook her head and a shaky laugh was drawn from her tight, aching throat.

'Don't you ever give up?'

'No.' This time there was no humour in his eyes; instead she saw something that made her stomach dip violently.

'I know it's no excuse but I was scared,' she began to explain hurriedly in a broken voice. 'You know, at the thought of someone taking the children off me.'

Luca saw the luminous eyes she raised to his face were filled with very real horror.

'In fact, you would have done anything to stop that happening, wouldn't you, Jude?'

He was right. When did that happen? she wondered.

Luca continued to hold her eyes with a steady, questioning gaze.

'*Oh!*' she exclaimed, when the penny dropped. 'You're saying that's why you...that's the way *you* feel...?'

'We have finally discovered some common ground, it would seem.'

'A few days ago,' she admitted, 'I would have been grateful if someone had taken the responsibility off my shoulders.' Tears of shame stood out in her eyes as she bit down hard on her lower lip to stop it trembling. 'I know you probably don't think my feelings can compare with those of a biological parent...obviously I don't know what it feels like to be a mother, but I just can't imagine I could feel more for a child of my own.'

'Do not assume to read my mind or know my opinions.'

There was a note in his harsh intervention that brought her frowning attention to his face. His brooding expression did not further enlighten her and she was left with the vague feeling she had just missed something that was significant.

'I know you care for the children,' he added shortly. 'That is not the issue here.'

'I thought David was mad making me their legal guardian...mind you, there isn't anyone else, except Mum.' The intensity of his regard made her nervous. 'Correction,' she added with a laugh. 'There isn't anyone else...' Her eyes widened in alarm. 'Oh, God, I left the children with Mum. I should go...' She turned towards the door but Luca, who moved remarkably quickly for a man of his size, got there before her.

She faced him warily, her heart thudding like a sledgehammer against her breastbone. 'I really have to go...' To her dismay the words emerged minus the necessary ring of conviction. In fact, there was a troubling note that suggested she wouldn't mind someone persuading her to change her mind.

'Would it not be worth some...sacrifice on your part to ensure that there are never, ever any knocks on the door in future? That the children have a secure future...' He held up his hand. 'Do not insult me by pretending you have not thought about my proposition, Jude. Even when you were ridiculing it you were thinking about it. You are an intelligent woman—do not let your prejudices stand in the way of you making the right decision.'

'Marriage isn't meant to be a sacrifice.' She was relieved to hear herself sound almost normal.

It was hard to speak, when he stood between her and freedom. On previous occasions she'd experienced the way her brain shifted down a gear when she was close to him, but this time it was debilitating. As if to compensate for her lack of brain function her senses became more acute; it made for an uncomfortable combination.

Under normal circumstances she would probably have

been blissfully unconscious of the male scent rising from his warm skin, but at that moment it filled her senses.

'Marriage is meant to be a great many things which it rarely, if ever, is, *cara*.'

The endearment, though she knew it had no significance, brought a lump to her throat. 'That's a very cynical thing to say.' Head tilted to one side in a questioning gesture he was beginning to recognise, she ran a finger across the arch of one feathery brow. 'Weren't you married to Valentina's mother?'

'I have never been married to anyone.'

'But did you want to be?'

'Please do not imagine me the victim of some ill-fated romance,' he commanded with a pained grimace.

'I wasn't.'

'You were,' he contradicted. 'I know what that misty look means on a female's face. Cloying sentimentality makes me queasy.'

'Thank you for sharing that with me. I'll try and remember in the future,' she promised. It was amazing, she reflected, that someone who looked so much like most women's idea of a romantic hero should actually be so totally and utterly unromantic.

'So you are finally admitting we have a future.'

'Your head is the only place we have a future.'

'I am not married for the simple reason I have never wanted to marry—until now, of course.'

'But you don't want to marry me...not *really*.' She scanned his handsome face worriedly in case he had detected the same wistful note her own ears had. Finding the most discernible expression on his face was mild irritation was actually quite a relief.

'What part of "will you marry me?" gives you that idea?'

'I'm an insurance policy.'

'Why do you keep throwing that casual remark back at me? You are a very beautiful woman,' he corrected, slick as silk.

Jude gave an angry snort; for a man who had had a lot of practice at saying the right thing to women that hadn't been very original. She had seen the sort of women he dated—did he really think she would imagine even for one second that he considered her anything more than average?

'Sure, I cause traffic jams when I walk down the street. And if I wasn't so *beautiful*, you wouldn't want to marry me, I suppose?'

'The fact you are is a plus point.'

Her curiosity wouldn't allow her to let the subject go. 'There must have been a few near misses marriage-wise.'

'No.'

'What are you—allergic to commitment? I mean, you're not exactly a spring chicken, are you?'

Luca blinked. 'I am thirty-two, if that is what you wanted to know. I still have all my own teeth.' He flashed them to prove the point. 'And my father still has a full head of hair, so genetically the odds are in my favour of keeping mine. I don't know if any of this influences your decision.'

'It doesn't.'

'There has never been any incentive before for me to get married. I already have a child, which is about the only possible reason I can see for marriage.'

'Love?' she protested, then blushed as his sensual lips formed a smile. She looked away from his dark, mocking eyes.

'*Love* is little more than temporary chemical imbalance. And marriage is based on the concept that that imbalance will last a lifetime.' He released a scornful laugh. 'You think, *cara*, because your heart beats a little faster when I am close to you that you love me? It is not love, it is sex that quickens the breath.' His dark lashes swept downwards as his attention moved to the outline of her heaving breasts. 'And raises the temperature.'

Jude placed a protective hand over her wildly thudding heart and shook her head. 'It doesn't!' she denied. 'I'm not,' she added in a shaky whisper.

'Of course it does, as does mine,' he rasped thickly. 'Do not go coy on me. I admired your honesty last night.'

'I wasn't myself last night,' she insisted as he moved towards her. 'I didn't mean a word of it...'

'Yes, you did, and so did I. I find you attractive—is this such a difficult concept for you to grasp?' he demanded.

Jude shook her head and covered her ears with her hands. 'I don't believe you,' she cried. 'You're just trying to confuse me.' And succeeding fairly spectacularly!

She was too shocked to resist when he caught hold of her wrist, white-hot heat like lightning zigzagged through her body from the point of contact. As she dazedly focused on his face he twined his brown fingers into hers and, pushing aside his robe, placed her fingers against the warm skin of his chest. Her nostrils quivered as she inhaled sharply in shock.

'No!' Her chest rose and fell rapidly in agitation as she desperately tried to pull away.

'You told me you want me.'

She closed her eyes and groaned. Was she *ever* going to live that down?

'But even if you hadn't, do you think I don't know when a woman wants me?' He traced the outline of her jaw with the tip of one finger. He smiled when she shivered. 'Jude?'

'I don't! This is s...self-delusion.' His or mine?

'The only person deluding themselves here is you.' He responded as if he'd read her thoughts. 'You're holding back from what you know is a practical and workable solution to both our problems,' he condemned.

If he carried on believing that was all she was holding back, she could live with it. She didn't want to contemplate the humiliation of his knowing her true feelings.

'And why? Because you're waiting for some romantic love that simply doesn't exist outside the pages of romantic fiction.' His expressive lips thinned in distaste. 'You've got to face facts.'

'Your facts!' she cried.

'I'm sorry to be brutal, but—'

'No, you're not sorry!' she cut in angrily. 'You *enjoy* making fun of people's dreams.'

'Don't be stupid.'

'Disagreeing with you doesn't automatically make someone stupid, Luca. You haven't got any dreams left and you don't want anyone else to have them either!' she accused.

A muscle clenched in his lean cheek as his flinty eyes locked down onto hers. She felt dizzy but was unable to break the mesmeric contact. It seemed to her feverish imagination that she could actually see smoking embers in the dark, velvety depths of his dark-lashed eyes.

'So what does this man you dream of have that I don't, *cara*? Does he have blond hair and blue eyes, the studious spectacles, perhaps, that indicate his deeply *sensitive* nature? Will he quote Shakespeare's sonnets by way of foreplay, or do you prefer someone who can mend fuses and bring you tea in bed?'

His savage sarcasm made her flinch. 'I can mend my own fuses and it's not important what he looks like.'

'Of course it's not,' he agreed. 'That's because you're going to fall in love with his beautiful soul. *Dio!* But I'm all choked up just thinking about it.' As he spoke he could feel the small hand he held within his tighten into a fist. 'I suppose it's your extreme indifference to something as trivial as looks that has had your eyes all over me like a rash? And it wouldn't bother you if I took this off...' he suggested, unpicking the loose knot on the cord of his robe.

'Don't you dare!' She gasped in horror. '*Please*, Luca.' She heaved a sigh of relief when his hand fell away. 'Are you happy now you've proved how damned irresistible you are?' she choked. 'Your problem—' she began, only to be interrupted by a staccato burst of his hoarse, incredulous laughter.

'*I* have a problem? Yes,' he agreed, his eyes raking contemptuously over her face, 'I do—*you*! My God, you are the most infuriating woman I have ever met!'

The pent-up breath escaped in a long hiss through her clenched teeth. 'You want to know who my ideal lover would be? Well, not you would be good to be going on with,' she declared, her eyes spitting fury. 'You have to be the most joyless person I've ever come across and that includes the ones who were suffering from clinical depression! Don't you ever *dream*?'

This time his eyes held no smoking embers but a conflagration. When she gave a scared little gasp and tried to look away he took hold of her chin between his thumb and forefinger and tilted her face up to him.

'I have dreams, but I don't think you're ready to share them just yet.' His voice, low and fascinatingly accented, had a hypnotic quality; it suggested exciting, forbidden things that sent an illicit shudder through her body.

'The state of your sordid subconscious is of no interest whatever to me.'

'I think it interests you greatly.'

'Well, you think wrong.' Her defiance disintegrated when he suddenly leaned down towards her until his mouth was on a level with hers. She felt the warmth of his breath on her skin.

'You tremble when I touch you,' he purred complacently.

Wave after wave of wanting rolled over her as she stared hopelessly into his incredible face. Her breathing slowed down to nothing, she was paralysed with lust, every muscle, every fibre of her body, each individual brain cell frozen in anticipation of his kiss.

His dark head bent lower and her eyes closed and then she heard him murmur.

'Could your ideal lover do that?'

It took a second for the mocking words to penetrate the sensual fog she was drowning in; when they finally did she stiffened.

'You bastard!' she cried.

Burning with mortification, she tried to turn her face away from his mocking gaze, but he held her fast. She closed her eyes but it didn't shut out the image of his face. In her head she could see his dark, compelling eyes burning through the delicate paper-thin flesh on her eyelids.

Slowly her fingers unfurled and her eyes flickered open. Like someone suffering from tunnel vision, all she could see was his face.

'I can't take my eyes off you,' she confessed in a driven, confused voice. 'You know that.' Tiny fractured gasps emerged from her lips as she tentatively began to stretch her fingertips until her hand lay palm down against his skin.

Something fierce and primal flared in Luca's proud, strong boned face. 'That's it, *cara*,' he sighed with husky approval as he released her hand.

She felt the shudder that vibrated through his body.

'You feel it. You feel my heart beat for you.'

'For me?' she said in a small voice.

He nodded. 'You are so beautiful.'

'You don't have to say that,' she replied, most of her mind concentrated on the heavy thud of his heart under her fingertips. His flesh was warm and hard with a texture like oiled silk—the intimacy was intoxicating. Her throat ached with emotions, her body light and strangely unconnected; she was floating.

'I *want* to say that.' He took her other hand and raised it to his mouth. Almost reverently he pressed his lips to the palm. 'Such a little hand,' he rasped in the sexy accented drawl that never failed to send a secret thrill through her. 'The chemistry, it has been there since the first moment you glared at me with those beautiful, hungry eyes.'

He bent his head and kissed the pulse spot at the base of her neck. Jude's head fell back, exposing the long, lovely line of her throat in an unconsciously submissive gesture to him.

It was when he wound his fingers into her hair that Jude lifted her head. Her eyes were half closed as she looked at him with slumberous longing.

'You think you can make me agree to anything if you take me to bed,' she accused.

His bold eyes laughed confidently down into hers. 'Only in the short term, *cara mia*. A priest would not approve of the groom making love to his bride at the altar.'

'Even if I *do* sleep with you it doesn't mean I'm going to marry you.'

'You do not have the personality of a mistress.'

'Well, I bow to your superior knowledge of the subject.'

'Before you start introducing conditions again, perhaps,' he suggested huskily, 'you should consider that two can play at that game.' Smiling fiercely down into at her bewildered face, he elaborated. 'I could for instance say if you won't marry me I won't make love to you.'

Every nerve in her body screamed out in protest at the suggestion.

'You're not serious!' She scanned his face for any sign this was an empty threat and found none. It was a very persuasive argument.

With a throaty murmur in his native tongue he suddenly pulled her close, crushing her soft body to him. 'Does this feel as if I have that sort of control?' he demanded roughly.

The bewilderment in her eyes was swallowed up by an expression of simmering sexual awareness when, placing a hand in the small of her back, Luca pressed her even harder against his lean body. His fingers splayed into the hollow at the base of her spine, effectively sealing their bodies together at hip level.

The thin robe he wore did little to disguise what was happening to his body. Feeling his arousal grinding into the softness of her belly drove the last rational thought from Jude's head. Eyes closed, lips parted, she squirmed ecstatically up against him and gasped as she felt his powerful body pulse in response.

'Do I feel like I could play hard to get?' he tormented softly.

Jude, weak with hunger for him, sobbed his name.

Luca scanned her face hungrily before expertly parting her trembling lips and sinking into her mouth with a deep groan. He did not kiss her gently, but tore at her lips frantically with a bruising hunger. Jude's response to the stabbing incursions of his tongue was equally wild and out of control.

'*Dio*, but that mouth,' he slurred thickly when they finally broke apart. His hot eyes ate up the delicate details of the flushed features turned up to him. Something primal buried deep inside her responded to the sexual challenge she saw blazing in the spectacular eyes of his.

In an unconsciously sultry manner she looked down and then allowed her slumberous gaze to travel up to his face. 'What about my mouth?' she asked innocently.

'It is made for kissing. Just as you are made for loving—for loving me,' he added, sliding his hand under her sweater and up across her narrow ribcage.

Her startled body jerked as the contact sent an electric thrill shooting all the way down to her curling toes.

From where Luca stood he could not see her eyes, just the heavy sweep of her lashes lying against the curve of her cheekbones. The tips he saw were pure gold. Her skin was milk-pale barring the thin ribbons of feverish colour slashed across her soft cheeks. The pupils of his eyes responded to the image of a deeply aroused woman and dramatically expanded until only a thin rim of iris remained visible.

As his fingers rubbed across the tight peak of the soft, warm flesh it pushed through the stretchy fabric that restrained it.

'I need to see you,' he told her thickly as he urgently peeled the cotton top off her. Firmly he unfolded the arms she had pressed protectively across her chest.

Embarrassment overcame her. 'I wasn't expecting…this isn't very…' The sports bra she wore was hardly a garment designed with seduction in mind.

'If you wish me to remove lacy undergarments I will buy you some,' he promised. 'However, *I* do not require such stimulus. I just,' he explained, holding her eyes with his needy gaze, 'require you.'

Tears started in her eyes. 'Truly?' she whispered.

'Absolutely.' Still holding her eyes with his own, he released the front fastening on her bra. His glance dropped as the fabric parted. 'You are perfect,' he gasped raggedly in a voice approaching reverence as his scorching gaze took in every aspect of the heaving, pink-tipped mounds of firm, soft flesh.

Jude moaned as he took one tingling mound, weighing it in his palm. His thumb rubbed across the engorged nipple, sending sharp currents of tingling sensation jolting through her body.

'See how well you fill my hand.' Luca shared the deep, primal satisfaction on discovering that her straining breast fitted so perfectly into his palm.

A soft, sibilant hiss escaped her parted lips as her head, too heavy now for her neck to support, fell bonelessly back. As it did so he twisted the loose curls that spilled back from her face into his fist. Then as it fell forward against his chest his hand moved to cup the back of her head.

'Oh, God, Luca, I didn't know it could be like this...'

He bent his head to her ear. 'And you like this?'

'Like?' She groaned and lifted her head. His dark eyes drew her restless gaze like a magnet. 'God, I love it...' I love you, she thought.

If she didn't tell him about her brilliant idea now she might never get around to it. 'Luca...?'

'Mmm...?'

'Have you thought that maybe we could just *pretend* we're married,' she suggested inventively.

She felt his body stiffen.

'No, I haven't.' His tone did not invite further discussion. *'Pretending* is not part of the bargain, but this,' he promised thickly, 'is.' Without warning he scooped her up into his arms and, carrying her over to the bed, lowered her onto the silk cover.

For a moment he stood just looking at her. The throbbing, expectant silence filled Jude's head like a drum beat. She actually read Luca's intention in the glittering challenge of his eyes about a split second before he began to loosen the belt on his robe.

She lay there dry-mouthed with anticipation as he shrugged it off. The sight of him standing looking like a magnificent statue of male perfection would have moved the most dispassionate of onlookers to awe. Jude felt as if her heart were in a vice.

It was remarkable to her that—for whatever reason—he wanted her. Of course, she knew *wanting* for a man was easy, but at that moment it was enough for her that he did.

Jude heard with a sense of detached disbelief the raw moan of longing that emerged from her bone-dry throat.

The sound made his smoky eyes blaze in male triumph and his already primed male body react in a way that made her gasp. She tried to imagine him moving inside her, picturing his bronzed body pressing down on her, the weight of his limbs pinning her...but stopped because the distant buzzing in her ears got noisily close and shoals of red dots had started to drift across her vision thickened to a thin red mist. Could a person faint from lust?

I could be the first. Well, this is a day for firsts.

Her inability to take her greedy eyes off him made Luca laugh and plead only half jokingly, 'If you look at me like that, *cara*, this thing might be over before it has begun.'

When the implication of his earthy observation penetrated her dazed condition a fresh flush of heat seeped through her already burning body. She shivered voluptuously when he leaned down to run his tongue along the valley between her bare rosy-tipped breasts. Lifting his head, he took her hands between his and ran the tip of his tongue along the moist edge of her parted lips. She wanted to feel his tongue inside her mouth, but none of her frantic, fractured pleas made him kiss her properly.

'Oh, God, Luca!' she panted in frustration when he drew

back. 'I'll die if you don't kiss me!' she claimed with total conviction.

'Slowly,' he soothed, raking an unsteady hand through his sweat-dampened hair. 'I want this to be special. I want you to remember this.'

The idea that there was even the remotest possibility of her forgetting this brought a strained smile to her lips. 'Forgettable isn't the first word that springs to mind when I look at you.'

'Tell me what word springs to your mind when you look at me,' he suggested as he placed his hands either side of her shoulders.

'I don't want to talk,' she said as he lowered himself down beside her—*finally*! She thought his soft laughter was pretty callous considering how she was hurting and might have told him so had he not chosen that moment to adjust her body so that they were lying side by side...thigh to thigh.

'What do you want to do?'

The light brush of his velvet hard erection against the waistband of her jeans sent a visible ripple of movement across her abdomen as the fine muscles beneath the skin contracted. Deeper inside everything just melted.

'You're very good at this, aren't you?' she whispered, looking deep into his eyes, eyes so dark and warm you could lose yourself in them.

'Would that be a bad thing?'

It might be if I turn out to be not so good at it. She was all right on the theory, but would she be able to put it into practice?

Luca, who had been trying as hard as he could to ignore the uneasy vibes he was picking up from her, found that he couldn't.

Jude was alarmed when without warning he rolled onto

his back and lay there with his crooked arm over his eyes. God, did I do something? Did I not do something…?

'Are you all right with this?' He held his breath. If she said no he didn't know what the hell he'd do because the five-miles run and cold showers he'd been taking on what seemed an hourly basis since he had first met this woman were not going to work today. There was only so far a man could run!

Jude found herself wishing she taken up some of the offers of meaningless sex she'd turned down over the years. Then she looked into his eyes and thought, No, I'm glad I didn't. This is going to be something special, something worth waiting for.

'I'm fine with this,' she announced firmly.

He rolled back in time to be on the receiving end of a sultry smile that made him just want to rip off her remaining clothes and to bury himself in her.

'Why don't you make up your own mind about me?' he suggested, curving a big hand possessively around her left breast. 'You like that?' he said, his voice thick with satisfaction as she moaned. When he ran his tongue wetly across one brazenly erect nipple her back arched and she cried out.

'Yes, I like it!'

When his lips and teeth continued the tormenting, teasing over her sensitised flesh, she lost what little control she had retained over what came out of her mouth.

'I've wanted you to do this for ever. I wanted you to do this from the moment…oh, God, I wanted you to do this *before* I even saw you!' A sigh was wrenched from somewhere incredibly deep down inside her. 'I just want you, Luca.'

His head lifted. 'Then take me, *cara mia*.'

She laid her hands against the warm skin of his shoulders. It felt smooth like oiled silk and the male scent of him was addictive—*he* was addictive. It was at that point sanity took a back seat. For several minutes they kissed and touched in a desperate, almost combative fashion.

There were two slashes of dark colour along Luca's cheekbones, nail marks on his shoulders and a feverish glow in his eyes when they finally broke for air.

'Perhaps I should have said earlier—assertive women scare me,' he explained in between gasps. 'I feel threatened.'

'You don't look threatened.' Part of her registered that he was shaking just as hard as she was. She brought her lips to the strong column of his brown throat and pressed a series of open-mouthed kisses to his damp flesh.

'How do I look?'

She angled her head so that she could see his face and holding his eyes, allowed her tongue to flick across his salty skin. *'Perfect.'*

He groaned something in Italian and continued to speak the same language in a deep, driven voice as he slid his long fingers under the waistband of her jeans. Her body tensed expectantly. His quest towards the moist heat was prevented by the constriction of her clothes.

There was no longer any pretence of controlling the pace about Luca's actions as he ripped urgently at the zip of her jeans. It gave way and he parted the thick fabric, revealing the thin lacy covering through which the soft fuzz of hair at the apex of her smooth thighs was visible.

Despite the fact that the strong hands that tugged her jeans down over her hips and legs were not quite steady, it only took a few seconds for Jude to be divested of everything but the tiny triangle of lace. His fingers slid under the insubstantial barrier.

For a split second her body tensed at the shocking intimacy of his touch, then as he began to stroke her she relaxed and was lost to everything but what was happening to her—what Luca was making happen. She barely even registered him sliding the damp lace down her thighs. Every cell in her body was screaming out for release by the time he settled between her smooth thighs.

The husky words that emerged in staccato bursts from his lips as he parted her thighs were an incoherent mixture of English and Italian, but the extreme urgency of his actions and the ferocious, raw tension on his strained face did not need translation.

'You're mine!' he breathed into her ear in the split second before he thrust powerfully into her. *'Madre di Dio!'* He froze.

Beneath him Jude hardly registered his shocked cry. She had too much else to concentrate on, such as the overwhelming and totally amazing sensation of feeling the hard, hot length of him inside her. Her eyelids lifted from her feverishly flushed cheek.

She gave a tiny triumphant smile. 'I knew you'd be good.'

'This isn't good,' he breathed back.

Jude opened her mouth to contradict him when he began to move slowly…again and again, sinking deeper inside her, and she was lost to everything but him and the incredible pleasure and the pressure building up inside her. Her teeth closed around his shoulder when the shattering climax hit her, convulsing every cell in her body with intense pleasure. Only then did she hear his hoarse cry and the pulsing heat of his release within her.

'That was good,' he sighed, slanting her a hot, complacent grin as he rolled off her.

Jude, who was panting almost as hard as he was, turned over onto her stomach and lifted a hand to his jaw. Her wondering eyes remained locked with his as she ran her fingers along his stubble-roughened lean cheek.

'That was *incredible*,' she corrected huskily. 'You were incredible.'

His dark head turned sideways on the pillow. 'I'm your first lover.'

Warily she nodded. 'Yes.'

'This was a…?'

'Listen, it just never happened, *all right*?' she challenged fiercely. 'I do not have any major hang-ups, I was not waiting for Mr Right, it just never happened; end of story!' With a final glare at him she rolled away from him.

'Do not turn your back on me!' he yelled, grabbing her shoulder and rolling her back to him.

'I'll do anything I damn well—'

A muscle in his lean cheek jerked. 'I could have hurt you.' The strong muscles in his throat worked as he swallowed. 'I wouldn't have…'

Jude's anger melted in the face of his concern, she touched a finger to his lips. 'You didn't hurt me, Luca, and you were perfect.'

For a long moment his eyes searched her face. 'I think you should marry me.'

There was something quite liberating about running out of options—you didn't have to make a decision, it made itself. Well, if that's your story, girl, stick to it like glue, the voice in her head advised drily.

'I think so too,' she agreed quietly.

Luca, who obviously possessed remarkable appetites and recuperative powers to match, decided they were already in the perfect place to celebrate their engagement.

Some time later she lay wrapped in both Luca's arms and the contented afterglow of his lovemaking.

'This wasn't what I planned today,' she murmured with

a smile as he swept the tumble of curls from her face to kiss her damp forehead.

'What did you plan?'

'I was going to take the...oh, my God, the children! *Mum!*' She shot out of bed and began running around the room in a frenzied effort to locate her discarded clothing.

'If the children are with your mother, surely there is no problem,' Luca mused, a hand tucked behind his head as he watched with an expression of amusement her frantic and clumsy efforts to fight her way into her clothes.

'You,' she told him darkly, 'have never met my mother.'

Luca had risen in a more leisurely fashion from the bed and pulled on his robe by the time she had finished dressing. It occurred to her as she walked to the door that, other than agreeing to marry, they had discussed very little of the practicalities.

She paused, her hand on the door handle. 'I was wondering if you'd thought about when we might actually...' she gave an awkward grimace '...you know, *do* it. I suppose there's quite a lot to sort out.' At least that would give her some time to prepare the children, not to mention herself.

'Saturday.'

Jude's jaw dropped. 'Saturday! You've got to be joking.' Suddenly this thing was running away, and she was losing control of the direction it was taking. You lost control the moment you met him, she reminded herself.

'Leave me to organise the children's passports. I assume that yours is up to date.'

'Of course it is, but what do I need a passport for? It's not like we'll be taking a honeymoon.'

'We'll be getting married at the chapel in my family home.'

'*Italy!*' she gasped.

He looked mildly amused by her open-mouthed astonishment. 'And we will be taking a honeymoon,' he added in a non-negotiable tone. 'Nothing about this wedding is to give anyone reason to think it is a marriage of convenience. *Nothing…*' he repeated, just in case she hadn't already picked up on the fact he meant what he said.

The enormity of the deceit they were undertaking hit her afresh. Luca could close the door on the rest of the world and drop the act; she didn't have that luxury, because she had to keep up the pretence in front of him too!

If she let her guard down he would guess that she had fallen in love with him, and that was clearly not part of the bargain as far as he was concerned. Jude exhaled gustily before lifted her apprehensive eyes to his. 'I don't think I can do this.'

'Nonsense.' Luca dismissed her fears with a shrug and the sort of high-handed attitude she had come to expect of him.

'People will know.'

'People will know what we want them to and see what we allow them. Think of it this way—all you have to do is act like you are fighting a constant, but losing battle to keep your hands off me.' A slow, intimate smile that made her stomach muscles quiver curved his lips as his dark eyes scanned her flushed face. 'It's what you might call a role you were born for,' he added softly.

'The next thing you'll be telling me I was born for you,' she slung over her shoulder as she walked out of the door.

CHAPTER NINE

LYN Lucas pushed her aching feet back into her four-inch stilettos at the sound of the door opening. 'Do you know what time it is?' she demanded, her normally beautifully modulated voice shrill. After flicking off the switch on the television she rose to her feet, smoothing down a crease in her skirt as she turned around.

'I came here to see you and what do you do? Disappear without a word. I call that thoughtless and inconsiderate. I had absolutely no idea where you were. The children wanted their supper and baths...' she related with an expressive little shudder. 'Have you *any* idea how exhausting it is to...?' She stopped, catching sight of her daughter's expression. 'What's happened to you?'

'I think...' A wash of soft colour tinged Jude's pale skin as she lifted her chin. 'No, I *know*,' she corrected firmly.

'Do you mind sharing what you "know"?'

'I just got engaged.'

'*Engaged?*' Lyn scanned her daughter's softly flushed face suspiciously. 'Have you been drinking, Jude?'

'No, but I think I might start.'

'Good God!' Lyn gasped. 'You're serious, aren't you? How could you get engaged dressed like that?' Her critical gaze slid over her casually dressed daughter. 'And your hair—having children is no excuse to let yourself go. Does he know about the children? No, I don't suppose he does.'

'Yes, he knows about the children, Mum.'

'What does he do? And is he solvent, Jude? Oh, I know

128

you'll say that money doesn't matter, but believe me it helps.'

'You can relax, Mum, he's financially secure. He's definitely not after my money.'

This information did not have the desired calming effect on her mother, who went deathly pale.

'Oh, God! This is *exactly* what I was afraid of…'

'What were you afraid of?' Jude asked, bewildered at this new tangent.

'You still think that if I hadn't divorced your father your childhood would have been so much rosier, don't you? Well, it wouldn't,' she rebutted bluntly. 'But we're not talking about my divorce here…'

'What are we talking about, Mum?'

'We're talking about you getting involved with some loser just to give the children financial security and a father-figure.'

There was *just* enough truth in this claim to make Jude look uncomfortable. Luca was the least 'loserish' man on the planet and she was madly in love with him, but there was no escaping the fact that they wouldn't be getting married if he hadn't needed a wife of convenience.

Lyn saw the guilty downward flicker of her daughter's eyes and clapped her hands over her mouth. 'I blame myself!' she announced dramatically.

Typical, after twenty-seven years my mum chooses to turn perceptive.

'I could tell you were desperate when you called me… I was too tough with you on the phone, I'm the first to admit it. That's why I had to come. I haven't been able to get the sound of your frantic voice out of my mind.'

'Mum…Mum, calm down!' Jude begged her distraught parent.

'I thought I'd taught you how important it is to retain

your financial independence. Relationships are temporary; your bank balance, Jude,' she told her daughter heavily, 'is for life.'

Jude struggled to retain her composure. In her own rather unique way her mum was clearly trying to look out for her daughter's best interests.

'Which is why,' Lyn continued, 'I've been discussing the matter with my accountant.'

'Your accountant?' Jude echoed, lost again.

'Yes, and according to him I might just as well give you the money that's going to come to you when I die now, when you genuinely need it.'

'*Mum!*' Jude cried, genuinely touched by this unexpected gesture from her normally less-than-open-handed parent. A tough, impoverished childhood, which she rarely spoke of, had made Lyn Lucas extremely careful with her money, and fearful of losing her financial security.

'It's not a lot, so don't get excited. So you see you don't need to settle for second best. Your problem is you don't believe in yourself...and what you have to offer. You're a clever, beautiful young woman, but if you don't rate yourself nobody else will, Jude.'

Jude went forward and threw her arms around her mother. 'That's the sweetest thing you've ever said to me,' she told her, planting a kiss on her mother's smooth cheek.

'Yes, well...' Lyn murmured, looking shaken but pleased as she emerged from the spontaneous embrace. 'There's no need to go overboard—it's not that much money,' she said gruffly.

'I'm just thanking you for caring,' Jude said with a watery smile. 'I don't want your money.'

'You're not still marrying this loser? I forbid it, Jude.'

'Mum, he's not a loser and he's *definitely* not second best.' The notion of Luca, who didn't have a word for lose in his vocabulary, being second *anything* was so absurd it was hard not to laugh out loud.

'I am most relieved to hear you say so, *cara*.'

Both women gasped in unison and spun in the direction of the deep, throaty drawl.

'What are you doing here?' Jude demanded, her face burning with embarrassed colour.

One dark brow adopted the satirical slant she was growing to know so well. 'I thought you might be missing me,' he suggested with an air of very unconvincing innocence.

'There's no need to look so unbearably smug,' she told the tall, vital figure who sent her pulse rate soaring. 'I was about to qualify my observation with what you *are*.'

'*Are* as in charming, adorable, incredibly intelligent?'

'*Are* as in infuriating, bossy, and overbearing.'

He grinned at her tart retort.

Lyn Lucas, who had been watching this interchange with slack-jawed astonishment, closed her mouth with an audible click and cleared her throat. 'Jude, are you going to introduce me to…?' As she spoke her eyes didn't stray from the tall, supremely elegant figure. 'My goodness,' she gasped with a laugh, 'you look just like—'

Jude cut in quickly. 'Mum, this is Luca. Luca Di Rossi.' Luca obligingly placed a hand on her shoulder and a faint choking sound emerged from her mother's open mouth.

'You're going to marry Luca Di Rossi.' Her mother's beautifully modulated voice was an incredulous squeak. 'Gianluca Di Rossi? This isn't a joke?'

Her mother's stupefaction was hardly flattering, but Jude could well understand it.

'It's no joke, Mum. Luca, this is my mother, Lyn Lucas. Mum, I'm *really* sorry to dump on you like that, I didn't intend to be so long.' She felt a guilty flush mount her cheeks.

'Do not blush, *cara*, your mother knows what it is like to lose track of time when you are with your future husband.' His enquiring glance slid to the older woman.

'What? Oh, yes, of course I do…' Lyn responded faintly.

'I'm afraid I'm the one to blame. I have so little opportunity to have Jude to myself it makes me selfish.'

As he spoke her name their eyes brushed and a tingling sensation passed through Jude's body, which still ached in a pleasurable way from their recent lovemaking. Of course, he was playing a part for the benefit of her mother, but it didn't make her own responses any less real.

He reached out and lifted a soft tendril of hair off her cheek. Jude flinched and apologised profusely as she stepped backwards and trod on his foot.

'I hope I didn't hurt you.' Under the cover of apologising she whispered. *'Go away!'*

'You didn't hurt me, *cara*. You have such delicate little feet. Mrs Lucas, I'm so glad I have the opportunity of meeting you at last. It's so good of you to give Jude a break this way. We both know that she's too stubborn to ask for help even when she needs it.'

'Oh, that's *so* true and she's always been that way even when she was a child.'

'I *hate* to interrupt but,' Jude interrupted sarcastically, 'in case you didn't notice, *I'm* here!'

'And so am I,' added her mother emotionally. 'I'm here for you whenever you need me, darling.'

Of course it was possible her mother had been replaced by an alien, but it was much more likely that this earth-mother role had something to do with a desire to impress Luca with her empathy. Jude almost immediately felt ashamed of her uncharitable thought. The fact that she was here proved that she did care.

'I think the likelihood of any of us forgetting that you

are here is remote.' Luca looked away and exchanged a conspiratorial look with her mother, who was almost visibly falling under his spell.

'So how long have you two known one another?'

'With some people you can know them all your life and never really know them at all...with others...' His gleaming jet eyes stroked suggestively over Jude's face. 'Others,' he sighed and gave an expressive shrug. 'A second is enough to tell you all you need to know.'

Jude wondered if her mother, whose eyes had misted over as he'd spoken, would even notice that he hadn't answered her question.

'That's so true!' Lyn sighed.

'Oh, *please*!'

Luca slipped an arm around her waist. 'Did you say something, *cara mia*?'

Lyn, watching them, sighed. 'What a lovely couple you make, though if you'd been blonde, Jude...' she mused, her eyes touching her daughter's dark brown hair regretfully. 'But not to worry. Have you set a date yet?'

'Saturday,' Luca supplied casually.

After the initial shock had worn off, Lyn went into full organisation mode, giving Luca lists of things that would need to be organised. Halfway through a discussion about the number of guests who would be able to attend at such short notice, she turned to her daughter.

'Why don't you go and make us a nice cup of tea, dear? Now, Luca...'

Jude was waiting for the kettle to boil when Luca walked in.

'What's wrong?' he asked, leaning against the wall as she brushed past him.

Jude set the carton of milk down with a bang. 'Nothing.'

'I hate women who sulk,' he observed, sounding bored.

'*Sulk?*' She swung around, her eyes flashing. 'This is meant to be *my* wedding, isn't it?' One dark sardonic brow lifted in response to her bitter query.

'Oh, I know it's not a *proper* wedding, but it would be nice,' she quivered, swallowing past the emotional lump in her throat, 'if I had *some* say in it. Actually I doubt if anyone would notice if I actually didn't turn up.'

'I would notice.'

Her wilful heart flipped at this soft interruption.

'You would?' She sniffed and raised her eyes to his. 'Well, of course you would, you need me.'

'I need you,' he echoed in agreement.

'For Valentina,' she added.

His wide, mobile lips formed a twisted smile. 'What other reason could there be, *cara*?'

Jude had finished her packing the night before. Her mother, who was still utterly intoxicated by the realisation her only daughter had netted the matrimonial catch of the century, had offered in a fit of grandmotherly fervour to take the children to the zoo to give her 'a bit of quality time, darling' before the flight.

'You're going to have the eyes of the world on you,' she announced portentously to her already nervous daughter, 'so you'll need to look your best.'

'Is that meant to relax me? Because I have to tell you—'

'Whatever made you think weddings were meant to be relaxing for a woman?' She laughed out loud at the notion, but almost immediately sobered. 'The fact is you owe it to Luca. I mean, you only have to think about the women he's used to being around. A man like that expects a certain sort of standard.'

'Actually, Mum, I'm trying to forget the sort of women

he dates.' If this maternal pep talk went on much longer she might just lose the will to live.

'What's this—a crisis of confidence?'

'What, with you around to bolster my ego?'

Jude's gentle irony went right over her mother's head. 'I'm here to help,' she agreed. 'But when you have doubts just remember: he chose you, not them…' A mystified expression entered her eyes as she shook her head.

Of course, she didn't know the real reason for the rush marriage so Luca's preference for a short, average-looking brunette was something her mum still couldn't quite get her head around, but then, Jude reflected ruefully, she never had let motherly love blind her to hard facts.

One of Jude's earliest memories was being taken to an eighth birthday party by her mother and being told in a hushed aside as she had had the smudges wiped from her nose that it didn't matter if she wasn't the prettiest girl there, she could be the most interesting.

She could smile about it now. At the time it hadn't been so easy—eight-year-old girls did not much want to be interesting! On reflection it was actually pretty amazing that she hadn't ended up walking around with a brown paper bag over her head!

'Then wouldn't it be a bit silly for me to try and look like them—even,' she added drily, 'if it was possible.'

'Well, I dare say the novelty factor comes into it…but you can't expect that to last for ever.'

A genuine laugh was torn from Jude's throat. 'So what you're trying to tell me is the honeymoon's over before the wedding has taken place?'

'I'm telling you, child,' Lyn replied, irritated by her daughter's refusal to take the matter seriously, 'that there's no harm making the best of what you have.'

It wasn't until after her mother had left that the real significance of this maternal remark became obvious, when in fact the entire staff—or so it seemed to Jude—of a well-known beauty establishment arrived on her doorstep armed to the teeth!

When they departed some two hours later Jude felt pretty much like a car that had gone through one of those automatic wax washes.

Her hair had been coaxed into its old pre-fizz sleekness. Her toenails and fingernails had acquired several coats of the latest shade of varnish, which, according to the manicurist, was so happening it was not going on sale to the general public until the autumn. Jude had dutifully expressed suitable gratitude and awe.

So here she was exfoliated, buffed and oiled until she was glowing. 'What now?' she demanded of the beautifully groomed frowning image in the mirror. 'Is this supposed to make him love me?' she mockingly continued. 'Oh, God, am I making the worst mistake of my life?' She was waiting in vain for the silent image to reply when she heard the sound of movement in the living room.

Assuming that one of the make-over team was still gathering their things, she tightened the belt on a fluffy towelling robe and padded through, barefoot, to the other room to chivvy them along.

'Did you forget something?' she began, then broke off. 'Marco!' she gasped as the blond-haired figure of Luca's sharply dressed younger half-brother was revealed.

Looking at him post-Luca, Jude could not help but compare him with his brother...it was automatic. Did people always do that to him? she wondered. It must be really terrible if they did. Did he mind living in the shadow of a brother who was *more* everything?

She asked the obvious question. 'What are you doing here?'

'I hope I didn't startle you. A guy with a hair-dryer let me in.'

'Blue hair?' He nodded. 'Ah, yes, that would be Rick. He said my hair was a challenge.'

'What a cheek. Well, I think it looks great.'

'Thank you,' she said, touching the bouncy bell of hair that swung around her face when she moved.

'If you're looking for Luca…' she felt herself colour and wondered if she was the only woman who felt awkward saying the name of the man she was going to marry '…he's not here… Well, he wouldn't be, we're not living together or anything.'

'No, you're just getting married.' His liquid brown eyes slid down her body admiringly. If Luca had done the same thing I'd have been toast, she thought, marvelling at the dramatic contrast to her response or, rather, lack of it when Marco employed one of his sultry Latin stares.

Marco sighed as his roaming gaze returned to her face. 'I had to see for myself it was true, and I see it is.' He nodded towards the square-cut emerald on her left hand.

'I suppose it seems a bit sudden.'

Marco grinned. 'Luca doesn't operate by the same rules as the rest of us. When he wants something he just goes for it, but then,' he added slyly, 'you already know that.'

His readiness to accept that Luca had fallen for her big time took Jude by surprise. She'd been geared up to face people's scepticism.

'It's been fast,' she agreed. 'I keep thinking I'm going to wake up,' she mused. 'I just can't decide yet whether it's a dream or a nightmare.'

Belatedly Jude became aware of Marco's startled expression. It was hardly surprising. Blushing brides-to-be didn't talk nightmares.

'The packing and organisation and everything—my feet

haven't touched the ground yet,' she explained in an attempt to cover her slip.

To her relief it seemed to work, but she acknowledged she was going to have to watch her tongue in future. Luca would be furious if something she said made people suspicious about this marriage. It defeated the purpose of the marriage if anyone saw through the charade.

The problem was she was just so relaxed around Marco, relaxed in a way that she could never imagine being around Luca. If it had been Luca standing there, and she'd been in a similar state of partial dress, there wouldn't have been a single second she would not have been acutely conscious that underneath the robe she wore nothing.

Catching the lapels of her robe together in one hand, Jude pinned a bright smile on her face. 'Can I get you a coffee or anything?'

'A beer would be good, if you have one.'

Jude went over to the fridge and pulled out an iced bottle. 'This do?'

'Perfect.' He accepted with gratitude, took a swallow and sighed. 'I just thought I'd touch base with Luca on my way through.'

'Have you been away?'

Amusement appeared in his eyes. 'You didn't notice. You really know how to kick a man when he's down.'

'Well, of course I noticed you were away, and you know perfectly well there was never anything happening between us.'

Marco accepted her remonstrance with a grin. 'I guess there was something happening with Luca. You always were immune to my charms, but whilst you were unattached I could hope. I guess it's too late now. Don't worry,' he cut in, 'I'm not about to make a clumsy pass.'

'Good, because it would not only be embarrassing, but pointless,' she told him frankly.

'You're a cruel woman,' he complained, wincing. 'But you don't need to worry, I'm actually quite fond of my face the way it is.'

'I had noticed,' she inserted innocently.

Marco laughed. 'Well, being the vain, shallow creature I am I'd never, ever try to muscle in on my brother's territory—not even for my lovely little English rose,' he added gallantly.

'I'm sure Luca wouldn't do anything like that,' she protested.

'You don't think so? Well, you'll learn.'

Jude, who didn't like the sinister sound of that enigmatic observation, frowned.

'To be honest I usually get away with a rap on the knuckles, but he's never planned to marry any of them. Actually I'm beginning to suspect the real reason why I've spent the last week clocking up more air miles than...' He shrugged. 'Not that I'm complaining—I've always said I wanted more responsibility.'

'What do you mean?'

Marco shook his head cheerfully. 'Just thinking out loud. Apparently Luca's got an army at work getting everything ready for the big day. He really wants to pull out all the stops on this wedding and, like everyone else, I've had my list of must-do things. So when you see him—I'm assuming he won't be able to keep away for long—I thought not,' he added drily when Jude blushed. 'Tell my big brother it's all in hand and I'll see him tomorrow. Until then, how about a sisterly kiss?'

Laughing, Jude presented her dimpled cheek.

'I'd say I deserve more compensation than that,' he murmured, turning her chin and planting a warm kiss on her lips. The smile died from his face as he scanned her up-turned features. 'It is just as well I am a shallow sort of guy, or it might take me a very long time to recover from this.'

A sudden volley of very furious Italian made Marco spring away from her as if he'd been shot.

Jude saw him close his eyes as if gathering his courage before he turned with a forced smile. 'Luca, I was hoping to catch you.'

His light-hearted tone didn't put a dent in his brother's stony expression. Luca's low response was in resonant Italian.

Jude, who heard her own name, found it deeply frustrating not be able to understand what was being said. Especially as whatever it was had such a conspicuous effect on Marco, who coloured deeply and began to shake his head. When he responded in the same language he sounded uneasy and his entire attitude was placatory. She wondered whether the brothers always acted this way or had perhaps had a recent falling-out.

The mystifying back-and-forth flow of words lasted a couple of minutes—minutes with Luca growing colder and Marco more subdued.

Finally Luca acknowledged her presence. Not before time, in her opinion.

His brows were drawn into a scowling line of disapproval as he scanned her face. 'What have you done to your hair?'

Jude blinked. 'I've had a make-over. Don't you like it?'

'No, I don't.'

She didn't cry because he didn't like her hair—that would have been just too pathetic. The fact that she *wanted to* filled her with despair. '*Marco* likes it.'

'*Marco* is just leaving,' Luca bit back without looking at his brother.

When he turned back to Jude, Marco's discomfort was obvious. 'I'm running late, I really have to be going. Thanks for the beer.'

Feeling for his embarrassment, Jude put some extra warmth into her smile to compensate for Luca's inexplicably hostile attitude. 'That's a pity. It's been really nice to catch up.' The defiant look she tossed at the tall, silent figure of her future husband shrivelled in face of the white-hot fury she encountered etched in the taut lines of his strong-boned face.

What on earth had Marco done to make him look like that? she wondered, pretty shaken by the dark brooding danger she had seen glittering in his incredible eyes. Well, she decided with a rebellious toss of her despised hair, whatever it was she damn well wasn't going to take the flak for it!

The moment he had gone Jude turned on Luca, her eyes flashing. 'What on earth did you say to him?' she demanded.

Luca, his shoulders pressed against the wall, continued to examine the toe of his handmade leather shoe as if it were more interesting than anything she might have to say. His indolent pose infuriated her even more.

'The poor thing looked really shaken,' she condemned. 'Everybody knows you're the boss...for heaven's sake, you never let us forget it! So is it really necessary to throw your weight around that way? Would it cost you anything to show a little bit of consideration?'

With an abrupt movement that startled her, Luca levered his lean body from the wall, drawing himself to his full and impressive height.

'*Consideration?*' His lashes lifted and Jude found the

stormy expression glowing in those stunning depths did not mesh one little bit with his soft, conversational tone. Oh, my God! She was wrong, he wasn't angry—he was *incandescent*!

'You were very rude,' she said with slightly less conviction.

'I heard your laughter from halfway up the stairs.' She had never laughed that way with him. Luca fought to contain the fresh lick of anger that surged through his veins. 'I walk in and find my brother drooling over my bride, who is flaunting her body…'

Rather unfortunately, this unexpected and ludicrous explanation for his mood drew a startled laugh from her.

Luca drew a harsh breath. 'You find this amusing… You think it is a joke to behave like a tart?'

'Tart!' she gasped in hot-cheeked protest as his smouldering gaze lashed over her.

'Well, are you going to tell me you've got anything on under that thing?' demanded Luca, who had begun to pace up and down in front of her like a panther with attitude.

Jude's eyes widened in indignant protest. Anyone would think from the way he was talking that she were parading around in a sexy G-string and nothing else, instead of an androgynous robe that was as revealing as a tent. 'No,' she admitted, 'but—'

'But *nothing*!' he rapped, coming to a halt directly in front of her. 'I can see you have nothing on, do you think that Marco could not? Or maybe you had less on a little while earlier.' His eyes slitted suspiciously. 'Just how long has he been here?'

Jude went rigid with shock at this preposterous suggestion. It took every ounce of her self-control not to hit him.

'If you actually believe that I would jump into bed with

your brother the moment your back is turned I think we'd better forget about this marriage.'

A visible shudder ran through his lean frame as he closed his eyes and rubbed an unsteady hand over his chin. 'No, I don't actually think that,' he admitted huskily.

The indentation between her feathery brows deepened as she studied his face. 'Well, why on earth did you say it?'

His eyes slid from hers. 'My brother has a reputation with women...'

Jude loosed an incredulous hoot of laughter. 'Whereas you are as pure as the driven snow?'

'We are not discussing me! Marco can be very appealing, but at heart he is an opportunist, and you standing there like that is an opportunity.' He raked a hand through his hair as he looked at her. '*Dio*, what man with blood in his veins would not be tempted?' he grated, closing his hand into a white-knuckled fist.

'And don't I have any say in the matter?' she began to demand, quivering with fury. Tears of humiliation filled her eyes. You could see where he was coming from—all he had to do was look at her to turn her into some sort of panting nymphomaniac, so he probably naturally assumed that she was like that with anyone who deigned to say he wanted her. 'I'll have you know...*oh*!'

The angry colour faded abruptly from her cheeks as his last comments penetrated her bubble of self-righteous indignation. 'You were *jealous*...?' she whispered.

His head turned so that she could see his chiselled golden profile. For a moment she felt he was going to deny it and her stomach muscles tightened in anticipation of the mortifying blow. Then he turned back.

'How could I not be?' His hands curved around her upper arms as he drew her towards him. The pressure of his fingers through the thick towelling just stopped short of painful. 'Italians do not share their women with other men and,' he added with an imperious movement of his dark head, 'I am Italian.'

And this proud heritage he claimed had never been more obvious than it was at that moment, she thought, gazing up at the stark male beauty of his chiselled features. A stab of sexual longing so intense it turned her knees to cotton wool shot through her body.

'And what does that make me?' she asked tensely.

'My woman and my wife…'

Goose-bumps broke out on the surface of her silky soft skin in response to this outrageously arrogant disclosure. Her stomach felt hollow and achy, her tender breasts tingled—this reaction went against everything she believed in.

A woman isn't a possession was an opinion she had voiced on more than one occasion, and she still believed it.

An image of all the 'uncles' she and David had hated over the years swam across her vision and panic gripped her—she was not her mother.

'We're not married yet.'

'Do not provoke me, *cara*…'

The tension drained out of her as their eyes clashed—it wasn't a clash, it was a connection. The exasperated warning carried no sinister overtones; in fact there was an expressive quiver of amusement in his rich, deep voice.

It suddenly hit her she was guilty of stereotyping. Even though Luca was undoubtedly imperious, arrogant and autocratic, he also possessed a dry sense of humour, had a thoughtful side and was incredibly sensitive to her feelings. And when had he ever treated her as less than an equal?

'Why do you bite?' The tear that had been suspended on the tip of a gold-tipped eyelash dislodged itself and began to slide down her cheek.

'You know I do,' he rasped.

The throaty reminder made Jude shiver. Her eyes closed as his dark head blotted out the light. Very slowly he dabbed his tongue to the single errant tear; she gave a fractured sigh.

'I love the taste of you.' He rested his forehead against hers. 'Why are you crying?'

'I'm not now,' she said, turning her cheek into the hand that was cupped her around her face.

'You *were.*'

It was impossible for her to explain the real why, so Jude said the first thing that came into her head. 'You hate my hair.' She sniffed.

She felt rather than heard him laugh at her petulant complaint. 'I don't hate your hair,' he contradicted, picking up a silky strand and letting it run through his fingers. 'I just prefer your curls. I like to bury my face in them.' Her drew her head against his shoulder. Jude's arms snaked around his ribs, and she revelled in the strength of the lean body she was close to.

'How strange you like them, almost as strange as you…' She just managed to bite back *wanting me*. Wanting me in her head could easily have come out sounding like *loving* me…? The last thing she wanted to do was put Luca in a position where he had to spell out what he didn't feel for her. 'Rick wanted me to cut it—he said my face wouldn't look so round and it would help to define my cheekbones.'

'You must never get your hair cut!' he thundered in a voice of outrage. Then— 'Who is *Rick*?'

Under the encouragement of a very firm hand she reluctantly lifted her head from its resting place.

'Rick is the member of the hit squad that my mum sent over to make me a bride fit for you…'

A spasm of astonishment crossed his face. 'You're joking.'

Jude shook her head. 'Her wedding present to me. Crazy, I know,' she admitted, blushing a little under his incredulous stare. 'But you have to remember she doesn't know why you want to marry me.' Jude was actually quite pleased that this explanation emerged without her sounding too obviously embittered. 'But don't worry,' she added as a strange expression flitted across his face. 'I won't tell her.' Solemnly she licked her forefinger and drew a cross over her chest. 'Cross my heart.'

Luca shook his head, his accent more pronounced as he went on to correct her anatomical inaccuracy. 'Your heart is not there, *bella mia*.' He brought her hand up and placed it on the left side of her chest, whether by accident or design directly over her breast. 'It is here.'

For once he was wrong—her heart had vacated her chest and was even now in her throat, restricting her breaths to shallow gasps.

'This is me made over.' Shakily she stepped back from him—never an easy thing to do, she was discovering—and gave a twirl.

For a few seconds Luca silently contemplated her display. 'Your mother is an idiot and so is this *Rick*,' he pronounced with withering contempt. 'You have a perfectly shaped face and your cheekbones require no definition.'

Jude's laugh was half surprise, half amusement. After a moment her gratified smile was replaced by a look of fretful concern. 'You didn't say anything *too* awful to Marco, did you? I'm scared enough about meeting your family as it is; I wouldn't want to lose the one friend there I have.'

He dismissed her concern with a shrug. 'My family need not concern you; they will treat you with the respect my wife deserves.' But what about when you're not around to see? she wondered uneasily. 'I didn't say anything too awful to Marco.'

'Oh, good,' she sighed, relieved.

'I just explained what I would do to him if he ever laid a finger on you,' he continued casually.

'Oh, God!' Jude wailed. 'You didn't. How could you? I'll never be able to look at him again.'

'I wouldn't let that worry you. I'm going to see to it you don't damn well have an opportunity to look at him,' he growled.

'How are you going to do that? Lock me in my room?'

'Marco works for me and I have very wide business interests…'

It took a few seconds for the implications of what he was saying to filter through. Then she recalled Marco mentioning the sudden travelling he had been doing. This was probably going to sound silly, but she had to ask.

'Did you *send* Marco away, because of me?'

Luca didn't seem offended by the question. 'He was already away, I just made sure he didn't come back. Your relationship with him was an unknown factor—it seemed the logical thing to do…'

The most shocking thing, she thought as she searched his face, was the fact nothing in his casual attitude suggested he considered he was saying anything outrageous. A spasm of unease slid through her at this chilling reminder that Luca had been planning everything in calculating detail almost before he'd even met her—in fact she could have been anyone! So long as I fitted the criteria, she concluded dismally.

Perhaps she needed this brutal wake-up, having been in serious danger of forgetting that, no matter how incredible a lover Luca was and how deeply she had fallen for him, this was at the end of the day a marriage of convenience.

'I wanted to marry you and he would have been a distraction. Now of course I know you weren't lovers.' There was a flash of primal male satisfaction in his eyes as they rested hungrily on her drawn face.

'And what if Marco and I had been lovers?' Jude queried, her anger mounting with each fresh casual revelation he made.

Luca didn't even take time to consider her taut question. 'I would have made you forget him.'

'You're totally ruthless, aren't you?' She took an angry step back from him. 'You treat people like puppets you can make dance to your tune! Well, you can't make me do anything I don't want to,' she quivered accusingly.

He studied her angry face for a moment before responding quietly, 'I know that, and I haven't.'

'How can you say that when I'm wearing this thing?' She waved her finger, which suddenly felt weighed down by the enormous ring, in front of him.

'You came to my bed because *you* wanted to. You are marrying me because *you* want to.' He saw Jude flinch and he smiled grimly. 'You cannot turn around and look at me as though I am some sort of Machiavellian monster who has compelled you to do these things against your will.'

He was right, of course he was, she thought, biting down hard on her lower lip. He had been persistent, but hadn't misled her or applied pressure. He hadn't needed to! Pretending he'd forced or tricked the ring onto her finger was easier than tackling the reason she'd accepted it. The compulsive need that she felt every time she looked at him.

'It is not my methods you object to,' he suggested in a harsh tone. 'It is my honesty. Now let me continue to be honest. If you wish you can turn your head away like a child,' he conceded. Jude flushed and turned back. 'But you *shall* listen to what I say. Though,' he added in a wry digression, 'whether you are in a mood to hear it is another matter. And *please* do not look at me as though you have been summoned to the overbearing headmaster's office!'

This last exasperated petition made her blink. 'You don't have to say anything else,' she told him with a resigned shrug. 'You're right, Luca. I...overreacted.'

Her unexpected capitulation caused the muscles in his lean dark face to tense with shock.

'So did I,' he responded after a moment's startled silence. 'With Marco. Marco has a history of trying to poach my women.'

She nodded. 'Which is why you were so mad with him.' That figured.

'And I have either ignored it,' he proceeded to elaborate, 'and let him get on with it, or told him to stop it, which he does. I have never felt the urge to rip him limb from limb before,' he revealed in a conversational tone.

Jude's eyes went round. *'Oh!'*

'I rather think my reaction to seeing him with you might have...'

'Scared the wits out of him?'

His lashes lowered over an amused gleam at her wry interjection.

'The idea of him or any man touching you does not make me think rationally...' He cleared his throat and added thickly, 'You are a passionate woman...' he began, his jet eyes brushing her face.

'Only with you,' an enchanted Jude replied without thinking.

He froze. And then slowly, like a complacent cat approaching its cornered prey, he relaxed. 'Is that so, *cara*?'

'What I was trying to say is I'm not attracted to Marco. And I'm not stupid, I know he is a charming love rat...' It was very hard to form a sentence, let alone string them together, when you were the focus of that unique lazy-eyed, gleaming scrutiny.

'I prefer the way you said it the first time,' Luca admitted, reaching for her.

With a sigh Jude walked into his arms and they closed tight around her. She felt his kisses in her hair, on her neck, moving along her collar-bone before finally finding her mouth.

The kiss sent her senses reeling into outer space. 'Make love to me.' Then, conscious her request had come out sounding like a command, she added on an apologetic note, 'If you have the time?'

'I think I might just fit it into my busy schedule,' he returned, straight-faced.

'Are you laughing at me?' she demanded, scanning his face suspiciously.

'It is fast becoming one of the great joys of my life,' he confirmed, taking her hand firmly within his.

She was still puzzling this enigmatic observation when he added, with one of his slow, sizzling smiles, 'Now let's go and enjoy the other one.'

CHAPTER TEN

JUDE'S concerns about flying with small children turned out to be unfounded. The only time they became restive was whilst they were waiting in the VIP lounge after Luca's private jet missed its original slot because she had insisted on going back to the flat because she couldn't remember if she had switched off her iron.

It was a subject she still felt pretty defensive about.

'We should be there by three.' Luca, who had been speaking to the pilot, said as he rejoined her.

'I suppose you're never going to let me forget it was my fault we're late,' she observed crankily.

'So far I haven't mentioned it once...' There was sardonic amusement in the dark eyes that drifted across her tense face. '*Your* last count was five.'

Jude frowned. 'Well, you were *thinking* it, I know you were. Maybe the iron wasn't on, but it *could* have been.'

'So you said at the time.' He reached across and pushed a curl from her cheek.

Jude despaired that even this casual contact had the power to make her stomach muscles clench.

'When we are an old married couple,' he confided in a soft voice, 'maybe then you will possess insight into my thoughts, but at this moment you are way out, *cara. Way out!*'

Something in his eyes made her decide it might not be such a good idea to ask him what he was thinking.

'*Coward,*' he whispered in her ear as she picked up a

glossy magazine thoughtfully provided by the eager-to-please cabin crew.

It seemed that Luca wasn't hampered by an inability to read *her* mind. Jude concentrated on the glossy photo spread and pretended not to hear the taunt until she realised she was looking at the latest society wedding when, with a sick feeling in the pit of her stomach, she slammed it down hastily. She looked up and found Luca's eyes were upon her. She looked away quickly, excruciatingly aware that the briefest contact could make her say stupid things. She was thinking along the lines of take me!

'It was the usual boring thing, celebrities in posh frocks,' she observed with a dismissive nod towards the discarded journal. 'God, what a way to live…' Her smooth brow puckered as she contemplated the apparent lifestyle of the people pictured in the pages. 'Living from one photo opportunity to the next. Never leaving the house without full make-up just in case someone takes a photo of you with your mouth open and sells it to a tabloid.'

She gave an expressive little shudder, which morphed into a look of wide-eyed anxiety as she realised she was talking to a man who had appeared in more than one glossy spread and was constantly stalked by the paparazzi.

'God, I didn't mean you!'

'My relief is boundless that I am exempt from your scorn.'

The sardonic amusement on his face made her facial muscles tighten as annoyance warmed her skin to a delicate soft pink. 'Silly me, I forgot I was talking to the man who doesn't require anyone's approval.'

'Except a judge who could decide Valentina would be better off with someone else.' His sombre, brooding gaze rested on his daughter, who was at that moment threading ribbons in Sophia's soft curls, a frown of charming concentration on her grave little face.

Jude's soft heart felt as though it were in a vice as she watched him. The tidal wave of love that swept over her was so intense that if she hadn't already been sitting it would have washed her away quite literally. Growing inside was a fierce determination that the thing Luca secretly feared would never actually come to pass. Impulsively she reached out and took the brown hand that rested lightly on his knee between her two hands.

'We won't let anyone do that, Luca,' she promised earnestly.

Luca turned his eyes, brushing first her small hands holding his before lifting to her face. It was only when he studied her face with a strange expression that Jude became aware that she had tight hold of his hand. Abruptly she released his warm hand, with an awkward little laugh.

'Sorry.'

'You've never apologised for touching me before.'

For a split second the image that flashed before her eyes—an erotic image of his golden body gleaming with sweat and need as she ran a finger lightly down his belly—blitzed every other thought from her head. She was shaking slightly as she refocused on his face.

Fighting to regain her composure, Jude resisted the temptation to draw attention to her hot cheeks by placing a cooling hand on them. She shrugged casually in an attempt to emulate his pragmatic attitude.

'Well, obviously that's not the same thing.' She hoped her response was sufficient to reassure him she wasn't going to overstep the unseen boundaries he'd erected and expect what they had in the bedroom to overflow into other parts of their lives.

He wanted sex, and he wanted shallow, so that was what

she would give him! And what makes you think you can do shallow with a man you are madly in love with when you couldn't do it with the ones that meant nothing to you?

'You mean it's not sex.' The pounding in his skull got louder when she smiled and looked relieved. *Relieved!*

'Exactly.'

She felt slightly uncertain when the flat, stony expression on Luca's face didn't alter.

'Maybe we should attempt to introduce such spontaneous gestures. They do lend authenticity to the image we wish to present.'

By not as much as a flicker of an eyelash did she reveal how much his comments hurt her. 'That's a good point,' she agreed cheerily. She knew that it was totally irrational under the circumstances to expect him to think of it any other way, but that didn't stop her wishing.

God, Jude, you can't start living in a fantasy world. He doesn't love you, he just fancies you, so live with it! she advised herself brutally.

'It was a silly idea *you* needing *my* help, I'm sure you've covered every angle.'

'You'd think so, wouldn't you?'

Whilst she couldn't quite pin down the elusive emotion that flickered across his face, she had the strongest feeling that it was somehow significant. As the moment stretched his unblinking scrutiny started to affect her control. For one crazy moment she even considered challenging him with her true feelings, then sanity intervened.

'You know, I've never been on a flight where there are more crew than passengers,' she told him brightly.

'Is that so?'

Despite his dauntingly uninterested manner Jude found she just couldn't stop talking; the words bubbled out of her.

'It all seems a bit decadent, though I've got to admit it's

something I could get used to, especially when travelling with small children.' Pleased to have a legitimate excuse to break eye contact, she glanced towards the older children, who were playing a board game with the minder. 'Carlo really is very good with them, but it's a lot more work with four of them. You can't expect him to take responsibility for all of them.'

Luca forced the tension from his muscles by sheer force of will. 'You think I'm taking advantage of him?' he suggested, linking his hands behind his head as he leaned back in his seat.

Nothing in the relaxed action suggested that at that moment he was planning the precise means he would use to illustrate to his bride, in a manner that not even *she* could misinterpret, that he wasn't going to be rationed as to when and where he could touch her! *To even suggest such a thing…*

Jude could no more *not* look at what his action displayed than she could not breathe; the draw of his lithe body was simply irresistible. Sometimes the violence of her emotions when he was around scared her—no, cancel sometimes, *always* was closer to the grim reality.

In future, she decided, there would be no more indiscreet disclosures concerning his sublime excellence as a lover! And the subject of her own blissful satisfaction with his efforts to please her would remain a taboo subject. If she carried on this way it was only a matter of time before she said something that couldn't be attributed to the heat of passion.

Despite this resolution, her eyes slid down his long, lean length terminating the covetous exploration at his shoes with an almost imperceptible sigh. It was just as well that leg room was not an issue here because Luca was not a man built for cramped spaces.

'Of course not,' she managed once she'd dragged her eyes back to his face. 'I just think you might not have considered the additional workload of three more children.'

'I have, which is why I have arranged for a nursemaid to be added to our staff.'

Our staff? Oh, God, do I know what the hell I'm getting myself into?

'I don't have any staff and I don't want any.'

'I thought the principal selling factor of this marriage, from your point of view,' he inserted drily, 'was to provide you with the means to continue with your career uninterrupted whilst the children were well taken care of.'

She waited for inspiration but it didn't arrive 'That was before,' she blurted, feeling pushed into a corner by his relentless logic.

A wolfish grin split his lean countenance. 'Before you started appreciating the other benefits of marriage to me?'

Jude flushed to the roots of her hair at the sly suggestion. 'You're so conceited,' she choked.

'A lot more so with being told how marvellous, extraordinary and the *best* I am on a regular basis,' he inserted innocently.

A hissing sound of exasperation escaped through her clenched teeth. 'You *are* incredible in bed; it's just out of it you drive me insane!'

His negligent attitude suddenly vanished as his dark eyes overflowed with amusement. His rich, warm laughter filled the enclosed space.

Jude closed her eyes and released her suspended breath. When she opened them the teasing quality had gone from his face.

'You've got to be realistic about this child-care situation, Jude.'

'I know I do...I just want the children to know who

their...' She drew a hand over the V of skin exposed at the base of her throat—she wasn't their mother. Even as she spoke—or tried to—she could feel the ugly blotches breaking out all over her neck. Which was hardly surprising, considering she was being pressurised to explain something she hadn't quite figured out herself yet.

'I want them to think of me as the person they come to when they need help. *Me*,' she emphasised, placing her hand flat on her breast. 'Not a nursemaid or nanny.'

'Can it be you have found parenting more rewarding than you imagined?' Luca, content to see the flicker of awareness chase across her features, did not actively pursue the subject. 'Accepting help with the children does not equate with renouncing your role. When we have children—'

Jude froze. 'Children?' she echoed in a strangled voice. She gulped. *'Us?'* she added in a barely audible whisper.

'You must have thought about the possibility, considering it is not something we've been actively avoiding.' One mobile brow lifted as all the colour drained from her face, leaving it milk-white. 'I'm assuming you are not on the contraceptive pill?'

She shook her head numbly.

'I thought not.'

Her thoughts were in total chaos. How could I *not* have thought...? God, I could be right now! Her eyes fell from his, drawn to the flat section of her midriff. There was something frighteningly seductive in the thought of Luca's baby growing inside her. This sudden revelation was just too much for her to assimilate; she held up her hand as if that could halt the chain that had been set in motion.

'Why didn't you...?' She faltered. Why didn't he? Why didn't *I*? A fractured sigh erupted from her throat as she squared her shoulders. She wasn't the type of person who passed the buck. 'No, it's not your fault.'

'Does it have to be anyone's fault?' he wondered.

Jude blinked. 'Pardon?'

'Would it be so terrible if you had a baby?'

The protective numbness washed over her afresh. '*Your* baby?' she heard herself whimper stupidly.

The lashes that any woman would have died for lowered, making it impossible for her to read his expression as he mildly observed, 'Well, if it were anyone else's baby I might be...*upset*.'

'Well, that's hardly likely, is it?' As if she were going to go from Luca into any other man's arms. With a sigh she pushed a shaky hand through the curls she had deliberately not tamed after Luca's comments on the subject. Is there *anything* you wouldn't do to make him happy? the irritated voice of her independence demanded.

But would having his baby be something that required a compromise?

Oh, my God!

'Babies?'

'Well, one would be fine to begin with.'

His flippancy caught her on the raw. Teeth gritted, she caught hold of his arm. 'This isn't a joke. I know you've already got a child but it's not something I... This is all new...'

Something moved at the back of his eyes that she couldn't define. 'A baby is never a joke, *cara*. It's a serious undertaking, the consequences of which last a lifetime.'

Her eyes widened to their fullest extent as his words introduced a horrifying possibility. 'You didn't *not* take precautions because you needed an ace up your sleeve if I decided to back out?'

This was one of those occasions when the moment the words were out you wished them unsaid. The expression of austere revulsion that contorted his chiselled features was proof enough that her instincts were correct—bad thing to say, Jude.

'Actually, I have never in my *life* been heedless and reckless enough to have unprotected sex with any woman, but you. So,' he added, making a sharp, stabbing gesture with his arm, 'I suggest you make of that what you will.'

'There's a little girl sitting over there who says otherwise,' Jude replied in a subdued, unhappy whisper.

A frustrated hissing sound issued from his compressed lips. 'Think what you will, but I meant what I said.' Rising in one elegant, fluid motion that made her sensitive tummy muscles flip, he moved across the cabin to the children.

Jude, following his advice, could only assume he meant that whereas Valentina was a child whose arrival had been planned, theirs—if there was one?—would be the result of a moment of reckless passion.

She spent the rest of the flight pretending she was asleep.

Carlo began to get into one of the limousines that had just brought the wedding party from the airport to the palazzo. Luca left Jude's side and placed a hand on the older man's shoulder.

A rather intense conversation then took place between the two men. Jude, watching the interchange from a distance, became increasingly curious as there was much armwaving from the normally phlegmatic Carlo as they spoke at length. She scooped up Amy, who had fallen onto the gravel in front of the ancient building Luca had identified as the palazzo.

'Is something wrong?' she asked in a low undertone as Luca came back to her side.

'Carlo has not been inside these walls for many years.' And then to Jude's intense frustration he didn't elaborate on this intriguing statement. She didn't have long to wait to see the reason for Carlo's reluctance.

'Our reception committee?' she asked when an elegant figure appeared flanked by a man and a woman both in uniform.

'My stepmother, Lucilla,' he explained in an expressionless voice.

'A fake,' her own mother whispered in her ear. 'The pearls are real, the smile isn't.'

Lucilla Di Rossi's condescending gaze swept over the visitors, halting dramatically when she reached the burly minder. Her loss of stately cool was quite dramatic.

'You cannot imagine that your father would allow you to bring this...*person* into the house!'

'Take the children up to the nursery, will you, Carlo? They are tired.' Carlo, his face impassive, followed the suggestion, leaving only Amy in Jude's arms.

You didn't have to understand Italian to figure out the gist of the words Luca's stepmother proceeded to spit at him were something akin to over her dead body.

Jude didn't have the faintest idea how Luca maintained his slightly bored attitude throughout the prolonged harangue. 'Carlo stays.'

This uncompromising response clearly infuriated the elegant figure who, with one poisonous look at her stepson, turned her attention to Jude.

'I suppose he has told you that creature you have left your children with has a criminal record?'

'*Mother!*' Marco, who had appeared in the doorway just in time to hear his mother's dramatic revelation, groaned in dismay.

Ignoring her son's warning, the older woman widened her thin lips in a vulpine smile as she observed Jude's shocked response. 'I see he didn't.' She shot a triumphant look at Luca, whose attention was fixed on Jude's taut profile.

'I'll go after them,' Jude heard her mother say as she started past.

Without taking her eyes off the figure in the doorway Jude caught hold of her mother's arm. 'That's not necessary, Mum. Carlo is quite capable of coping.'

'Shall I tell you what he did?'

'*No!*' Jude smiled and moderated her forceful tone. Her chin lifted. 'If Luca trusts Carlo then I don't need to know anything else,' she said quietly.

'Jude, darling, are you sure?' her mother's fretful voice hissed.

Jude's frantic heartbeat slowed as she took a deep breath. 'I'm totally sure, Mum.' And she was. Her eyes flickered towards the tall, silent figure standing a little apart.

Their eyes touched. Jude, mesmerised by the message in his stunning eyes, barely registered that for once Luca actually looked less than his usual urbane, controlled self.

The moment passed and Luca was making the formal introductions and, like everyone else, she was acting as though the nasty scene had not occurred.

Whilst on the outside she was smiling and making the right noises, inside she was in a state of total confusion. Could what she was thinking be true? Did he care? Was she a fool to read so much into one look and a silence?

'She's heavy—shall I take her?'

Jude started and realised that Luca was talking to her. Feeling ridiculously shy, she nodded and placed the toddler in his outstretched arms. Their hands accidentally touched and for a moment they neither of them moved, they just stood there, their fingers brushing softly. The moment was broken when the little girl curled her arms about Luca's neck and placed a loud kiss on his lean cheek as they mounted the wide, curving staircase.

'Where's Mum?' Jude asked, looking around and finding all the other members of their party had disappeared without her even noticing!

'They've put her in the east wing. I can have her moved closer to you, if you wish?'

'No, I'll be fine.'

'It'll only be for the one night; tomorrow we will spend the night in the tower room.'

If she thought that far ahead she might well freak out on the spot. 'Can you see the Grand Canal from there?' The sardonic look he slanted her made Jude frown defensively. 'Well, you might take all this for granted, but I've never been to Venice before and it seems a shame not to see a few things whilst I'm here. Think of me as a tourist.'

This cheery suggestion drew a choking sound from his throat. 'I believe you can see the Grand Canal, but actually I hadn't planned on spending much time admiring the view.'

Jude took one look into the challenge shimmering in his silver-flecked eyes and took the next two steps together. Then stopped dead.

'My mother,' Luca explained, seeing her staring at the portrait of a luminously beautiful woman that overlooked the hallway.

'She was very beautiful, and you look very like her,' Jude concluded, comparing the eyes and the full lips on the woman in the portrait with the man beside her.

'I'm beautiful?' he teased.

Jude didn't smile. 'I've always thought so.'

Though she made a point of not looking to see how he reacted to this revelation, she did hear his sharp inhalation. This time she took the lead in their slow progress.

It wasn't until they reached the top that Luca spoke. 'About Carlo…'

'It doesn't matter.'

'It does,' he countered flatly. 'When I was in my teens Carlo was my father's driver. He befriended me; his friendship made life more…bearable,' he revealed quietly. 'My stepmother didn't like the fact he was kind to me, and even defended me upon occasion. Some items went missing…'

Sensing what was coming, Jude shook her head.

The eyes he turned to her held the smouldering remains of a deep sense of anger and injustice that she suspected would stay with him for ever.

'They were found in his room,' he confirmed. 'She as good as admitted she planted them there when I accused her, but I was a boy and my voice was not heard. Carlo was given a suspended sentence, but a record doesn't make it easy to get a job.'

'Couldn't your father…?'

'I think he knew what she had done, but my father does not concern himself with anything much but his books.'

'Including you? Don't shrug as if it's trivial!' she cried. 'It isn't! I think—'

'Jude—'

'No, let me say this, Luca. I know he's your father, and I don't care how heartbroken he was when your mother died. What sort of a man isn't there when his son needs him?' she demanded on a quivering note of outrage.

'A father who doesn't perhaps deserve that son?'

This harsh explanation originated from just behind her. Jude spun around as if shot. A little under six feet, with dark hair heavily streaked with grey and a thin face that was deeply etched with lines, the man standing there had the saddest eyes she had ever seen.

Luca's explanatory, 'This is my father. Father, this is my future wife, Dr Jude Lucas,' was kind of redundant.

The dark eyes surveyed her flushed face silently for a moment. 'Not at all what I was expecting, Luca,' he observed cryptically before nodding to his son and moving away.

'Why does this sort of thing always happen to me?'

Luca didn't vouchsafe an answer to her anguished question; instead he put forth one of his own. 'Do you intend to fight my battles often?'

'I'm s...sorry,' she stammered apologetically. 'I know it's none of my business, but when I thought of you...' Her throat closed over emotionally.

'So I'm the object of your pity.'

Jude's teeth grated in exasperation as she held out her hands for Amy. 'Come to Aunty Jude, darling,' she coaxed. Over the toddler's head she added, 'How do you manage to twist everything I say?'

A look of total astonishment appeared on his face. '*Me* twist what *you* say...?' he began when a uniformed figure appeared at his side and apologetically informed him the call he had been expecting had arrived.

Luca nodded. 'Could you show Dr Lucas to the nursery and then to her bedroom?' His eyes touched Jude's face as he handed over Amy and he nodded again.

Watching him go, Jude felt as if her only friend in the place had gone, friend in this instance being a relative term.

'Luca!' she called suddenly.

He turned at the sound of her voice.

'Will I...will you be there later...at dinner?'

Even before the forlorn question reached him Luca was striding towards her. He took her face between his hands and kissed her until the world was spinning.

'I'll *always* be there for you.'

CHAPTER ELEVEN

'CAREFUL of your hair!' Lyn remonstrated as her daughter slipped the champagne silk satin gown over her head.

'I haven't put the flowers in yet.' Jude held her breath as the slim garment slid over the curls that had been loosely confined on the top of her head. 'And I am being careful,' she promised as the rich, heavy fabric pooled around her feet. 'How do I look?' She craned her neck to see her rear view in the mirror as she struggled to reach the zip.

'For heaven's sake!' her mother protested watching her daughter's efforts with an expression of exasperation. 'If you're going to marry the man who's going to inherit all this—' her gesture took in the incredibly grand surroundings '—you're going to have to cultivate a more regal manner.'

'It's pretty imposing, isn't it?' Jude sighed. Walking through the echoing stone corridors, she had felt the oppressive weight of the generations of Di Rossis, many of whom stared at her from the walls bearing down upon her. Knowing of Luca's background and actually seeing it were different matters entirely.

'The plumbing leaves much to be desired.'

This practical observation made Jude laugh. 'That's better,' Lyn approved. 'Now, stop fidgeting whilst I get this zip. You really don't want to let his family intimidate you—from what I hear, if it wasn't for Luca the whole place would have fallen back into the canal by now. Apparently half those priceless works of art on the walls had been sold off,' she revealed in a confidential manner as she struggled with the long zip.

'I dread to think how much it cost him to buy them back. Mind you, he can afford it,' she concluded with a touch of complacency.

'I don't think his father likes me,' Jude, who hadn't told anyone about her accidental meeting with Stefano Di Rossi, commented.

'I really don't see how you could tell, darling. I didn't see his expression change once at dinner. And I doubt if he said more than two words all through the meal. Perhaps he was disappointed that Luca wasn't there?' she suggested.

Jude focused on her toes. 'Perhaps.' It was ironic really that she'd read so much into Luca's 'I'll *always* be there for you' when he'd actually not even managed to be there for her at that interminable family dinner!

'Breathe in a bit…that's it. Did you notice when we were taking breakfast that the room was full of photos of Marco, but there wasn't a single one of Luca?'

'I didn't go down to breakfast, Mum.'

'No, but you really should have—we don't want you fainting.'

'I won't do that.'

'You know, the first thing I'd do if I was married to the very sexy Stefano would be to take down that dirty great portrait of my predecessor. My God, but Luca is the living image of the woman, isn't he?'

'Stefano is married, Mum.'

'Good God, child, I'm not *interested*. He may be attractive, but he's far too cerebral for my taste. I prefer my men to be a bit more physical; of course *both* is nice but we can't all be as lucky as you.'

Jude, who was becoming increasingly uncomfortable with this frank exchange, sighed with relief when Lyn cried, 'That's it,' as the zip shot safely home. 'You look very beautiful,' she added huskily when Jude turned around.

'*Really?*'

'Look for yourself.'

Jude was amazed to see the tears standing out in her mother's eyes. 'You can't cry—you'll ruin your makeup, Mum.'

'Good point,' sniffed her mother with a watery grin as she dabbed a tissue to her eyes. 'I'll see you there, then.'

'You're leaving?' Jude felt a flare of panic.

'Don't worry, you won't be alone,' Lyn said, casting a last emotional look at her daughter. 'He's on time!' she exclaimed when there was a loud knock on the door.

'Who...?' Jude began as her mother opened the door with a flourish. From where she was standing she couldn't see who it was, just the shocked expression on her mum's face. Clearly this was not the person she had been expecting.

'Well, of course...I was just going,' Jude heard her say in a flustered manner before she blew her daughter a kiss and stepped out of the room.

'Signor Di Rossi!' she exclaimed as the distinguished figure entered the room fully. She didn't have the faintest idea why Luca's austere father should be paying her a visit. The only half-possible explanation she could come up with was this was some sort of last-ditch effort to prevent the marriage...a personal plea to beg her not to sully the blood line. Or maybe he was going to try and buy her off?

'Jude—I may call you Jude?'

'Of course,' she agreed warily.

'You look extremely beautiful.'

'Thank you.'

'You are wondering why I am here? Of course you are.

I just wished…I hope that you will accept this from me.' He held a velvet box out to her. When she didn't make a move to take it he nodded. 'Please?'

With unsteady hands Jude did as he wanted. Inside the box was a heavy gold ring; it was intricately carved and looked extremely old.

'It's beautiful,' she said, flicking him a questioning look.

'My wife, Luca's mother, gave it to me on our wedding day. I thought perhaps you would like to give it to Luca? I have given him his mother's wedding band to give to you.'

The gesture was so unexpected her eyes filled with tears. 'Thank you, I would like that very much,' she said quietly. The significance of this gesture was not wasted on her.

He only said, 'Good,' but Jude had the impression he was pleased. Hand on the door handle, he turned back. 'I can see why my son has fallen in love with you.'

Only he hasn't!

The irony reduced Jude to tears, which she desperately fought to hold back. When a short time later there was a second knock on the door she took several moments to compose herself before answering.

'The flowers, how lovely,' she began when she saw the figure carrying her bouquet. Then she stopped, the blood draining from her face. 'Dad?' she whispered incredulously. 'You're here?'

'Just stepped off the plane—literally,' the tanned figure who looked very like her brother explained.

'But how?'

'Your husband is a very forceful bloke when he puts his mind to something.'

'Luca did this?' she breathed, her thoughts racing.

'He seemed to think you might like to have your old dad at your wedding?'

For the first time Jude recognised the diffidence in her father's manner for what it was—he wasn't sure of his reception. 'Luca thought right!' she cried, throwing her arms around him.

'Watch the flowers, girl, you'll crush them,' her father remonstrated huskily as he pushed her a little away. 'My,' he said, a catch in his voice. 'I'd fly around the world twice over to see you looking like that.'

Jude shook her head. 'I still can't believe you're here.'

'It's been too long, but maybe it's not too late for us to get reacquainted?'

'I'd like that.'

'But not now, I think you've got a previous appointment.'

Jude took a deep breath, accepted the bouquet of gypsophila and white baby roses and laid her hand in the crook of the arm he presented her.

'Ready?'

Jude lifted her chin. 'Ready.' She just hoped that when the time came she would be able to deliver her vows in an equally confident fashion, that she wouldn't stumble or stutter.

Her worries proved unfounded. The ceremony went without a hitch. The tiny chapel was filled with the aroma of flowers and incense. Through the sea of faces Jude saw only one. The entire service had a dreamlike quality; it was only when it was over and she and Luca were making their way to the salon overlooking the Grand Canal where the wedding breakfast was to take place that it hit her.

'You're shaking.' Luca, a groove of anxiety between his dark brows, examined her face, which was a shade paler than her dress. 'Do you want to sit down?'

'I could do with some fresh air.'

Nodding, he led her outside into a small private court-

yard. Flowers spilled from pots on the tiny wrought bal-
conies of the rooms above and water from a tiny fountain
tinkled softly. Luca pushed her down onto a wrought-iron
bench.

A few deep breaths later she lifted her head.

'Feeling better?'

She blinked. 'I did it...I went through with it. Sorry, you
know that—you were there.' She gave a shaky laugh.

'It's customary to wait until after you've cut the cake to
start having regrets.'

Jude's eyes widened. 'I don't have regrets.' Then, regretting the vehemence of her rebuttal, added quickly,
'Why—do you?' Belatedly she registered his uncharacteristically strained air and added, rising jerkily to her feet,
'Well, *do you*?'

'The only thing I regret is that we have to go back in
there. This party is going to go on for ever and the only
person I want to share today with is you.'

The way he was looking at her made her heart thud faster. 'Well, you invited them...talking of which, bringing
my father, it was a lovely thing to do, Luca, thank you,'
she said huskily.

'I hoped it would please you.' Suddenly he took her
hands in his and drew her towards him. 'I want to say a
lot of things to you, but if I start to someone will inevitably
come and interrupt—the things I wish to say should not be
interrupted.' Frustration filled his lean face as he looked
hungrily down into her upturned features. 'Meet me here
later tonight at...eleven...?'

Mutely Jude nodded.

She told herself there was absolutely no point speculating
about what he intended to tell her, but of course she did.
Whilst she smiled, laughed and danced and acted like a

carefree bride she thought about little else. Frequently when her eyes drifted towards Luca's tall, dynamic figure—they did this fairly often—she found that he was watching her.

On each occasion the effect of the contact on her nervous system was dramatic and sometimes embarrassing. She dropped two glasses and trod on a diplomat's toes.

Late in the evening she found herself dancing with Marco, who was a very accomplished dancer.

'Don't worry, I asked Luca's permission.'

Jude couldn't decide if he was joking or not. 'That woman over there, the one in purple.' Marco's glance followed the direction she tilted her head. He looked away quickly, his colour slightly heightened. 'Who is she? She's been watching me all night.'

'That's Natalia Corradi, Valentina's grandmother and a stiff-necked old battleaxe. The guy sitting next to her is her son, Laurent, the blonde is his wife.'

Jude nodded. That at least explained the unfriendly vibes she'd been picking up.

'Listen, Marco, if you could dance me towards that door, I'm just going to slip away to say goodnight to the children.'

'Sure thing,' he agreed, whirling her lightly around.

She spent half an hour with the children, promised Valentina and Sophia they could press the flowers in their posies and keep them for ever, agreed that Joseph would never have to wear a page's outfit again and found the corner where Amy's favourite teddy had fallen.

By the time she slipped out of the building there was still a margin of carmine along the horizon, though the first stars were beginning to pierce the velvety night sky. Jude shivered and drew the cobwebby lace wrap up over her bare shoulders as she picked her way across the damp grass to the fountain.

The day had been magic and the night promised to be even more so. Luca's words kept going around in her head. Could she have read more into them than was actually there…?

Lifting her skirts to protect the fabric from the slightly longer grass, she reached the steps that led up to the secret courtyard. At the top she stopped, the breath nagged in her throat; it was a magical scene. The cobbled courtyard and the balcony of the ancient stone building behind it were artistically back-lit by strategically placed spotlights.

As she walked forward the tapping of her heels on the cobbles was mingled with the trickling sound of water as it splashed onto the ancient stone. The air she breathed was filled with the scent of night-scented stocks and jasmine. As her long gown brushed the floor she felt as though she'd stepped into the pages of a fairy-tale book, but then the entire day had had an air of unreality about it.

She drew the wrap a little tighter as a soft gust of wind stirred the leaves of the trees above her head. Suddenly several spotlights that had been inactive flickered into life. It took her eyes a couple of seconds to adjust to the extra illumination.

When she did she saw the detail these lights had been positioned to softly highlight. Her enchanted gaze took in the small table and two chairs set discreetly in one corner. She walked towards them, a soft smile curving her lips. When she reached the table she picked the bottle of champagne set on the mosaic surface from the ice bucket it nestled in and pretended to study the label before returning it.

She flicked one champagne flute with the tip of one pearly fingernail and a bell-like tone rang out across the courtyard.

'Well, are you going to come out or should I drink this alone?' she called out teasingly to the darkness.

Even though she had been expecting to see him, a frisson of shock ran through her body when a tall figure separated out from the shadows.

'You knew I was here?' His face was in shadow so she couldn't see his expression.

'I always know when you're there,' she explained simply.

He drew a harsh breath and as he stepped into the light he looked into her soft glowing eyes. 'You look very beautiful tonight, *cara mia*.'

'I feel beautiful,' she admitted.

'Perhaps you are learning to see yourself through my eyes,' he suggested, taking her arm and drawing her back to the table.

Jude liked the feel of his heavy arm across her shoulders. Instead of backing away from the raw, intoxicating masculinity he exuded, she embraced it.

'Champagne?' he asked, lifting the bottle from its cradle.

'I already feel a little drunk,' she confided.

'You haven't had anything to drink. I know—I have been watching you.'

'What—all the time?'

'Every second,' he confirmed throatily.

'I'm not drunk on wine, just the air, the magical air. This has been a marvellous day, Luca. I keep pinching myself to check I'm not dreaming,' she confided.

He came towards her and pressed the glass full of sparkling liquid in her hand. Standing so close their thighs almost touched, he raised his own glass. 'To much more pleasurable ways of convincing you you're not dreaming,' he proposed, brushing a soft curl from her brow. 'Are you cold?' he added solicitously as a shiver ran through her body.

'No, just excited,' she admitted, swaying gently towards him.

'Now isn't this romantic?'

The slurred voice made Jude start. She would have pulled back from Luca if the hand firmly placed in the curve at the base of her spine had not prevented her. After a moment she relaxed and leaned into his hard, lean body.

'Is this a private party?'

As the older woman tottered towards them on shaky legs it was evident she had been taking advantage of the lavish bar facilities.

As she got closer Jude was shocked by the appearance of the sophisticated woman Marco had identified for her earlier that evening. Natalia Corradi's smooth chignon had become unanchored, leaving her silver-grey hair to fall in wild disarray around her face. Her once perfect make-up was smudged and smeared. The fresh application of scarlet lipstick had obviously been applied with an unsteady hand.

Jude experienced a wave of compassion for the woman, her own happiness contrasted so dramatically with this woman's dejection. This must have been an incredibly hard day for her, to see another woman take her daughter's place, and no matter what her argument with Luca was she must love her grandchild, she thought.

How much better it would be for everyone if they could put their differences behind them. Her eyes narrowed thoughtfully; there was the possibility that coming fresh into the situation she could act as some sort of mediator. Surely there was a middle ground that both parties could live with for Valentina's sake. Luca was an intelligent man—he would see that, surely.

'Why don't you have a seat?' Jude suggested, slipping

away from Luca's side and drawing one of the wrought-iron chairs from beside the table.

'Ah, the little wife.' The depth of malice in the harsh voice was reflected in the feverish glittering eyes that hazily focused upon Jude.

'Nobody wants to keep you from your granddaughter. You can see Valentina any time you want, can't she, Luca?' Jude appealed to her husband.

'No, she has abused that privilege.' Luca stepped forward, interposing his body between the older woman and Jude as though to protect her.

Jude was far more dismayed by the total inflexibility in her husband's hard voice and the grim remoteness of his expression than she was by any threat offered by the pathetic, rather sad-looking female he was shielding her from. How could he be so unfeeling?

'But, Luca, wouldn't it be better to…?'

Luca's cold eyes flicked across her face. *As if I'm a stranger*—the thought slid into her head. 'You have not the faintest idea what you are talking about, Jude, so leave it alone.' His attitude was blightingly dismissive. 'Natalia,' he said, inclining his head fractionally.

'Only two glasses…what a shame.'

'I think perhaps you have had enough,' Luca observed in a voice of deadly calm.

'Well, how else was I meant to get through this day?' she hissed. 'Is she in on your plan?' Her bleary-eyed attention switched to the slender figure clad in cream silk standing just behind him. What she saw made her shake her head. 'No, she's too stupid. I suppose the little fool thinks you married her for love.' High tinkling laughter rang out. 'She's obviously besotted with you; it's written all over her,' she sneered. 'Is that a blush? How quaint,' she trilled.

The sound that issued through his clenched teeth drew

Jude's attention to Luca's arrogant chiselled profile. She saw his jaw clench just before he responded in his native tongue. Despite the obvious strength of his emotions he expressed himself in an even, carefully measured manner, which, despite his soft voice and the fact she hadn't the faintest idea what he was saying, chilled Jude to the bone.

She saw that the older woman looked pretty shaken by what he had said too. That Luca could employ such brutal tactics to browbeat a woman who was obviously emotionally fragile shocked and disgusted Jude, whose soft heart went out to the distressed grandmother. Hand extended in an instinctively comforting gesture, Jude stepped forward, ignoring Luca's harsh warning growl.

Just as she was about to lay her hand on the hunched shoulder of the grey-haired figure the other woman's head came up. There was such malice in the eyes that raked her face that Jude stepped backwards, almost colliding with Luca. His arms went around her, drawing her to him. She sank into him, drawing strength and comfort from the contact.

'He thinks he can silence me.' The thin lips compressed in a mean smile. 'Well, not this time. I want justice for my baby. I'm going to tell your precious bride what sort of man she has married and none of your threats will stop me. The world should know what sort of man he is. It's only for my granddaughter's sake that I have kept silent up until now.'

Luca spun Jude around. For a moment he looked down into her pale, confused face as if he was committing what he saw to memory. 'She is poison, Jude.'

'Perhaps you should get her son to help. I'll stay with her.'

Luca shook her gently as her attention drifted back towards the other woman. 'You must not listen to what she says.'

'It doesn't matter what she says, I can see she's upset.'

'Has he told you about Maria…my baby girl?'

Jude pushed away Luca's restraining hand. 'Luca told me that she suffered bad post-natal depression.'

'And that's why she killed herself, is that what he told you? Oh, the doctors said that too, but he paid them to say it!' she accused, stabbing a shaking finger towards the tall, silent man who appeared to have distanced himself from the entire hostility. His air of icy detachment seemed to inflame his adversary.

'It was tragic,' Jude, her eyes filled with tears, said softly. To lose a child had to be the ultimate tragedy—no wonder the poor woman had been driven to making crude and wild accusations.

'Tragic was being seduced and left pregnant when she was seventeen.'

'Seventeen—but that can't be right?' Jude turned to Luca confidently expecting to hear his denial; his silence sent an icy chill through her body. *'Seventeen?'* she whispered hoarsely. 'And you were…?'

'He was eight years older! Not that we even knew who the father was until after she'd died and we read her diary. It told it all—how he'd seduced her and deserted her when she told him she was pregnant.'

Jude felt as if her world was falling apart around her ears.

'And now,' continued the relentless voice of retribution, 'he is taking away from me the child he never wanted anyway.'

'Luca, tell her…' Jude caught his arm, her beseeching eyes fixed on his stony face. 'Tell her it's not true.'

'Go and get Laurent, Jude. Tell him his mother is drunk.'

'Tell her, Luca!' Jude's voice rose to a shriek.

'He can't tell you because it's true.' And leaving Jude momentarily speechless, Natalia Corradi stormed away in bitter triumph.

Jude turned her back and tried to tune out the spiteful comments. She focused all her attention on Luca. 'Say something, Luca?' she begged, frustrated by his lack of response.

'Valentina is not an unwanted child and never has been. As for the rest you will have to trust me.'

'Trust you?' she echoed as though he were speaking a foreign language. 'That's a big trust, Luca.'

'Marriage is based on trust.'

'Meaning I should just accept your word that you did nothing wrong? That would be convenient,' she agreed. Only Luca could take the moral high ground at a time like this. 'Whilst we're on the subject of marriage, maybe it's the time to remind you that ours—' she choked '—is based on lies.'

His jaw tightened another notch. 'Originally maybe,' he conceded stiffly.

She shook her head; he was saying what she wanted to hear, but too late. 'You're not denying that Maria was seventeen?'

'How can I?'

She scanned his face and saw no remorse, no humility. There was not going to be any coming clean, admitting he'd done wrong but had been trying to make amends since. *No, I will live with this thing on my conscience for the rest of my life. Just a take-it-or-leave-it trust me! Did he even accept there was anything to forgive? Maybe he thought he was above the rules that applied to lesser mortals.*

'Strength is about admitting when you've made a mistake. I want to hear your side, Luca.'

His lip curled. 'That's incredibly decent of you.'

His attitude was the final straw. 'How dare you sneer at me? You're not the slightest bit sorry, are you?'

Disgust curdling in her belly, disgust with him for what he'd done and disgust with herself for still loving him.

She turned and began to walk away. She heard him call after her, but carried on walking.

She managed to make it to the tower room where her belongings had been moved without actually seeing anyone else. Someone had already been in to switch on the lamps and turn back the bed.

It was the rose petals romantically scattered over the bed that released the tears. She sank onto the floor, a puddle of cream silk and antique lace, and sobbed her heart out. When she was eventually cried out she unzipped the dress and let it fall to the floor; her silky undies followed it.

Naked, she walked through to the *en suite* bathroom and stepped into the shower. The initial blast of cold water took her breath away. By the time she reached for the temperature control she had almost got used to the icy needles stabbing at her flesh.

'You feel the need of a cold shower too?' Well, if he hadn't before he did now, Luca thought as his own body reacted lustfully to the sight of her naked body.

She stood there like a figure carved from marble. Though Luca doubted any sculptor, no matter how talented, could convey in inanimate stone the beauty of the living flesh. He might capture the form but not the spirit behind it. The cold water had given her creamy skin a delicious pinky glow, but through it the blue tracery of fine veins under the skin on her breasts, with their tight, erect pink buds, was clearly visible.

'Or is this part of a Spartan lifestyle you haven't told me about? Should I expect hair shirts next?'

She raised a hand to the leaping pulse at the base of her neck and cleared her throat.

'No.' She relaxed slightly at hearing her own voice, though relaxed was perhaps too generous a term. Being relaxed in the true sense was a non-starter when you were standing stark naked with Luca Di Rossi's eyes all over you.

'No,' she repeated with slightly more force. 'Compared with you my life is an open book.' Her teeth were chattering partly from cold, but mostly, she suspected, from the shock of seeing him. 'What are you doing here?'

'Where else would a groom be on his wedding night but by his bride's side?' He picked up a bath sheet and held it open between his hands.

'I can see it might excite comment if you weren't and someone might even get the idea—God forbid—that this marriage is a joke.'

'Heaven knows, I'm the very last person who would ask you to cover up but if you don't get dry soon you're going to freeze. But as I can see my presence offends you I will take the couch in the other room.' Laying the towel on the bed, he walked out.

By the time Jude picked up the towel the moisture had evaporated from her skin. There was an expression of resolution on her face as she wrapped it sarong-wise around her body.

The adjoining sitting room was in darkness. When her eyes adjusted she saw a figure sitting on a chair beside the window.

'*Luca?*' she called out, moving towards him. 'Ouch!' she

cried as her knee glanced against the corner of a piece of furniture.

A lamp was flicked on. 'What are you trying to do?' an irritable voice demanded harshly.

'I'm trying,' Jude declared, rubbing her bruised thigh, 'to talk to my husband.'

'I've said all I'm going to, and I've heard quite enough of what you have to say.'

'Oh, for heaven's sake, don't be a stubborn prat!' The tall figure snapped to rigid attention. Well, if nothing else her outburst had got his attention. 'Everyone says stuff they don't mean—even you! And you might as well listen because I'm going to say it anyway. What that woman said shocked me,' she admitted. 'But I've been thinking about it.'

'And you think flogging is too good for me?'

'I know it can't be right. I know there has to be an explanation.'

'And what explanation did you have in mind, Jude?'

'I didn't have anything in mind.' The questioning note in her voice crystallised into conviction as she stated positively, 'I just know you wouldn't do that.'

Silence greeted her words and frustratingly the shadow from the lamp fell directly across his face so she didn't have a clue how he was taking her declaration. She took a deep breath.

'I know you're not going to tell me what really happened, because,' she added, a note of exasperation entering her voice, '*you* don't explain yourself. Anyone who *dares* to question your precious integrity is instantly shunned. Well, let me tell you, Luca Di perfect Rossi, it's all very well to be proud but I'm only human and I…I thought I could take loving you and not being loved back even though it just about killed me.' His audible gasp momentarily made her lose her tenuous thread, but, determined to talk for as long as it took to make him start listening, she gave a loud sniff and gulped before doggedly picking up where she'd left off.

'And then tonight, just when I thought you m...might actually feel something for me and everything was perfect, that woman said those vile things. I just wanted you to tell me it wasn't true...but you just stood there looking all noble and remote...' She exhaled and gently slapped both her cheeks to focus as her feelings threatened to overwhelm her. 'You want trust? Well, it may be a bit late, but you've got mine. And if you don't forgive me for being credulous enough to listen to that woman you're the biggest fool ever born! Because you need me, Luca Di Rossi!' she ended, finally running out of steam.

'Have you finished?'

She looked at the tall, shadowed figure and nodded. Well, I suppose it would be fair to say I've laid my cards on the table, she thought, unable to quite believe she had just said what she had just said, but not sorry.

What the result of such reckless honesty would be remained to be seen, but, she realised, holding her breath as Luca moved out of the shadow towards her, I'm about to find out. He stopped about a foot away from her and took her tear-stained face between his hands. He looked down at her, an expression of adoration that took her breath away stamped on his hard features.

Jude, propelled into instant bliss, felt a smile of relief spread across her tear-stained face.

'Of course I need you, *cara mia*, I've known that for some time. I was just waiting for you to realise it, and if I let you go I would indeed be the...*prat*?' Jude laughed and nodded. '*Sì*, the *prat* you accuse me of being. The fact is you have crept into my heart and if you left I think it would break.'

'I've no intention of leaving, Luca, unless you boot me out.'

'I couldn't afford to—you'd take me for all I'm worth, or at least half of it.'

'So this is a purely financial arrangement.' She laughed.

'This is a purely loving arrangement,' he corrected huskily.

'Why didn't you say something?' she cried, thinking of all the misery she might have been saved.

'Like you did?' he suggested drily. 'Not once did you say you loved me; you acted like I was a sex object.'

Jude giggled at his indignant expression. 'Well, you are, but I love you for your beautiful mind too.'

With a growl he drew her to him and kissed her hair, the curve of her neck, the tip of her nose, before finding her mouth. With a sigh of pleasure Jude wound her arms around his neck and gave herself up to the kiss.

'This is our wedding night…?' she murmured in shocked discovery when they drew apart. 'Gosh, this morning seems a lifetime ago,' she mused.

Luca nodded as his hands continued to move constantly over her, as though he couldn't bear not to be touching her. 'This is our wedding night—I think it is almost obligatory to make love.'

'Well, if it's obligatory…' Her laughing shriek as he swept her off her feet was smothered by his lips.

'You're awake?' Luca asked, picking a rose petal from her hair.

Jude opened her eyes and stretched lazily. 'Have you been asleep at all?'

'I prefer watching you.'

The unqualified love shining in his incredible eyes made her sigh with amazed contentment. How did I get this lucky?

'About Valentina.'

A shadow appeared in her eyes as she raised a finger to his lips. 'You don't have to tell me, Luca.'

'I want to,' he said, taking her hand and kissing the palm. 'What I am telling you is known by only one other person and it must never leave this room,' he told her solemnly. 'The fact is Valentina is not my daughter; I never even met her mother.'

Jude gasped. 'She isn't your daughter—then who...?'

'I am not trying to excuse what he did, but Marco was very young.'

'Marco! Marco is Valentina's father.' Jude was stunned by this revelation.

Luca nodded. 'When the Corradis approached me I realised immediately what must have happened. It wasn't the first time that Marco had used my name, though parking tickets and speeding fines were not quite in this league.'

'But why didn't he own up? Why let you bring up his child?'

'When I confronted him he admitted everything. As far as he was concerned he'd had a one-night stand. When the girl told him she was pregnant he'd panicked. His mother has always idolised him and he was terrified of her finding out.'

'So you took responsibility for his mistake.'

'It wasn't a mistake, *cara*, it was a baby,' he corrected in a gentle voice that made her eyes fill. 'Marco was not in a position to bring up a child either emotionally or financially. If I had told the truth what would have happened to Valentina? She is a Di Rossi.'

'So you kept quiet.'

'The Corradis didn't make waves then as they will now, because they didn't want the precious *family name* dragged through the mud. They hushed up the suicide for the same reason, and were only too glad to hand over the baby to me. I may be on shaky moral ground…lies are wrong, but the truth can be cruel, Jude,' he reflected grimly. 'And no child should have to live with a father's rejection.'

Like you did, my darling, she thought, smoothing the hair from his forehead with a loving hand. 'Anyone who questions your integrity will have me to answer to,' she announced fiercely as she caught hold of his dark head and pressed her lips to his.

'As far as everyone is concerned she is my daughter.'

'*Our* daughter,' Jude corrected huskily. She shot him a questioning look from under her lashes. '*Our* family. Some people might think that four children is enough to be going on with…'

'And do you care what people think?' he asked, drawing her soft, pliant body on top of him.

'Not any more!' she discovered happily. 'I would like to have your baby, Luca.'

She was crestfallen to see that Luca did not look particularly gladdened by her shy disclosure. 'I want a child, Jude, you know that, but this is not something you should be doing for me. If it is too soon for you…I am prepared to wait.'

The cloud vanished from her face. 'I'm not,' she told him simply.

With a groan he drew her to him. 'It might not happen straight away,' he warned her as his breath fanned across her lips.

'Think of all the fun we'll have trying.'

'Later I'll think, now I need you.'

Jude, who could find no fault with this plan, gave herself up to the wonder she had discovered in his arms.

THE BILLIONAIRE
AFFAIR

Diana Hamilton

Diana Hamilton is a true romantic and fell in love with her husband at first sight. They still live in the fairytale Tudor house where they raised their three children. Now the idyll is shared with eight rescued cats and a puppy. But despite an often chaotic lifestyle, ever since she learned to read and write Diana has had her nose in a book – either reading or writing one – and plans to go on doing just that for a very long time to come.

Don't miss Diana Hamilton's new novel, *Virgin: Wedded at the Italian's Convenience*, out in April 2008 from Mills & Boon® Modern™!

CHAPTER ONE

'THE resemblance is quite remarkable, Caroline. You could have been the sitter—come here, take a look.' Edward Weinberg's slender, long-boned hands beckoned her and she put the guest list for the up-and-coming private viewing down on the beautiful, fastidiously uncluttered expanse of his desk and went to join him in front of the painting a uniformed porter had just brought up from the strongroom and placed on an easel.

Her employer's remark regarding the likeness was irrelevant, but she was consumed with curiosity to at last see the masterpiece that Michael, Edward's son, had acquired at a small, country-town auction a few months ago.

Carefully cleaned, painstakingly authenticated, the lost work by the pre-Raphaelite painter J. J. Lassoon had caused deep ripples of acquisitive excitement amongst the select band of collectors who could afford to pay serious money for the pleasure of owning a thing of covetable beauty.

Caroline had been in the north of England advising the new heir to one of the great houses on what he could dispose of, with the most profit and the least pain, to pay death duties, and had missed out on all the excitement.

'Which will be the more important, the prestige or the profit?' She glanced at Edward from black-fringed, deep violet eyes but his expression gave nothing away. He had the face of a mournful aesthete, his tall, elegant figure looked fragile enough to be bowled away by a puff of wind. But he was as tough as old boots. If she had been asked to put money on his true feelings she would have put prestige as his prime concern.

The London-based Weinberg Galleries had a fiercely guarded reputation for offering art and artifacts of the finest quality. The acquisition of the Lassoon painting could only add to his reputation.

'I'll leave you to ponder on that.' Edward smiled as he turned away and Caroline gave her attention to the newly discovered masterpiece only to have her breath freeze in her lungs because he was right. The resemblance was remarkable. More than remarkable. It was uncanny.

Set against a riot of lush greenery, the artist's model cupped a white lily in her curving hands and it was the very image of her, exactly as she had looked twelve years ago at the age of seventeen. The cloud of glossy black hair reaching almost to her waist, the youthful translucence of the milky skin, the thin patrician nose, the over-full rosy lips parted in a secret smile, the dreaming, drowning deep violet eyes. Dreaming of love, drowning in love.

Even the title was apt. *First Love.*

A shudder of bitter anger rippled down her spine. That was exactly how she had looked all those years ago when she had loved Ben Dexter with all her passionate being. So much love, she had thought she might die of it.

Yes, that was how she had looked before she had learned the truth, before he had turned his back on her and had walked away from their turbulent love affair, her father's money in his pocket, more money than the boy from the wrong side of the tracks had ever seen in his life, his gypsy-black eyes glinting with the satisfaction of a bargain well struck, his whip-thin, virile body swaggering with heartless triumph.

She swung abruptly from the painting. She felt sick. She wished she had never set eyes on the wretched thing. It had brought back memories she'd buried deep in her psyche, memories she would have to struggle to inter again with even greater determination before the internal, unvented anger could do more real and lasting damage.

Edward's immaculately barbered silver head was bent confidingly over the phone as she walked past him, avoiding her office, going to Michael's to discuss the final gallery arrangements for the imminent private viewing, only breaking off when her secretary, Lynne, located her on the internal line just before lunch-time.

'The letters are ready for your signature and the balance sheets from the accountants have just come through. Mr Edward will want to see them. Oh, and he wants you to stay on this evening. He left a message. He's got a client for *First Love*. The usual drill.'

Champagne and canapés, followed—if the client showed serious interest and was willing to pay top dollar—by an elegant dinner at one of London's more select eating houses. As Edward's executive assistant it was her job to ensure that the evening went smoothly, his to extol the virtues and provenance of the piece the client was interested in.

'So he's not putting it in the private viewing,' Caroline mused as she came off the phone. 'Someone must be keen.' She leant back in her chair and raised one finely drawn brow at Michael.

The private viewings were as near the vulgarity of a public auction as Edward Weinberg would allow. None of the items were ever priced but amounts were discreetly mentioned, offers just as discreetly made and just as quietly topped until, at the end of the day, the original sum mentioned would have rocketed sky high.

Though occasionally, a particular client would make it known that he was prepared to go to the limit, and above, to acquire a particular piece and a private evening meeting, as the one scheduled for tonight, would take place.

'The old man plays his cards close to his chest,' Michael pointed out. 'He must have put feelers out— or waited to see what came up after the heavier broadsheets published that photograph of the painting. Who knows?'

He lounged back in his chair, his warm hazel eyes

approving her elegant, softly styled suit, the gleam of her upswept black hair. Caroline Harvey was quite something. Beautiful, intelligent, articulate. And a challenge. Her beauty was cloaked in inviolability. He wondered if she had ever allowed any man past a chaste kiss at the end of a date. He doubted it. He picked up a pencil, rolling it between his fingers, and wondered what it would take.

She returned his warm approval, hers overlaid with affectionate amusement. Edward's son was stockily built, almost good-looking. He affected a casual style of dress—bordering on the sloppy. Mainly because, she guessed, he knew he could never compete with his father in the sartorial stakes so went the other way.

She gathered together the papers she needed and Michael said, 'Lunch? There's a new place opened round the corner, just off Berkeley Square. I thought we might suss it out.'

He was already on his feet but Caroline shook her head. Since his divorce, over twelve months ago now, they often lunched together when they were both back at base. To begin with they'd talked shop, but recently their conversation had reached a more personal level. Without actually saying as much, he had hinted that he would like their friendship to deepen into something far more intimate.

She sighed slightly. Approaching thirty, she had choices to make: whether to remain single, a career woman with no family, just a small circle of friends;

or whether to become part of a couple, have children, trust a man again…

'Sorry,' she declined softly. 'I'll have to work through. I'm going to have to squeeze in the arrangements for this evening and I'm already pushed for time.'

She worked quickly and efficiently, gaining enough time to leave an hour early. She needed to go home to her small apartment near Green Park, change and be back at the Weinberg Galleries in Mayfair by six-thirty at the very latest.

She would have rather spent the mild April evening at home with a good book, and that wasn't like her. She lived and breathed her work. But she wasn't looking forward to this evening and wasn't stupid enough to pretend she didn't know why. The sooner *First Love* was off their hands the better. The memories it had forced into the front of her mind tormented her. She had believed she had forgotten the pain of heartbreak and betrayal. But she hadn't.

She dressed carefully because it was part of her job to look as good as she could: claret-coloured silk trousers topped by a matching tuxedo-style top, a slightly lighter toned camisole underneath, garnet eardrops her only decoration, high heels to add to her five-ten height. And she was back at the gallery to approve the caterer's efforts before Edward and his client arrived.

'Elegant, as usual, Ivan.' Her heavily lidded eyes swept the small but exquisite buffet, concentrating on that because she couldn't bear to look at the painting on its display easel, cunningly lit by discreetly placed spotlights. Just thinking about it, the shattering resemblance that reminded her of the passionate but clueless young thing she'd been, made her feel ill with anger.

'There's no need for you to stay on.' She made herself smile at him. 'As soon as you've opened the champagne you can fade away. One of the security guards will let you out.'

She squared her shoulders, forcing painful memories to the back of her mind. It was only a painting, for pity's sake! Ben Dexter had meant nothing to her for twelve long years and the residue of anger she hadn't realised she still felt had to be nothing more than a self-indulgent fancy.

It had to stop!

'Everything's in hand for the private viewing later this week, I take it?'

'Saturday. Yes, of course.' Ivan gave the bottle of champagne a final twist in its bucket of ice and stepped back, his hands on his slim hips. He had a dancer's body and soulful brown eyes. Caroline wondered wryly how many hearts he'd broken in his young lifetime as the brown eyes flirted with her. 'Everything will be perfect, especially for you—for you, anything else would be unthinkable.'

'Such flattery,' she mocked. Everything would be perfect because he and his small, hard-working team were the best money could hire, and inside that handsome Slavic head lurked an astute business brain.

The small moment broke the unease of not wanting to be here at all, and she was grateful for that until, from the open doorway, Edward said, 'Caroline, my dear, let me introduce Ben Dexter. Ben, meet my invaluable right hand, Caroline Harvey.'

She closed her eyes. She couldn't help it. The panelled walls were closing in on her, the luxurious Aubusson tilting beneath her feet, the tumultuous beats of her heart suffocating her.

Ben Dexter. The man who had taken all she had had to give—her body, heart and soul—then, Judas-like, had sneaked away with her father's pay-off. She should, she thought savagely, be thankful that, unlike Maggie Pope from the village, he hadn't left her, literally, holding the baby.

She forced her eyes open, scrabbling for the slim hope that two men could bear that name, made herself look at him and met the bitterness in his darkly eloquent eyes, saw the slight, contemptuous curl of his handsome mouth, the proud lift of his dark head, and wanted to hit him for what he had been, for what he had done.

He'd been a thorn in the sides of the parents of daughters, the bad boy of the village, disappearing for months on end to goodness only knew where, reappearing with his wild, gypsy looks, his whippy grace, his devil's eyes, to quite literally charm the pants off the local girls!

Only she hadn't known that then, all those years ago. He'd said he loved her, wanted her for always, until the stars turned to ashes. And she'd believed him. Then.

She felt herself sway with the force of her anger, scathing words of condemnation bubbling in her throat, choking her. But Ivan's steadying hand on the small of her back brought her back to her senses, and she smiled for Edward, met Ben's cynical eyes as Ivan moved discreetly away, and extended a hand towards the man she despised, dreading the touch, the clasp of those slim, strong fingers on hers, the warmth of his skin.

'Mr Dexter.' The almost painful clasp of his hand pushed whatever inanity she might have followed up with right back in her throat. His skin was cool, yet it burned her. She couldn't pull her hand away quickly enough.

'Miss Harvey.' Formal. Yet beneath the veneer something about his voice, something sensuous, like dark chocolate covered in rough velvet, sent her nerve endings skittering to life. How well she remembered that voice, the things he had said…the wickedly seductive things…the lies, all lies…

He turned away, his mouth indented, as if he were mocking her, saying something to Edward now, casually accepting the flute of champagne Ivan handed him and strolling towards the painting on display. So he wasn't about to acknowledge the fact that they knew each other, that they'd made wild, tempestuous love during that long-ago summer when the world, for her, had been touched by magic.

Well, why would he? She hadn't explained that

they knew each other when Edward had introduced them because, heaven knew, she was deeply, abidingly ashamed of her younger, stupidly gullible self. And he'd probably forgotten her entirely. Just one in a long line of silly, disposable females who'd been only too eager to lie on their backs for him!

The deal had been done over the canapés and champagne. Caroline didn't know how the boy who'd been brought up by his widowed mother in a near-derelict cottage could have come by that amount of spare cash. Well, however he'd come by it, she figured the means would have been unsavoury. But she wasn't going to waste mental energy trying to work it out.

Edward was giving them supper in the exclusive restaurant currently in favour. Caroline faced Ben over the elegantly appointed table, watching him covertly beneath the dark sweep of her lashes.

Twelve years had changed him; his shoulders were broader beneath the expensive tailoring, his honed body more powerful, his ruggedly handsome face less expressive than it had been at nineteen years of age, his tough jaw darkly shadowed and his sensual mouth touched with a recognisable line of determination.

She shivered slightly and forced her attention to the sole in white-wine sauce she'd ordered. She hadn't wanted to come, had even, for a moment, thought of crying off, pleading the onset of a migraine as an excuse to cut and run.

But the moment had passed. She wouldn't let Dexter turn her into a coward.

Edward had ordered champagne. He never drank anything else. Hers, untouched, had gone flat. The relaxed conversation between the two men ranged over subjects as diverse as politics and the theatre. She was barely listening, just wishing the evening would end.

'And how did you become attached to the prestigious Weinberg Galleries, Miss Harvey. Or may I call you Caroline?'

The hateful drawl pricked her violently back into full awareness. The question could have been interpreted as an insult, implying amazement that any respected firm would employ her!

'Through the usual route, Mr Dexter.' Her eyes clashed with his. If there'd been a hidden slur behind his words then he'd better realise she was up to any challenge. 'A postgraduate course in the history of art, alongside another in museum studies.' She laid her cutlery down, not bothering to hide the fact that she'd barely touched her fish. 'Fortuitously, Edward was looking for an assistant. I happened to fill the bill.'

'A dedicated career woman? Never married, Caroline?'

She caught the dark glitter of his eyes. He had never called her Caroline, saying that he'd have needed a mouthful of plums before he could have pronounced it properly. He'd called her Caro. Softly, sweetly, oh, so seductively.

Her heart thudded painfully. Oh, to have the ability

to erase memories at will! She made her voice cool, disdainful, 'No, I've yet to meet the man who could satisfy my exacting standards. And you, Mr Dexter— are you married?'

She saw his mouth tighten. She'd touched a nerve. Just feet away, she felt rather than saw Edward frown. One was not supposed to descend to personal levels with clients!

Tough. Dexter had started it.

'The married state has never appealed. I'm not into voluntary entrapment.' Urbanely said. The prick of annoyance obviously forgotten, his slow smile was unsettling.

No, you prefer to change your women as often as you change your socks. The words were on the tip of her tongue but she swallowed them. Spit them out and she'd be fired on the spot.

Taking advantage of the waiter's arrival to clear their plates, she excused herself and headed for the rest room. Of course he recognised her, she'd seen it in his eyes. She hadn't changed much. She had fined down a little, had acquired a veneer of sophistication, had cut her hair to shoulder length and had coiled it into a smooth knot on top of her head.

So she must have had something memorable about her, she thought wryly. Or did he remember the faces of all the women he had bedded and had discarded over the years?

It wasn't important, she told herself as she held her wrists under the cold tap to cool down. A few more minutes of his miserable company and she would never see him again. Then she took her mobile from her slim leather bag and called the cab firm she always used.

Moments later, she slid back into her seat. Edward handed her the dessert menu but she closed it and laid it down on the table. 'I'll pass,' she told him. 'And leave you two to enjoy the rest of your meal. I've a hectic day tomorrow.' No problem there, Edward knew what her workload was like, especially when there was an invitation-only viewing on the horizon.

She got fluidly to her feet, putting on a polite, social smile. 'So nice to have met you, Mr Dexter.'

Both men had risen. Ben Dexter said smoothly, bland self-assurance in his dark, honeyed voice, 'Humour me, Miss Harvey. My driver's due to pick me up in ten minutes. I'll drop you off. We'll have coffee while we wait.'

Once she would have tied knots in herself for him. Now she took great satisfaction in telling him sweetly, 'How kind. But my usual minicab driver is probably already parked outside. Enjoy your coffee.'

And allowed herself a small smile of satisfaction before she swept out.

She had no idea why he'd offered to drive her home. She certainly couldn't accuse him of having gentlemanly instincts! And he could hardly have wanted to reminisce over old times. Whatever, she had very politely pushed his offer back down his throat.

It was high time Ben Dexter learned he couldn't always get what he wanted.

CHAPTER TWO

THE alarm clock was a welcome intrusion. Caroline
rolled over, silenced it, and slid her feet out of bed.
She'd had a lousy night.

Dreams or, more specifically, nightmares of Ben
Dexter weren't conducive to restful sleep. Especially
when they featured such graphic images as his sweat-
slicked olive skin against the white femininity of
hers, his mouth exploring every inch of her body
with hungry, all-male dominance. And his voice, that
honeyed, sexy voice of his, telling her he loved her.
Lies, every word of it...

She made a rough, self-denigrating sound at the
back of her throat, headed for her small bathroom
and took a shower. She wouldn't think about him
again. She would not. No need. He'd bought the
painting that had brought him briefly back into her
life and today it would be crated and dispatched. End
of story.

The morning was just pleasantly hectic, leaving no
room for brooding over those erotic dreams and she
made time to accept Michael's invitation to lunch.
The new, much publicised restaurant lived up to expectations as far as the food went but the service
was slow.

'I don't know about you, but I'd better be getting back,' she declined when he suggested coffee to round off the meal. She was on the point of rising but he reached out and clasped her wrist.

'We're already late, a few more minutes won't make much difference. Besides, there's something I want to say to you.'

From the look in his eyes, the softening of his mouth, she knew what it was. And she didn't want to hear it. She wasn't ready.

His hand slid down to capture her fingers. 'You must know I'm attracted to you,' he said quickly. 'We already have a good relationship and I want to take it further. I don't know what you think about me, and I won't put you on the spot by asking, but you're all I admire in a woman. I'm pretty sure we could build something good and lasting together. You might not think so right now, but will you give it a try?'

Carefully, she slid her fingers away from his. What to say? Only yesterday she'd caught herself listening to the ticking of her biological clock again, knowing her pleasant working relationship with her employer's son was on the point of developing into something deeper, balancing the prospect of a lonely old age against the warm, emotional security of having a husband and family.

Yesterday she would have been comfortable with what he'd just said, agreed to go with the flow, find out if they would make a compatible couple.

So why the hesitation? What had changed? Something had.

'You don't fancy me at all?' he muttered into the suddenly spiky silence.

She smiled at him. He looked like a sulky child.

'I've never thought about it,' she said soothingly, lying smoothly to cover the lack of enthusiasm that was obviously upsetting him.

'But you will?' He made it sound like an order. 'Why not have dinner with me tonight? Since Justine left me I've learned to cook a mean steak. But, if you prefer, I could rise to beans on toast. Take your pick.'

His sudden, boyish grin gave her pause. She didn't know why his marriage had broken down after only a couple of years. Edward had voiced the general opinion that it was a blessing there were no children but apart from that he'd said nothing about the cause.

Whatever, Michael didn't deserve to be hurt again. She said with rare impulsiveness, 'I'm allergic to beans! Make it Monday, shall we, after the viewing!' She stood up, hitching the strap of her bag over her shoulder. 'One condition, though,' she warned. 'Friends. Nothing more, not yet. Nothing personal, Mike. I'm simply not ready for commitment.'

Not ready? When for weeks she'd often caught herself brooding about her long-term future. Children. Happy, family life. Not that she knew much about that...

'Condition accepted.' He stood up too, leaving

folded notes to cover the bill. 'But don't blame me if I try to change your mind. Eventually.'

She knew she'd made a mistake when she caught his satisfied smirk. Lunch was fine, but supper at his flat near the Barbican?

Misgivings shuddered through her. A week ago she would have seen the invitation as a natural progression of their deepening comradeship, would have pleasantly anticipated getting to know him on his home ground. Now she'd accepted his invitation because he was her friend, a nice guy, and she hadn't wanted to upset him with an outright refusal.

Back at the gallery there was a message for her at the front desk. Edward wanted to see her. Now.

Enclosed in the silver capsule that whisked her directly into Edward's office she filed the problem with Michael away at the back of her mind. She'd handle it as smoothly as she'd learned to handle everything else since she'd left the parental home at eighteen.

Handled everything except—

'Ben Dexter,' Edward said as the lift doors closed behind her. 'He needs you to appraise the contents of a property his company—or one of them—acquired relatively recently. About eighteen months ago, if I remember correctly.'

He arranged a few papers into a neat pile and then tapped it with the ends of his long, thin fingers, tilting his silver-grey head he asked, 'Are you unwell? You

look a bit green around the gills—lunch upset you?
Do please sit down.'

The shock of hearing that name slotted into her
uncomfortable thoughts had driven what colour she
did have out of her skin. It had nothing to do with
what she'd eaten at lunch or her unfathomable
change of attitude over her relationship with his son.

Besides, what company was Edward talking
about? From what she knew of Dexter it was probably dodgy. Should she warn her boss, confess she
knew Dexter to be a cheat and a liar? It was something to think about.

'I'm absolutely fine,' she claimed, gathering herself, slipping into the chair on the opposite side of
his desk. 'You were saying?'

She wouldn't do it. If he wanted bits and pieces
of antiques, paintings, whatever, appraised then
someone else would have to do it. Her stomach
churned over at the very thought of having to have
anything at all to do with him.

Edward gave her a long look and then, as if satisfied, told her, 'His company, Country Estates,
bought up this run-down house and land in
Shropshire. They've sorted out the business end—
planning permission for a golf course, clubhouse and
leisure centre and a small heritage farm, and now
they're turning their attention to the house itself.'

Caroline felt the shock of that like a physical blow.
There could be few people who hadn't heard of the
ultra-successful Country Estates, admired by big
business and the environmental lobby alike. She must

have misjudged him, having believed him to have obtained his wealth by nefarious means. The thought wasn't comforting. The idea of Ben Dexter as a liar, cheat and betrayer had been with her for so long that having to rethink it was like an amputation.

But what place were they talking about here? Suddenly she was sure she knew. Had Dexter's company acquired more than one run-down estate in Shropshire around eighteen months ago? It was possible, of course, but not very likely.

'Are we talking about Langley Hayes?' The smile she manufactured was just right. Borderline interested. Only she knew how heavily her heart was pounding.

'You know it?''

The slightest nod would do. She'd been born there, had lived there—apart from when she'd been away at boarding school—until she'd been driven out by misery and one dictate too many from her authoritarian father.

Of her mother she had no memory. Laura Harvey had died shortly after giving birth to Caroline. Only the occasional photograph in a barely opened album had shown her just how beautiful her mother had been.

She had never been back. She'd been warned not to show her face again. Attending her father's funeral out of duty, Caroline had not gone back to the house. It and the land had been sold to Country Estates, the bulk of the purchase price repaying the mortgage her father must have taken out on the property, the small residue going to Dorothy Skeet, his housekeeper, the woman who had also been his long-time mistress.

Apparently her non-commital nod had sufficed. Edward said, 'Dexter tells me the entire contents of the house were acquired at the time of the sale. Some of the things are fine, others definitely not. Though as he admitted, he's no expert. Which is why he wants you to do an appraisal.'

Careful, she told herself. Be very careful. Otherwise you might find yourself throwing your head back and howling out torrents of rage.

'This was discussed last night, after I left?' she asked levelly, crossing her long, elegant legs at the ankles, clasping her hands loosely together in her lap. They looked very pale against the dark sage of her tailored skirt. She knew what Dexter was doing— exactly what he was doing. And despised him for it.

'No, he phoned this morning. He left last night almost as soon as you did. It's been arranged that his driver will pick you up from your apartment at ten on Monday morning. I don't think you'll need to be away for more than three or four days. However, spend as much time there as it takes. Dexter's a client I'd like to hang onto.'

Just like that! 'It's my stint on the front desk next week, and with the extra work following a viewing I can't afford to be away,' she pointed out calmly.

All the qualified staff took it in turn to man the front. Hopeful people walked in off the street, carrying things in plastic bags or wrapped in newspapers, hoping to be told that granny's old jug or the painting they'd put up in the attic decades ago was worth a small fortune.

'Edna will cover for you at the front and, as for the rest, we'll cope without you. Dexter asked specifically for you, most probably because he'd already met you last evening.' He steepled his fingers, his eyes probing. 'Do I sense a certain reluctance?'

Too right! A deep reluctance to do Dexter's bidding, to let him pull her strings and put her in the position of sorting through the detritus of Reginald Harvey's life. It wasn't enough that the wild, penniless lad from the wrong side of the tracks who'd broken hearts with about as much compunction as he would break eggs, had bought up the lord of the manor's property—he wanted to put her, Caroline, in the position of humble retainer.

He wanted to turn the tables.

'Only in as much as it affects my work here.' She couldn't tell him the truth. She had shut her troubled past away years ago and refused to bring it out for anyone now.

'It won't. You're my right-hand man, but no one's indispensable.'

'Of course not,' she conceded, her smile too tight. She could refuse to go, and earn herself a big black mark. Edward was a wonderful employer but cross him and he'd never forgive or forget. She'd seen it happen. Resigned now, hoping Dexter wouldn't be at Langley Hayes, but prepared for the worst, she half left her seat but resumed it again, asking, 'I gather Dexter has personal financial clout? The price he paid for the Lassoon wouldn't be counted as peanuts in anyone's book.'

Know your enemy, she thought. And Dexter was hers. Leaving aside the way he'd treated her in the past, there was something going on here, some dark undercurrent. She felt it in her bones.

Edward could have refused to discuss his client but thankfully he seemed happy to do so. 'His cheque won't bounce,' he said drily. 'Rich as Croesus apparently. Came from nothing.' His smile was tinged with admiration. 'That's according to the only article I've ever read about him—financial press a year or so ago. He built a computer-software empire and is reckoned to be some kind of genius in the field. That's rock solid and growing, but he needed more challenges. That was when he diversified into property and now he's reputed to be a billionaire.'

'And he never even got close to being married?' She could have kicked herself for the unguarded remark. It wasn't like her. Her descent into what her boss would term idle tittle-tattle shamed her and Edward's displeasure was contained in his dismissive, 'I know nothing about the man's personal life.'

Taking her cue, Caroline rose, smoothed down her skirt and collected her bag. Back to business, she asked, 'Do you know whether or not he intends to dispose of anything of value?' There had been some lovely things she remembered. Although if her father had been in financial difficulty he might have sold them.

'From what I could gather he aims to keep the best

in situ. It will be up to you to report on what could be kept as an investment.' He began to shuffle the small pile of papers, a clear indication that her presence was no longer required.

Caroline left, wondering why the unknown details of Dexter's private life were like a burning ache in the forefront of her mind.

That Langley Hayes was in the process of restoration was not in doubt, Caroline thought as the driver parked the Lexus on the sweep of gravel in front of the main door. Scaffolding festooned the early-Georgian façade. The parkland through which they'd approached the house—unkempt in her own recollection—had been smoothly manicured and, in the middle distance, she'd seen two men working with a theodolite.

Surveying the land for the golf course? The clubhouse? The—what was it—leisure centre? Whatever, it was no longer any concern of hers. Her life here, largely lonely, hadn't been a bed of roses. She felt no pangs of nostalgia or loss. Only that nagging internal anxiety—would Dexter be here?

'A lot of work in progress,' she remarked, as she stood on the forecourt in the warm April sun as the driver opened the boot to collect her baggage, saying the first thing that came to mind to smother all those uncharacteristic internal flutterings.

'Mostly finished on the main house,' he answered, closing the boot. 'Structurally, anyhow.' His bushy eyebrows rose a fraction. 'You should have seen the state it was in. But the boss got everything moving—once he makes his mind up to something he don't hang about.'

He lifted her bags. 'If you'll follow me, miss, I'll rouse the housekeeper for you—Ms Penny. She'll look after you.'

The rows of pedimented windows gleamed as they had never done when she'd lived here and the main door had been newly painted. So Mrs Skeet hadn't been kept on, she pondered as she entered the spacious hallway. Ben Dexter obviously believed in making a clean sweep. His restlessness would push him towards the principle of out with the old and in with the new. And that went for his women, too, she thought with a stab of bitterness that alarmed her.

There had been no other car parked on the forecourt. Just the builder's lorry and a giant skip. Which didn't mean to say that his vehicle wasn't tucked away in the old stable block.

She asked, trying to ignore the tightness in her throat, the peculiar rolling sensation in her stomach, 'Is Mr Dexter here?' And held her breath.

'Couldn't say, miss. I generally take my orders from his PA. I'm just the driver. Now…' he set the cases down '…if you'll wait half a tick I'll go find Ms Penny.'

Caroline closed her eyes as she expelled her breath and slowly opened them again to take stock. The central, sweeping staircase had been freshly waxed, as had the linen-fold wall panelling. And the black and white slabs beneath her feet gleamed with care.

All vastly different from the dingy, increasingly neglected house she had been brought up in.

But echoes of the past remained. If she listened hard enough she could hear her father's acid voice. 'You will do as I say, Caroline, exactly as I say.' And even worse, 'I will not tolerate it. Village children are not suitable playmates. If you disobey me again you will be severely punished.' And Mrs Skeet's voice, pleading, 'Don't cross your dad, young Carrie. You know it isn't worth it.'

Her full mouth tightened. She had crossed him in the end. Monumentally. Had been forbidden the house. And had been glad to go, the legacy her mother had bequeathed her enabling her to continue her studies.

Might things have been different if her mother had lived? If she'd been the son her father had wanted?

'So you swallowed your Harvey pride. I more than half expected you to refuse to turn up.'

The soft dark voice punched through her like a body-blow. Her breath tensed and trembled in her lungs as she turned reluctantly to face him. He had entered by the main door behind her and although the hall was large by any standards he dominated it.

Gypsy-dark black eyes hinting at a wildness only superficially tamed, soft black hair fingered by the breeze, lithe body clothed in black, of course, to match his soul, snug-fitting jeans, topped by a fluid fine-cotton shirt.

Her heart stung deep in her breast. But she could hold her own. No longer in thrall to his seductive magic she was his equal, or more than, and not his willing toy.

The possibility that he might be here had had her dressing for effect, making a statement. Beautifully tailored, sleek deep blue suit, high-heeled pumps, her hair coiled into a knot at her nape, her stockings sheer and disgracefully expensive, her only jewellery a thin gold chain that shone softly against the milky-pearl skin of her throat. Where, to her deep annoyance, a pulse had started to beat much too rapidly.

'Where my work's concerned I have no prejudices. You hired a professional, Mr Dexter.'

'So I see.' A hint of amusement tugged at the corners of his long, sensual mouth as his dark eyes swept from the top of her glossy black hair to the tips of her shoes and back again to lock with hers. 'Such elegant packaging—exquisitely understated of course—such control. Every inch the daughter of the landed gentry.' His voice deepened to a honeyed drawl. 'I recall times when—'

'Mr Dexter.' She cut in firmly, desperately trying to ignore the way his lazy, explicit appraisal had set her skin on fire, had made the blood fizz alarmingly in her veins. 'Might I suggest we stick to why I'm here?' She broke off, sheer relief making her feel light-headed as a woman in her early thirties walked briskly towards them from the back of the house.

Short blonde hair curved crisply around an open, cheerful face, her short, wiry body clothed in service-able blue jeans and a navy sweatshirt. Ms Penny? A far cry from the billowy, faded prettiness of Dorothy Skeet.

'Sorry to have kept you; Martin couldn't find me. Unblocking a drain.' Brisk voice but a warm smile. 'Lunch in fifteen minutes, boss. Breakfast room.' Bright grey eyes were turned on Caroline. 'I'll show you where you'll sleep, Miss Harvey.' She picked up the luggage and headed for the stairs.

Caroline followed, still light-headed enough to have to hold onto the banisters. It was bad enough that Dexter was around when he didn't need to be. She could have done the job she'd been hired to do without having him under her feet.

But if he was going to try to dredge up the past, make pointed comments on the way she looked then the next two or three days would be intolerable.

CHAPTER THREE

'HERE we go, then.' The housekeeper pushed open a door at the far end of the corridor that ran the full and impressive length of the house. 'No *en suite*, I'm afraid, but there's a bathroom next door.'

Caroline sucked in a sharp breath as she stood on the threshold. Was it coincidence or had Dexter issued instructions that she should be given this particular room?

He knew it had been hers. How many times had he tossed pebbles at the window to wake her? Countless. But she'd never been sleeping; she'd been waiting for his signal, full of longing for the arms of her secret lover, racked with anxiety in case he didn't come, ready to fly silently down the stairs to be with him, to melt with him into the magical beauty of the soft summer night.

A wave of ice washed through her, followed by unstoppable drenching heat. She shook her head, annoyed by her body's reaction, then firmed her mouth, a flicker of scorn darkening the deep blue of her eyes. She was too strong now to let him get to her on any level. In any event, the atmosphere of the room felt entirely different.

The faded nursery paper had been replaced by soft primrose-yellow emulsion and there was a pale ferny-green carpet instead of the cracked linoleum that had shrivelled her bare feet in wintertime—

'You'll have lunch with the boss—the breakfast room's the third door on the left, off the hall.' The housekeeper put the bags down at the side of the bed. 'He'll give you instructions on what he wants you to do, of course. But if there's anything else you need, you just let me know.'

'Thank you. It's Ms Penny, isn't it?'

Really, she had to get a grip, not go to pieces simply because she'd be using her old room for a night or two. She made herself smile, walk through the door instead of hovering like someone being urged to enter a chamber of horrors! For pity's sake, she didn't have to remember if she didn't want to!

'Call me Linda. I only come over Ms-ish when I'm on my dignity!' A disarming grin then a square, capable hand was extended and was taken.

'And I'm Caroline. Tell me, is Mr Dexter staying too, or is this a flying visit?' She hoped it was the latter, but she wouldn't put money on it.

'Staying, as far as I know. He comes and goes. Usually he just drops by from time to time to keep an eye on work in progress. But this time he arrived with a heap of luggage. Now...' a quick glance at the man-sized watch she wore '...I'll get lunch on the table. It's cold; I'm not much of a hand when it comes to cooking. Admin's my line and there won't be a cook in residence for another month, so you're going to have to take pot luck, I'm afraid.'

A live-in cook as well as a housekeeper to ensure

the smooth day-to-day running of the house. Dexter must have decided to make Langley Hayes his permanent home she mused as Linda left the room. Showing that the wild, penniless youngster could lord it over the village just as her father had done? Only in better style, with far more money to throw around.

Sucking her lower lip between her teeth Caroline methodically began to unpack. In a way she couldn't blame Dexter for what he was doing. Brought up by his mother—a rather fearsome woman, she remembered—paying a small rent for the dubious delights of living in a near derelict cottage on her father's estate which no one else would dream of inhabiting, the unconventional pair had been looked down on by the majority of the villagers. It would take a strong-minded man to resist the temptation to come back and display his new-found affluence.

Not that his motives interested her, of course. They didn't. Her only concern was getting the job done and getting back to London.

Aware of the passage of time, she squashed the childish impulse to refuse to go down to lunch at all. Refusing to face problems wasn't her style.

And he was a problem, she admitted as she opened the breakfast-room door a few minutes later. He was waiting for her, his back to the tall window that framed a view of newly manicured parkland. Tall, tough, beautifully built, even more compellingly handsome than he had been twelve years ago.

But there was something missing. There was no

sign of the former tenderness, or the sexily inviting
smile that had captivated her, had bound her to him
during that lost, lazy, loving summer. The man he
had become was arrogant, his slight smile insolent,
the dark glitter of his eyes speaking of derision overlaid with the bleak menace of an anger she couldn't
understand. If anyone had the right to be angry it
was she.

'So you decided not to ask for a tray in your room.
Bravo!'

The nerve-pricking insolence deepened his smile.
Caroline went very still. This had to stop, this nee-
dling. She opened her mouth to tell him as much but
her lips remained parted and silent as he gestured
with one finely boned, strong hand, 'Shall we eat?'

The small circular table had been haphazardly set
with earthenware plates of cold-cut roasts and unin-
spired salads. But there was wine, an excellent mus-
cat, she noted as she reluctantly took her place, vowing not to touch a drop. She needed to keep a clear
head when dealing with the man who carried such
an aura of danger.

She shivered suddenly and if she'd hoped she
could keep that betraying reaction to herself she was
doomed to disappointment.

'Cold?' An upwards twitch of one straight black
brow. 'I thought it was unseasonably warm for mid-
April.' He lifted the wine from the ice bucket, but
she quickly placed her hand over her glass.

'No?' He poured sparingly for himself, his movements deft, undeniably pleasing. 'Then do help your-

self—I think we've been given beef.' A semi-humorous glance at her pale, set features. 'And I apologise for the cheap plates and cutlery. But that's the way the cookie crumbles. Your father must have sold all the family silver along with the Royal Worcester.'

They'd eaten from Minton, not Worcester, the pieces mismatched but beautiful, the silver flatware heavy, with richly decorated handles. She felt colour stain the skin that covered her cheekbones.

'Cut it out!' she ground out unthinkingly, her lips tightening at his undisguised taunt. She hadn't meant to rise, had decided to ignore any sly jibes coming from him, but it hadn't happened; she hadn't been able to help herself.

Her hands knotted together in her lap, she added heatedly, 'I know why you wanted me to come here, so let's take it as read, shall we? Then perhaps I can get on with the work you hired me for.'

The urge to get to her feet and walk out of this room was strong. But she wouldn't do it; it would be another display of regrettable temperament, letting him know just how easily he could get to her.

So she sat mutinously still, hoping her features displayed nothing but boredom now. Until he leant back, one arm looping over the back of his chair, lazy mockery in his dark velvet voice.

'So you tell me—why did I want you here?'

Anger kicked inside her again and she said good-bye to all her remaining control for the first time in years, huge, thickly lashed violet eyes snapping as they clashed with the black enigma of his. 'Because my father called you the scum of the earth.' She recalled his exact words, spoken contemptuously so long ago. 'You stole from him, you were a danger to the morals of the village girls—'

That didn't hurt her, not now, not after so many years! How could it?

'You lived in squalor. So when father died, in debt, and you were able to buy up his property, you decided to drag me here and rub my nose in it!'

Suddenly running out of steam she sagged back. Since his callous betrayal of her younger self she'd learned not to have strong emotions, certainly not blind, unthinking anger. Still, she supposed, it was better said than not. Bottled anger festered, left scars.

'Wrong,' he said lightly, his long mouth twitching unforgivably, her tirade and character assassination not causing him a moment's discomfiture. 'But interesting. My mother and I lived in squalor because when we arrived in the village we couldn't afford anything else and it gave your father a very small income while the cottage was in the process of falling down.

'And as for stealing from him...' long fingers played with the stem of his wine glass, the dark, hypnotic depths of his eyes holding hers '...I was fourteen when we came here and was under the mistaken impression that the trout in the stream that ran behind our hovel were free for the taking. Your father put me right with the aid of a rather threatening shotgun.

'That said…' his mouth hardened '…I didn't bring you here to rub your disdainful little nose in my financial success. Your presence here is a necessity.'

'Now,' he inserted coolly, handing her the platter of cold meat, 'I suggest we eat, and then you can get down to work.'

Once, he'd told her she was necessary to his happiness; now, her expertise was the only thing he wanted from her. She swallowed convulsively, wishing her mind didn't stray into the past, comparing it to the uncomfortable present. Another impulse came to cut and run. But Edward would not be pleased, and that was putting it mildly. Dexter was paying handsomely for her presence here. Walk out and the gallery would lose a potentially valuable client, acquire a black mark against its venerable name.

Grimly, she speared a slice of beef, added a tomato and wondered if she'd be able to force any of it down. He hadn't countered the claim that he'd been a moral danger to the village girls simply because he couldn't.

Did he know he'd left at least one fatherless child behind him when he'd disappeared from the village, richer by the several hundred pounds her father had paid him to leave, an amount that must have seemed like a fortune to him back then? Of course he did. Maggie Pope had told him her baby daughter was his. He hadn't wanted to know.

'As I'm here to sort out the dross from the remaining good pieces, perhaps you would tell me where you'd like me to start. Or do I have a free hand?'

She did her best to sound brisk and business-like, to put the regrettable disturbance of the personal behind her. But recalling the part of her life that had left her disillusioned, hurt and betrayed had sapped her energy, had made her feel drained.

She was hardly in a fit condition to endure the long appraisal he gave her expensively tailored, slim jacket, the fine fabric and sophisticated style discreetly announcing a coveted designer label before he stated, 'Start at the top and work down. I don't think the contents of the attics have been looked at in years. And, I'll warn you, you'll find a fair amount of builders' rubble—part of the roof had to be re-tiled—among the dust and grime of decades. It can be properly cleaned out once you've decided if there's anything up there worth keeping.'

He finished the wine in his glass and said with a flicker of impatience, 'If you've finished mangling your food perhaps you would make a start.'

He was vile! Caroline thought as she stood in the open attic doorway. He had looked at the way she was dressed and had deliberately sent her up here.

It was even worse than she'd remembered, lumps of fallen, crumbling plaster littered the cobweb-shrouded disintegrating boxes, weighed down the laughably named ragged and torn dust-sheets that only partly covered old, unwanted bits of furniture.

She had removed her stockings and replaced the

high heels with Gucci loafers but they, and her suit, would be ruined.

Had he guessed that the things she'd brought with her were all beautiful and expensive, that she'd been determined that if he should show up he would see a cool, elegantly sophisticated career woman—in direct contrast to the wild, uninhibited young thing she had been when he'd held her in his arms, had made love to her, whispering of his adoration.

How he had changed! But, there again, maybe he hadn't. That streak of cruelty had been inherent in his nature. He couldn't have used and betrayed her, lied to her, if it hadn't. Or abandoned the woman who had given birth to his child.

She turned abruptly on her heels and backtracked down the twisty attic staircase. Linda was at the kitchen table, making notes in a ledger.

Taking in the new quarry-tiled floor, the huge state-of-the-art cooking range, immense dishwasher and commercial-sized fridge, Caroline wondered briefly if Dexter intended to settle down to marriage, raise an enormous family, then dismissed that from her mind as something of no consequence and asked, 'Do you have an overall I could borrow? I've been asked to clear out the attics.'

'Oh lord, they're filthy, aren't they?' Linda laid down her pen and gave her a sympathetic smile as she got to her feet. 'I said the whole lot should be put on a bonfire, but the boss said there might be something of sentimental value. Apparently, this house was owned by some monumental old snob—

been in the family for generations. He's dead now, but there was a daughter. The boss said to leave it as it was. She might come back some time and be gutted if she found family stuff had been destroyed.'

Had Dexter really been that thoughtful? Something twisted sharply inside her. Had he really believed she might return at some time in the future? Had he taken his opportunity to force her to return to the family home when they'd eventually met up again because he wanted her to have anything of sentimental value?

And where did that leave her theory that his prime motivation was to turn the tables on her?

But she was too shaken by what she'd heard to try to work out his motives. She said heavily, 'Then, he can't have sent me to work in the attics solely because he wanted to see me get my hands dirty. I am the daughter of that monumental old snob.'

A heartbeat of silence. Linda gave her a startled look. 'I'm sorry. I had no idea—'

'Don't worry about it. He was an incurable snob. He believed he had a position to uphold, but the problem was he didn't have the wherewithal to sustain it.'

That had been common knowledge, he hadn't known that the people from the village had laughed at him behind his back. She didn't add that he'd been authoritarian, cold and unloving. He had been her father, after all. She owed his memory some loyalty.

'I—well—' Linda was clearly embarrassed by her *faux pas*. 'I don't go in for overalls, but I think the previous housekeeper left some behind. Hang on a tick, I'll see what I can find in the box of stuff put out for the next jumble sale.'

Moments later she was back carrying a small pile of laundered, folded garments. Flimsy nylon, flower-patterned overalls. Very feminine, very Mrs Skeet.

'Do you know where Mrs Skeet is now?' Curiosity and a slight, lingering affection for the woman who had looked after her—in a fashion—prompted Caroline to ask as she tucked the overalls under her arm.

'Rents the cottage next to the village stores,' Linda supplied. 'When the renovation work started here she came up two or three times to clear out your father's clothes. Nice woman, a bit prone to flap. You could tell she was gutted by your old man's death.'

The question, Why hadn't his daughter undertaken that sombre task? lurked at the back of the other woman's eyes but Caroline wasn't answering it. 'I'll make time, one evening while I'm here, to visit her.' Her accompanying smile was small and social as she turned and walked away. She knew why her father had forbidden her the house, had said he never wanted to see her again. But she would never know why he had been unable to feel any affection for her at all. Maybe Dorothy Skeet could supply the answer.

Caroline hung up her suit and buttoned one of the overalls over her black satin bra and briefs. The skimpy fabric was virtually transparent and the splashy blue and pink roses were a nightmare. Plus, the thing itself was oceans too large.

Not to worry that she looked completely ridiculous; no one would see her and her suit would be saved from certain ruination.

Back in the airless space beneath the roof she began to work methodically, clearing an area at one end where she could stack rubbish, hauling boxes of chipped china and battered saucepans, a collapsed Victorian whatnot, over the uneven, dusty boards, wondering why people hoarded useless objects, then remembering how in her childhood she had found magic up here, the perfect antidote to many a wet and lonely day.

There had been a dressing-up box, at least that was how she'd thought of it: A tin trunk full of old clothes, probably once belonging to her great-grandmother and her mother, most of the things beautiful and all of them fragile. Period dresses could fetch big money, especially if they were in good condition and, remembering back, most of them had been.

After some searching she found the trunk, lifted the lid and found it empty, apart from a bundle of letters tied up with faded ribbon. Her father must have sold the things when money got tight. At Dorothy Skeet's prompting? She could remember the housekeeper's voice as if it was yesterday, 'I thought I'd find you up here. It's time for bed. And mind what you're doing with those things—they can be really valuable. Still, if dressing up keeps you quiet and out of the way—'

Caroline sank down on her heels. Her shiny black

hair had come adrift from its moorings. She pushed it back off her face with a dusty hand, leaving a dark smudge on the side of her milky-pale face.

If only her father could have swallowed his pride and sold Langley Hayes instead of re-mortgaging it, moved to a much smaller place, then he could have spent his final years free from financial worry. But his sense of self-importance wouldn't have let him do that.

Sighing, she reached for the letters. They were from her father, written to her mother before their marriage. She selected the one at the top of the bundle and began to read. A few lines were enough to tell her that they'd been deeply in love with each other, a few more told her that the young Reginald Harvey had adored and worshipped his beautiful bride-to-be.

She slipped the letter back in its envelope and bound it back with the others, her fingers shaking. This was personal and private and showed her a side of her father she had never known existed. He had been capable of a love so strong and enduring it practically sang from the faded pages.

Clutching the letters, she got to her feet, her eyes blurred with sudden tears. And saw him. She couldn't breathe.

She hadn't given Ben Dexter a single thought for the last couple of hours but now he was standing in the open attic doorway, watching her. And he filled her head, the whole drowsy, dusty space. The atmosphere was charged with his presence.

If she'd explained to her father— the thought came
fleetingly—just how deeply she'd been in love with
Ben Dexter instead of stubbornly remaining mute,
her eyes defiant, then perhaps he would have understood. He had known the type of love that could
enthral, that could bind one person to another with a
special kind of magic.

Just as swiftly that thought was replaced by something much more cynical: it wouldn't have made a
blind bit of difference. Even if her father could have
been persuaded to approve of her relationship with
the village wild boy instead of threatening fire and
brimstone there wouldn't have been a happy ending.
The black-eyed, half tamed, young Dexter had never
loved her. Had just lied about it because he'd wanted
sex with her, happy enough to go find it elsewhere
when he'd had a fistful of her father's money as a
pay-off.

Now the downward sweep of his eyes, the curl of
his long, hard mouth told her that he'd noted her
weird appearance and had fastened on what was obvious: the clear outline of her svelte body showing
through the ghastly overall, modesty secured, but
only just, by the tiny black bra and briefs.

Quelling the impulse to run right out of here, she
lifted her chin a fraction higher and coolly asked,
'You wanted something?'

'You.'

Eyes like molten jet swept up and locked with hers
and for a moment she thought he meant it. Meant
just that. Her bones trembled, heat fizzing through

her veins, her breath lodging in her throat. Until a deep cleft slashed between his dark brows, the lazy, taunting smile wiped away as he moved closer.

Of course he hadn't meant he wanted her the way he once had. Wildly, passionately, possessively. He just wanted to check the hired help was actually working, not sitting somewhere with her feet up, painting her nails.

Which was just as well because she didn't want him, most certainly she didn't. Until he touched her, the merest brush of the backs of his fingers as he stroked the heavy fall of midnight hair away from her face and everything inside her melted in the shattering conflagration of present desire and remembered ecstasy.

Dry-mouthed, she could hardly breathe, the air tasting thick and heavy on her tongue as he touched the wet spikiness of her lashes with the tip of his forefinger and said heavily, 'You're upset, Caro. I didn't mean that to happen, I truly didn't.'

Concern in those black, black eyes, a bone-melting softness. She remembered how that look could slice straight into her heart. Remembered that time, all those summers ago, a moonlit night, she'd collided with a sapling oak because when she'd been with him she'd seen nothing else. The same look as then, as he'd stroked the soft white skin of her shoulder, as if his touch, his love, could have stopped the slight abrasion from hurting, prevented a bruise from forming. She hadn't doubted the sincerity of his concern for her then.

But she should have done.

'I thought there might be something here of sentimental value,' he told her softly. 'Souvenirs of your childhood, photograph albums, whatever; things you might like to keep. Mrs Skeet has your father's personal effects. I know she intended to contact you. I'll arrange for the two of you to meet up while you're here.'

His hand lay lightly on her shoulder and her whole body tightened in rejection of what he was now and what he had been. Unwittingly, her eyes came up and levelled on his mouth. It looked as if he'd kissed more women than he'd had hot dinners. And as a well-worn cliché it probably hit the mark.

'No need,' she answered, keeping her voice steady, hard, even. 'I'd already decided to contact Dorothy. So far...' she shrugged his hand away '...I've found nothing of any value or interest apart from these letters which I intend to keep. But I'll continue looking.'

Oh, how she wished she didn't look so darned ridiculous! That Dorothy's cast-off overalls had been made from good, solid cotton, something, anything, that didn't reveal her skimpy underwear to eyes that were now hard, definitely ungiving. Because she'd rejected his concern as certainly as if she'd physically pushed the words back down his throat?

'Not now.' He turned away from her. 'Carry on in the morning. I told Linda we'd eat out this evening; she's got enough on her hands without having to feed us.' He paused in the doorway, turned to look at her, his voice hovering between frustration and amusement, 'Change out of that whatever it is—nightdress?—and be ready to leave in thirty minutes.'

CHAPTER FOUR

'I'M SURE you must be hungry by now. You barely touched your lunch.' No hint of that deeply unsettling caring in his voice now, just a smoky curl of amusement.

It was eight o'clock and the light was beginning to fade from the clear, evening sky. His teeth gleamed whitely against the olive tones of his skin as he switched off the ignition and gave her the self-assured, chillingly predatory smile that sent a rapid succession of shivers down the length of her spine.

She could have said with truth that she was absolutely ravenous, that it was his fault she hadn't been able to swallow more than a mouthful of her lunch. But she gave a brief dip of her glossy dark head and told him, 'Slightly,' instead.

Expecting the village pub she'd dressed as down as she could, given the selection of clothes she'd brought with her. But they'd ended up on the forecourt of what looked like a formidably exclusive eating house in the depths of the country and if the female clientele were all wearing little black numbers she'd stick out like a sore thumb in her cream linen trousers, toning Italian sweater and Gucci loafers.

Not that she was going to let it bother her, she decided as her assumption proved correct. In any case, Ben Dexter, immaculately suited, with his darkly virile looks, his obvious sophistication, stole all the attention. And sitting opposite him as they were handed menus as large and difficult to handle as broadsheets she wondered why he was bothering to try to impress her.

For the same reason he'd wanted to impress the locals when he'd bought the Langley Hayes estate— despised poor boy makes good?

He'd impressed her far more twelve years ago when he'd had two burning ambitions: To make her his wife and to achieve the financial success to keep her in style. At least, that was what he had said, and she'd believed him. Gullible fool that she'd been!

Oh, the success had come, no doubt about it, and she hadn't been interested in being kept in style— but as for making her his wife, nothing had been further from his lying, cheating mind.

She handed her menu to a passing waiter, glad to be rid of it. She said, lightly, coolly, 'I'll be a little late starting in the morning. I need to walk down to the village to see if Angie Brown still carries a stock of jeans and shirts. I need something serviceable if I'm going to spend half my time rooting around in the attics. And I was wearing one of Dorothy Skeet's overalls. I don't go to bed in billowing yards of flowery stuff.'

Suddenly the black eyes were laughing at her, his mouth a sinful curve, and she knew it had been a huge mistake to remind him that he'd suggested she was wearing her nightdress when he said, 'What do you wear to bed these days? Tailored silk pyjamas? There was a time when our bed was the softest, coolest moss we could find, if you remember. Or, if it rained, and it rarely did, the sweetly rustling hay in your father's stable loft. Neither of us wore a stitch back then.'

And then, without missing a beat, while thick hot colour swept into her cheeks and something nameless twisted viciously inside her, he said, 'The village store altered five years ago when Angie retired. The new owners don't stock clothing. But I need to drive into Shrewsbury tomorrow; you can come with me. You can shop while I keep my appointment with my solicitors.' He broke a bread roll with those long, strong fingers, buttered one ragged half and added softly, 'There's a rather good trattoria in Butcher Row. We can meet there for lunch.'

Just like that! Oh lord, let me get my composure back, she prayed, willing her pulse beat back to normal. Dropping explicit reminders of the past into everyday conversation was going to do her head in if he persisted. Best to ignore it. Hope it was a one-off.

'I would have thought you'd have used a firm of slick city lawyers.' She took up the conversational ball, ignoring his reference to the long, stolen nights they'd spent together, hoping that in future he would do the same. If he didn't then she'd be forced to have her say, and she didn't want to have a stand-up fight with him, risk him complaining to Edward, putting the job she loved in jeopardy. Much better to try to hold her tongue on the vexed subject of their past and keep their present relationship as businesslike as it was possible to be under the circumstances.

'No. I believe in supporting local firms—now.' As their waiter approached, he added, 'What will you have?'

She recited her order of Danish tartlets followed by red mullet with mushrooms abstractedly. By referring to himself as local he'd made it plain that he intended to settle at Langley Hayes. Being surrounded by his company's golf course and leisure centre would be a small price to pay for the self-aggrandisement of living in the home of his former enemy.

A home large enough to house a wife, a growing number of children and an army of servants. The thought that he might be contemplating marriage made her feel almost terminally ill.

Though it shouldn't. He was less than nothing to her now and she pitied his future wife. Once a liar and cheat, always a liar and cheat where women were concerned. She refused his offer of wine, ate well, made banal conversation and was thankful when they left.

The headlights made a sweeping golden tunnel beneath the newly leafing trees that overhung the narrow lane. Soon the Queen Anne's lace would foam on the verges and the wild roses and honeysuckle would bloom, filling the air with fragrance.

Her childhood had been lonely and often miserable

but even so she loved this part of the country. But her life was in London now, her home, her work, her friends. She didn't want or need to feel this utterly surprising, aching pang of nostalgia.

Without thinking, as they swept onto the driveway of Langley Hayes, she said tartly, 'I'm sure the area has a need for a golf course and leisure facilities—your company wouldn't have gone for it if they hadn't done their homework—but won't you mind being surrounded by people? Father would have had a fit if he'd found what he called the *hoi polloi* wandering around his property.'

'I'm not your father,' he observed coldly and she tightened her mouth in mute acknowledgement. He was far more handsome and charismatic than her father had ever been, worked hard—he must do to have acquired what was obviously a massive fortune where her father had lived on dwindling capital, and had mismanaged what had been left of the once enormous estate. But both men possessed a streak of cruelty, a complete disregard for other people's feelings.

'And I won't be here that often to be troubled by the masses,' he added sardonically. 'However, I will keep a suite of rooms here.'

He parked the gleaming Jaguar perilously close to the builder's skip, the tyres crunching on badly targeted lumps of plaster and brick ends. Caroline, getting out before he did, wondered if he was always as careless with his possessions as he was with other people's emotions.

She entered the house before he did but he caught up with her. 'Share a bottle of wine with me?'

His voice had lost that sharp edge and here in the soft silence of the house his presence was sensationally male and potent. And dangerous.

She shuddered inside. How easy it would be to give in to the temptation. Just be with him, get to know the man he had become. Wonder if he still made love as generously as he had done all those years ago or if he'd become jaded, taking his physical pleasure perfunctorily.

She slammed the door of her mind shut on that thought and shook her head slightly. 'Thank you, but I'll pass. What time do you leave for Shrewsbury tomorrow?'

'Ten. We should be back here by three. Are you sure about that wine?'

'Perfectly sure.' The best part of tomorrow would be wasted if she went with him. Spending more time with him than was absolutely necessary wasn't on her agenda. Why hadn't she had the foresight to bring something rough-and-ready to wear? Because none of her clothes fitted that category.

She smothered a sigh and said, 'I'll pass on the shopping trip, too. I'll manage with what I have.' Better to ruin her clothes than the image of a cool and collected professional. There was a limit to how much time she could spend with him without giving in to the temptation to tell him how much he disgusted her.

She turned her back and headed for the stairs and

heard him say softly, 'Running scared, Caro? I wonder why?'

In her room she closed the door and leant back against it, breathing heavily, her heart banging against her ribs. She felt as if she'd run a marathon with the devil on her tail. And the devil was Ben Dexter.

Once she'd adored him; he'd become her sole reason for living and her life had fallen apart when he'd betrayed her. But that betrayal didn't alter his incredible physical appeal. It should do, but it didn't.

She pushed herself away from the door, more than annoyed with herself for the direction her thoughts were taking. Furious.

Selecting an aqua silk nightdress and matching robe she went to the bathroom and ten minutes later, belting the robe around her narrow waist, she walked back and found Linda tapping on her bedroom door.

'I thought you might like to borrow these. They'll be too wide and too short, I guess, but they'll be more practical than those wispy flowery things.'

Caroline gave her heart-stopping smile. She could have hugged the other woman. She wouldn't have to ruin her own clothes and, more to the point, she wouldn't have to wonder when Dexter might walk in on her to make a point of looking at her underwear!

'Thanks, Linda!' She accepted the neatly folded jeans and faded green sweatshirt, debated whether to ask why Dexter, with the whole house at his disposal, would be keeping just a suite of rooms for his occasional use, and then thought better of it. Questions like that would only display an interest she desperately wanted to deny, particularly to herself. 'This is really thoughtful of you,' she said instead.

'Think nothing of it,' Linda gave a slight shrug, asking, 'Did you enjoy your evening?'

'The food was excellent.' She evaded the question, one hand going to the doorknob, turning it, opening the bedroom door. She didn't want to talk about it.

'Good.' Linda took her dismissal with an easy smile. 'I'll say goodbye in case I don't see you again. I've got the rest of the week off—family christening; my sister's first and I'm godmother—so you might have finished here before I get back.'

So she'd be alone here with Dexter, Caroline thought sinkingly as she smiled and said all the right things, and closed her bedroom door behind her telling herself staunchly that the other woman's absence wouldn't really matter. She could handle Ben Dexter all by herself; she didn't need backup.

He could no longer be remotely interested in her sexually. Been there, done that; his past history showed he was that kind of man. He had only insisted she come here so that he could demonstrate how well he'd done for himself, show her that he now had the upper hand.

Well, that she could handle, no problem; in fact she admired his financial acumen. As for the other, the unwanted sexual pull she was unable to hide from herself, well, she hated to admit it, but she was having difficulties.

And instead of being able to dismiss them from her wakeful mind she found herself lying in the darkness actually listening for his signal, the pebbles he'd lightly tossed against the window-pane, calling her down to him.

How willingly she'd gone...

She sat up, squirming to the edge of the bed, flicked on the bedside lamp and pressed her fingertips to her aching temples.

She had to pull herself together, stop remembering. They were different people now and she knew what a heartless bastard he really was. The man she'd loved all those years ago was nothing but a figment of her imagination, a silly romantic dream.

Her watch told her it was just gone two o'clock and she knew she wouldn't sleep. Why lie sleepless in bed, agonising over the past, when she could be working, bringing the time of her departure that little bit closer?

The decision made, she slipped her arms into the aqua silk robe once more, tied the belt securely and reached for her notebook.

She'd visit the dining room first she thought as she slipped silently down the great staircase. The Regency dining table with its twelve chairs had been sold long ago. She'd been about fourteen years old, home for the Christmas break and, when she'd questioned him, her father had said sarcastically, 'How else am I to pay your boarding school fees? Rob a bank? Ask the tooth fairy?'

Useless to tell him, for perhaps the fourth time,

that she'd have been happier at the nearest comprehensive. He'd given that withering look he'd seemed to reserve for her alone. 'Remember who you are!'

Who she was. Suddenly she had the unnerving feeling that she didn't know. A successful woman in her own right or a rootless shadow, pining for a lost love? Being back here with the boy who had been forbidden in the grounds, now transformed into a hard-eyed man who owned everything around her, made her feel unreal.

Shrugging off the unsettling feeling she turned her mind back to business. The table had gone, never replaced because her father had never entertained. But there had been a mahogany serving table— George III she thought—and a large dresser of around the same period. Both would be valuable and would represent a sound investment.

Pushing open the double doors and quietly closing them behind her she unerringly found the light switch and stood for a moment, transfixed by what she was seeing, wishing she had swallowed her distaste at seeming to be interested, and had asked Linda what plans Dexter had for the house.

The ugly, dark red flocked wallpaper had been stripped away, replaced by warm primrose-yellow emulsion. The boards beneath her feet gleamed and two refectory tables, complete with long bench seats, took up the centre of the room while comfortable but functional armchairs surrounded the huge fireplace.

Remembering the catering-size kitchen equipment, the extra, functional bathroom that had been made in what had once been a bedroom next to her own, she began to put two and two together. But a country house hotel didn't make real sense. Everything was too basic.

Hearing the double doors behind her open she stiffened, holding her breath, praying that it was Linda doing the investigating, not Dexter.

But her luck was out, as it always had been with him, and he walked into her line of vision, dressed in black, a soft V-necked sweater over well-worn jeans, his feet bare, as were hers.

Her heart thumped, a bolt of electricity zapping through her bloodstream. He looked so unfairly sexy, his dark hair rumpled, his jaw shadowed, his black eyes glinting beneath heavy, brooding lids. How well she remembered that look, the promise it offered— and delivered.

'You couldn't sleep? I wonder why,' he uttered silkily, his eyes sweeping the length of her body, lingering on the soft curves and hollows that the tightly belted, slithery robe did precious little to conceal. He made her so aware of how little she was wearing.

'Something I ate at dinner. Indigestion,' she lied, desperately trying to ignore the quivers of sexual response that were careering right through her. She didn't want this to happen to her, to feel anything for him other than utter contempt.

And, the pity of it was, no other man had ever had this effect on her. She'd dated, of course she had; she hadn't turned into a man-hater. But no one had ever come near to invoking the intense emotions, the devastating physical needs Ben had awoken within her.

The notebook she was holding shook in her hands. She made herself open it, remove the pen that was clipped inside the spiral of metal that bound it together, and said, 'As I couldn't get to sleep I thought I might as well do some work. I hadn't meant to disturb you.'

'Meant or not, you did. And do,' he responded drily. 'And did you? Work?'

Wildly, she cast her eyes round the room that was now so different from how she remembered it, gathered her scattered mental resources and said, 'There used to be a serving table. Father probably sold it, unless you've moved it somewhere else.'

'Nope.'

She wasn't looking at him but she had the distinct impression he'd moved closer. Much closer. Her skin prickled. She said, her voice thickening deplorably, 'The dresser's still here. Georgian. Valuable. Hang onto it if you're looking for an investment.'

'At the moment all I'm looking at is you.'

Caroline gulped, her breath fluttering in her throat. What he'd said was true. She could feel his eyes on her, burning her flesh. She wanted out of here. Now. But her legs wouldn't move. Then she felt his hand on her waist, searing through the fine layers of silk, sending flickers of fire to her pulse points, each and every one of them. Don't, she wanted to say. Don't touch me. But her tongue was cleaving to the roof of her mouth.

'You're cold; the central heating's turned down to the minimum. Let's go. Warm milk should settle your—indigestion.'

The pressure of his hand increased, she could feel the exact placement of every fingertip. Now was the time to tell him she didn't want his hot milk, or his manufactured concern, to take herself back to her room. But she didn't. She simply went where he led, appalling herself by her mindless regression to that summer all those years ago when she would have followed him to purgatory and back if he'd asked her to.

'You haven't asked why I found it impossible to sleep,' he said as they entered the warmth of the kitchen. 'Don't you think that would be the correct response in the course of polite conversation?'

The dark rub of irony in his voice touched a raw nerve. What lay between them precluded normal polite conversation. But then, she remembered, he'd always had beautiful manners, despite his wild ways, always seemingly highly tuned into the feelings of others.

Seemingly.

She said nothing, just hovered, her slender body as taut as a bowstring, watching as he poured milk into a pan and reached for two mugs, a bottle of brandy. She knew she should walk out of the room, break this strangely prickly intimacy but some dark compulsion kept her where she was, just as much in thrall to his male vitality, his smouldering sexuality as she had ever been.

'Then, I'll tell you, since you don't seem inclined to ask.'

The mere sound of his voice made her catch her breath, her teeth sinking into the soft flesh of her lower lip. If she'd had her wits about her she would have said, Don't bother, I'm not interested. But her wits had gone on holiday, along with her common sense.

And he told her, 'Thinking of you, sleeping under the same roof, wasn't conducive to a peaceful night's rest. I needed something to read to take my mind off it. That was when I saw the strip of light under the dining-room doors.' He shot her a brief, frowning glance. 'I thought it would be easy, but it isn't.'

He poured the hot milk into the two mugs and Caroline drew her fine brows together.

What wasn't easy? Having her around? Was his guilty conscience pricking him? Why didn't he say what he meant? He always had before. He'd had deep emotions and he'd expressed them freely, had been totally up front about what he'd wanted. Her.

Just for a time, she reminded herself tiredly. Another notch on his bedpost, the sheltered daughter of the local landowner who had treated him like scum, no less. How he must have been laughing at her father!

And how he had changed. Not an emotion in sight. A puzzling flicker of anger once in a while but nothing else. Watching him rinse out the milk pan and put it in the cavernous depths of the dishwasher she determined to get at least one straight answer out of him: an answer to the question that had been teasing her mind.

'What plans have you for this house?'

'Ah.' His smile was slightly cynical. 'I wondered when your curiosity would get the better of that aloof mantle you assume for me.' He picked up the steaming mugs. 'I suggest we drink this in the comfort of the library. And I'll tell you what I have in mind for Langley Hayes. And in return you can tell me what messed up your relationship with—what was his name?—the Honorable Jeremy Curtis, wasn't it? You were due to celebrate your engagement on your eighteenth birthday. Quite a catch for the only daughter of an impoverished local squire. So what went wrong? Did he find out you'd been enjoying a bit of rough trade and call it off? You must have been devastated, especially when you'd been so insistent that we keep our meetings so carefully secret.'

CHAPTER FIVE

CAROLINE couldn't believe he'd said that!

Almost tripping over herself in her rush to catch him up, she followed him to the library, a small book-lined room furnished with the scuffed old leather sofas that had been here for as long as she could remember.

He knew why they'd kept their affair secret, damn him! He knew what her father had been like! And how dared he imply that she'd been using him just for sex!

He'd made space for the mugs on the cluttered top of a low table and now bent to flick on the electric fire. Caroline watched him through narrowed eyes, biting back the scalding torrent of recriminations.

If he'd made that insulting remark twelve years ago she would have responded with passion, hitting out, probably biting and scratching too! But she was older now, a hell of a lot older and in total control.

The angry thump of her heart threatened to push a hole in her breastbone, but she picked up one of the mugs in both shaking hands and sank down into the corner of a sofa.

She was not going to let him see he could still reach her on any emotional level. No way. Unlike her younger self, she could control her reactions to whatever he did or said.

So, treating his insulting remark about rough trade with the contempt it deserved, she ignored it and said, her voice tight and hard with the effort of masking her angry emotions, 'Any engagement was in my father's head, and Jeremy's, not mine.'

'Really? An engagement was arranged without one side of the happy couple being aware of it?'

Plainly, he didn't believe her. He was standing a few paces away, facing her, a straddle-legged stance. The way he'd hooked his thumbs into the low-slung waistband of his jeans drew her riveted attention to the narrow span of his hips, his tautly muscled thighs.

She wrenched her eyes away, fastened them on the mug she was cradling in her hands and lifted it to her lips. A hefty swallow told her that his lacing of brandy had been far more than generous. Nevertheless, it did begin to take the sharp edge off her anger.

She pulled in a breath. For some no doubt non-sensical reason, she wanted him to believe her. What he thought of her shouldn't be important but on some deep, troubled level it was.

One more mouthful of the potent liquid, and then she explained tightly, 'Dad was at Oxford with Jeremy's father and they kept in touch. After all, they only live twenty-odd miles away. Dad was Jeremy's godfather and when I was young I used to spend school holidays with them. I think Lady Curtis thought I needed mothering, and Dad was glad to get me out from under his feet.

Then, when I was around thirteen, Lady C. was killed in a riding accident, and my visits stopped. But we still saw Jeremy. He and his father were about the only people we ever saw socially. Dad wanted me to marry him.'

She shrugged slightly, memories clouding her eyes. Marrying Jeremy, and the Curtis fortune, would have been the one and only thing she could have done to actually please her father.

'Was the poor devil in love with you?' Ben demanded. His voice was harsh, a strand of bitterness threading through the obvious scorn.

It was a question he had no right to ask. Besides, she didn't know the answer. Oh, she'd caught Jeremy looking at her in ways that had made her feel uncomfortable and she'd been the unwilling recipient of a couple of clumsy, slack-lipped kisses. But love—no, she didn't truly think so. Lust was more like it and a willingness to fulfil their respective fathers' wishes in that rather spineless way he'd had.

She merely shrugged, took another gulp of the brandy-spiked milk and widened her eyes in shock as he castigated abruptly, 'Still a heartless bitch!' Then his voice flattened, as if control had been sought and found, and he said, 'Your letter telling me my services were no longer required was obviously written a little too late. Because by then he must have found out that you'd been having some fun on the side and the engagement never took place. The man must have been gutted.'

He took a pace forward, bending to thrust his face close to hers, his black eyes brimming with contempt. 'And all you can do is shrug!'

Anger as hot and sharp as his pulsed through her. How dared he act this way! Putting her mug down on the faded Persian carpet she got to her feet, the tilt of her chin mutinous as she countered scathingly, 'You're trying to put the blame on me for what happened to hide your own guilt—it's what people do, isn't it? Why should you be any different?'

His dark eyes flared as he took a step towards her. Caroline stood her ground. The situation was explosive but she wasn't going to run away from it. He had been guilty of almost every sin in the book, not she!

The palms of her hands were slick with sweat and the heat of his body consumed her, as if the fire of their anger was pulling them closer instead of pushing them further apart.

His lips curled thinly in a parody of a smile. 'Is that so? Then you deny writing to tell me you never wanted to see me again? You didn't even do me the courtesy of telling me to my face.'

Of course she couldn't deny it! She wanted to hit him for trying to put her in the wrong. 'You weren't around.' She spat the words out scornfully. 'After my father had been to see you, you'd taken off, remember?'

Even now she could hear her father's thin, sarcastic voice, 'You can forget your loutish lover. I offered him money to make himself scarce, and he couldn't take it fast enough. He won't be back and, if that's not enough to cool your ardour, ask young Maggie Pope who fathered that brat of hers.'

Caroline expelled a shaky, emotional breath. She hadn't wanted this bitter confrontation, or the dreadful effect it was having on her body, making her aware of every pulse point, of every inch of burning, sensitised skin. The adrenalin flooding through her was turning passionate anger into a dark and dangerous pleasure.

'So I wrote you a letter and left it with your mother. What else did you expect?' she said, her voice a low, tortured growl.

She was out of here, she had to be, before she said something that would rob her of her pride, something that would tell him how much, and for how long, his cruel betrayal had affected her.

As if he'd read her intentions, Ben's hand curved sharply round the back of her neck, his black eyes burning into hers. 'What did I expect?' He repeated her words, his voice thick now. 'You tell me! But there was a time…' the fingers that had been like talons on her neck gentled with the suddenly lowered tone of his voice '…when you more than fulfilled all my wildest expectations. Remember?'

The soft, stroking movement of his fingers on her skin held her far more effectively than that earlier threatening grip. Sensations she had denied for so long were springing to demanding life, making her head spin giddily when he repeated thickly, 'Remember, Caro? Remember how we only had to look at each other? How looking was never enough? How we had to touch naked skin, move our bodies in the dance of love, how you couldn't wait to take me inside you?'

'Don't!' The word was a moan of denial, issued from quivering lips. Her whole body was shaking with all the old dark magic, uncomfortably mixed with the aching sense of loss and betrayal that still echoed through the years. 'Let me go,' she said thickly, her mind horrified by her body's sensual anticipation.

'I would if you wanted me to.' His voice purred softly. 'But you don't. You're as ready for me now as you ever were. Deny it all you like, but these don't lie...' Gently, he rubbed the ball of his thumb over her parted, pouting lips, the soft friction setting up a primal ache deep inside her, making her need to draw his thumb into her mouth take on a forbidden and self-destructive urgency.

He dropped his hand as if he'd read the need in her eyes, his fingers finding their way along the angle of her jaw, sliding down her throat and slipping beneath the edge of her robe where the soft silk trembled with the panicky force of the beats of her pulse.

'And neither do these,' he added, his voice slow, sultry, infinitely disturbing as long fingers grazed the crests of her blatantly peaking breasts, lingering, easing beneath the insubstantial barrier of fabric.

Caroline couldn't breathe. His caressing fingers

sent shafts of exquisite pleasure through her, just as they always had. Whatever he'd done in the past was obliterated for just this moment when the ties of passion were the only memories.

Her lips parting, she lifted her suddenly leaden eyelids and met the harsh, hungry lights in the narrowed blackness of his eyes. Her breath juddered on a soft whisper of sound, the atmosphere was so emotionally charged it stung—a million pinpricks of sexual awareness; sharp, intrusive, deeply exciting.

She could taste all the old need and raw desire on her tongue, here and now, not something left over from the past, sternly pushed away if it dared to float into her consciousness on the wings of memory. Here, binding her to him as it always had, here in the assured claim of his night-dark, compelling eyes, in the slight, slow smile that curved his undeniably beautiful mouth, a sizzlingly sexy smile that robbed her mind and body of all strength of character.

'So…' He expelled a long, slow breath, his thick lashes sweeping down as he gazed at her mouth. 'No denials, Caro?' His dark head bent, his mouth a breath away from hers. 'Good. That's good.'

Her lips parted in helpless invitation. She could smell the fresh almost savagely male scent of him; it made her giddy. And then his mouth touched the corner of hers and she turned her head, instinctively, urgently seeking the remembered heady magic of his kiss, that total surrender to the ecstatically wild passion that no other man had ever come near to making her feel.

But he merely touched her full lower lip with the tip of his tongue then lifted his head, both hands fastening lightly around her narrow waist, keeping his control where she had lost hers entirely, and she was almost sobbing with cruel frustration as he said wryly, 'Like taking candy from a baby.'

Ben released her, stepping back, his mouth compressed as his dark eyes swept over the evidence of her body's arousal, from her peaking breasts, her softened, parted lips, the haze of sexual desire that clouded her deep violet eyes. 'Round one to me, Caro,' he added, then jerked his head towards the door, his voice clipped, impersonal. 'Get some sleep. You'll need it. At seventeen you could be up all night and still look ravishing in the morning.' He gave a slight, humourless smile. 'But things change, don't they?'

The implication was that she would look like a raddled hag in the morning, that she was over the hill and, just as shaming, that she had lost everything that had once driven him to wild passion, unable to look at her without needing her with a desperation that had consumed them both.

How she managed to walk in a straight line, get out of the room, she didn't know. The humiliation was so intense it turned her bones to water and filled her head with a fiery red mist that blinded her.

When she woke Caroline was mildly surprised that she'd managed to sleep at all and not at all surprised to note the dark rings around her eyes. Her normally pearly translucent skin was grey and dull in the bright spring light that flooded the small bedroom.

No, she was no longer seventeen. His taunt came back to sting her. She was twenty-nine years old and should have known better than to let a deceitful, lying louse like Ben Dexter rouse her so effortlessly, rouse her to the point of being on the verge of pleading with him to make love to her.

A hot tide of shame raged through her, making her feel nauseous. Her own body had betrayed her as surely as he had done all those years ago.

She shook her head then pressed her fingers to her aching temples. So, OK, she thought wearily, she'd behaved like a fool, like the gullible teenager she'd been when she'd emerged from the cool canopy of the woods on that long-gone, hot summer afternoon to find Ben perched on the top of the drunken wooden gate that led to one of her father's neglected hay meadows.

He'd been wearing cut-off shabby denims and, apart from scuffed canvas deck shoes, nothing else. The skin that covered his whippy frame had been nut-brown, glistening, his dark unruly hair flopping over his forehead, his black eyes dancing with a million seductive lights, his smile dangerous and sexy as he'd dropped to his feet and had walked with slow deliberation towards her.

She'd felt it then, the sizzling chemistry; it had made her breathless, so she could barely answer when he'd said, 'So school's out. Something tells me it's going to be a great summer.' His eyes told her he liked what he saw, her slenderness cloaked in soft summer cotton, her black hair tumbling down to her waist.

She'd never been this close to him before. The effect was shattering. Of course she knew that he and his mother lived in the decrepit cottage down by the stream, had done for several years. And she'd seen him in the village once or twice and heard the mutterings about his wild ways. And she could understand them, the mutterings, almost sympathise with the staid village matrons because Ben Dexter was something else: too drop dead gorgeous, too charismatic. An untamed male.

All she could do was give him a wide smile of glorious recognition and take the hand he held out to her. And so it had begun...

Caroline gave a shaky sigh then tightened her lips. She'd been such a gullible fool then, and last night she'd have gone down the same path if Ben hadn't demonstrated that he wasn't remotely interested.

But it was no use brooding about it or wishing it hadn't happened. It had and she had to put it out of her head, salvage some pride, do her job and get out of here as quickly as she could.

A shower helped a little. No way was she going to dress in the old jeans and top Linda had lent her and scrabble around in the dusty attics. Today of all days she needed to have all flags flying, to retrieve some of her pride and somehow try to wipe away the shame.

Ben wouldn't be around to see what she looked like but she needed to look her best for her own sake.

Teaming the elegantly cut linen trousers she'd worn to the restaurant with an oyster silk shirt and a narrow tan belt she spent far longer than usual on her make-up, achieving a discreet and perfect mask. Then she fixed her glossy hair into her nape with a mock-tortoiseshell comb.

Linda was at the kitchen table, a sheet of paper in front of her. She got up, smiling, as Caroline entered. 'Good—I was just about to leave you a note; now I don't have to bother. There's cold stuff in the fridge and loads of tins in the wall cupboards. So help yourself. I guess the boss will do the same—he's already left for Shrewsbury... And don't tell me you're going to tackle the attics in that outfit! Didn't the jeans and top fit?'

'I'm sure they will.' Caroline followed her nose to the coffee pot. 'I thought I'd give the attics a miss today and make a start on the first floor.' She lifted the pot. 'Like some?'

Linda wrinkled her pert nose. 'Go on, then, twist my arm! I should be on my way, but another ten minutes won't make much difference.' She sat down again, watching as Caroline filled two mugs. 'Tell me, how do you manage to look so flippin' stylish? It's something you're born with, I guess. Me, I look all wrong whatever I wear!'

'I'm sure that's not true.' Caroline sat opposite the other woman and handed her the milk jug and sugar bowl. She felt really mean; Linda obviously wanted to settle into girl talk but she herself had other ideas.

Last night she'd fully intended to satisfy her now burning curiosity and ask Ben what his plans were for Langley Hayes. And now, after what had happened, she would make sure that she had as little to do with him as possible during the remainder of her time here. So that precluded any conversation longer than one syllable.

So before Linda could start talking about clothes and make-up she said, 'I can't help noticing that the house has a rather institutional look. Comfortable and much brighter than it ever was when I lived here— but functional. What does Mr Dexter intend to do with it?'

'Don't you know?' Linda widened her eyes then gave a wry smile. 'No, of course you don't, or you wouldn't be asking!' She took a sip of her coffee then added more sugar. 'He's set up a trust, put a whole load of his own money in, and the income from the golf club and leisure centre will help with the upkeep, pay the helpers' wages. It's for disadvantaged kids—holidays, weekends. It's a brilliant idea— There'll be indoor activities as well as outdoor, a small farm, organic-produce gardens, riding, boating, fishing— It will let inner-city kids know there's more to life than hanging round street corners and getting into trouble.'

Long after Linda had left Caroline stayed in a mild state of shock. What the housekeeper had told her didn't gel with the picture of Ben Dexter she had built up in her mind: an arrogant, self-serving deceiver—a picture reinforced by his behaviour last night; his announcement that he'd won round one, as if he'd brought her here to engage in a battle. An announcement she'd been too filled with shame and embarrassment to question.

Had she been totally wrong about him? Had she misjudged him?

She pushed herself to her feet, putting the enigma that was Ben Dexter out of her mind. She had a job to do and it was pointless to waste her mental energies on a man who had as good as declared himself to be her enemy.

Bracing herself, she climbed the staircase to the room that had been her father's. The cumbersome Victorian wardrobes were empty as was the solitary chest of drawers, cleared out by the grieving Dorothy Skeet. The only piece of any value, the Italian, carved giltwood tester bed, which the housekeeper had sometimes shared, brought a lump to her throat.

She made a note of its likely value in the pad she carried and made a swift exit. Why had her father never loved her? Why had he actively disliked her?

Making a mental note to see Dorothy before she headed back to London she forced the memories of her troubled childhood to the back of her mind and carried on. The rooms that had been unused when her father had been alive were now cheerful and bright, either furnished with twin beds and colourful, functional chests and hanging cupboards, or made into bathrooms, ready for the youngsters who would be spending time here.

Ben must have invested a considerable amount of his private fortune in this charitable enterprise. Because he remembered his own deprived childhood?

The state had supported his mother, but only barely. Janet Dexter had tried to supplement her benefit by growing and selling fresh fruit and vegetables but the villagers, suspicious of the hard-eyed, grim-faced woman and her wild son, had refused to buy. Someone, she remembered now, had once threatened to report her pathetic entrepreneurial efforts to social security.

Life must have been tough for both of them, and what had brought mother and son to the village in the first place was unknown. Close as they had been during that long-ago summer, he had never talked about his earlier life. There were always things he'd kept hidden, even then.

Admiration for what he had made of himself, for his altruism where similarly disadvantaged children were concerned, made her bite her lip. She didn't want to think well of him. She couldn't afford to; she could so easily fall right back under his mesmeric spell, she admitted honestly. Last night had shown her that much.

Needing to keep her mental image of him sullied she reminded herself of the child he had fathered and had callously abandoned. Her own father had told her that Maggie Pope was a slut, had warned her not to have anything to do with her, ever, because if she did she'd be locked in her room until it was time to go back to school. Yet during those last traumatic days he'd said, 'Ask Maggie Pope who fathered that brat of hers. Dexter. You don't believe me? Well, just go and ask her!'

Caroline shuddered, her body suddenly cold, as if she'd been immersed in icy water. It had been the worst day of her life and she didn't want to relive it, but couldn't stop the pictures that flashed into her mind.

The baby girl, around two months old at that time, had had silky black hair, just like Ben's, and Maggie had said sourly, 'Sure she's his. Only he don't want to know—that's his sort all over. Drop a girl as soon as the novelty's over, or someone tastier comes along—no sense of responsibility!'

Swallowing hard, Caroline forced her mind back to the job in hand. At the far end of the corridor, where the old Tudor wing joined the main part of the house, there had been a handsome mahogany linen press. But, like most of the other pieces of any value, it had gone. Irritation pricked her. Her professional appraisal was unnecessary. The few pieces of any value would be obvious to anyone. Ben Dexter had got her here under false pretences.

But why?

Automatically, her hand lifted to the latch on the oak-boarded door that led to the old wing. These rooms, over the kitchen regions, had been forbidden to her as a child. 'Full of spiders and creepy-crawlies, and the floorboards are rotten,' Dorothy Skeet had warned, and she'd been eight years old before she'd plucked up the courage to poke her nose in.

Now all was changed. Crumbling timbers had been replaced with silvery oak beams and sunlight streamed in through the windows, enriching the colours of the Persian rugs on the polished floor of what was clearly the sitting room of the suite Ben had reserved for his own use, the attractively furnished room dominated by the painting that had thrown them together again. *First Love.*

She caught her breath, her heart starting to thud. If Michael hadn't recognised the lost Lassoon masterpiece for what it was, or if Ben hadn't wanted to own it, then her life would have gone on smoothly, the old, painful yearnings would never have resurfaced so strongly because she and Ben would not have met again.

Her bones tightened rigidly as she stared up at what could have been her mirror image. She and Ben had spent a couple of blissfully happy, ecstatic months together and his betrayal had been cruel. But it had been twelve years ago, for pity's sake. It should have been written off to experience, forgotten.

But it hadn't.

'You approve?' His voice was silky-soft.

Caroline gave an involuntary jerk of her head, startled out of her tormenting thoughts. Then she turned reluctantly to face him, her violet eyes huge in the delicate pallor of her face.

He was looking particularly spectacular in a beautifully cut dark blue suit, crisp white shirt and sober tie. At the back of the house she hadn't heard his car draw up outside. If she had she would have taken evasive action. As it was she could only answer his question, 'It's your painting, it's up to you where you hang it. Though I hope you have some sort of security system.'

'There speaks the prosaic Caroline Harvey.' He was smiling, just slightly, but his eyes were cold, like splinters of polished jet. 'But let's take the larger view, shall we? Don't you agree that the portrait should be here, back at home, as it were?' Laughter was lurking in the curl of his voice now. It incensed her.

'Rubbish!' she said stoutly. He was playing games with her and she wasn't going to let him amuse himself at her expense. 'You're talking as if that's a portrait of me hanging on that wall—and you know damned well it isn't. Now, if you'll excuse me—'

'But it could be, couldn't it?' he inserted smoothly. 'You, as I remember you. After I'd read the article about its discovery, saw the photograph, I knew I had to have that painting and hang it here. As a reminder that things aren't always as they seem. The sitter looks like you, but she isn't. Just as you, when I knew you, weren't what I thought you were.'

'That's a case of the pot calling the kettle black if ever I heard one!' she said in sharp retaliation. This was a man with a serious grudge. Had he resented so badly that letter saying she never wanted to see him again? Was his ego still smarting over being dumped for once, after all this time?

This was getting far too deep for her. She was leaving. This very minute.

'Mr Dexter,' she said, schooling her voice to what she hoped would pass as icy coolness. 'There is no point in my being here any longer. My professional services weren't required in the first place. As far as I can see you've already disposed of most of the worthless furnishings and kept less than a handful of good pieces. I'll let you have Weinberg's evaluation of their worth in writing.'

'How kind.' One dark brow was elevated mockingly. He was blocking the doorway and to get out of here she'd have to brush right past him. Close to him. She couldn't face that. Just being in the same room with him made her feel weak all over.

Caroline swallowed convulsively and Ben drawled, 'You were right about your professional services not being needed. But I have other needs, Caro, and you are going to satisfy every last one of them. Only then will you be free to go.'

He gave her a slow, thoughtful look, 'I suggest we stop pussy-footing around and start right now.'

CHAPTER SIX

'Now, why would I agree to do that?' Caroline queried, facing him with a poise she was miles away from feeling. Her heart was thumping wildly, her flesh quivering on her bones.

A long time ago they'd satisfied each other's needs completely—was that what he was suggesting? Had last night been a slow, cruelly teasing prelude to an inexorable seduction? The palms of her hands were slick now and drops of perspiration beaded her forehead, gathered in the cleft between her breasts as she was torn between jangling nervousness and helpless excitement.

'Because you owe me,' he retorted heavily, his narrowed eyes holding hers then dropping to rest on her mouth. 'You owe me for twelve, wasted years.'

Her brain told her to walk out of here, pack her bags and phone for a taxi. He couldn't hold her here by force. But her heart was beating in compelling opposition, telling her to stay.

That their long-ago tempestuous love affair had left an indelible mark on him too, given his love-'em-and-leave-'em attitude to women, was shattering. Perhaps it was mischievous fate that had brought them back together because it was finally time to close the circle and at last shut the past away where it belonged.

She couldn't walk away from this, this final confrontation, if that was what it was. 'Judging by your impressive achievements, the last twelve years can hardly be called a waste,' she managed to say, desperately striving to bring an air of factual normality into a conversation that was in danger of becoming unreal: Unreal to believe that she could have wounded his psyche as he, she now admitted helplessly, had so deeply wounded hers.

'That's not what I'm talking about, and I think you know it.' Two paces brought Ben to stand directly in front of her, his wide-shouldered stance overpowering her senses. Holding her huge violet eyes with the shadowed darkness of his he removed his suit jacket, slowly tossing it onto the nearest armchair, then loosened his tie.

Caroline's mouth went dry. She took a quick, ragged intake of breath. She could feel the heat of that intensely virile body just inches from her own, and the heat was melting her.

Instinctively, her tongue peeped out to moisten the aridity of her lips, lips that suddenly felt too full and lush. And his brooding eyes followed the involuntary, betraying movement and he said soberly, 'Ah, yes, I remember that nervous little gesture from moments before the first kiss we ever shared. And exactly how I helped—like this, remember, Caro?' His dark head dipped as his mouth met hers, no other part of their bodies touching, his tongue laving the quivering fullness of her lower lip, leaving the sensitised skin slick and supple, finding the parting, making an easy entry to the helplessly willing sweetness within.

Her blood sang, the electric brush of his lips and tongue was just as she remembered, the pleasure almost too much to bear. As much as she wanted to close the tiny distance between them, to wrap her arms around him, press her aching breasts and thighs against the hard maleness of him, she resisted. The slow, seductive melding of their mouths was exquisite torment enough.

And it should not be happening, the last dying vestige of common sense reminded her, acidly recalling his off-hand rejection of the night before.

But the voice died, drowned in the clamour of her raging pulse beats. His love-making had always been a drug, something she couldn't do without. Something her body had been silently crying for during these last barren, lonely years.

When he lifted his head after timeless, delirious moments his breathing was as ragged as her own, his fingers not quite steady as he reached to take the tortoiseshell clip from her hair, setting it free to fall in midnight-dark glossy abandon to her shoulders.

'It used to be much longer,' he murmured thickly. 'It used to cloak your breasts with silk, inviting me to kiss the rosy buds that hid behind it. You knew how to tantalise me, Caro. Do you remember?'

Remember? How could she ever forget? Memories of how wonderful and perfect they'd been together had always been buried deep in her mind, not taken out and examined—she'd learned more control than that—but there all the same, indelibly imprinted, denying her any sexual interest in any other man.

Had it been the same for him? The concept was difficult to take in, especially as her brain seemed to have stopped working.

Slowly, with explicit intent, he began to undo the tiny buttons of her shirt, his eyes focused on what he was doing, the backs of his fingers grazing her burning skin, making her incapable of any coherent response when he said darkly, 'Twelve years is a long time, Caro. Too damned long to be left in limbo.'

He slid the shirt from her shoulders and bent to briefly suckle her blatantly engorged nipples through the creamy lace of her bra and she whimpered softly with the tormenting pleasure of the short, insistent tugs of his mouth. She laid her hands against his chest, palms down, feeling the heat and vibrant strength of him, the heavy beats of his heart and knew she would soon be unable to stand without support because every last one of her bones had turned to water.

'Years of wanting what most men want, a wife, a family,' Ben asserted, his voice holding a trace of bitterness. His knuckles pressed against the softly feminine curve of her tummy as, having disposed of her belt and dealt with the zip he began to slide her trousers down over her hips. 'Of wanting a good, long-term relationship and not being able to deliver, of being unable to commit to any other woman because no other woman came close to what I remembered of you.'

Naked now, apart from insubstantial briefs and bra, she was open to his darkly anguished eyes, vulnerable, captivated by him as she always had been, but pricked to suspicion by the strong note of torment in his voice.

Treachery! her internal warning system whispered and she said, almost incoherently, 'You bought that painting—'

'As a reminder that things are not always what they seem, or what you want them to be,' he repeated. And then, as if he saw the beginnings of understanding, of resistance in her eyes, he laid a finger across her mouth, 'Don't speak. Just give yourself to the moment,' and enfolded her in his arms, his mouth finding the tender hollow just below her ear, his lips moving with slow eroticism as he murmured, 'You always liked this, and you still do, don't you? Admit it, Caro.'

As if the tiny moan that escaped her was admission enough he lifted her in his arms, holding her close as he carried her into the adjoining bedroom.

A hazy impression of a cool masculine atmosphere, the tiny-paned windows open to the warm spring air admitting the perfume of early-flowering honeysuckle, a carved oak bed. A huge bed.

Her unresisting body sank into the soft duvet as he laid her down and removed the last scraps of creamy lace. 'As perfect as ever.' His dark gaze caressed her nakedness. 'The years have been kind to you, Caro.'

The slight catch in his voice touched her heart with pain. Instinctively, she held out her arms to him, needing to hold him close, to banish whatever it was that was hurting him. But he straightened up, his beautiful mouth forming the command, 'Wait', and began to unbutton his shirt, removing it, and then those elegantly tailored trousers, tossing the expensive garments aside as if they were old dusters.

His lean, whippy young adult's body had matured spectacularly; His shoulders wide and strong, his chest deep and faintly dusted with dark hair. Yet there wasn't an ounce of spare flesh beneath the olive-toned skin that gleamed with health and vitality.

Caroline swallowed awkwardly around the sudden lump in her throat. Fully aroused, he was magnificent and the air throbbed with expectancy, with the inevitability of what was happening between them and, as he lowered himself beside her, laying his hand on the heated mound of her aching desire she searched his face for the lover he had been, longing to find him again, to hear the words of white-hot passion he had bewitched and had captivated her with, longing with an intensity that shook her slight frame and set her veins on fire.

But as his gently questing fingers found the slick core of her and just before his mouth took hers in a drugging kiss, he murmured raggedly, 'You want me, and I need this. I need, finally, to prove to myself that what you were to me is only in my mind. That you're no different from any other woman.'

She must have fallen asleep. The earth-shattering, multi-climaxes of their love-making, coupled with the near sleepless night had exhausted her. Caroline struggled to come properly awake beneath the light warmth of the duvet. Twilight filled the room and she was alone.

Of course she was alone. Tears stung the back of her eyes and tightened her throat. Ben had calculatedly used her, had got her out of his system. It was as simple and as devastating as that.

When he'd told her exactly how and why he was using her she'd been too far gone in the sexual delirium that only he could make happen to do the right thing: to slap his sinfully beautiful, arrogant face and walk away.

Tears coursed unheeded down her pale cheeks. They were both damned: he for so cold-bloodedly using her, she for allowing it to happen.

But his blood hadn't been cold, had it? Hot, white-hot passion had driven him and she—she had been incandescent.

Angrily, she swiped at her wet cheeks with the back of her hand and scrambled off the bed, snatching up her bra and briefs and scampering through to the sitting room to collect the rest of her discarded clothing. Throwing them on all anyhow, not because she was afraid Ben might walk in on her—he had got what he wanted and probably wouldn't want to see her any more than she wanted to have to face him—but because she had to get out of this house, the house that had never, in all of her life, held any happiness for her.

It was too late now to make the necessary arrangements to get back to London. Besides, she felt emotionally wrung out, in no fit state.

Tomorrow she would feel better. Later tonight she would pack and first thing in the morning she would phone for a taxi to take her into Shrewsbury, get the inter-city back to London, get her life back on track again.

Ben wouldn't complain to her boss, she decided cynically. She'd satisfied those needs he'd talked about and he'd be more than happy to see her go.

Outside the air was cooler than she'd expected but she wasn't going back in to fetch a jacket, not when it meant risking running into Ben. Hell would freeze over before she could meet his eyes without cringing with shame.

Unthinking, her mind pre-programmed, Caroline skirted the property, crossed the walled kitchen gardens and let herself out onto the green lane beyond the wooden door in the far wall. The grass was soft beneath her feet and soon she was under the dim canopy of the trees that bordered the stream.

The sound of the water as it chattered over its stony bed soothed her a little. The rustle of ferns as she brushed through them and the cry of a distant owl eased some of the tension from her shoulders.

She rubbed some warmth into her arms, the thin

silk of her shirt offering little protection from the cool evening air, and stepped into a grassy clearing. The mist from the water made softly moving grey patterns against the dark background of the trees.

She saw him then and stopped breathing. Too late she realised where she'd come, instinctively making her way, as she had so often done in the past, to the secret place. The secluded, magical place where their love had been consummated, where dreams had been born and nourished. Dreams that had turned into a nightmare of betrayal and deceit.

How could she have been so thoughtless? And, more to the point, why was he here?

Ben had his back to her, standing on the bank of the stream, seemingly intent on the dark waters as they swirled around the partly submerged rocks. Caroline turned swiftly to retrace her steps but he must have heard her.

He called her name.

The sound of his voice sent shock waves through her. Her feet felt as if they were rooted to the ground. She could hear his approach and still couldn't move.

'Don't go.' He sounded weary, as if something had happened to drain away his life force. 'I have to talk to you.'

Caroline didn't want to hear what he had to say, whatever it was. He diminished her utterly, made her so ashamed of herself.

Clinging onto what little dignity that remained, she said dully, 'I'm going back. It's getting very dark and I'm cold.'

'Then, I'll walk with you,' he said firmly, adding, 'Wait!' as she took a blind step back into the woodland. The touch of his hand as he laid it on her shoulder was sheer torture, the warmth and strength of it sending sparks through her that were part pleasure, part agonising pain.

He turned her round, his eyes searching her face and even in the fading light she could see the faint, almost reluctant, smile that curved his mouth. 'Your shirt's buttoned up all wrongly and your hair's gone mad—you look exactly like the wild thing I used to know. Here—' Releasing her briefly, he slipped out of the soft leather jacket he wore over a body-hugging dark T-shirt and draped it over her shoulders.

The masculine warmth of him, stored in the supple leather, almost defeated her, but not nearly as much as the sudden shocking and heart-stopping realisation that, whatever he had been in the past, whatever he was now, she still loved him.

Her stomach churned sickeningly. But he didn't love her. He never had, despite his youthful protestations. The sex had been brilliant, that was all.

Today he'd admitted that his need to form a committed relationship with any other woman had been stifled by the memory of their tempestuous, perfect love-making.

She could understand that, sympathise. Memories could be dangerous, distorting things. So he'd made love to her, had used her to satisfy himself that she was just an ordinary woman, no different from any other.

She had set him free, free to do what he'd said he wanted—commit himself to one special woman, marry, raise children. Did that explain his gentler mood, the care he was taking on her behalf as he guided her through the growing darkness? Resignedly, she supposed it did.

Emerging from the trees she caught her foot on a root and would have fallen had the guiding arm around her waist not tightened, pulling her against his body.

She heard the rough tug of his breath, felt the heavy beats of his heart beneath the palms of her hands that had automatically splayed out, seeking support. Felt the immediate masculine stir of his body and pulled away. Easy to go with the flow, take what there was to take of him in the short time they had left together. But dangerous for her future peace of mind. What had happened this afternoon must not happen again.

Away from the trees the going was easier, the light from billions of stars making his guiding, protective arm redundant. She mourned the loss though she knew she shouldn't and the silence he kept—in spite of his saying that he needed to talk to her—was like an intolerable ache.

She would be leaving early in the morning she reminded herself so perhaps this was their final good-bye. Recriminations for the heartless way he'd used her—both in the past and since their paths had crossed again—would achieve nothing.

No one was all bad and, as they reached the house, she knew she had to tell him how much she admired what was good in him.

Caroline waited while he closed the door behind them and flicked on the lights, the aching sadness inside her robbing her voice of all vitality as she said, 'Linda told me what you're doing with this house— helping children from deprived backgrounds. I think it's wonderful—'

'You do?' His eyes, the set of his mouth was dismissive. Plainly he wasn't interested in compliments, not if they came from her. 'Ironic, isn't it? I saved your revered family home from falling into complete disrepair, only to plan to fill it with young tearaways from run-down estates. Your father would turn in his grave if he knew that his precious daughter would have to face such a situation.' One brow rose mockingly. 'The villagers used to call you Princess Caroline, did you know that? Shut away in your ivory tower, too good to mix with the likes of them.'

This barely veiled antagonism was enough to break her heart, especially as she recognised the truth that she'd so carefully hidden from herself for such a long time. She could never love another man as she loved this one: warts and all.

Misery, coupled with anger at the hand fate had dealt her, made her voice thick and throaty as she countered, 'Of course I knew! It was unfair and it hurt! And as far as my father was concerned I would never be coming back here. He finally disowned me and threw me out when I refused to fall in with his plans and get engaged to Jeremy.'

She saw his quick frown, heard the sharp intake of his breath as he asked, 'Is that true? Your father said the engagement was planned for your eighteenth birthday—only a few weeks away, that the marriage would take place early the following spring.'

'Really!'

She couldn't entirely blame her father. He had only been saying what he'd believed to be the truth, that he could, as usual, coerce her into doing exactly what he told her to do. But she could blame Dexter for taking her father's statement at face value and deciding that she'd been using him, having a sneaky affair on the side, enjoying—what had he called it?—rough trade!

'And when did that conversation take place?' she queried bitterly, 'When he offered you money to make yourself scarce?'

'Yes.'

The simple, unrepentant affirmative rocked her. Stupidly, she'd been hoping that he'd categorically deny ever having taken that pay-off, that his betrayal hadn't been as thorough and as cruel as she'd believed, that her father had lied.

Her shoulders slumping, she removed his jacket and dropped it on the floor. She felt so tired and empty now it was an effort to stand upright. Bed. Sleep. That was what she needed. Tomorrow the traumatic happenings of this day would be behind her and she could go on.

She took a faltering step towards the staircase and heard him say gently, 'What happened this afternoon was a shock for me, too, Caro. I guess I'm only just coming out of it. No, don't go—' She took another jerky step towards the escape route of the stairs. 'Hear me out, please. I want you to forget we have a history. I want you to marry me.'

CHAPTER SEVEN

CAROLINE turned quickly. Too quickly. Her head swam dizzily. She would have fallen if Ben hadn't slipped an arm around her and held her, pulling her against the broad, hard wall of his chest.

His blunt, out-of-the-blue proposal was the very last thing she'd expected. Her acceptance, should she be crazy enough to give it, would throw up implications she didn't think she'd be able to handle.

Marrying Ben Dexter had once been her most precious dream but now, after all that had happened and the passage of so many years, it was totally out of the question. Her shoulders shook with the onset of hysteria and her sudden, unstoppable and totally humiliating tears soaked the front of his T-shirt.

'Don't cry,' he said soothingly. 'Please don't. I shouldn't have landed that on you so suddenly.' Strong hands on her slender shoulders held her slightly away, his fingers brushing away the wetness from her cheeks, his dark eyes sweeping over her troubled features. 'I don't expect an answer right now, Caro. You'll need time to think about it. I've been mulling it over ever since you fell asleep in my arms, so I've had a head start.'

He dropped a light kiss on her quivering mouth, his eyes smiling now, bringing all his forceful charisma into play as he slipped an arm back around her waist and insisted wryly, 'We'll both feel less disorientated if we eat. I'll throw something on the stove while you choose the wine.'

Resisting the strong desire to disintegrate into further hysterics Caroline dragged air through her pinched nostrils and blurted, 'I can't marry you, you know I can't—it was a crazy thing to ask!'

She felt utterly confused and deeply upset and his lazy 'Why?' did nothing to help. Breathing unevenly, she pulled away from him. Ever since she'd returned to Langley Hayes she'd lost her grip on reality. Somehow or other she had to regain it.

'Because,' she said more steadily, determined now to gather her defences against the man her treacherous body and stupid heart craved so desperately, 'what you feel for me is simply lust—not to mention contempt. Marriage couldn't possibly work out.'

'Contempt; yes, there was that,' he admitted softly after a pause no longer than a heartbeat. 'For a long time now I've believed you were planning to marry the Curtis fortune while having a furtive affair with me. That sort of conviction is difficult to shake off. You see, way back then, I wanted to ask you if it was true, about Curtis, but when I got back I found that letter telling me it was all over between us, that you never wanted to set eyes on me again. As far as I was concerned it confirmed everything your father had told me.'

He walked into her line of vision, his hands bunched into his trouser pockets, his dark eyes moody. 'I had to go that day; there was no choice. With hindsight I know I should have told you of my plans, explained why I used to disappear for days, but I wasn't sure things would work out.' His mouth compressed wryly. 'I guess I was misguided but I wanted to present you—everyone—with a tangible success, not a pipedream.

'For over a year Jim Mays—an old friend from up north—and I had been trying to set up in the software business. We met up now and then to develop ideas. Then, that day, right after my disastrous meeting with your father, Jim phoned me, told me to drop everything and get down to London because he'd found a potential backer who would only be available for a few hours that day. But all the while we were pitching I was desperate to get back and get the truth from you.

'But the moment I did get back Mother gave me your letter—giving me the brush-off in no uncertain terms, and from then on I thought you were every kind of bitch. Now I prefer to believe your version of events, that your father threw you out because you refused to marry Curtis. As for your Dear John, looking back I guess we can put that down to cold feet. You were very young at the time. So forget the contempt side of it, Caro, it no longer exists.'

He shrugged slightly, his mouth indented. 'And, as for lust, what's wrong with that? It's nature's way of ensuring the survival of the species, so don't knock it. OK, I admit to the crass sin of getting you here under false pretences. I wanted to prove to myself that you were nothing special and all I did was prove that you were very special indeed. We're dynamite together; no other woman comes near you as far as I'm concerned. You're a singing in my blood, a desperate hunger—this afternoon proved that much.' His voice thickened. 'And I think—no, I know, you felt it too. It's not finished Caro; it's lasted twelve long years; it's an undying fever.'

His words bewildered, delighted and terrified her. She could so easily ignore common sense and give in to the craving to marry the man she loved, to take what she could of him for the time it lasted.

She put her fingers to her temples in the age-old gesture of despair. The time it lasted would be short. How could it be otherwise when he was motivated only by lust and long memory of an incomparable, magical summer, and she by a love that was tainted with mistrust?

True, he had come back to find the truth from all that time ago. But that underlined his deceit. He had come back despite having taken a wad of her father's cash in return for the promise to stay away.

Unconsciously, she shook her head. 'Sex isn't everything, no matter how brilliant it is. So, OK—' she gave him a tired smile '—I admit that what we once had made such an impression that, like you, apparently, it's hard to find a partner that measures up. But the bottom line is, Ben, you deceived and cheated on us all—Father, Maggie Pope, me. People don't change, not basically. I would always be waiting for it to happen again.'

And when that happened she would be destroyed. Utterly, totally and completely.

The hall clock struck the hour, nine sonorous beats, and Ben said darkly, 'What the hell are you talking about?' Then he swore softly, almost inaudibly as the doorbell chimed. 'Wait.' He flung the word at her tersely. 'I'll get rid of whoever it is and then you can tell me what you meant.'

She registered the irritated set of his wide shoulders, the impatience of his long-legged stride as he crossed the hall, and she shivered.

He was everything she'd ever wanted and the white heat of their young passion had ruined her emotional life for years as, so it would seem, it had ruined his. That being the case, she could understand and even forgive his cold-blooded attempt to get her out of his system.

But that hadn't happened, had it? Their love-making this afternoon had been better than ever, spiced with a deeper, sweeter poignancy. So, to use that hoary phrase 'marry or burn' he had decided to propose.

And she was burning now, flames of forbidden excitement leaping inside her because despite knowing it would be emotional suicide she wanted to accept his proposal so badly it was like an invisible hoist, drawing her inexorably to him.

Perhaps, after he'd sent the caller away, they could sort things out.

If he should tell her he deeply regretted his behaviour towards Maggie and now gave her and the daughter he'd turned his back on all those years ago financial and moral support...

If he told her he had had every intention of returning the money her father had given him, admitting that he wasn't prepared, after all, to stay away...

But he was holding the door wide, his inborn politeness to the fore as he said, 'Of course you're not being a nuisance. She's right here. Please do come in.'

Dorothy Skeet emerged slowly into the lighted hall. The years had solidified her plumpness into corpulence and her once blondish fluffy hair had turned to dull pepper and salt. She said uncertainly, 'I heard you were here, Miss Caroline, but I didn't know for how long. It's a bit late, I know, but I didn't want to miss you.'

Caroline's heart skipped a beat and, awkwardly at first and then more surely, she crossed the floor to hug the older woman. Her throat felt clogged with the tears that now seemed perilously and uncharacteristically near the surface. The only kindness—albeit casual—she'd known in this house had come from this lady.

'Why don't we all go through?' Ben said into the ensuing, emotionally charged silence. 'I was about to make supper, why don't you join us, Dorothy?'

'Oh, I couldn't!—I mean, I've already had my tea,' she said, flustered, her round face turning pink. 'I didn't want to intrude, I only came to hand over your dad's things.' She fumbled at the catch on her capacious handbag, suspiciously over-bright eyes now clinging to Caroline's.

The older woman was clearly ill at ease and Caroline didn't know what to say to make her feel more comfortable. It was Ben who came to the rescue, his smile as irresistible as ever as he suggested, 'Then, come and sit with us while we eat. Enjoy a glass of wine—or coffee if you prefer, and spill all the village gossip. I know Caro wants to catch up with everything that's been going on these last few years.'

That was news to her, but the fabrication was worth it, Caroline thought as Dorothy's eyes lit up at the prospect and she became instantly more relaxed.

Her father's former housekeeper had an incorrigible and unrepentant appetite for gossip and she wondered if the older woman had somehow found out about her and Ben's secret affair, or had heard gossip in the village and had passed it on to her father. If so it would explain why she'd initially appeared so uncomfortable when encountering the two of them together.

Trailing behind Ben and Dorothy as they headed for the kitchen, Caroline dismissed the thought. It was no longer important. Let the past stay in the past.

Even if her father had remained ignorant of what had been going on and she and Ben had married quietly as soon as she was eighteen, as she'd suggested on more than one occasion, the result would have been the same: their relationship would have broken up in pain and disillusionment when the inevitable happened and she learned of his abandoned little daughter.

The sobering knowledge was something she was going to have to keep in the forefront of her mind. Something to stiffen her resolve to turn that astonishing proposal of marriage down flat and not give in to the weakness of her love for the deceiving monster that kept creeping up on her whenever she let her mental guard down.

How could she, even in a weak moment, contemplate marriage with a man whose past record made her cringe, whose only real interest in her was the slaking of a lust that hadn't died, despite all their years apart?

But despite her angst-ridden thoughts it was hard to stay in a sombre mood whilst Dorothy Skeet, sipping at the mug of hot cocoa which was her preferred tipple at this time of night, regaled them with the latest village gossip, sometimes hilarious and often downright slanderous, while Caroline herself, finding an appetite that surprised her, tucked into the succulent grilled gammon and tomatoes Ben had rustled up.

'Don't believe half of it.' Ben grinned as he refilled both their wine glasses and motioned Dorothy to stay where she was when she made to clear the table. 'Every time a story's told it gathers a whole new and highly coloured dimension!'

'Too true!' Caroline smiled right back at him over the rim of her glass. The relaxed atmosphere, the simple food and superb wine, the laughter, Ben's comical mock-horror as he threw up his hands and rolled his eyes at some of Dorothy's more wicked comments, had taken the stress out of the situation.

So when the older woman took a tissue-wrapped bundle from her handbag and handed it to her Caroline was able to view her father's few personal effects without the familiar clutch of misery in the region of her heart.

The silver fob-watch he had always worn tucked into his waistcoat pocket complete with chain and onyx seal, the gold signet ring that had come down from his father and was now thin with age, two fountain pens—not much to show for sixty-odd years of living.

But her sense of loss was deep as she folded the tissue over the pathetic mementos. However she did her best not to let it show as she placed the package back into Dorothy's hands.

'I know my father would have liked you to keep these,' she said gently.

Dorothy had been Reginald Harvey's bed companion for many years. On her part it had been love, on his a blunt and probably infrequently expressed affection. Seeing the doubt in the other woman's eyes, Caroline insisted. 'He was fond of you, he was closer to you than anyone. He—' her voice faltered, thickened, but she forced the words out '—he actively disliked me. I know he would rather you had these keepsakes.'

She heard the intake of Ben's breath followed by

a beat of a silence so thick she could almost taste it. Strangely, although she knew it should be otherwise, his presence gave her the strength to add, 'In return, you could tell me why—why he never seemed able to stand the sight of me. You must have gathered some clues over the years. And maybe—' she tugged in a deep breath, feeling Ben's dark eyes on her, feeling his unspoken compassion '—maybe if I knew why, I could forgive him.'

'Yes,' the older woman concurred, her eyes darkening with sympathy even as her fingers tightened around the keepsakes. 'He was close-lipped where his feelings were concerned but he adored your mother—anyone who saw them together knew that—he worshipped the ground she walked on. Jane Bayliss—you'll remember her, she married old Hume the butcher—worked here at the time, cleaning and such; she said she was sure he had mixed feelings when your mum got pregnant with you. He didn't want anyone, even his own child, to have any of her attention. He wanted it all for himself.'

Caroline's brow furrowed. Had her father really loved that obsessively? Then she remembered the letters she'd found in the attic and knew that he had. He'd loved her mother as single-mindedly and deeply as he'd disliked his only child.

Her eyes misting, she said quietly, her voice barely audible, 'And she died when I was very small.' That much she did know. Her father had never talked to her about her mother, apart from angrily stating that bald fact when she'd pressed him for details. Truth to tell, he'd rarely spoken to her at all, except to issue curt instructions and even curter reprimands.

'She died an hour after you were born,' Dorothy supplied, shaking her head. 'It was the talk of the area at the time, a terrible tragedy. You came three weeks early, at the beginning of November.

'There'd been a surprise heavy snowstorm overnight. Appalling drifts—your dad couldn't get your mum out and no one could get through. You came quickly and your mum haemorrhaged badly, and by the time the emergency helicopter and paramedics arrived it was already too late—all this came out at the inquest.

'When I got the job as housekeeper I saw how your dad treated you and it's my guess he bitterly resented the fact that you had lived and his wife had died.' She gave a heavy sigh. 'You grew up to be the living image of her, but you weren't her.'

'So he couldn't bear to have me around,' Caroline said huskily. 'He blamed me.'

'I thought the world of him. Well, you know that, but I wasn't afraid to let him know he was treating you wrong—even if he did tell me to mind my own damn business,' Dorothy conceded. 'It wasn't your fault, you didn't ask to be born. I did tell him that, more than once. And later, he started to soften up a bit. But by then it was too late. You'd grown prickly and defiant. A terrible shame, really.' She got slowly to her feet. 'I really should go now, but I'm glad we talked.'

'I'll drive you.'

Even as Ben made the offer Caroline was conscious of his smouldering gaze; it burned her where it touched. When they'd been together all those years ago he had known she and her father didn't get along but had been unaware of how deep the rift was. She hadn't wanted to talk about her unhappy home life, only about the future they'd planned together.

'No need,' Dorothy stated. 'I came in my old rattle-trap.'

'Then, I'll see you out.'

Caroline smothered a groan. Right now she didn't want Ben's sympathy or his company. She needed time to herself to come to terms with the mess she and her father had made of their relationship, to mourn that final interview when she had screamed at him, vowing she'd rather die than do what he wanted and marry Jeremy, telling him she didn't care if he carried out his threat to throw her out because she never wanted anything more to do with him.

Seventeen going on eighteen, her heart broken and bleeding because of her lover's betrayal, she'd been in no mood for conciliatory words, to soberly tell him that she could never marry the Curtis wealth because she didn't, and never would, love Jeremy Curtis. In too much pain herself to consider her father's possible hurt when she'd declared that she hated him and always had.

It was too late now to retract the bitter words, to tell him she forgave him for not having been able to love her as a father should have because, at last, she understood the reason for his resentment of her.

Her shoulders shook as she buried her head in her hands, her sobs overwhelming her. Only when she felt the light touch of Ben's hand on the top of her head did she make a determined but not too successful effort to pull herself together.

'Don't,' he said softly as he cupped her elbows and pulled her to her feet, his arms holding her close. 'Tonight you learned something you hadn't known before and naturally enough it's upset you. But your father treated you abominably, Caro. His memory doesn't deserve this amount of grief.'

He framed her tear-stained face with long-fingered hands, his thumbs stroking back tendrils of raven-dark hair. 'He was a man obsessed by the memory of his one great love and I can understand that, but not his treatment of an innocent child. If the two of you were estranged for the last years of his life it wasn't your fault.'

Caroline shook her head mutely, her breath shaking in her lungs, her fingers clutching his shoulders convulsively, as if she could take strength from the warm solidity of muscle and bone. The compassion and caring in his beautiful eyes, in the tender set of that sensual mouth, made her tremble, taking her back through the years to the place she had been when he'd not only been her first and devastatingly exciting lover but her very best friend, a rock she could have clung to in any storm.

Her soft lips parting, she managed a shaky, 'No.' Then, more steadily, she confessed sadly, 'When I was little I wanted him to love me more than anything in the world. But I knew he didn't. Sometimes I saw him looking at me as if he hated me. I thought it was my fault, that there was something horrible about me.'

She shook her head, silencing him when he gave a growl of repudiation deep in his throat. 'Dorothy was right on two counts. At one time he did try to build bridges, to take an interest when I was home for school holidays, asking about the friends I'd made, what books I was reading.'

She scooped in a shaky breath. 'But it was too late. I was a defiant fifteen by then, used to being pushed away, ignored. I shrugged away any overture he tried to make, stuck my nose in the air and walked away, letting him know I didn't need him, didn't need anyone.' She gave a shaky sigh. 'That was the end of any hope of any harmony in our spiky relationship. I bitterly regret it now.'

His body tensed against hers and there was the shadow of a catch in his voice as he told her, 'That reaction would have been entirely natural, given the circumstances. You truly don't have to regret it. The only thing you should regret is the fact that his treatment of you made you wary of—or incapable of—committing to a permanent relationship. I understand that.'

He didn't understand at all, she thought wearily. She would have committed the rest of her life to Ben if things hadn't gone so badly wrong, if he hadn't deceived her. But right now she was too drained to put him straight on that score, and her head fell forward, resting against the solid expanse of his chest.

All she wanted was the oblivion of sleep, to rid her tired brain of aching regrets, of the confusion of her heart and body wanting and needing this one man with something approaching ferocity and her brain telling her in no uncertain terms that he wasn't to be trusted.

So when he murmured, 'You're emotionally drained, sweetheart. We'll talk again in the morning. Right now you need sleep,' she could only nod in thankful agreement and push away the admonitory voice in her brain that told her to object when he scooped her into his arms and carried her up to his room.

CHAPTER EIGHT

His bedroom. His bed. The covers still rumpled from this afternoon's wild love-making. Something electric quivered all the way through her.

Why had he brought her here instead of taking her to her own room? Silly question. He aimed to take advantage of her while she was stricken...

A low, self-denigrating moan escaped her as he slid her down the length of his body and set her on her feet. Who was she trying to fool? There was a fatal weakness in her where he was concerned, a deep craving that banished sanity and pride. And if he stayed this close to her one moment longer it would be she who would be taking advantage of him!

Wanton heat was already pooling between her thighs and something caught at the back of her throat as she raised the sultry heaviness of her lashes and let her glazed eyes roam the savagely handsome planes of his face, meeting the slightly frowning, brooding intensity of those gypsy dark eyes.

She shuddered convulsively as a wave of fierce longing flooded right through her. She needed to feel that sensually carved mouth on hers again, to take the thrusting masculine pride of his body into hers again—a need so desperate it ravaged her chaotic senses...

Her bones shaking, she reached out to him, but...

'You're out on your feet, sweetheart,' Ben remarked softly, placing his hands lightly on her shoulders, holding her upright as she swayed involuntarily towards him. 'Skip the shower tonight. You need sleep.'

The caring in his voice brought fresh tears to her eyes, mortifying her. She who never cried had shed enough to float a battleship over the past few hours.

Nothing to do with the trauma of at last learning just why her father had so bitterly resented her existence, nor the painful memories of that final interview—just Ben, his compassion. His caring for her well-being during their long-ago love affair had been one of the things that had made her love him so.

Yet that didn't gel with the way he'd washed his hands of any responsibility towards Maggie Pope and his baby daughter...

She muffled a sob as he began to undress her, peeling away her blouse then undoing the waistband of her linen trousers, the backs of his fingers grazing the soft, sensitised skin of her tummy.

Caroline gasped, her stomach muscles tightening as he slid the fabric down her hips. Did he know what he was doing—the effect he was having on her? How every nerve in her body leapt? How her heart was thundering wildly sending fire to every part of her in a raging torrent of need? How her breasts were swelling, the rosy peaks hard, aching for his mouth?

Risking a glance from under her lashes she saw that he didn't show even a casual interest in the twin globes he released as he unclipped her bra, merely dropping the filmy garment to the floor before turning his attention to her briefs with a smooth efficiency that made her burn with frustration.

Was he totally unaware of how wildly aroused she was, of how much she needed him? Did he think he was being considerate, leaving her in this state?

She thought she heard the sharp tug of his breath as she held onto him for balance while she shakily stepped out of the briefs he'd slid down the length of her legs, her engorged breasts brushing against him. And then she was sure she had to have imagined it when he laid almost clinical hands on her shoulders, turning her round then briskly plumping up the pillows, holding back the lightweight duvet, telling her levelly, 'In you get. I don't think you should be alone to brood tonight. So I'll be right beside you if you feel the need to talk, for someone to hold you. Just hold you, OK, Caro?'

A catch in her throat, she stumbled into the bed, felt the duvet settle upon her, heard him move away, heard the gush of the shower in the *en suite*, turned her face into the pillow and bit it. Hard.

It seemed hours before he joined her, the raging torment of wanting him so much it hurt making the sleep she needed impossible to come by.

He hadn't said a word when he'd finally exited the *en suite*. He'd simply walked across the room, switching off the light, closing the door to his private suite of rooms quietly behind him, leaving her alone in this room for what must have been ages.

Now Caroline heard the rustle of his clothing as he undressed in the darkness, felt the mattress dip as he slid in beside her, taking care not to disturb her.

Disturb her? She was disturbed enough to be in a white-hot sexual frenzy!

He settled down, his back to her, an aching void away in the huge bed. And she commanded thickly because she couldn't help it, because she was driven, 'Hold me, Ben. Please, hold me!'

She sensed him stiffen, the darkness around them tensing for one brief second before he turned and gathered her to him, folding his arms around her, tucking her head into the angle of his shoulder, his warm breath fanning her cheek as he murmured gently, 'I'm here, sweetheart. You'd like to talk?'

He too was naked. Her skin ignited against his, her blood exploding in her veins. Talk? They had to, of course they did. About Maggie, his child, the money he'd taken from her father. But not now.

Now she wanted him. Just him. The utter perfection of their physical mating, the bad things forgotten, just for now. Tomorrow would be soon enough for this fantasy of love to end, to tell him that she could never marry a man she couldn't trust.

'No!' she uttered hoarsely. 'Make love to me. I need you.' And she pressed her tingling breasts against the hard wall of his chest, wrapping her legs around his, drawing one of his thighs between hers, melting with delirium as she felt his instant, leaping response against the frantically quivering flesh of her abdomen. 'Now, Ben! Now!'

She heard him take a sudden breath and knew the control he'd been keeping had been fractured when he turned her on her back and straddled her. Then, with tormenting slowness he ran his hands down the length of her writhing body until he found the warm, secret dampness at the juncture of her thighs.

Caroline moaned aloud, his skilful fingers driving her to the point of no return and when his mouth replaced them she arched and bucked and cried his name as waves of ecstasy convulsed her, over and over, until she reached out and caught his head between her hands and kissed him, her breath sobbing raggedly in her lungs.

His own breathing was raw as he pulled her down with him and kicked away the duvet. Linking his fingers with hers he said with sultry confidence, 'That was for you. Now we do it my way, sweetheart. Slowly, very, very slowly...'

When Caroline woke she half expected to feel ashamed of her behaviour, but all she felt was a glorious wave of happiness and a sweet, drenching contentment.

She stirred and stretched lazily, voluptuously, and Ben's deep, honeyed voice said, 'Just like a lithe little cat.'

Lifting her lashes her soft amethyst eyes located him. Standing above her, clad in a short terry robe, his hair damp from the shower, he looked utterly gorgeous, the harsh, proud planes of his face curiously softened, his mouth a sultry, kissable curve.

Her heart wrenching over she hoisted herself back against the pillows as he put the two mugs of coffee he'd been carrying down on the bedside table then perched on the edge of the bed beside her.

'Now, there's a sight a man would gladly kill for,' he remarked silkily, his black eyes roaming her nakedness with languorous attention to every detail. 'Perfection against his pillows.'

His smile was so sexy it took her breath away, and she couldn't breathe at all when he dipped his dark head and lapped each tingling, pouting nipple then took her parted lips with an intimacy that blew her mind.

Her hands flew to his head, fingers tangling with the thick dark strands, as his tongue mimicked the staggering activities of the night, her body leaping with immediate, feverish response. But he drew away, his hands capturing hers, his eyes glinting wickedly beneath the lowered fan of his thick, spiky lashes.

'I've a proposition to put to you.'

Caroline dragged in a much needed breath as her heart twisted sharply. A proposition, not a proposal, thank the lord. She did not, most definitely not, want to have to think about his proposal of the evening before.

She didn't want to think of anything at all. The focus of her world, just for these few precious moments, was this man, the love for him that had burgeoned into strong, new life.

'We make today a holiday. We don't talk or think about anything but the two of us, the way we are now. The past, the future, won't get a mention.'

She saw a brief flicker of uncertainty in his eyes and gave him a glorious smile, assuring him throatily, 'That's absolutely fine by me!'

Couldn't be finer, in fact. Another magical twenty-four hours when reality didn't get a look in, when nothing bad marred the magic of letting herself drift with the flow of loving him.

'Then—' the wicked confidence was back in his eyes now, in the smile that curved the beautifully sculpted mouth as he reached over and put one of the delicate china mugs in her hand '—coffee first, followed by a shower—and it will be my pleasure to help you—and we'll take it from there.'

The shower took longer than any shower she'd ever taken before, the touch of his long fingers on every part of her soap-slicked body a new and decidedly erotic experience, just begging her to do the same to him, to share with him the intense pleasure she was feeling. And when he eased her back against the marble tiled wall, parted her trembling thighs and thrust possessively into her waiting body she knew that heaven couldn't offer a sweeter experience than this.

'I can't get enough of you.' His voice was still hoarse long after their mingled cries of rapture had been swallowed by the hiss of the water. 'It was always like this for us, remember?'

'Don't.' She placed her hand over his mouth to silence him. The writhing tendrils of steam made his features blurred, out of focus. 'We don't mention the past. We are simply what we are,' she reminded him, refusing to remember those long-gone good times because then she might have to remember the bad.

'And we are spectacular.' He grinned, conceding her point, reaching up to turn off the shower head.

And that she had to agree with, Caroline thought as he helped her out of the stall and wrapped her in a fluffy towel that smelt of sunshine and flowers. Cuddling into the folds she watched him, with dreamy eyes towel himself dry, drinking in the pagan splendour of his male physique, making one more memory to add to all the others.

As if he'd seen the sudden wistfulness behind her eyes, he reached out to cup the side of her face with one gentle hand. 'Mop yourself up and dress, sweetheart. I won't offer to do it for you because we wouldn't get breakfast before supper time if I did. Will toast and tea be enough, or shall I boil eggs?'

'Just toast,' she said croaking around the sudden lump in her throat. Was it still the lingering remnant of steam or had her eyes misted with tears? She certainly felt like weeping all over again. Today was meant to be a stolen slice of paradise, wasn't it? No room for looking back, or forward, no room for regrets, for tears.

She moved away, plucked a fresh towel from one

of the heated rails and wrapped it around her dripping hair, rubbing vigorously. When she emphasised, 'Tea and toast will be fine,' she sounded nicely cheerful.

Apparently satisfied, he walked through to the bedroom and she gave him ten minutes before she made her way to the room she'd been using. Passing the place where the mahogany linen press had once stood she had a sharp pang of conscience.

She really ought to get in touch with base, tell them she'd be returning in the morning. In view of the small amount of actual work she'd had to do here they'd wonder why it had taken her this long.

But she pushed the thought to the back of her mind. She'd phone first thing in the morning, before she set out. Today was hers. And Ben's. One more day out of a lifetime wasn't too much to ask, was it?

Tossing the things she'd worn the day before into her empty suitcase she slipped into clean silk undies and pondered what to wear as she stroked the brush through her damp hair. She didn't know what Ben's plans were but there was no one else in the house. The builders had removed the scaffolding yesterday morning, and the men currently at work making the golf course were on the opposite side of the estate.

Just the two of them, and whatever she put on wouldn't stay on for very long, she was sure of that. Her stomach wriggled at the thought, excited anticipation already building up inside her again. Just like the old times...

She brutally strangled the thought and picked up the faded, much washed jeans Linda had lent her.

They were indeed too wide and too short in the leg but she took the narrow leather belt from her own linen trousers and anchored the denim waist to her own much narrower one. Teamed with one of her own blouses, pale blue crêpe with short sleeves and a smooth V neckline, her bare feet pushed into her loafers, her hair a wild cloud falling to her shoulders, she looked nothing at all like the aloof, elegantly packaged career woman who had arrived here only a few short days ago.

The sudden rush of relief as she gazed at her haphazardly attired and comfortably unsophisticated reflection made her grin. She felt and looked more relaxed than she had done for years. Eschewing her usual, perfect make-up, she left the room, her feet on wings as she sped down to the kitchen.

Ben had gone ahead and boiled eggs anyway and the aroma of fresh coffee and warm toast made Caroline's mouth water. They were using the butcher's-block table beneath one of the sun-warmed windows and he'd produced honey and orange juice too.

'I can't remember ever eating such a huge breakfast,' she confessed, as she accepted a second cup of coffee after they'd stacked the used crockery in the dishwasher, wondering if she should loosen the narrow leather belt by a couple of notches.

'Then, maybe we should walk it off,' Ben suggested, smiling, as she drained her cup.

'Good idea.'

A beam of spring sunlight gleamed in his hair, touched the side of his forcefully handsome face and her heart swelled inside her breast. He was so gorgeous it sometimes hurt to look at him, and her body melted, just melted when he came to stand behind her, slipping his hands around her waist then slowly lifting them to cup her breasts.

He leant his face against the side of hers, his lips warm on her pinkening skin and she felt her breasts harden and fill the palms of his hands.

'Then, we'll head for the woods,' he murmured, adding silkily as his thumbs stroked her pouting nipples, 'Unless you have another form of exercise in mind?'

'Walk,' she said chokily, moving away. 'To begin with,' she added, but her smile was thin. They had always met in the woods, relishing the dark secrecy, their own precious privacy. The reminder put a heavy slab of sorrow in her heart.

She didn't want reminders, not today. Today was all they had left, and she would only be able to make it a happy memory if she didn't remember the past. So she wouldn't remember it. They were different people now and all she had to do was to pretend, just for today, that they'd only just met, had just fallen in love.

Tomorrow would be soon enough to get back to

normal, to get on with the life she knew and could rely on.

'Fine.' Black eyes glinted wickedly as he took her hand. 'I'm ready for the afters whenever you say the word. Let's get the "begin with" over.'

They were still holding hands as they wandered slowly beneath the cool green canopy, taking the rarely trodden paths, the only sound that of their feet in the undergrowth, the music of birdsong and the ever-present murmur of the stream.

Idyllic, Caroline thought, or at least it should have been. But it wasn't working. Every step brought back memories of that long-ago summer when she'd believed she'd met her soul mate, when she would have trusted him with her life. How could she divorce herself from the reality of his callous betrayal?

'I've got something I want to show you,' he said as they emerged into a clearing on the banks of the stream. 'Remember Ma's falling down rented cottage?'

Seemingly oblivious of her now sombre mood, he strode ahead of her, holding back the branches of a hazel, his boyish grin lighting his face.

She had no option but to follow, her heart sinking as she recalled that dreadful day. It had taken her a while for everything to sink in. Her father had paid him to go away and stay away. Maggie Pope had confirmed that he was the father of her baby, had confirmed that he'd shrugged, had laid all the responsibility on her and had swaggered away.

So she'd written that letter, in case he'd already

left the area, and it had been easy. All the hurt and bitterness had spilled out onto the paper. And of course he'd already gone.

'Not here,' his austere-featured mother had answered her enquiry. So Caroline had pushed the sealed envelope into her hands. 'Then, give him this if and when you see him again.'

Now the cottage had been transformed, she registered numbly. Before, it had been barely habitable, the extensive garden filled with the produce Mrs Dexter had grown to sell and which had remained unsold. Now the stonework was sturdy, the leaking roof re-thatched and a sizeable, sympathetic extension added, an extension so well executed it might always have been here.

'Well, what do you think?' Ben turned to her, tucking an arm around her, pulling her close to his side.

Caroline pulled away, her features pale and serious. So much for their precious stolen day, for pretending they had no shared past. 'Does your mother still live here?' she asked dully.

The cottage didn't look lived in and the once productive garden was a jungle of weeds, so she didn't think she did. She sighed heavily. She'd tried so hard to block out thoughts of his past betrayal, just for this one day, but being here had made that impossible. 'She never did like me.'

'She was afraid of you,' Ben commented lightly as he took a door key from the pocket of the stone-coloured jeans he was wearing. 'She knew how I felt about you and kept telling me it would all end in tears!' He had opened the carefully restored oak-plank door and it swung back easily on its hinges. 'She was always telling me that the young lady from the big house would never settle down with the local tearaway who had a bad reputation and even worse prospects!'

He loomed over her and Caroline felt something wither and die inside her as he traced the line of her cheek with a caressing forefinger and added gently, 'You didn't ditch me out of snobbishness, Caro. But because of your upbringing you were unable to make a long-term commitment, I understand that now. And you were very young.'

He had been young at the time, too. And sooner or later he would have abandoned her as he'd abandoned Maggie and their baby; sooner rather than later if her father had demanded the return of that money because, typically, he hadn't kept his side of their bargain. Yet he was talking as if she had been the one to blame for everything that had happened.

Ben put a hand beneath her elbow, urging her over the threshold and as if he sensed her resistance he said lightly, 'To answer your question, Ma now lives with her sister Jane in Derbyshire on what used to be the family farm. The land was sold off when their parents died within six months of each other around five years ago. They share the farmhouse.'

They were in the main living room and it seemed much larger and lighter than it had been on the only occasion she'd set foot inside the cottage. Her eyes must have been showing her bemusement because Ben told her, 'When Ma and I lived here, this room was divided by a hardboard partition. She slept behind it and I had a room upstairs with crumbling floorboards and a leaking ceiling.'

So there was light coming from two windows now, and lots more space. The rusty old cooking range had been taken out, revealing a wide inglenook where logs would blaze in the winter. The overhead beams had been cleaned of their peeling layers of black paint and were their warm natural colour.

'The place was a pigsty when we lived here,' Ben confided. 'But because of that the rent was low. We couldn't afford any better.' He had drawn her to the deep window-seat at the far side of the room and she had let him, reluctantly, too low-spirited now to argue. 'You would have seen her around after we came to live here but you never knew her. I think you should. I'm sure you'll get on like a house on fire when you get to know each other properly.'

He had taken her unresisting hand and they were sitting close in the confined space but Caroline didn't feel anything. Just numb.

'People thought she was hard, unfriendly,' he admitted. 'But that was simply a defence mechanism. She called herself Mrs Dexter but she was never married. She simply allowed people to think she was widowed or divorced.

'My father worked with a travelling fair. She and Jane, the sister she was closest to, had sneaked away to the forbidden and "wicked" fairground when it first arrived. That was where she met him. A week later they all packed up and moved on and a few weeks on she found she was pregnant.

'Her parents didn't throw her out but they made life uncomfortable. They were devout members of a narrow religious sect and made no secret of the fact that she had shamed them. She stuck it out until I was two.'

He gave her a wry, sideways smile. 'By then she'd stopped waiting for the fair and the man who'd fathered me to return to the area. So she cut her losses and took off and supported me by taking what work she could. We had a settled period in Manchester—I guess it would be around eight years. Then we moved down south and ended up here.

'She had a tough life but she never let it get her down.'

It must have been hard for both of them, Caroline conceded silently. Ben's father had seduced a young girl and had moved away, never giving her another thought. Like father like son? But then, his father hadn't known he'd sired a child.

Ben had. And still he'd walked away.

She shifted uncomfortably on the window-seat. She felt utterly drained and very slightly nauseous. What a fool she'd been to imagine that they could share just one perfect day.

Ben's fingers tightened around hers as he sprang lithely to his feet, his smile radiant with enthusiasm as he invited, 'Come and see the rest—I originally had it restored and enlarged for Ma but she tells me she's settled up north with Jane. If you like it, I could give up my suite at the house—there'd be room for more children if I did—and we could use the cottage when I visit. Or—' his smile deepened to a grin '—if you prefer motherhood and country living over a career in the city, we could make this our permanent home and keep my London apartment on for when we fancy a dose of the bright lights. It's entirely up to you, sweetheart.'

Caroline caught her breath. In this light, completely relaxed mood he was damned near irresistible. She shuddered as a cold wash of misery swamped her. He was obviously taking her acceptance of his proposal for granted after the way she'd turned to him in the night.

It was tempting, more tempting than she wanted to admit, but how could she trust him? She'd trusted him before and look where that had got her. She'd be a fool to fall into the same trap twice,

'Sweetheart?' The question in his voice, the way he probed her eyes as if he were looking deep inside her soul, unglued her tongue.

She stepped away from him, folding her arms around her body and told him sombrely, 'We can't divorce the past from the present, pretend it never happened. You can't, either. The very fact that you brought me here when you'd said we wouldn't give it, or the future, headroom today, proves it.'

'I know what I said.' His tone was serious now, his eyes narrowing as he moved closer again and stroked with the tip of one finger the tiny frown line that had appeared between her eyes. 'I was wrong. We can't forget the way we were, what we had, any more than we can ignore the future.' His hand dropped as he traced the delicate line from the arc of her slanting cheekbone to the angle of her jaw. 'And as for today, right here and now, we're the bridge that connects the two.'

She pulled in a sharp breath, her eyes holding his. They had no future. 'I have thought it over—' Her voice failed but under the pressure of his still narrow-eyed scrutiny she found it again. 'Your proposal, that is. Ben, I can't marry you.'

CHAPTER NINE

FOR long seconds Ben simply looked at her, his features stony. Then he asked rawly, 'So what was last night all about?' His mouth thinned. 'And let's not forget this morning. Just sex was it? Not used to going without and I was handy?'

'No!' Caroline's sharp denial was filled with pain. She couldn't let him think that of her, but she couldn't confess she still loved him. If she did that then the pressure he would put on her to take their relationship into the future, make it as permanent as he wanted it to be, would be intolerable.

It was time for the truth, to be as honest as she could be without revealing the depth of her feelings for him. She gave an involuntary shudder but her lush mouth was firm as she told him. 'When we're together it's as if nothing else matters, as if the rest of the world doesn't exist. It was always like that for me, I admit that freely. And if I could keep it like that, then believe me I would.'

She turned her back on him because she simply couldn't bear to see the eyes that had revealed so many things about him—humour, caring, passion— turning to slits of cold, hard jet.

And there would be worse, she knew that, when she'd explained her position. No man who had created a fortune, his company an international byword, his name highly respected in both business and social spheres, would like to be reminded of his cheating past.

Her eyes on the tangled garden, her heart gave a pain-filled judder. With a lot of hard work and a great deal of pleasure it could be turned into a place of riotous beauty. But of course she would not be the one to make the transformation.

She flicked her tongue over dry-as-dust lips and tried to ease the tension from her shoulders. But it wouldn't go and she forced out thickly, 'After the way you betrayed us all I could never really trust you. I might want and—' she bit off the words, love you, and substituted, '—find you attractive, but I wouldn't trust you not to do the same again.'

'Ah. So we're back to that word betrayal again.'

She heard him move closer, his feet making very little sound on the wide oak boards. She wondered if he'd touch her, but he didn't.

'You were about to tell me what you meant last night, but events overtook us, as I remember.' There was a firm edge of determination in his voice. 'So spit it out now, Caro.'

'Look I know it was a long time ago,' she said tiredly. 'You were young, unprincipled and wild. You might be twelve years older now, successful, extremely wealthy and respected, but people don't change, not basically.'

'Cut to the chase,' Ben instructed, his voice a warning, and she dragged in a breath, wondering why she had to be so stubborn, why she had to be so darned particular. Couldn't she have at least tried to wipe the slate clean, take as much happiness as she could for as long as it lasted?

But trust was important. Too important to be brushed aside as if it didn't matter.

She swallowed to ease the tightness in her throat and stiffened her already tense shoulders. Start with the easy one, the sin he'd already put his hand up for, she told herself.

'My father paid you to go away and stay away. That was bad enough, showed how much I really meant to you. But you went back on the deal, on your own admission. You came panting back to ask me if I was going to marry Jeremy Curtis. I guess your ego couldn't stand the thought that I might have used you the way you'd used me. You went back on that mercenary deal you made with my father. That shows a complete lack of moral integrity.'

A few beats of silence followed, fraught with menace. Caroline felt the hairs on the back of her neck stand on end. She turned swiftly, facing him, just as he snapped out, 'Your father offered me money but I didn't take it. I told him what he could do with it. I didn't renege on any bargain because none was made. If he told you differently, he lied, just as, apparently, he lied when he informed me you were only a couple of months away from announcing your engagement.'

She dropped her lashes. The dark, accusatory glitter of his eyes hurt so much.

'Had you so little faith in me?' Ben demanded heavily. 'I've already explained why I had to head to London at a moment's notice, how I couldn't wait to get back to hear your side of the engagement story. Couldn't you have done the same? Waited to hear what I had to say? Why take your father's word as gospel, write me off?'

Put like that, he had every reason to look so quietly, forbiddingly angry, she acknowledged miserably.

And if the alleged exchange of money for a promise had been the only thing she'd had to worry about at that time then everything would have been different. She would have waited at Langley Hayes to see if he did come back and would have asked him if what her father had said was true.

But it hadn't been the only thing, had it?

'There was more to it than that. I know what you did to Maggie Pope and your baby daughter.' She could hardly get the words out, the memory of the shattering blow she'd endured still had the power to hurt and appall her.

She drew in a deep, ragged breath and said heavily, 'When my father told me I didn't want to believe it. But Maggie confirmed it. You got her pregnant but refused to take any responsibility. You washed your hands of both of them; you didn't want to know. And turned your attention to your next willing victim. Me.'

She watched the colour drain from his face and flinched. The truth hurt, didn't it just. Strangely, she ached to touch him, to make her peace with him. Love, she supposed, was responsible for this almost primal urge to offer comfort. When it came to the crunch love forgave everything, she acknowledged with a tremor of shock.

Instinctively, she reached out a hand but he shook his head abruptly and walked to the door, his voice tight as he bit out, 'I have never touched Maggie Pope, much less fathered a child on her. You have to make a choice whether or not to believe me.' He swung round, his black eyes impaling her. 'In the end, it all comes down to trust, doesn't it?'

The brisk walk back through the woods was accomplished in a silence so intense it set Caroline's nerve ends jangling and made her mouth run dry.

She wanted to tell him she couldn't condone what he'd done but she did understand. He'd been young, highly sexed and his father had set him a terrible example. And maybe, just maybe, he'd been living up to his own reputation as the village Lothario.

She wanted to beg him not to lie about it, especially not to her, not after the passion they'd shared. She wanted to suggest he made amends by getting to know his daughter, helping to provide for her.

Perhaps, that way, they could finally put the past behind them and go on...

The pace he'd set had made her breathless and her voice snagged as she began, 'Ben—listen—please don't lie to me—'

But he cut her short with one slashing movement

of his hand. Scornful eyes stabbed into hers. 'I have *never* lied to you. I suggest you start listening to your heart instead of your cold, judgmental brain. And while you're doing that, you can finish up your work here.' He pulled his lips back against his teeth in a humourless smile. 'You might not have the time, or the inclination, when I'm through thrashing things out with you.'

Stung by his dictatorial, contemptuous tone, hurt by his refusal to trust her enough to admit he'd lied, she glared at him with tear-glittered eyes.

Ben swung round and stalked away, his stride long and rangy as he crossed the gravelled forecourt of Langley Hayes, his aggrieved pride showing in the tense set of his shoulders.

'Wait!' she cried, finding her voice, her tone every bit as dictatorial as his had been. But to her teeth-grinding chagrin he ignored her, striding to his car, gunning the powerful engine, wide tyres scattering gravel as he drove away.

Caroline gritted her teeth and stumped back into the house. The man was impossible. Was his ego so huge he couldn't face humbling himself, admitting he'd done wrong? Did he have to lie about it?

Did he take her for a total fool?

Because twelve years ago Maggie Pope couldn't have been lying. The girl, only a few months older than Caroline herself, would have had no possible reason to tell lies about the identity of her tiny baby's father.

The perfect day she'd planned—they had both

planned—had turned into a nightmare and there would be no going back, no reclamation of the stolen hours that had seemed so enticing earlier on.

Which was possibly just as well, she consoled herself crossly, hoping that if she whipped up enough anger then the heat of it would counteract the icy pain in her heart. It might have been twenty-four hours of paradise, but it would have been a paradise for blind fools.

The phone was ringing as she headed across the hall. Frowning, she decided to ignore it then rapidly changed her mind. It might be one of the contractors Ben had hired to reinvent the estate, and she wasn't going to emulate him and throw a tantrum, regardless of normal everyday duties, nor storm off in a huff!

She took the call in the room that had been her father's study and such was her jagged emotional state it was a full sixty seconds before she registered the identity of the caller.

'Michael,' she responded shortly.

'The one and only! Listen, Caroline, I'm in the area—a big-house sale just outside Shrewsbury. If you're finished up your end, and as hacked off as you sound, you could come back to London with me. Yes?'

She had no further excuse for staying here but the mere thought of leaving Ben, putting their bitter-sweet reunion behind her, was like the pain of a thousand knives twisting in her heart.

But it had to be done.

'Yes?' Her boss's son repeated his query. 'I say, are you still there, Caroline?'

'Sorry—just thinking.' She pulled in a breath and went on more firmly, 'I've done all that could be done here.'

'Great! I should be with you around four. We can stop off for something to eat on the way...' his voice lowered huskily '...and continue the conversation we were having before you had to go away. *Ciao*, sweetheart!'

She flinched at the endearment Ben had used so effectively during the last twenty-four hours, sounding as if he'd really meant it, and replaced the receiver with unsteady hands. She didn't want any other man to call her sweetheart. She didn't want any other man, full stop.

And what conversation had Michael been referring to? The getting-to-know-each-other-better one, she supposed with a spurt of misery. Remembering her almost clinical detachment at the time when she'd vaguely supposed that her friendly relationship with Michael Weinberg was worth exploring further, she grimaced. How objectively she'd weighed up the pros and cons: to remain single or form a relationship and a family.

It would never happen for her. There was nothing wrong with Michael: he was intelligent, nice-looking, they had much in common. But like the few other men she'd dated during the past twelve years, he wasn't Ben.

Caroline put her fingertips to her aching temples,

her glossy head bowed. Right from the start, all those years ago, Ben had spoiled her for any other man. She dragged her lower lip between her teeth, her breath burning in her lungs.

Hadn't he admitted it had been exactly the same for him? Confessed to having brought her back to Langley Hayes with the intention of finally laying those memories they had of each other to rest, proving beyond any shadow of doubt that what they'd had was nothing special?

And hadn't he admitted frankly that it hadn't worked that way? And what had he told her? She pushed her jumbled hair away from her face. 'I suggest you start listening to your heart.'

As he'd listened to his when he'd excused the hateful letter she'd left with his mother just hours before she'd left this house for good. Excusing it, putting it down to a seventeen-year-old's panicky reaction against making a serious commitment. He'd been wrong, of course, but he had been trying to understand and make allowances because there had been love in his heart and he'd listened to it?

Could she have misjudged him?

Something sweet, a tender fledgling certainty, blossomed in her own heart. Maybe he hadn't driven away in the middle of a temper tantrum, furious because he'd been shown up as far less than perfect. But had gone because he'd needed time on his own to figure out how he was going to convince her he'd been telling the truth.

Caroline walked from the room, closing the door quietly behind her, her mind made up now.

She could readily accept that her father had lied about Ben accepting that pay-off. He would have done anything, said anything, to break up their affair, put a stop to it before Jeremy Curtis got to hear of it. His plans for marrying her off into a wealthy family would have been put in jeopardy.

That left Maggie Pope.

Letting herself out of the house Caroline noted that dull grey clouds had covered the sun, the fickle English spring veering back to winter. She shivered, but began a brisk walk into the village.

There was plenty of time before Michael arrived to collect her to find Maggie and demand the truth. Provided she hadn't left the area.

But that wasn't likely. Her widower father kept the village pub, as his father and grandfather had before him, and Maggie had helped out ever since she'd left school the minute she'd reached sixteen. Continuing to live and work there would be the ideal answer for a single mother with no qualifications.

Even as a chilling wind blew out of nowhere, Caroline's heart sang and she listened. Ben hadn't lied, he wasn't callous now—witness his plans for Langley Hayes—and he hadn't been callous when she'd first known him and had fallen in love with him.

Ben had wanted to marry her way back then and he wanted to marry her now! And they wouldn't have wasted twelve long years if she'd been more mature, refusing to believe those lies until she'd talked to him and had heard what he'd had to say, keeping her faith in him despite her father's insistence that he'd gone for good.

Vowing she'd make it up to him, she lengthened her stride, hugging the hedgerows for protection from the increasingly steady drizzle.

The only enigma was why Maggie had lied. Out of spite? Because the wild, sexy Ben Dexter had never touched her and she'd wished he would?

Caroline had known of his reputation, who hadn't? Sometimes, home from boarding school for the holidays, she'd visited the general store, had heard a group of village girls drooling over the hunky Ben Dexter, giggling and preening if he'd happened to roar by on the old motorbike he'd used to get around on, some of them boasting that they'd ridden pillion with him, implying a whole lot more.

Had Maggie been jealous because she hadn't been one of the lucky ones? Deciding to get her own back by telling everyone that she had?

Whatever. Speculation was getting her nowhere. She had to have the truth, discover what had lain behind the lie that had done so much damage, and she knew she was going to have to wait a short while longer when the heavens opened as she reached the outskirts of the village.

Scurrying, her head down, she headed for the store where she could shelter until the worst had passed.

A violent tapping on a window-pane had her skidding to a standstill.

Dorothy Skeet beckoned her frantically and Caroline dived thankfully under the porch of the pretty cottage and pushed on the open front door.

'You've got drenched!' Dorothy clucked as she emerged from a door on the right. 'I saw you coming down the lane—you can see everything from my front window—and I said to myself, Poor Miss Caroline will get a right soaking! Now, come and dry off by the fire and I'll get you a towel for your hair. And what about a cup of tea? I could fancy one myself.'

Acquiescing gratefully, Caroline entered a cosy, cluttered room and rough-dried her hair in front of the fire that crackled in the tiny hearth while Dorothy went to make the promised tea.

'You've made it very comfortable,' she remarked when the older woman returned with a tray of tea things. 'You're happy here?'

Her father's death must have hit Dorothy hard. She'd lost the man who'd been the centre of her narrow life for years, had lost her home and her livelihood. Caroline felt a nagging sense of responsibility. If Dorothy was having difficulty making ends meet— the legacy wouldn't have amounted to much after her father's debts had been paid—then something would have to be done about it.

'Oh, yes.' Dorothy filled two cups from the squat brown teapot, handing one to Caroline who had put the damp towel aside and was watching the steam rise from her borrowed jeans. 'I miss your dad, of course I do, and I thought I'd be lonely, but I'm not really. There's always someone to talk to and, like I said, I can see all the comings and goings from my window.'

And report them, innocuous or not, to the first willing ear she happened to come across, Caroline thought with a wry smile as she refused the sugar bowl. She probed gently, 'I know you won't be pensionable age, Dorothy. So how are you managing? Don't be afraid to say if you're not. I'll probably be able to help.'

'Bless you, I'm managing fine.' The other woman sank into a roomy armchair, beaming. 'When Mr Dexter's company took over the house he explained why he couldn't keep me on, not as full-time house-keeper anyway. He needs someone young and street-wise to keep up with all those energetic young tear-aways he's going to take in. But as soon as the first lot arrives I'm to go there for a few hours each day and just help out here and there, get to know them, be a sort of temporary granny, he said. And until they do arrive he pays me a handsome retainer.' She stirred her tea reflectively. 'He's a good man, that.'

Of course he was, Caroline conceded silently, a lump in her throat. The best. So why had it taken her so long to admit it to herself? She'd been so intent on clinging to the misconceptions of the past that she'd been blinded to the truth.

Her father hadn't been able to love her. So had she, subconsciously, believed that, because he couldn't love her, no one else could, either?

Was that why she'd so easily believed the lies

about Ben, convinced in the dark, hidden parts of her mind that he had never loved her, had merely used her?

She set her empty cup down and rubbed at the frown that had appeared between her eyes. She wasn't into self-analysis. Up until now her thoughts had run in a straight line—no looking back—mapping out her life, building her career, seeing things as black or white, no shades in between acceptable.

Huffing out a breath, she smiled for Dorothy, glancing at the window. She wouldn't be going in search of Maggie now; let her keep her secret. There was no point in hurling recriminations for the damage that had been done in the past. Caroline had to look to the future, the possibility of sharing it with Ben because she knew now that he hadn't lied when he'd stated categorically that he had never touched Maggie Pope.

She said briskly, 'I think the rain's stopped.'

She went to investigate and Dorothy joined her at the window. 'Yes, you're right. But you don't have to rush off, do you?'

'Afraid so.' She grimaced at her crumpled, borrowed clothes. 'I have to get back and change.' Michael was coming at four, but hopefully she wouldn't be leaving with him. She had to see Ben, retract all the hurtful things she'd said, ask him to forgive her and tell him she loved him.

A watery sun was turning the raindrops on the grass of the village green to sparkling diamonds and from where she was standing she could see the picturesque but shabby Poacher's Arms. And partly hidden by the stand of trees in the centre of the green the sleek profile of a Jaguar. Ben's?

As if in answer to her unspoken question the main door opened and Ben strode out, his face grim, followed closely by Maggie, her blonde hair tousled as if she'd been trying to pull it out by the roots, her eyes red and puffy.

And then, dancing around the adults, a tall, coltish child, dark plaits flying around her animated face.

'Maggie's child.'

Caroline hadn't realised she'd spoken the instinctive words aloud until Dorothy confirmed, 'That's right. She'll have grown a bit since you were last here! Gone twelve now, she is. Angela, they call her—though she's no angel—up to every mischief she can find! She's the image of her dad, though, don't you think?'

The giant hand that squeezed her heart made Caroline feel nauseous. The dark braids were a shade or two lighter than Ben's raven hair, but the wiry, coltish grace, the half-tamed joy of living that animated the lively face...

Caroline couldn't answer but Dorothy didn't need confirmation of her remark, her voice avid with her love of gossip as she said, 'Wild horses wouldn't make him admit he's Angie's father but everyone knows it. They've been caught at it, if you take my meaning, more than once. He'd never marry her and make the kid legitimate, of course. Our Maggie's too far beneath him. Well, she's slow on the uptake...'

Dorothy tapped the side of her head meaningfully '...a bit rough and ready, so he wouldn't tie himself to the likes of her. You know him well enough to see that, what with his position and everything.'

Caroline bit down hard on her bottom lip. She desperately wanted to make her excuses and leave but she couldn't move.

Rooted to the spot, she saw Ben grin as he said something to the child, dig in the pocket of his jeans and count coins out into the small, outstretched palm. Watched the little girl skip across the green towards the store, watched Ben turn back to Maggie, his face frigidly serious now.

And Dorothy droned on, oblivious to Caroline's turmoil, 'Mind you, he visits now and then, I'll say that for him. You can see him come and go out of opening hours, usually this time of day. Probably helps out a bit financially, I wouldn't know. But so he should, he's not short of a bob or two, as you know.'

Caroline caught her breath as the hand around her heart squeezed tighter but she managed to uproot her feet from the floor, unglue her tongue from the roof of her mouth, rasping, 'Sorry, I really must go.'

To get away from the words that were drilling holes in her head.

'Must you?' As always, Dorothy Skeet was enjoying her gossip. She dipped her head towards Ben, his face emphatic as he spoke to Maggie. 'Mr Dexter can give you a lift back when he's ready.'

'No!' The negative was torn from her. She turned and fled.

CHAPTER TEN

CLEARING the sharp bend in the narrow lane which put her safely out of sight of the entire village and Dorothy's no doubt astonished eyes, Caroline stopped to catch her breath and let her thumping heartbeats settle down to a more sedate pace, her silky, fine dark brows pulling together in an exasperated frown.

She was doing it again, wasn't she? Running away just as she'd done twelve years ago. Assuming the worst about the man she loved without stopping to hear his side of the story.

Dorothy's opinions weren't conclusive evidence, were they? Opinions formed by village gossips, who had nothing better to do with their time than speculate, elaborate and embroider on the doings of others, weren't to be taken as gospel truth.

And she, Caroline, wasn't going to make the same mistake twice. She would speak to Ben, tell him what Dorothy had said—implied—and listen to what he had to say with an open, trusting mind.

Briefly debating whether to retrace her steps, head back to the village and find Ben or flag him down if he happened to pass her on his way back to Langley Hayes, she glanced down at her wrist-watch.

In just under an hour Michael would arrive to pick

145

her up so it would probably be better—less of a half-way-to-hysterical impulse—if she carried on up to the house, got cleaned up and changed so that when Ben turned up she could face him with some dignity and poise.

Looking as she did, her hair hanging in straggly rats' tails, her blouse crumpled and the borrowed, too wide, too short jeans still damp and spattered with mud, she must look like a particularly unappealing tramp.

She would have time for a quick shower, she decided as she walked on up the lane trying to avoid the puddles and the rainwater that dripped off the overhanging trees. She'd probably change into the suit she'd arrived in, blow dry her hair and—

She cut her thoughts off with a muffled groan, aware of what she was doing—filling her mind with unimportant trivia to crowd out the terrible doubts.

That he had lied to her and would go on lying.

That the things Dorothy had said were the truth, that everyone knew he was the father of Maggie's child.

She didn't want to have doubts about him, she really didn't, she didn't want them festering in her mind so she'd been trying to blot them out.

She wanted to recapture that earlier faith, the blossoming of certainty that had filled her heart with such sweet joy.

Her throat tightened and thickened with tears as she turned into the Langley Hayes' driveway and walked on towards the house. After what she'd seen and had heard, that earlier certainty was impossible to recapture, but she wouldn't let herself dwell on these negative thoughts before she'd heard what he had to say.

The final bend in the drive brought her in sight of the house and of Michael's blue BMW. Caroline bit back a groan of stark annoyance. Her employer's son was leaning against the bonnet, perfectly relaxed, his legs crossed at the ankles, the hem of his pale green shirt coming adrift from the waistband of his crumpled grey chinos.

She would have much preferred him to be late rather than early. She was going to have to tell him that she couldn't leave until she'd talked to Ben, that he could go on without her and she'd make her own way back to base.

Reluctantly, she returned his wave of greeting and he levered his stocky body away from the car and walked to meet her. His hazel eyes crinkled with laughter as he threw an arm around her shoulders.

'You're early.' Caroline heard the accusatory tone in her voice and tried to moderate it. None of this was his fault. 'I have to—'

No need to go on, the crunch of tyres on gravel told her that Ben had returned. The big car slowed as it drew level. She saw one comprehensive look from narrowed black eyes as Michael grinned and hugged her just that little bit closer, 'What have you done to yourself, my darling? You look more like a scarecrow than my beautiful, elegant partner!'

She wasn't his partner in any sense of the word;

she was his colleague. She fumed inwardly, impatiently shrugging his arm from her shoulder and tucking a straggle of hair behind her ear as Ben shot her a fulminating glare then gunned the engine and ended up parking beside the BMW in a shower of gravel.

Caroline surged forward, her jaw at a determined angle, but Michael captured her waist in what felt like a grip of iron. 'Hang on, what's the rush?'

'I need to speak to Ben—Mr Dexter—'

'Fine. I'm in no hurry, and he doesn't seem to be going anywhere.'

He wasn't. He was waiting. Feet apart, his extravagantly handsome features austere. Caroline's stomach clenched as her heart turned over. The force of his anger was almost visible. She had never, ever, seen him look quite so forbidding.

But Michael seemed blithely unaware of it as they approached the waiting man. His hand outstretched, he acknowledged, 'Dexter—good to meet the guy who gave my find a home!' And at Ben's blank, tight-lipped stare, he elaborated. '*First Love*—the find of the decade.'

Eliciting no response he belatedly introduced himself. 'Michael Weinberg. Caroline told me on the phone that she's finished up here and I offered to drive her back. I'm a tad earlier than I said I'd be, but that's probably a bonus, because I get the impression she's anxious to get under way.'

He turned smiling eyes back to her, and to her ears his voice sounded decidedly intimate. 'We'll stop off for an early supper. I got on the mobile and booked a table at a rather good restaurant just outside Banbury—it will go some way towards making up for the dinner date we had to cancel when you came up here.'

Only when his hand gave a proprietorial squeeze did Caroline become aware that he still had an arm around her waist. Michael was giving entirely the wrong impression. About everything. Wanting to slap a hand over his mouth to stop him saying another word she felt herself redden with frustration then go cold all over as Ben turned contemptuous, half-hooded eyes on her for a long, blistering second before turning back to the other man.

'Yes. I see now.' His voice was flat, the pent-up anger disappearing, making him seem weary. He made a gesture with one hand towards the house. 'Perhaps you'd like to wait inside, Weinberg? I'm sure it won't take Miss Harvey too long to make herself beautiful for you. And would you like her to make you some tea to drink while you wait?'

All cool urbanity now, and then some. Caroline fumed as she escaped Michael's clutches and stalked ahead of them into the house. Ben was savagely angry with her, that much was obvious. Less obvious was the reason.

Because she'd as good as called him a liar, impugned his integrity?

Because, from the way Michael had put it, he'd made it sound as if she'd contacted him and had begged him to fetch her away?

Or because of Michael's overfamiliarity, the way he'd spoken to and about her, his arm possessively around her waist?

Or an explosive combination of all three?

That seemed more than likely and, looking at it that way, she couldn't blame Ben for being so angry, she decided glumly as she walked through to the kitchen to make that dratted tea. They both had a lot of explaining to do. But was he in any mood to listen to anything she said? she questioned, her nerves beginning to shred.

Wondering whether to ask him for ten minutes of his time before she showered and changed, or afterwards when she'd look less messy and ridiculous and just might feel more in control of emotions that were getting more dangerously unstable by the moment, she filled the electric kettle and plugged it in.

Assembling the tea things on a tray was almost impossible, her hands were shaking so much. One of the cups slithered from her fingers and shattered on the tiled floor, when Ben walked in and shouldered the door shut behind him.

The silence after she'd muttered something distinctly unladylike was intense, prickly, painful. A silent accusation hanging in the air, so many things to be said, retracted, so many questions to be asked.

Feeling gauche and incredibly clumsy, tongue-tied because there were so many things to be said and she didn't for the life of her know where to start, Caroline hunted for the dustpan and brush, found it eventually and swept up the mess.

And all the time he said nothing, watching her with those cold, narrowed eyes. The kettle was boiling furiously as she tipped the shards into the waste bin.

At least the question of when they would talk had been taken out of her hands. It was Ben who broke the silence that was making her feel like a halfwit on the edge of hysteria as he went to deal with the kettle, pour the boiling water onto the leaves she'd already spooned into the pot. 'If you'd been ready to leave with your gallant rescuer before I got back, would you have left me another Dear John letter, I wonder?'

He arranged the milk jug and sugar bowl on the tray with neat precision, his hands perfectly steady, his voice like an arctic night as he answered his own question before she had a chance to make any reply, 'No, I suppose you wouldn't. As your partner has already let slip, you can't wait to get way, you wouldn't have wanted to waste the time putting pen to paper. You'd already told me exactly what you thought of me.'

The tea preparations finished, he picked up the tray and Caroline said tautly, 'I know you're angry, but I'm not feeling too euphoric, either.' She searched his impressive but chilling features for some sign of the closeness they had so recently shared. She found none. So she reminded herself that she was a grown woman of above average intelligence and said emphatically, 'We really do need to talk.'

The look he turned on her said he found her statement completely incomprehensible. His head tilted slightly to one side, he uttered, 'I can't think why, when there's nothing more to say.' He gave a slight, insouciant-seeming shrug. 'But if you insist I'll give you five minutes of my time when you're ready to leave.'

He walked to the door then turned to face her, 'I'll serve tea to your partner while you get your things together. Oh, and just one more thing, I spoke to Maggie Pope this afternoon. She admitted that your father paid her to name me as the father of her child, should you ask.' He gave her a mocking smile that was totally devoid of humour. 'He certainly put the money I refused to take to good use.' His beautifully shaped mouth hardened, 'Not that you'll believe me, of course. That would be too much to ask. You've probably already decided that I somehow twisted her arm to persuade her to say that.'

He left as swiftly and silently as he'd appeared, left before she had time to even begin to respond to what he'd said.

It was the best she could do, Caroline thought as she nervously scanned her reflection half an hour later.

Deciding against the suit she'd arrived in as being too formal, too much like the hard-nosed career woman she'd done her best to portray when she'd arrived here, she'd dressed in a sleek-fitting, beautifully tailored sage green skirt, topped by a lighter toned fine cashmere sweater. But not even her skilled application of make-up could disguise the haunted look in her eyes or the lines of strain around her mouth.

Ben's stress on the word 'partner' told her a lot. He thought her relationship with Michael was much closer than it was. Bleakly she recalled what he'd said earlier when he'd asked her what last night and this morning had been about, implying that she'd been missing regular sex and he'd been handy.

Implying that she was some kind of nymphomaniac!

Michael's words and attitude would have reinforced that rock-bottom opinion.

Casting a final look around the room that had been hers for the first, almost eighteen, years of her life she told herself to think positively.

She loved Ben and, more importantly, she trusted him now, implicitly. What he'd told her about Maggie Pope made perfect sense, made everything else slot into place.

Her father's plan to buy Ben off had failed; so what better way to blacken his character and put an end to what he'd thought was his daughter's infatuation with an unsuitable man than to use the spurned money to pay Maggie to tell those lies?

The girl wasn't too bright and ever since the drink-drive laws her father had barely scraped a living, only the immediate locals using the bar at The Poacher's Arms. Money was tight and Maggie'd had a small baby to care for.

Yes, it did make perfect sense; it was just a pity Ben had been too angry to hang around long enough to hear her tell him she believed every word of what he'd said.

Still, he'd promised they'd talk before she left. They'd work things out; they had to. Then maybe she could stay—unless Ben needed some time to think things over. She loved him so desperately and, even if he hadn't said he still loved her, he did have deep feelings for her. He'd asked her to marry him, to share his life, and he wouldn't have done that if all they had was fantastic sex.

Ben would be waiting. Caroline picked up her bag and walked through the door. A trillion butterflies were performing acrobatics in her stomach.

'That's more like it—well worth waiting for!' Michael's warm hazel eyes swept over her with male approval as he laid the newspaper he'd been reading aside and got to his feet, levering himself out of the deep armchair. 'If you're ready, we'll get moving.' He took her bag from her suddenly nerveless fingers. 'It will be good to have you back at base. I've missed you.'

Caroline ignored that. 'I can't leave yet,' she stated firmly. 'I have to speak to Ben.' She scanned the study, as if expecting to see him emerge from behind the shabby furniture, but only the used tea cups testified that he'd ever been here.

'He's gone,' Michael relayed blithely as he walked to the door. 'No worries—he said to tell you goodbye and thanks.'

Goodbye? A final goodbye? And thanks? For what? A few sessions of out-of-this-world sex?

Her heart plummeted down through the soles of her shoes and the butterflies in her stomach went into panic mode. 'Gone where?' she demanded hoarsely, pattering after Michael as he crossed the main hall.

He'd promised they'd talk before she left. He couldn't have simply gone. Unless he'd been so disillusioned and disgusted by her lack of trust he'd decided he never wanted to have to set eyes on her again, much less to have to listen to her accuse him of being a liar.

Michael shrugged. 'Couldn't say. He said he'd just remembered an appointment and shot out. And we're not to worry about locking up. Apparently he was going to ask the site manager to do it before he leaves this evening.'

This evening? Did that mean she could sit around waiting for him all night and he still wouldn't turn up?

Probably, she conceded numbly. If he really had suddenly remembered an appointment too important to cancel, if he really had wanted to thrash things out with her—as he'd intimated much earlier—then he would have left a different message, something along the lines of getting in touch at a later date.

He'd invented that appointment, she was sure of it, she decided, feeling limp and sick to her stomach. He just couldn't be bothered to argue his case with a woman who'd made it plain what she thought of his morals.

And Michael confirmed it when he joined her in the car. 'Dexter asked me to invoice him for your time, but you're not to bother with an evaluation. He can decide for himself what's worth keeping and what's not.' He fastened his seat belt and turned the key in the ignition. 'I don't know why he wanted you up here in the first place. Still, if he wants to waste his money, that's his affair.' The car drew smoothly away. 'Was there much of interest around the place?'

'Not much.' Automatically, Caroline mentioned the pieces that would be worth keeping as an investment, her mind functioning on a different level entirely.

Was there a hidden meaning behind his statement that he could decide what was worth keeping and what was not? Meaning *she* was not worth keeping?

Probably. But there could be no doubt that his instruction regarding her written evaluation meant he wanted no further contact.

Ben Dexter had washed his hands of her and, looking at the sorry mess from his point of view, she couldn't blame him.

He had finally done what he'd set out to do. Got her out of his system.

CHAPTER ELEVEN

SITTING opposite Michael in the small but elegantly appointed restaurant on the outskirts of Banbury, Caroline wondered miserably how she could ever have imagined that their close and friendly working relationship could have developed into something so very much more. Marriage, home-building, children—leading eventually to a companionable old age.

She would never have been able to love him. How could she love him, or any other man for that matter, when Ben had captured her heart and had never let it go? Michael deserved far better than that.

She stared unseeing at the plate of green salad she'd ordered, bleakly looking into a lonely, loveless future and Michael said, 'Aren't you going to eat that? I must say, it certainly looks pretty boring to me—you should have gone for the duck, it's brilliant.'

'Sorry.' Caroline gave him a wan smile and picked up her fork and speared a dressing-slicked leaf without any enthusiasm. 'I'm tired, I guess.'

Although drained was more like it. Drained of energy and hope. Too listless to have been able to tell Michael she'd much prefer to get straight back to London rather than take an early supper break.

Besides, that would have been selfish. Michael must have been ravenous if the way he'd demolished his meal was anything to go by.

'Tired? What brought that on?' A sandy brow lifted enquiringly as he laid down his cutlery and relaxed back in his chair. 'From the little of real interest you say you found at Langley Hayes, I wouldn't have thought you've been overworked exactly.'

There was no getting around that. It was time to be honest and open, to explain why his suggestion that they get to know each other better on a personal level was a non-starter. She owed Michael that much at least.

Caroline laid down her fork and confessed numbly, 'I don't want this to go any further, but Ben—Mr Dexter—and I go back a long way, Mike. We had an affair twelve years ago. It ended after a couple of months or so. I didn't see him again until he came to look at the Lassoon painting.' She pulled in a breath then went on doggedly. 'The last few days have been pretty traumatic.'

'Good God!' He looked stunned. He stared at her for long, assessing moments then stated bluntly, 'You're still in love with him, aren't you?'

Her throat too tight to allow her to speak, Caroline nodded and Michael said slowly, 'If it's lasted that length of time, with nothing to feed on, it has to be the real thing.' He gave her a twisted smile. 'I guess that puts me right out of the frame.' He lifted his shoulders then slowly let them drop. 'But then, I don't suppose I was ever really in it, was I? And you were too polite to tell me. Still friends, though?'

'Of course,' she answered, on a rush of gratitude, glad he was taking it like this, even more relieved to know that his feelings hadn't taken a thorough battering. As hers had done. She wouldn't wish that on her worst enemy.

But she wasn't going to think of that, of bruised and battered feelings; she wouldn't let herself. If she allowed herself to think of what she had almost had and thrown away with her lack of trust, she would put back her head and howl like a dog and embarrass both of them. But then Michael asked, 'Does he feel the same?'

An iron fist clenched around her heart, the pain unbearable, her voice a ragged whisper as she got out, 'Once, perhaps. Not any more.'

'I thought I detected a bit of an atmosphere. Had a fight, did you?'

'Something like that.' She didn't want to say any more on the subject but Michael wouldn't let it go.

He inched towards her, his forearms on the table, his fingers touching hers, just briefly, as he told her, 'He'll get over it—whatever you fought about. Caroline, he isn't a fool. And—' he cleared his throat and added uncomfortably, his face going pink '—I don't know, but I might have put my foot in it. Well, we were talking while we waited for you. He was asking questions, about your position at the gallery, whether you were wedded to your career—that sort of stuff.' He fell silent as their waiter approached to clear the main course and Caroline gave an inner groan of despair.

Had Ben, even at that stage, still wanted to marry her? Why else should he have tried to find out how much her work meant to her? He'd given her a free choice earlier, when he'd made that stunning proposal of marriage: continue with her career, live in London and use the cottage for weekends, or make it their permanent home.

Her throat clogged with tears. She made a determined effort to swallow them. Of course he hadn't still been thinking of marriage. He'd been disgusted by her, by her total lack of trust.

Michael was saying something. Caroline hauled herself out of her pit of misery and said thickly, 'Sorry?'

'I asked if you would like the dessert menu.'

She shook her head, unable at the moment to trust her voice. She couldn't eat, she simply couldn't. She just wanted to get out of here, get back to London and lick her wounds in private.

But Michael had ordered coffee. Caroline smothered a sigh of sheer impatience and Michael mumbled, 'I feel a fool. I had no idea you and he—well, why would I? I'm afraid I gave him the impression you and I were an item. That when Dad retires next year and I take over you'd be a full partner.' His face turned bright red. 'And my wife. Well,' he said brusquely, on the defensive now, 'I did have hopes in that direction, and I guess I was jumping the gun. Over-confidence is my one big failing, or so the old man keeps telling me. Look,' he offered grimly, 'if it'll help heal the rift I'll swallow my pride and call Dexter first thing tomorrow to put him straight.'

'I'd rather you didn't,' Caroline returned stiffly. It was over. Ben had already let her know in no uncertain terms how disgusted he was with her before that conversation had taken place.

The wrong impression Michael had given Ben made her stomach churn queasily but it wasn't anything to make a song and dance about. It would have been nothing more than the final nail in the coffin of their already doomed relationship.

'It wouldn't make a scrap of difference,' she said dismissively with a fatalistic sigh. She looked pointedly at her watch. 'If you're ready, could we make a move? I need a good night's sleep if I'm going to be fit for anything in the morning.'

A good night's sleep was difficult to come by, Caroline decided edgily four weeks later, as she ran a duster over the uncluttered surfaces in her minimally furnished small sitting room.

By armouring herself in designer suits and the mask of her make-up, absorbing herself in her work, she got through the days. And weekends she spent with whichever of her friends happened to be free. But the nights...

The nights were unadulterated torment. Ben took the starring role in dreams that grew ever more sexually explicit and she would come partially awake and reach for him, but he wasn't there, and never would be.

And she'd spend the remaining hours until daylight telling herself that it was over, making herself accept it, facing the fact that Ben would have put their ill-fated relationship firmly behind him, finally ridding himself of her, of his memories of her. Because what man in his right mind could want a woman who openly stated that she didn't trust him?

She was coming dangerously close to hating herself, unravelling round the edges, unable to eat or sleep, tormented by the thoughts of her lost love.

She tossed the duster aside, angry with herself. If her life was a mess she had only herself to blame. So something had to be done about it. And no one else would do it for her.

When Edward Weinberg had said, 'You look dreadful. You're either terminally ill and not telling anyone, or I'm working you too hard. I'm inclined to believe the latter, so take two weeks off. Go to the continent and lie on a beach', she'd wanted to dig her heels in and refuse to do any such thing.

But perhaps the enforced break was just what she really needed to straighten herself out, to do something positive. But what?

Lying on a beach held no appeal. Too much time to think, to brood. She needed hard, physical work.

Casting a look around her sterile living quarters, she made up her mind, grabbed a jacket and walked out.

And two hours later she was back, weighed down

with tins of paint, brushes, fabric swatches, cheap denim jeans and T-shirts from the local street-market.

The apartment she'd previously viewed simply as a place to sleep was going to be turned into a proper home.

'Talk about a sea change!' Danielle Booth, Caroline's neighbour from across the hall, poked her sleek brown head around the open door. 'You've worked your socks off all week so how about a girls' night out—you're not going to work all weekend, I forbid it! You'll give yourself painter's elbow!'

Warm apricot emulsion had transformed the vestibule—formerly an uninspiring pale grey—and the partly open door through to the sitting room revealed the same colour but in a slightly deeper tone.

'Do you like it?' Caroline, on her knees, putting the finishing touches to the skirting board, wanted to know because this was her first attempt at home-decorating and she wasn't sure she'd got it right.

She scrambled to her feet and Danielle said, 'I love it. But I would never have put you down as a hands-on sort of person. Have the decorators in and stay at an hotel until they'd finished would be more your style. And I've never seen you look anything but perfectly groomed before—'

'There's always a first time.' With difficulty Caroline returned her friend's grin. Danielle wasn't to know that she was having to keep herself occupied every minute of her time to stop herself brooding. Over what might have been, over what she had so briefly had and had stupidly thrown away. 'And it's nice not to have to bother about the way I look. Coffee?'

'I'd love some, but I can't. Hair appointment,' Danielle stated. 'Now, what about tonight? We could take in a film, have supper.'

'Sorry,' Caroline declined. She wasn't ready for a relaxed evening out; she'd be terrible company. 'I've got a bedroom to paper. We'll hit the town some other time?'

Danielle planted her hands on her curvaceous hips, her chin going up at an angle as she huffed, 'Caroline Harvey—you are the most stubborn creature—' and fell silent as another, harder voice intervened, 'A sentiment I most sincerely endorse.'

Ben!

Caroline didn't know whether she'd spoken his name aloud or whether it simply rattled around inside her head. In any case, her heart had stopped, she was sure it had. Danielle was staring with wide grey eyes, her mouth partly open, her cheeks flushed.

Caroline could understand that reaction because Ben Dexter was something else: six feet plus of sizzlingly virile masculinity clothed in a silvery grey suit that fitted the lithe body to perfection; dark, dark hair, beautifully groomed, and eyes as black as night, fringed by those extravagant lashes.

And he was still angry, she recognised with a shock of icy sensation that ran right down her spine and all the way back up again. The atmosphere positively thrummed with it, although he cloaked it with the urbanity of the smile he turned on Danielle, who went pinker and burbled, 'Well, I'll be off, then.' And behind Ben's back she rolled her eyes expressively, grinned and gave the stunned Caroline the thumbs-up sign.

'Am I to be invited in?' His voice was all honey-smooth on the surface but quite definitely laced with ice. Caroline put a hand up to where a pulse was beating madly at the base of her throat.

She had dreamed of being with him again, yearning, aching, desperate dreams, but the reality filled her with a deep and dark foreboding. He had the face of an austere stranger. He looked as if what they had been to each other, the glimpses of paradise they'd shared, had been ruthlessly wiped from his memory.

Wordlessly, she stepped aside, her heart flipping over because it was there, and always would be, the fateful, deeply ingrained physical recognition that made her body ache for his.

His taut profile grim, he strode ahead of her into the sitting room, a single raking glance taking in her few pieces of shrouded furniture, the paint-spattered newspapers spread all over the floor. And then his eyes flowed over her, making her suddenly and horribly aware of the sight she must present. Cheap baggy jeans and sloppy T-shirt, liberally splashed with paint, her hair caught back from her make-up-less face with a piece of string.

But the sheer length of his scrutiny, the slow gleam of something sultry in those narrowed black eyes sent her dizzy with hope. Maybe, just maybe, it wasn't dead for him, either.

The violent sexual attraction, the meeting and mating of souls that had lasted through twelve, long years of separation, making them both unfit partners for anyone else on the planet, couldn't have been wiped out overnight. Surely it couldn't.

Her head still swimming, her lower limbs suddenly feeling like cotton wool she forced herself to say something, anything, to break the charged and spikey silence. And the breaking of it would enable him to open up, tell her why he was here when he hadn't wanted to have to talk to her at all on that dreadful last day at Langley Hayes.

'Can I—' her tongue felt as if it were twisted into knots. Her milky skin burned with fierce colour as she forced out the words '—offer you coffee?'

'This isn't a social call.'

His voice was flat, the eyes that pinned hers were hard and dark. His feet planted apart, he pushed his hands into the pockets of his trousers, his superbly cut jacket falling open to reveal the pale grey silk of the shirt that covered the broad plane of his chest. 'It's been long enough—a full month. I used no protection. Although knowing now of your relationship with the younger Weinberg, I guessed you're more than likely to be on the pill.'

His staggeringly handsome features were blank but his eyes brimmed with unconcealed contempt. 'However, I need to know if you're pregnant. And if you are, I need to know if it's mine, or Weinberg's.'

His lips pulled back against his teeth in a smile that wasn't a smile at all. 'Tell me you're not and I'll leave you in peace. And I promise you'll never have to see me again.'

Caroline swayed on her feet, the final frail hope snatched away from her. Her soft mouth trembled as her blood roared in her ears. So much pain coming on the top of all that had gone before. She didn't know how she was going to bear it.

Darkness closed in on her and she felt herself falling.

CHAPTER TWELVE

GRATING out a harsh expletive, Ben's voice sounded as if it were echoing over some vast distance, and his face, hovering over her, was fuzzy, as if the bright May morning had spawned a thick November fog.

Caroline shook her head and her vision cleared; she had to be imagining the sharp stab of concern in the night-black eyes.

Of course he didn't care about her, not any more, and she wasn't going to be pathetic or crazy enough to let herself even begin to hope that he did. If he hadn't been too lost in passion when they'd made love to remember to use protection he wouldn't be here at all, she reminded herself wretchedly.

Struggling to escape the arms that were holding her upright, she gave a strangled, anguished sob. Being held so close to the hard heat of his body was torture, all the more painful because her own body was flooding with a wildfire heat of its own, her pulses racing, her breath coming in shallow gasps.

'Stop it!' His command was rough-edged as he subdued her feeble efforts by sweeping her up into his arms and shouldering his way through doors until he found her bedroom.

With a muted hiss of impatience, Ben swept the rolls of wallpaper off the narrow single bed and low-

168

ered her down onto it. 'Stay right there,' he stated emphatically. 'I'll fetch you a glass of water.'

A piercing glance from under lowered brows reinforced her opinion that concern for her well-being had been a product of her own demented imagination, an immature grasping at non-existent straws. He simply and obviously regarded her as nothing more than a nuisance, her unprecedented collapse something he had to handle but could very well have done without.

She turned her face into the pillow and shuddered. She wished he'd go away. It was better to be alone, struggling to accept that everything was finally over, rather than have to see him the way he was now. She didn't want to have to remember him like this, so cold, so contemptuous, so forbidding.

How he must hate her!

'Drink this.'

Unwillingly, Caroline dragged herself up against the pillows, not meeting his eyes. She couldn't bear to see that raw contempt, that stinging impatience.

'You fainted,' he said tonelessly as she clutched the glass in both hands and lifted it shakily to her mouth. 'Women in the early stages of pregnancy often do, so I believe.'

A savage spurt of temper got her kick-started. Colour flooding her ashen face, she swung her legs over the side of the bed, putting the glass on the floor before she gave into the temptation to throw it at him.

Out of a sense of duty he'd come here with the sole purpose of finding out if she was pregnant.

That was chastening.

But he had also come to find out—if her answer was in the affirmative—whether he or Michael was the father.

And that was disgusting, infuriating!

How could he think that of her? Oh, how could he?

'What do you think you're doing?' His question was laced with a good dose of aggravation as he caught hold of her ankles.

And before she could answer, Getting ready to strangle you before I throw you out, he swung her legs back onto the bed and told her, 'You need to rest. You look dreadful.'

Thanks a bunch, Caroline fulminated silently. While he, of course, looked immaculate, remote as the moon, forbidding and utterly, utterly, heart-stoppingly gorgeous. And deserving of some hefty punishment for marking her down as a slut!

'So what will you do if I confirm my pregnancy?' she asked out of sheer wickedness, watching for his reaction beneath lowered lashes.

'Marry you, if it's mine—make sure my child's properly cared for.' Not a flicker of emotion, nothing, just a bland statement of intent.

'And if it's Michael's?' Caroline turned the screw, increased the punishment in an anger-fuelled and completely ignoble attempt to pay him back for his lower-than-low opinion of her.

She saw his jaw clench, a white line of anger appear around his compressed lips, as he ground out between his teeth, 'That would be entirely up to him. Apparently, the poor sucker already thinks he's going to lead you up the aisle. He hasn't yet worked out that you're unable to commit to a long-term relationship.'

The contempt in his eyes deepened. 'When push comes to shove, you back off in a panic, write a Dear John letter or pick one hell of a fight. As I should know. And I somehow doubt if he's got the strength of character to make you toe the line.'

And Ben had?

Of course he had. Commitment to him would never have been a problem; it had been her inability to trust him that had turned everything sour. Her fatal mistake.

Her dark head drooped, her tear-filled eyes fastening on her hands which appeared to be trying to rip the hemline of her paint-spattered T-shirt to shreds.

This had gone far enough.

'I'm definitely not pregnant,' she told him in a voice that was flat and cold and thin. And she closed her heavy eyes and waited to hear the bedroom door shut behind him as he left. He now had the information he must have been desperately hoping to get. There would be nothing to keep him here for one more moment.

She heard nothing, just the silence, until his voice sliced at her, 'Then what the hell was that all about? The ''what if it's yours, or what if it's his'' spiel?'

Caroline risked a glance beneath the thick sweep of her lashes, her mouth dropping open in astonishment because she'd been so sure he'd stalk straight out the moment he had the reassurance he'd come for.

He still looked coldly, furiously angry. She looked away, her heartbeat thundering in her ears, and she lay back, turning her face into the pillows.

She couldn't stand much more of this. 'I wanted to pay you back for thinking I'd do something like that,' she muttered wearily, her voice scarcely above a whisper. The anger had gone, leaving a sense of loss that utterly overwhelmed her. 'Make love with you while supposedly in a serious relationship with Michael Weinberg.'

'And that made you angry, did it?' The query was laced with something approaching sarcasm. Then Ben's voice thickened, 'Then, you know what it feels like, don't you? Not to be trusted. To have someone you loved think you're capable of every slimey trick in the book.'

'Loved.' Past tense. So final. The door labelled Hope that had remained stubbornly ajar closed with a definitive bang in her mind.

Caroline hauled herself into a sitting position and swung her feet to the floor. Somehow she had to put an end to this nightmare. And she could cope. Right?

She would never forget him but eventually the terrible pain would leave her. The scar tissue on her heart would grow hard, letting her get on with her career because that was all she had, with never a hint that she had once been capable of any kind of emotion.

And she knew what she had to do to get the process started.

She wiped the moisture from her cheeks with fingers still sticky from the paintbrush and said with a calmness that belied all the anguished turmoil inside her, 'You can go now. I'm fine. I don't know why I passed out.' She gave the hint of a tight, impersonal smile, a small hike of one shoulder. 'It's not something I've done before. Probably down to the paint fumes.'

And being unable to eat, nor sleep; and seeing him again, coupled with the brief resurrection of hope and it's inevitable demise. But she certainly wasn't going to mention that.

'Then, perhaps we should open some windows.' And he moved around the flat, doing just that. Caroline got wearily to her feet. When he'd finished he'd leave, nothing surer than that. Her legs felt unsteady and she had to hang onto the door frame when she'd tracked him down in the kitchen.

Please go, she whimpered, in her mind. I need to start the long, slow, agonisingly painful process of getting over you again.

He was taking in the frantic muddle: the opened tins of paint; emulsion brushes soaking in her stainless-steel washing-up bowl; the ones used for gloss paint standing up to their necks in white spirits; the old dusters she'd used to wipe up all the splodges she'd made screwed up on the floor. And the pizza she'd ordered ages ago and hadn't been able to eat because just looking at it had turned her stomach.

'When we met again, that evening, I would have staked my last penny against you ever deigning to get your pretty white hands dirty.'

Which was why he'd taken one look at her, her make-up a perfect mask, not a hair out of place, her designer suit a statement of her status as a cool, efficient career lady, and had sent her to grovel in the dust of the Langley Hayes attics, she thought with a reluctant inner salute for his ability to cut her down to size.

Caroline merely shrugged. It seemed to take the last scrap of energy remaining to her, but she managed to say, 'You can go now.'

Ben ignored her. He turned his back on her, filled the kettle and plugged it in, searching for mugs and tea bags. There was no milk, just a curdled couple of inches in the bottom of a carton. He tossed it into the pedal bin. 'Empty fridge, an untouched pizza wearing a mouldy wig—you certainly know how to look after yourself.'

He moved aside a pile of old newspapers, a roll of masking tape, the ancient pizza, and put two mugs of milkless tea on the small square table. Pulling out two chairs he ordered, 'Sit.'

She complied because it seemed easier than arguing, but she told him, 'There's no need for you to do this—make tea, hang around. I can look after myself.'

'Obviously!' His tone was dry. Then, his voice

lower, gruffer, he admitted, 'I don't like to see you like this—washed out, exhausted.'

His words made her heart contract and twist, but she wasn't going to let herself read anything into them that wasn't there. Lifting her mug in both hands she took a sip of the strong, hot brew and then another, and felt for the first time since he'd walked in on her just a fraction more than half-alive.

Revived enough, she asked the question that had been lodged in the back of her mind. 'Who is the father of Maggie Pope's daughter? Did she tell you?'

'You've already decided I am,' he reminded her brusquely and pushed his mug to one side with an expression of deep distaste. Whether for the milkless tea or for her, she didn't know. The latter, she supposed.

'No.' Her mug had left a damp circle on the surface of the table. She rubbed at it with her forefinger. 'Not now, not after you told me what she'd said, that Dad had paid her to tell that lie. I do admit,' she went on tiredly, 'to believing her twelve years ago, and going on believing her. When he—my father, that is—said he'd given you money to go away and stay away, I couldn't believe it, not of you. I thought you really loved me, the way I loved you.'

A final rub with the heel of her hand and the ring of moisture disappeared. 'Then, of course, came the final blow. He suggested I ask Maggie who had fathered her child. Maybe I shouldn't have done, but think what it was like—I was only seventeen, all churned up emotionally. You'd disappeared, Dad had planted those doubts in my mind. I had to know. Well, you know what she said, and why she said it. She was very convincing.'

Caroline lifted her eyes to find Ben watching her, his burning gaze roving over her face. She felt the muscles in her shoulders relax. Even if he had no strong feelings for her now because her lack of trust had killed them stone dead, it felt good to get it all off her chest.

She pulled in a deep breath. 'That awful day—when I'd said I couldn't marry you because I couldn't trust you—after you drove away I went to see Maggie and get the truth out of her. The real truth,' she stressed. 'You'd told me to listen to my heart, do you remember? And I did. My heart told me you'd been telling the truth, that you were no-where near callous enough to betray anyone. The only question was, why had Maggie lied? I was going to drag the truth out of her. But it started to pour with rain and I sheltered at Dorothy's. We saw the three of you. Maggie, you and the child. Dorothy was looking at you and talking about the child's father, talking as if I knew him.'

'And that put me back in the frame?'

'Not entirely.' She shook her head. 'I went back to the house to wait for you. Michael had phoned, he was in the area, and was to drive me back. I knew we didn't have much time, I knew we had to talk; and I knew—' she met his eyes, willing him to believe her, '—that I would believe, implicitly, whatever you told me. You were still angry, but you did say we'd talk before I had to leave. But you'd gone when I came down after changing.'

For long, aching minutes he didn't respond, the silence putting her nerve ends on the rack. She stood up jerkily, clearing the mugs for something to do to end this nail-biting stasis and Ben shot to his feet.

Caroline's teeth bit into her lower lip. He was leaving. Her garbled attempt at self-justification, apology, had cut no ice. But then, had she really expected it to, she thought wretchedly. She half turned away and Ben took the mugs from her clenched fingers, dumped them back on the table and pulled her round to face him.

'Jeremy Curtis is Angela's father. Presumably that was why Dorothy was talking as if you knew the man. That's the drill when it comes to serious village gossip—name no names. Simply imply. Don't run the risk of being sued for defamation of character.'

Jeremy? Oh, sweet heavens above! He'd been having an affair with the unsuitable Maggie while her father and his had been planning her own marriage to the Curtis fortune! Jeremy would have gone along with it because she, Caroline, was suitable-wife material and poor Maggie wasn't. It might have been funny if the consequences hadn't been so devastating.

The hands that had gripped her upper arms gentled. His thumbs stroked her skin beneath the sleeves of her T-shirt, hypnotic, holding her immobile, her power of speech wiped out by the hot pressure of emotion building up around her heart.

'It was a shock when I saw you were getting ready to leave, presumably without hanging around long enough to say goodbye,' Ben admitted rawly. 'I'd finally got the truth out of Maggie and I was determined to get you to accept it, trust me enough to be my wife. But I left because I couldn't bear listening to young Weinberg for a moment longer. The things he was saying did my head in. I would have smashed his teeth through the back of his neck if I'd stayed,' he said roughly.

His hands came up to cup her face, his eyes holding hers with an intensity that made her mouth run dry. He murmured, 'Think back, Caro. You said that I'd thought you'd made love with me while you were supposedly in a serious relationship with young Weinberg. Supposedly, being the operative word.'

Caroline drew in a deep, shuddering breath that racked her slender frame. So Michael's laid-back over-confidence had done the damage after all. Ben hadn't washed his hands of her; he'd just gone out to find the truth and would have done his damnedest to make her believe it.

Tears flooded her eyes. The temptation to lay her head against his chest was immense. Resisting it, she said thickly, 'Michael and I always worked well as colleagues, and after his divorce we became friends. Just friends.' Caroline swallowed round the sharp, painful lump in her throat.

Would Ben discount what Michael had said and accept in his heart that she was telling the truth? But why should he, when she had believed the worst of him for so long? It really didn't bear thinking about. 'We have never been more than colleagues and friends, I promise you.'

She twisted away from him before he could move away from her and thus let her know that what she was saying was very far from convincing. Her slight shoulders slumped, she folded her arms around her body, holding in the misery, the sheer trepidation.

'To be completely honest with you, I did begin to realise that he wanted more than friendship. And because my wretched biological clock had started ticking loudly I even thought that he and I could progress to a closer relationship, given time. Then—then you came back on the scene.'

Her voice snagged in her throat, but she pressed on. 'And I knew it couldn't work, not with Michael, not with any other man. You haunted me. And it wasn't long before I knew I'd never stopped loving you, and never would, despite what I thought you'd done. Michael told me what he'd said to you. He knew something was wrong, and I ended up confessing that I was in love with you. He said he'd put his foot in it—offered to phone the next day and explain he'd jumped the gun. But I thought I was beyond forgiveness.'

One, two, three heartbeats of silence.

Caroline felt her already shaky control begin the tight spiral that would end in explosion and disintegration. And then she felt his hands gently touch her shoulders. She expelled a long, shaky breath of relief and sagged weakly back against him, her eyes drifting shut as his hands lifted to untie the length of string that bound back her hair.

Fanning the dark mass over her shoulders he turned her to face him, his voice unsteady, 'You've got paint in your hair.'

'I know.' Her eyes were dreamy, a misty deep violet. Her hands splayed out against his chest, parting his jacket to find the vital, living warmth of him through the silk of his shirt. 'Probably on my teeth, too.'

'I guess.' He lifted one of her hands and placed a kiss on the inside of her wrist, just where her pulse began a crazy tattoo.

'I look a complete mess.' She found it difficult to speak when her heart was thundering, her body quivering as he pressed the hard span of his hips against hers.

'Do you? I hadn't noticed.' His voice thickened as she captured his hand and pressed fervent, dancing kisses on the back of each finger in turn. 'I just love you.'

He drew in a harsh breath then kissed her with a savage hunger that drew a wild and wanting response from her as she clung to him, the whirlwind of passion making words unnecessary. They were together, just as fate had intended them to be; they were home, soul mates; they understood. They were complete.

She could feel the drum beats of his heart as he lifted her and carried her to the bedroom. Laying her on the top of the duvet he slowly shrugged out of his jacket, his cheekbones flushing darkly as he said,

'I'm going to bind you to me for the rest of my life, love you and care for you for the rest of my life. And I'm going to make love to you, now, with no hidden agendas, no fantasies, just you and me and what we feel for each other.'

His shirt followed his jacket. The dark eyes he kept fixed on her drenched with burning emotion, and Caroline bounced back up, dragged her T-shirt over her head, and held her arms wide for him. 'My darling, come to me, come home...'

The warm, late May sunshine tempted Caroline out of the cottage before she'd even started on the customary morning chores. An internal wriggle of sheer pleasure made her screw her eyes shut and beam, her grin stretching from ear to ear.

The surrounding woods were full of birdsong and the garden was showing promise of becoming as fabulous as she meant it to be. And in two days' time she and Ben would be celebrating their first wedding anniversary.

A year of bliss, sheer unadulterated bliss. She would never have believed two people could achieve such closeness: never parted for more than an hour or two until now.

Travelling with him to wherever he needed to be, brief sojourns at the London apartment, attending glittering social events, longer periods here at the cottage, making it a real home, checking up on the youngsters up at the big house.

That had been her life up until now, and a wonderful life it was, too, she thought contentedly, lifting her face to the sun, breathing in the soft, clean, scented air. Tomorrow morning Ben would be home, and she would break the news, the news that she herself had found hard to believe.

For the first time ever she'd shaken her head when he'd invited her to hop on the company jet and fly with him to Amsterdam. A flash of disappointment had clouded his eyes at the thought of being parted for over a week. But then he'd grinned, 'What will you do with yourself?'

'Oh, this and that. Spend a few days shopping.' It was the first time she'd lied to him and it wasn't a good feeling. 'Then drive down to the cottage. Tackle the weeds before they swamp the garden.' That part at least was the gospel truth. 'Join me there?'

And so he would, tomorrow. She couldn't wait. Couldn't wait to tell him, to confess that she'd lied, to explain that it had been necessary because even she hadn't been able to absorb the truth.

Meanwhile, there was all that weeding to be done...

Two hours later Caroline got up off her knees, easing the stiffness out of her back. The sun was scorching her bare arms, and white cotton jeans hadn't been the ideal choice for a stint of dedicated gardening, she decided as she brushed ineffectually at the stains on her knees and tucked the straying hem of her ice-blue sleeveless shirt back beneath the waistband.

Hooking her hair behind her ears, she headed for shade; down the path, skirting the cottage and the meadow and through the gate in the picket fence. And she stood quite still in the clearing in the woods, then wandered down to the edge of the rushing stream.

She and Ben always spent time here when they were at the cottage. It was a sort of pilgrimage, she supposed, a ritual visit to their special place, the place they'd always come to on those long-ago soft summer nights.

They had so nearly lost each other. A shiver rippled her skin and then her breath caught in her throat. She hadn't heard him come but she knew he was here.

She spun round, her face alight, just as he entered the clearing.

'Ben!' She ran lightly towards him, into his arms, and he lifted her, spinning her round, then kissed her as if he was starving.

'I didn't expect you until tomorrow,' she uttered breathlessly when they both gulped in much needed air.

'I bunked off.' He grinned at her, ruffling her hair. 'You weren't inside, and you weren't in the garden— just all those weeds piled up on the paths which, no doubt, I shall be required to put on the compost heap. I knew you'd be here.'

Smiling, she kissed him again, and 'I've got something to tell you.'

They both spoke together. Caroline said, 'You first. Mine's got to be better than yours!'

'I wouldn't bet on that!' He drew her down onto the soft, mossy bank of the stream. 'Now, am I right in thinking you look on this place as our real home, our special place? I know I do.'

She nodded, mock serious, but her eyes were dancing. 'True. Is that it? Right, my turn!'

'Shh.' He laid a finger across her mouth to silence her. She nipped it with her teeth. Grinning, he told her, 'I wasn't too miffed when you said you didn't want to come to Amsterdam. I missed you like crazy but it did give me the opportunity to get things moving without you breathing down my neck. I wanted it done and dusted, then spring the surprise. I'm going to work mostly from home—here—in the future. No more jetting round the continent at the drop of a hat. Any travelling we do in the future will be for pleasure—holidays—in any part of the world that takes your fancy. Of course—' he traced the outline of her mouth with a delicate, sensual finger '—it will mean building on. Just a room to house the usual electronic communications systems. Is that OK with you?'

'Couldn't be better.' She looped her arms around his neck and gently touched his mouth with hers. 'It fits in so well with what I've got to tell you.'

'Which is?'

'I'm pregnant. I wasn't sure but now I am. I didn't go shopping, why should I? I have everything I could want or need. I had it confirmed. I had a scan.'

Ben just stared at her. Caroline said, 'Aren't you pleased?' knowing he had to be. She knew him as well as she knew herself. And he confirmed it, his face lighting up in the grin that had the power to stun her.

'I'm ecstatic, my precious darling! Over the moon! Well done, Caro!'

'It takes two,' she said, laughter lurking behind the prim expression she plastered on. 'And that's not all. We're expecting twins.'

A breathless, adoring hug later she emerged from encircling arms that would have held onto her for ever. 'We'll have to build on a rumpus room. And being country babies they'll grow up to want ponies. And that means building a stable, and fencing off a paddock. And if we have more we'll need another bedroom. Or two. And an extra bathroom. The place will just get bigger and bigger. Do you mind?'

For answer he slid an arm back round her waist and drew her down with him onto the soft mossy grass. 'I can put up with everything getting bigger— and better.' A softly stroking hand slid over her still flat tummy, commanding fingers finding the button of her waistband. 'Just like my love for you—bigger and better in every way, day by glorious day.'

Queens of Romance

The Wedding Ultimatum

Rich and ruthless Rafe Valdez was way out of Danielle's
league. She'd turned to him as a last resort to help her family
but his solution was outrageous! The devastating, sexy
man gave her twenty-four hours to decide if she would
marry him, share his bed and give him an heir.

The Pregnancy Proposal

Tasha is overjoyed to discover that she's pregnant with
sensual tycoon Jared North's baby, but telling him is the
hardest thing she's ever done. For three years they've shared
an intensely passionate relationship – but marriage has
never been on the agenda.

Available 1st February 2008

Collect all 10 superb books in the collection!

Danger and desire collide...

When FBI agent Garon Grier sets up home in
Texas, the strong, silent loner is certainly not
looking for love when he meets Grace Carver,
a lovely young woman unmarried and
untouched because of a dark, tragic past.

Then Garon has to tackle the most difficult case
of his career, hunting an escaped convict, whose
former child victims are all dead. All except one.

Now a desperate lawman and a proud woman
must decide if secrets will come between them
forever...or free them to love at last.

Available 15th February 2008

1880s Yorkshire brought to vivid life

For Sarah-Louise, life in the big city of York is all she's ever wanted. And when her employer decides to move away, he helps Sarah-Lou find a new position. Unlike in her old work, Sarah-Lou is treated as nothing more than a skivvy, but there is one ray of hope in her life: Gideon, the son of her employers.

Sarah-Lou and Gideon become close and their friendship blossoms into something more. But could a love affair between Sarah-Lou and Gideon ever really work?

Available 18th January 2008

www.millsandboon.co.uk

MILLS & BOON
100
YEARS
of pure reading pleasure

100 Reasons to Celebrate

2008 is a very special year as we celebrate Mills and Boon's Centenary.

Each month throughout the year there will be something new and exciting to mark the centenary, so watch for your favourite authors, captivating new stories, special limited edition collections...and more!

Celebrate 100 years of pure reading pleasure with Mills & Boon®

To mark our centenary, each month we're publishing a special 100th Birthday Edition. These celebratory editions are packed with extra features and include a FREE bonus story.

Now that's worth celebrating!

4th January 2008

The Vanishing Viscountess by Diane Gaston
With FREE story The Mysterious Miss M
This award-winning tale of the Regency Underworld launched Diane Gaston's writing career.

1st February 2008

Cattle Rancher, Secret Son by Margaret Way
With FREE story His Heiress Wife
Margaret Way excels at rugged Outback heroes…

15th February 2008

Raintree: Inferno by Linda Howard
With FREE story Loving Evangeline
A double dose of Linda Howard's heady mix of passion and adventure.

Don't miss out! From February you'll have the chance to enter our fabulous monthly prize draw. See special 100th Birthday Editions for details.

www.millsandboon.co.uk